**Resounding praise for the year's
most remarkable debut thriller**

GORDON CAMPBELL'S
MISSING WITNESS

"Campbell breaks new ground in a legal thriller that
explores the alchemy of the law and truth. . . .
Missing Witness is a searing look at the law on the cusp
of change and of idealism churning into corporate greed.
Not since Scott Turow's *Presumed Innocent* has a
legal thriller been so enthralling."
Ft. Lauderdale Sun-Sentinel

"[A] top-notch legal thriller. . . . Campbell isn't afraid to
delve into the intricacies of the law, but his simple,
down-to-earth writing style makes it all flow smoothly.
As interesting as the plot is, the authentic,
multidimensional characters, especially McKenzie,
are the real thrill of the story. *Missing Witness* is one
of the stronger debuts of the year."
Chicago Sun Times

"Reminiscent of John Grisham's *The Rainmaker*. . . .
True fans of legal dramas will relish the depth
of Campbell's knowledge."
Tampa Tribune

"Deserves to be ranked with masterpieces of the craft. . . .
It's a riveting tale."
Seattle Post-Intelligencer

MISSING WITNESS

GORDON CAMPBELL

HARPER

An Imprint of HarperCollinsPublishers

HARPER

An Imprint of HarperCollins*Publishers*
10 East 53rd Street
New York, New York 10022-5299

Copyright © 2007 by Gordon Campbell
ISBN 978-0-06-164663-8

First Harper paperback printing: January 2009
First William Morrow hardcover printing: October 2007

10 9 8 7 6 5 4 3 2 1

For Mona

You don't have to be an asshole to be a trial lawyer. That having been said, you never want to lose sight of the fact that you are part of the milieu.

—Thomas J. Gallagher, *Esquire*
Phoenix, Arizona, January 1, 1974

PROLOGUE

DAN MORGAN *had a tattoo. How is it that, after all these years, that's the first thing that always comes to mind when I think back to the whole mess? It certainly isn't that I can't remember all the rest of it—every last detail. And it isn't that I don't think about the whole thing. I seem to do that more and more these days. It's just that when I do return to it all, it's the tattoo, that ugly stain that had branded him since the war, his war, that always comes back first.*

OCTOBER 21, 1973. It was just after sunrise that they rode the horses to the house. They dismounted. They tied the horses to the fence. They walked up the dusty little path. They climbed the two small steps. They went inside. And then they closed the door. Juan saw all that. He saw them ride up. He saw them go inside. He saw them close the door. And, in time, he heard the shots. He saw them come outside. And when he went to them, after the gun had hit the ground, he saw on the ragged rug beyond the open door the hand he knew so well and the blood beginning to pool.

About the event, the shooting itself, that is all we knew, what the old sheep man, Juan Menchaka, my lifelong friend, had said he saw and heard. Juan told the truth.

There never was any real question about that. But then he only heard the shots; he didn't see which one of them fired the gun. I look back to that day and I wonder how much differently my life might have gone if only Juan had seen who pulled the trigger. If only there had been a bigger window. If only they had not closed the door.

1 THE PRESIDENT OF the Arizona Golf Association carried a battery-powered megaphone. He didn't need it. At the hour we were starting, there were only a handful of people around the tee. Still, he raised it to his mouth, and his voice carried all the way across the San Marcos Country Club.

"Ladies and gentlemen, the final match of the 1973 Arizona Golf Association Men's Amateur Championship. On the tee the defending champion, Dr. Winthrop North."

Winthrop North stood confidently beside his caddie and his huge, hand-tooled golf bag. Harvard educated and, at least by any Arizona standard, patrician, he seemed almost to pose in his madras pants and wing-tipped golf shoes. He wore a white shirt with a crocodile on it and over that a white cashmere cardigan. It all could have been a scene from the cover of *Golf Digest,* save for the old flat course whose Bermuda fairways were beginning to turn yellow with the coming of winter. After announcing his name, the president rapidly cataloged the doctor's biggest golf accomplishments: the United States Amateur, the British Amateur; his years on the Walker Cup team, multiple state championships. I fiddled with my head cover and wondered how on earth he'd managed all that while conducting a medical practice.

"Dr. North."

The president lowered his megaphone, and my opponent took two precise steps to where he had already teed his ball. He hit a driver, a low, controlled fade to the right side of the fairway. He couldn't have walked out and placed it any better.

Could I beat him? Sure I could. I had as many clubs in my bag as he had in his. We played the same course under the same conditions and the same rules. Besides, when you've joined a law firm to work for one partner and that partner hasn't shown up for work in the two months you've been there, and you've spent almost every afternoon with another partner entertaining insurance adjusters at various country clubs around the valley, your golf game tends to sharpen dramatically. Why shouldn't I beat him? I commend those sorts of thoughts to anyone who might find himself in the situation I was in that morning. A more realistic question dominated my consciousness, however: It was to be a thirty-six-hole match; could I take him to twenty-seven?

"On the tee. Mr. Douglas McKenzie. Phoenix City Junior Champion, 1959."

I hooked it. I did all the things they tell you to do to get rid of the butterflies. An extra practice swing, an extra deep breath, a long and focused look at my target. Then I swung, and I watched the ball go left and held my breath as it rolled close by a small barrel cactus that used to be on the left side of the first fairway at San Marcos. Winthrop North and his caddie and his enormous golf bag started quickly up the fairway. Berating myself at not having shelled out for a caddie, I turned and picked up my little bag that had BEN HOGAN printed on the side.

"That'll play!" I swung around just in time to see a golf cart careen off the path in front of the pro shop and plow through a bed of flowers. I saw beer splash out of a can and all over the passenger, and I heard the passenger yell, "Jesus H. Christ, Tom!" The cart took a dive through a sprinkler, and as it emerged, I could make out the two occupants. Uncombed and grizzled, they both wore suit pants and white dress shirts that looked like they'd been slept in.

A big swing to the right, and the cart skidded sideways to a stop directly in front of me. I looked down into the bulging eyes and the unshaven face of Tom Gallagher, the man for whom I'd been working, the one with whom I'd been entertaining insurance adjusters. I knew instantly that he was more than just a little drunk. "That'll play," he said for a second time. "You didn't hit it very well, but you've got a shot at the pin."

"I hope I do," I said with my mouth hanging open.

"Doug McKenzie," Gallagher announced, "Dan Morgan." My gaze jumped to the other side of the cart. He looked worse than Gallagher. He hadn't shaved for days. His eyes were veined with red. His shirt was splashed with beer. "You say you want to work for him, Douglas. Well, here he is. Back from two months in the country."

Dan Morgan put the cigarette he was holding in his hand into his mouth and squinted from the smoke. He shifted a can of beer to the left and put out his right hand. He nodded one time, not saying a word. I managed to get my golf bag around on my shoulder so I could shake his hand. And there it was, on the third Sunday in October, on the first tee at the San Marcos Country Club, that I finally met him.

"Throw your clubs on here," Gallagher ordered. "We'll caddie for you." I strapped my bag onto the back of the cart, and as I did, I saw a tub full of ice and beer. Then they were gone, bouncing up the fairway with their beer and my clubs, and I was walking far behind them shaking my head in disbelief.

That may have been the first time I met Dan Morgan, but it wasn't the first time I'd seen him. I had indeed been forewarned, back on a day in August when I sat, for the first time, in the lobby of the offices of Butler and Menendez. Paul Butler had insisted that I let the firm fly me down to Phoenix so he could propose a substantially larger salary than I'd been offered in San Francisco. I sat there that August morning, waiting for Butler, sensing the onslaught of a summer day in Arizona, and feeling the fresh press go out of my brand-new Brooks Brothers suit. I watched Josephine, the octogenarian receptionist whose skin resembled the onionskin paper upon which she typed. I surveyed the room. I saw on the only wall not covered with bookshelves the single piece of art the firm owned in those days, the oil portrait of the great Apache, Geronimo.

And I saw the aged Indian sitting beneath the painting, huge and silent. He sat so still that for a moment I thought he might have been another piece of artwork, a sculpture made of space-age material looking so real that you could see each graying hair in the bun tied behind his head and the fibers of felt in the big, flat-brimmed Stetson hat and the weave of the denim in his Levi's. Perhaps, I thought, he, too, was Geronimo, Geronimo when he was old. But then I heard a sound from his direction, a low, round, mellifluous sound. Then I heard it again. And then I sniffed the air. In some astonishment I turned to Josephine, and she leaned in my direction.

"A client," she whispered across our end of the room. "All we may do is pray for olfactory fatigue."

I turned the pages of a year-old issue of *Arizona Highways,* resenting the cold shoulder I was receiving from the man named Paul Butler who had implored me to come but had kept me waiting for more than an hour. The day had seemed to hold only one pleasant promise: I would at last meet the legendary Daniel Morgan. After all, he was the real reason I'd accepted the invitation to return to Phoenix for the interview, and I had decided to make the trip not because he was a folk hero among law students and professors but because the judge had spoken of him with such admiration. "Daniel Morgan is a trial man," the judge had told me. "The real thing." Paul Butler had promised that I would meet him. I turned the pages, looking at the pretty pictures of the blooming saguaros and ocotillos, and almost went to sleep. Suddenly I was wrenched from the doldrums by a harsh, flat Arizona drawl.

"Jesus H. Christ. Who in hell has been fart—" I looked up just in time to see Josephine put her finger to her lips, then slowly turn it in the direction of the old Indian. The man standing before me had thick brown hair shot with gray that stood up as though he'd been running his hands through it. His eyes were a reddish brown, the color of a fox, and when he narrowed them down, they looked like a fox's eyes. He widened them, and they flashed all over the room, then at me in a way that made me flinch. He wore a striped shirt unbuttoned at the top, with a loosened tie. Chest hair showed above the tie. He carried a file folder and had a plaid jacket draped over his arm. Wiry and very thin at the waist, he stood stock-still, yet some hidden energy gave the impression that he was moving. He looked over at the old man, then leaned his head way back, raised his eyes to the ceiling, and very softly, in some great despair, he let escape, "Oh, Lord." He lowered his eyes, and the fierce glare that had been in them seemed to dissolve. Shaking his head, he chuckled without mirth, and then he spoke again. "Come on, Mr. Apadaka," the man said, "we've got to go talk to that judge."

The old man rose and slowly followed toward the elevator. "You gonna take care me, lawyer?" the old man asked in language as abrupt and broken as his wind.

"I'm going to do my best, sir," answered the younger man.

"That sonabitch had a asskick'n com'n."

"That's what we have to make that judge understand."

The elevator doors closed upon the two. I turned to Josephine. "Is that man a lawyer here?" I asked.

"Yes."

"What's his name?"

"Morgan."

"That's Daniel Morgan?"

"That's Danny." Josephine gave me a searching look. "You seem disappointed."

"I guess I'd been expecting something else," I finally said.

I guess I'd been expecting Orson Welles or José Ferrer or Gregory Peck. Well, what I saw was Dan Morgan with his flat drawl and his uncombed hair and his wild eyes and some strange electricity that made me nervous. I never got to talk to him that day, but I did see him. And I saw the offices of Butler and Menendez, the old, tattered offices in the Luhrs Building. And I saw their rude manners in the form of one Paul Butler. And I saw a sample of their clientele in the form of the flatulent Native American. And still I had come home to Arizona. My God, what had I done? I guess the answer to that question was fairly simple. I had rejected an offer of employment from a great big blue-chip law firm in San Francisco in favor of what I saw slumped and splattered with beer on the right side of that golf cart. I had turned up my nose at sophisticated legal work in elegant offices filled with great art. All that and a promise of membership in one of the finest golf clubs in the world. Oh, God! What had I done? No. I knew what I'd done. The question was, *Why had I done it*?

Over the years I've thought about that question more than I care to remember, and still I don't have an answer. Perhaps it was that I knew I was just an Arizona boy who'd be out of his depth in the big city. Or perhaps I knew, given what it had done to Ben Hogan and Arnold Palmer, what the Olympic Country Club would do to me. Then again, it might have been something else. Maybe, just maybe, it was the kindness in the voice of the man with eyes like a fox when finally, just before the elevator doors closed, he softened completely and put his arm around the old Indian and said, "Don't worry, Mr. Apadaka, I think everything's going to be all right." Well, whatever my unfathomable reasons, I was back in Arizona, and I was following Dan Morgan up the first fairway at the San Marcos Country Club. And I was having profound second thoughts about my decision.

When I reached my ball, Gallagher stood beside it. He motioned the president of the golf association to his side. "Hey, Red," he slurred unsteadily, "under the rules, so long as I'm caddying for McKenzie, I can give him advice. That's right, isn't it?"

"That's right, Tom. A contestant may accept advice from his caddie, but only from his caddie."

"All right," Gallagher said, keeping his bleary eyes on Red Atkinson. I waited, expecting advice on yardage or club choice. Gallagher rocked back and forth unsteadily for a time, then turned in my direction. "Knock that son of a bitch close." Slowly he lowered himself onto the cart and backed it away to give me room to swing.

Strangely, I do believe that Gallagher's advice helped. As I watched him stare at me and then heard him bark his order, I felt the butterflies leave. And when I hit the shot, I struck it pretty well, and when the ball found the green, it danced a couple of steps and stopped twenty feet below the hole. The trouble was, Winthrop North followed Gallagher's mandate precisely. He knocked it four feet from the pin, then drilled it through the light dew that was still on the green into the center of the cup. One down. My fear of slaughter was already coming to fruition.

Our entourage moved on. Neither Gallagher nor Morgan bothered to tell me why they were there or where they'd been. Tom would just drive along, then pull the cart close to my ball, and once I had taken a club, he would move away a respectful distance so I could hit my shot. Then I would follow them along, hole after hole, as the cart bounced and they drank their beer.

I tried not to think about Gallagher and Morgan. I kept telling myself that I should be thinking about my golf game, not about my need to go and prostrate myself before the hiring committee at 111 Sutter Street in San Francisco. But Gallagher and Morgan were there, and it is very difficult not to think about what you're trying not to think about, and at last, as I was standing next to their cart just off the fifth tee, I let my curiosity get away from me. "How did you guys get in this condition?" I asked, trying to make the question sound lighthearted.

"What condition?" Gallagher demanded. He smiled. Then he just left me wriggling there, feeling like I was pinned to the little saguaro cactus behind me. I believe that for all the years I've known him now, it was the only time Tom Gallagher ever did anything to me that was even remotely unkind. But unkind he was at that moment, when his fixed smile became almost treacherous and sustained his demand to know what I thought his condition was. "What condition?" Gallagher asked again. He smiled again, too. I squirmed, knowing I had to move to the tee and hit my shot and knowing also that I could not move until something was said.

It was there, as I had my back to the cactus and I was squirming, that Dan Morgan spoke the first words he ever said to me. "It was my birthday yesterday," he said. "Some friends threw a party for me." He said it in a level, matter-of-fact way, but when I turned and looked at him, I saw him nod. Then he winked at me and by doing so let me off the hook.

I said, "Oh," and I hit my shot. I didn't ask Morgan how old he was that day. Nor did I ask where that party had been thrown. I know those things now, though. That's because there came a time when finally I had the courage again to ask Tom Gallagher how the two of them had gotten in that condition. That was just last night, after a firm dinner, after everyone but Tom and I had left the Arizona Club, and the two of us remained with the crumbs on the linen and the dregs in the bottom of the last bottle of wine.

"Tom," I said to him, "do you remember that day you and Dan showed up drunk at San Marcos, when I was play-ing in the State Amateur?"

"Of course I do."

"How did you guys get that way?"

This time he neither asked embarrassing questions nor smiled disquieting smiles. He just got a faraway look and told me what happened. "That was the day he came home from Europe," Tom said. "It was when he'd been over there giving that series of lectures on habeas corpus to all those English barristers and French *avocats*. It was his fiftieth birthday. And, for God knows what reason, he wanted to spend it in Arizona." The memory touched something. Tom's words began to catch in his throat, and he had to look out to South Mountain. "I think he heard that Kath-erine was looking for him in France. I think he ran away from her. I picked him up at the airport, and we had a couple of drinks here." Tom was looking around the room we were in. "Then Danny said he wondered if they still had a Saturday-night poker game at the Baseline Tavern. They did, and we went, and when we left, the sun was up."

"You spent the whole night in the Baseline Tavern?" Tom paid no attention to my small exclamation of incredulity; he seemed lost in his memory. "He called that a birthday party?"

"We were out in the parking lot," Tom continued. "I was going to drive him home. Up to the house in Paradise Valley. But as I was unlocking the car, he said, 'Tom,' and I looked across the top of the car, and he said, 'I don't want to go home.' "

I remember every shot I hit during that round and every shot Winthrop North hit as well. Lamentably, after seven holes, he had hit three fewer than I. And I wasn't playing badly either. After the first hole, I'd hit every fairway, and I'd hit every green. It was just that North had made that birdie at one and then stroked a forty-foot putt at five that broke my heart when it rattled to the bottom of the cup. I three-putted seven. One over par. Three down.

But then at eight, the par three, there came a small turnaround. I hit a high six iron that covered the flag right from the time it left the tee. The ball landed six feet past the hole, and it backed up, and for a moment I thought it was going in. It stopped a foot from the cup.

Gallagher yelled, "Great shot, Doug!" And I heard Dan Morgan whisper, "I'll be damned." And the little gallery, which by then had begun to grow, applauded quietly and politely. North conceded my putt. Two down. As I was walking off the green, I heard Dan Morgan whisper to Gallagher, "I never knew that this goddamned stupid game could be interesting."

As I took the club back on the ninth tee, I got my weight all the way to my right side, and I could feel my hands high, and I could tell that the shaft of my driver was parallel to the earth and pointed right up the middle of the fairway. Then I started down with my left hip, and I could feel my left side clear and the club head strike the ball flush and then my shoulders go all the way around. The ball exploded off the tee. "Holy shit!" Morgan exclaimed. And when we finished the front side, I was only one down.

"Douglas!" Gallagher yelled as I walked off the ninth green. "Come over here." I walked to where he stood apart from the rest of the gallery. "I have some real advice."

"Yes?" I said.

"You just keep showing off for Danny."

"What?"

"Make him react."

"I'm not showing off." *What does he mean, showing off? For that guy? In his condition?*

"Sure you are. And you just keep it up. You spend the rest of this day teaching Dan Morgan what this game is all about, and you may just have a chance against Winthrop North. You start making that goddamned ball talk. Now, get on it."

Winthrop North and I exchanged birdies for the next four holes, leaving me one down.

Then I heard something that made me realize that neither Tom Gallagher nor Dan Morgan was paying as close attention to the match as I'd thought. At the fourteenth tee, I went to the cart for my driver only to catch Gallagher speaking to Morgan with remarkable sobriety. "Make no mistake about it, Danny. That asshole's got you right in his crosshairs."

"Oh, come on, Tom. He can't pull that off."

"The hell he can't. I'm telling you the little son of a bitch is Machiavellian."

"I need a case, Tom. I need a good case."

"That's right," Gallagher said. "One that's got some money in it."

Gallagher didn't say who it was that was taking aim at Morgan, but then he didn't have to. I knew instantly that he was talking about Paul Butler, managing partner at Butler and Menendez, the small firm with the tattered offices in a crumbling old building in Phoenix, Arizona, the law firm for which I'd left San Francisco. What should I say about Paul Butler? That he was short? That he was going prematurely bald? That he had a voice like a chain saw and breath that made me think he used the saw to cut something really rotten? I didn't dislike him in those days. Feared him, perhaps, which I now realize was silly. He was only three years older than I, but he had risen to managing partner in the firm, and that caused me to be just a little afraid of him. But I didn't bear him any ill will. It was Tom Gallagher who did that. Tom hated him, and he was in no way afraid of him.

Not long before Morgan returned from Europe, I endured a very uncomfortable coffee break during which I learned a number of things about Paul Butler. The lawyers' lounge had filled that morning, with lawyers carrying chairs from their own offices so they could crowd in for coffee while they read their mail. Paul Butler showed up, the only time I ever saw him in the lounge. He hadn't come for coffee or for mail, however. He'd come to make a simple announcement. "You should all be aware that Elias will be out of the office until the first of November," Paul Butler advised us.

Tom Gallagher, who had not found a chair, slowly bent down and put his mail on the low-slung coffee table. He stood back up and cleared his throat. "You know, Paul," Tom said, "I've always wondered why you call your father by his first name. I mean, why is it that you don't call him 'Dad' or 'Pop' or 'Father' or something like that?"

"I don't know, Tom. I just always have."

"I guess I just wondered if you hoped that we'd forget you came in here as the son of the boss."

Butler took off his glasses and rubbed his balding head.

Gallagher put his hands on his hips and bent forward at the waist in a way that always made him appear slightly dislocated. He stood on the balls of his feet, and, looking very much the graying, aging athlete that he was, he fixed Paul Butler with his bulging eyes. (In those days I suspected a thyroid condition.) "Let me ask you this, Paul. Did you leave orders for Josephine to route all Elias's calls to you while he's away this time?" Gallagher's bulging eyes pulsated, almost like a fire-control radar.

"I don't know what you're talking about," Paul Butler said.

"The hell you don't," Gallagher shot back. Gallagher

maintained his virulent glare for a time. Finally he turned to Walter Smith. "Did you know he does that, Walter? Did you know he makes Josephine forward all his father's calls to him when Elias is in Palm Springs?"

Walter Smith pulled his pipe from his mouth. His red face became a little redder. "Maybe we should save this for the management committee, Tom," said the senior litigator.

"To hell with the management committee," Gallagher said. Then he looked at me. "How about it, Doug? How would you like to be able to take all Elias Butler's calls when he's away on these extended trips?"

"I don't get it," I said. "I don't know what you mean."

"Just think a minute," Gallagher pressed. "Just put yourself in the place of some corporate counsel in New York or Chicago whose company needs a lawyer in Arizona. And you get referred to this firm. Or you look up Phoenix in *Martindale & Hubble* and you like the cut of our résumé. Who at this firm are you going to call to talk about sending us your company's business?"

I was about to tell him that I got it, but before I could get the words out, something made me look up, and I saw that many of the lawyers had stood in preparation to leave but that they had not left. Instead they'd formed something close to a circle. Suddenly I had the feeling I was back at Mesa High School and a fight had broken out behind the boys' gym, and I was about to be pushed from the circle that always formed at those times into the middle where the dust and the fists were flying and the kicking was about to start. I looked at Paul Butler. He put his glasses back on and used them to look at me. I felt my teeth grip together.

"You get it, Doug," Gallagher assured me. "The guy in New York calls the senior partner, the top man. He wants to know he'll get attention. He does it damned near every time. So if we let you field Elias's calls for about six months, you know what would happen?" My teeth remained clenched. "I'll tell you, Doug. If you could handle yourself with a modicum of finesse, you'd have so much new business at the end of your six months, so much client control, that we'd have to make you a partner. Then, if you wanted to be a real prick, we'd have to set your draw above the rest of ours. And then, if you really wanted to be an asshole, we'd have to put you on the management committee."

With that he turned his fierce glare back upon Paul Butler, who immediately walked out of the room. Gallagher shouted after him, "You can have my vote on your latest proposal right now if you want it, Paul!"

The lounge cleared. Only Chet Johnson and I remained. "Jesus," my fellow associate breathed through his droopy mustache. "They usually save that kind of stuff for partners' meetings."

"That scared me," I said.

"There are a lot of skeletons in these closets."

"Do you know what Gallagher was talking about when he said he would vote on Butler's proposal?" I asked him.

"Yeah," Chet allowed.

I waited. "Well, how about telling me?" I said.

"Butler circulated a memorandum," Chet revealed tentatively, "a memorandum to all the partners, proposing that they change the way they give origination of business credit."

"What's that?" I asked him.

Chet explained what he'd learned about how the firm divided up the money, how partners were given credit for bringing business to the firm. It was such that if a lawyer had "origination" for a given client, it didn't matter whether he did work for that client. He still got half of every fee paid. "So somebody like Elias Butler who has developed such a large clientele over time can spend half the year in California, while other lawyers do all the work for his clients, and still be paid a handsome salary."

"What would Butler's proposal do?"

"Up until now whenever a partner has died or left the firm, his clients, the ones for whom he had origination credit, have just gone to the firm, and no individual partner gets credit for them. Butler wants it changed so that when someone leaves, the lawyer controlling the work for each of that lawyer's clients will get origination credit for them."

"So," I reasoned, "when Elias Butler retires, Paul Butler will get credit for his father's clients."

"Those whose work he's doing," Chet advised. "But that won't make much difference. It's something else."

"What is it?"

"Frank Menendez has a client named Ferris Eddington. He's the biggest cattleman in Arizona. He's a very important client."

"Yes, I know that," I told him.

"Frank is sick. They had him at Mayo Brothers, then at some fancy cancer clinic in Pasadena. Nobody talks about it, but I heard he came home the other day."

"Yes?"

"Under Butler's new proposal, if Frank dies, Paul Butler gets the Eddington Ranch."

"What? Why?"

"The writing's on the wall. The ranch will have to be sold."

"Why?"

"The land is worth too much as a potential residential development. Someone will come along and turn it into another McCormick Ranch. You know, one of those developments with lakes and golf courses and quaint shopping centers and condos and patio homes. When that happens, if we can hold on to Ferris Eddington, this firm will be drafting condominium agreements and trust deeds and ground leases and restrictive covenants into the next century. And the lawyer who has origination credit for all that work will never have to do a thing he doesn't want to do for the rest of his professional life. And that lawyer, under his proposal, would be Paul Butler, since he heads the real estate section."

I sat back in my chair, and certain things began to come a little clearer, things to do with the anxiety in Paul Butler's voice the day he called and begged me to fly down from San Francisco for an interview. I had certainly wondered why he so readily outbid the Sutter Street salary. Ferris Eddington must have mentioned my name.

"When Frank Menendez dies," Chet Johnson informed me, "there's going to be a war around here."

"Is Dan Morgan going to be in the fight?" I asked.

"Dan Morgan is in deep trouble in the firm."

"Why?" I demanded. "That seems crazy to me. Someone with his reputation. I mean, he's the architect of the *Martinez* decision. That case is read in every law school in the country. Morgan expanded the law of federal habeas corpus more than any lawyer in the history of American jurisprudence."

"That's true," said Chet. "Ironic that it's probably one of Dan's lesser accomplishments."

"Then how can he be in trouble around here?"

"First, Butler is out to get him. Second, Morgan's vulnerable."

"Why?"

"Why is he vulnerable? He has no permanent clientele. No origination-of-business credit."

"I guess that stands to reason."

"You bet it does," Chet said. "When State Farm or Allstate sends business to Tom Gallagher, he can look forward to more business from them in the future, growing business for lots of us, not just for himself. It's the same when the hospital retains Walter Smith or when Westinghouse comes to Elias Butler. And it's especially true when Ferris Eddington stays with Frank Menendez. It isn't the same with Morgan's clients. A good murder case or a juicy contested divorce is usually a onetime piece of legal business for a client. The whole idea is that the client never returns. Because of that, Morgan has no meaningful origination-of-business points."

"Why does Paul Butler have it in for him?"

"Trust me, Doug. They ain't the same kind of men. Butler wants money, lots of it. Hell, Morgan gives away more legal work every year than most lawyers in this town live on." Chet pointed to one of the many photographs that hung on the walls of the lounge. "And then there's that," he said. "Maybe it's just a matter of personal style." The picture showed Dan Morgan at a formal firm dinner party thrown years before. He wore a tuxedo and slouched at a table after dinner with a brandy snifter in his hand. He gazed approvingly at a pretty young woman with a beehive hairdo who sat next to him. The woman extended a fist toward the camera. From her fist she extended upward her middle finger.

"That's Morgan's second wife."

"I know," I said. "I think her name is Frankie."

"That's right," said Chet. "I met her once. I can tell you she's still a very foxy lady. But I'll tell you this, too. If Frankie walked into a bar and started talking, sailors would run out. Paul Butler tried to take that picture down when he first came here, and his father told him if he tried it again, he was out of the firm. Elias really liked her."

"What do you think of Morgan?"

"I love him. I'd carry his briefcase to the end of the world. He'll treat you like a mushroom occasionally, but he'll take the time to teach you things, and he's the best guy I've ever worked for. Be advised, though, that there are people around here who won't work for him."

"What do you mean, 'he'll treat you like a mushroom'?"

"Sometimes he keeps you in the dark and feeds you shit."

"Who won't work for him?"

"Ann Hastings, for one."

"Why?"

"She doesn't like being treated like a mushroom. Lee Goodman for another. They held up his partnership for a year because Morgan couldn't collect for a bunch of his work. Hell, Morgan taught Lee everything he knows. He even let him have his manual on cross-examination. Now Goodman won't even speak to him."

"What's Morgan's manual on cross-examination?"

"He wrote a book. It catalogs everything Arizona law allows you to do on cross. West Publishing Company wants to publish it, but Morgan won't let anybody see it."

"Why won't he publish it?"

"Who knows? But he let Lee have it for a while. Now Lee won't give him the time of day, and that's after Morgan made him into one of the best young trial lawyers in the state. All because Dan let a little money get away. Shit, as far as I'm concerned, I'd rather learn what Morgan can teach me than make partner in this place any day."

I sat sipping from the bottom of my coffee cup, letting the realities of law-firm economics soak in. I guess I knew that Dan Morgan needed a good case even before he did.

Back at the golf course, while we waited for a ruling on whether Winthrop North could move his ball from a cart path, I came once again within surreptitious earshot of the cart. This time it was Morgan who spoke first, and he spoke very tentatively. "How's Frank?" he said.

Gallagher didn't look at him. He reached forward and picked up a golf ball from the cart. He turned the ball in his hand. "He's dying, Danny."

"No."

"Yes. You'd better get used to it. This time it's for real. They sent him home to die."

North and I both parred fourteen and fifteen, and I remained one down. At sixteen he left himself six feet for birdie. He lined the putt up from all sides while I braced myself to lose another hole. Then, as the doctor stood over the ball about to draw the putter back, I heard a pop and then a hiss. I turned and saw Dan Morgan, out of the cart for the first time, leaning against a palm tree. He had just opened another can of beer. North stepped away from his ball. He glared at Morgan. Morgan stared straight back at him without a hint of embarrassment. Then Morgan did something I hadn't seen done since I got out of the United States Navy. He bent down, raised his pant leg, and pulled a pack of cigarettes from his sock. He shook one up, clenched it between his teeth, and flipped open a Zippo lighter. He lit the cigarette and let it dangle from his lips. Smoke rose, and his eyes flashed as he studied my opponent. At last North moved back over the ball. He left the putt two inches short. He stood in the same spot looking down at his putter. "That's good," I said, and his caddie picked up the ball.

After a few more seconds, North began to walk off the green. As he moved by, he spoke the only words he had for me that day. "Whoever he is," Winthrop North said, "why don't you ask him to be quiet?"

A few minutes later, I was standing in the middle of the seventeenth fairway. I'd hit a good drive about ten yards past North's, long enough that I knew I could reach the green on that par-five hole in two. North unfortunately had already hit his second shot to the front edge of the green, and I knew there was no way he wouldn't make a birdie. Suddenly Dan Morgan appeared beside me and touched my elbow. "You can beat this guy," he whispered. I stared at him. "It's true," he affirmed. "I know about these things. Hell, I could beat him if I knew how to play this game."

I pulled out a four wood. I stayed down and through the shot, and it felt like the club head brushed the grass for a foot after it hit the ball. The ball started low, then climbed, then hung high above the flag, shimmering in the Arizona noonday sun. "It's going in!" Tom Gallagher yelled while the ball was still in flight. "The goddamned thing's going in!"

The ball did not go in. It landed just short, and it stopped right where it landed, about three feet below the hole. It was the best golf shot I'd ever hit in my life, and when I stroked the putt that followed, I hit the ball with the sweet spot of the putter. And that's how it happened that Winthrop North birdied the seventeenth hole at San Marcos Country Club in the finals of the Arizona State Amateur and lost it.

We both parred eighteen, and we walked to the clubhouse for lunch. Now the truly unimaginable had happened: Not only had I qualified and then made the finals, but I had played eighteen holes with Winthrop North himself, and I'd held him even. As I walked toward the clubhouse, I felt Dan Morgan's hand at my elbow once again. "You beat this turd," he told me, "and we'll have a hell of a party." He shook his head one time in a gesture of finality. "I mean it."

We took a table on the patio near the dining-room door, and Winthrop North sat down on the other side, as far from us as he could get. I had almost grown accustomed to the way my lunch companions looked, but when North moved so far away, I regarded them again. Morgan might have been handsome, I thought, if he hadn't been in the shape he was that day. He had acne scars on his cheeks, and his eyes may have been set a shade close together, but his nose was fine and straight, flaring slightly at the nostrils, and his chin was square and strong.

A waiter brought menus. "Better be careful, Danny," Gallagher warned. "I see that spare tire you brought back from France." Morgan chuckled and rubbed his belly. We ordered cheeseburgers all around.

"I always wanted to see that guy," Morgan said, looking over at my opponent.

"Why?" asked Gallagher. "You don't follow golf."

"No. No, it isn't that," Morgan said. "He's the pathologist who did the autopsy on Homer Many Goats. He's the guy who called it homicide."

"Oh, that's right," Gallagher remembered. "That's right. I'd forgotten, but you're right."

"The bastard's incompetent," Morgan all but shouted. "He ought to turn in his ticket. He ought to do nothing but play golf, and he knows it."

Across the patio Winthrop North sat alone at his table. He had a glass of milk in front of him. Beyond him, out on the first tee, his caddie sat on the big golf bag, smoking a cigarette as he unwrapped a sandwich. I turned back to Morgan with his uncombed hair and his bloodshot eyes and his beer-soaked shirt that stuck to his belly. I bit my cheeseburger and, chewing on an onion, I turned and watched my opponent and felt a strange vacuum.

"Tom tells me that you passed up an offer from Brobeck, Phlegher and Harrison to come down here, Doug."

"That's true," I said.

"That's a hell of a fancy firm."

"Yes," I said.

"Tom says you did it on a promise by Paul Butler that you'll be working with me."

"Yes," I said.

"Funny," said Morgan, "nobody ever said anything about it to me."

"I . . . I hope," I stammered, "it's—"

"Did Butler let you know I don't have much work right now?"

"No. He said—"

"Well, look who's here," Tom Gallagher suddenly piped up in a nasty tone.

I looked up, surprised to see Paul Butler walking hurriedly toward our table. He stopped before us, took a moment to catch his breath, and said something that, given the things I'd been hearing, seemed quite odd.

"Oh, Dan, I am glad to see you," Butler said. He sat down. "I heard you were back. Elias said he saw you both at the Arizona Club last night. I've been looking all over for you, Tom. Finally I remembered hearing you say you might come out to watch the golf match. I was hoping you were here, hoping you'd know where Dan made off to. I have—"

"So what happened?" Gallagher barked, interrupting this stream of consciousness.

Paul Butler caught his breath once again. "Ferris Eddington's son was murdered this morning."

"Holy Christ!"

Then a protracted silence. I lowered my cheeseburger. Now it was I who was trying to catch his breath. And it was I who finally spoke. "Travis?"

"You knew Travis?" Morgan asked.

"Yes."

"Well, Paul," Morgan said, "you didn't come all this way just to tell us that."

"That's right, Dan. I came to tell you that Ferris Eddington wants you to defend Travis's widow." Morgan leaned back in his chair. "She's the one who killed him," Butler finally said, as if to restart the conversation.

"Ferris Eddington wants me to defend the woman who killed his only son?"

"Yes," Butler told him. "That's what he says."

"Why?"

"I don't know, Dan. I just know what he said when he called me."

"What happened?"

"I really don't know that either. Just that the wife—I didn't even think to get her name—"

"Rita."

They looked at me.

"Her name is Rita," I reiterated.

"You know her, too?"

"Yes."

"Well," Butler went on, "apparently Travis had moved out of the house and was staying in one of the old irrigator's shacks on the ranch. Rita, is it? Rita went out there this morning and shot him. Ferris said she had her daughter with her when she did it."

Morgan looked at me quizzically.

"Miranda," I said.

"How do you know all these people?" Morgan asked.

Tom Gallagher stepped in. "Didn't you know Doug's father, Dan? Bill McKenzie?"

"I don't think so."

"He was Ferris Eddington's accountant. The comptroller for the ranch. He worked with Frank on all Ferris's matters. He died a few years ago."

"I sort of grew up on the ranch," I told Morgan.

"When he wasn't playing golf over at the Mesa Country Club," Gallagher added.

"Ferris told me that there was a witness who didn't see the shooting but heard it," Paul Butler said, trying to get back to the matter that brought him there. "The manager of his sheep operation."

"Do you know him, too?" Morgan asked me.

"Yes. His name is Juan Menchaka."

"That's all I know, Dan," Butler said. "Will you defend her?"

Morgan reached for his sock and lit another cigarette, watching the smoke drift upward. He put down his can of beer and yelled across the patio. "Hey, waiter! I'd like a cup of coffee."

The assistant pro walked by the table and leaned in toward me. "Fifteen minutes, Mr. McKenzie."

"Huh?"

"You're on the tee in fifteen minutes."

"Oh. Yes. Thank you."

A large gallery was gathering at the first tee.

"There'll be problems," Morgan said to Butler.

"Such as?" Butler asked suspiciously.

"You've got ethical problems, Paul, when you're paid by one person to defend another person in a criminal case. It's in the canons."

"Well, those things can always be worked out," said Butler. Morgan stared at him. "With informed consents and all." Morgan continued staring. "Isn't that true?" Butler demanded. Morgan took a long drag on his cigarette and let the smoke drift thickly through his nose. Then he sipped some coffee. "Well?" said Butler.

"Maybe," Morgan ventured. "Maybe."

"Well, assuming those sorts of problems can be worked out, will you take the case?"

"Maybe he will and maybe he won't," Tom Gallagher interjected. Paul Butler spun around and stared. "I mean, maybe I'll just veto it," Gallagher added.

Butler bristled, and Morgan said, "What?"

Gallagher turned. "There's something I haven't told you, Danny. While you were away, Paul got a new policy passed. Any member of the management committee now has the right to veto the taking of a criminal matter."

"Come again!"

"Dan," Butler pleaded, "we have to get control of our billing practices."

"Right," said Gallagher. "And on account of that duplicitous little theory, I have veto power. Paul, my friend, I may just have to hoist you on your own petard."

"I don't understand."

"Oh, come on, Paul, we know what's going on here, you and I."

I sat stock-still, unable to move.

"I do *not* know what you're talking about, Tom."

"Yes you do," Gallagher said. "Yes you do. You know that when that woman pulled the trigger, she didn't just shoot Travis. She got you, too. For some reason, and only God knows why, Ferris Eddington wants her defended. And you know that if Danny doesn't do it, Ferris will go somewhere else. Maybe to Ramsey and Elliot. They do criminal work over there. And while Ferris is over there, Frank could die. And if that should happen, Ferris Eddington just might not come back to us. They do real estate work, too. You know that. Damned good real estate work. Lots of it. And if that should happen, if Ferris should leave us, all that origination credit you're salivating over would evaporate."

"Ten minutes, Mr. McKenzie," I heard from behind me.

Paul Butler's face was aflame. "Are you telling me, Tom, that you would risk the firm's losing Ferris Eddington just to injure me?"

"I'm telling you that I will do something that I feel is for the good of the entire firm. I'm telling you that I will veto Dan's taking this case unless you agree to something."

"What's that?"

"That if Dan Morgan represents this woman, then, upon Frank Menendez's death, origination credit for every bit of the Eddington business goes to Dan Morgan. After all, we both know that if anybody can hold that client right now, it's Danny. Isn't it you who wants to do things fairly, Paul?"

Butler's jaw slackened.

"Tom," Morgan interjected, "you don't need to do this."

"The hell I don't," Gallagher said, still looking straight at Butler. "The hell I don't."

"That would take the agreement of the entire partnership," Butler stated.

"And they'll agree. To hold that client? It'll be unanimous. You're the only one with reason to object. Hell, Paul, they'll agree to it just to see that you don't get the points, and they'll laugh while they do it."

Butler glowered.

"You need to make a decision, Paul. And you need to make it quickly. If we're to take the case, we'll need to arrange a partnership meeting to get it straight. But if we're not going to take it, I want to watch the end of this golf tournament. Young McKenzie here is going to win it."

Butler jerked his chair around, and with his back to us he studied the pro shop door.

"I know you've thought about your own interests a lot more than I have, Paul, so I won't make a speech. I won't mention how much of that Eddington work you'll still get to do. And I won't talk about how there'll be peace in the valley." For the first time since he'd started, Gallagher looked at me. He smiled and winked. "Instead of talking about all that stuff, I think I'll just go pee." Gallagher rose and headed for the clubhouse.

Morgan turned to me, seemingly oblivious to Paul Butler's dilemma. "What's Rita Eddington like?" he asked.

"She's beautiful," I told him.

"No," he said with an impatient edge. "I mean, what's she like? Would she kill him?"

"Oh," I said. "I don't know. I mean, I wouldn't think so. But I don't know."

"Why wouldn't you think so?"

"She was about the nicest girl I ever knew."

"Where did you know her?"

"In high school. At Mesa High School. She was a few years older, but she was always nice to me."

"Miranda. The daughter. What's she like?"

"She's emotionally disturbed," I told him. "She's been in hospitals."

"Like where?"

"I know once they took her to the Menninger Clinic in Kansas."

Morgan shook his head, pursed his lips, and whistled without sound. "How old?"

"Twelve, I think. Maybe thirteen."

He held his cigarette between his fingers and slowly scratched his chin with his thumb.

Suddenly Winthrop North approached our table. "Hello, Paul," he said.

"Dr. North, how are you?" Paul Butler stood up. They were friendly and obviously well acquainted.

"Missed you at the Harvard Club meeting last week," the doctor said.

Butler made some excuse, and their talk turned to when next they would get together for squash and where in Phoenix they might find a decent court.

While they chatted, Morgan bent toward me. He narrowed his eyes like a fox. "Hey, Doug," he whispered, "with what Butler just said happened, how can they be so sure Rita did it? How can they be so damned sure the little girl didn't kill him?"

"I don't know," I said. "Maybe Juan Menchaka could tell who did it."

"Right," Morgan said.

Gallagher returned from the restroom. He sat down next to me and watched Paul Butler and Winthrop North with an insolent expression. He warmed and lit a greenish cigar. The conversation between the two alumni returned to the Harvard Club. "Spare me, sweet Jesus," Gallagher whispered in my direction. "I think I'm going to throw up."

Butler urged Winthrop North closer to our table. "Of course you know Doug McKenzie, Win." My opponent and I nodded at each other. "And Tom Gallagher."

"We've met before," Gallagher said, waving his cigar toward the doctor.

"And have you met Dan Morgan?"

A strange expression came over Winthrop North as he and Morgan shook hands. "The lawyer," North said.

"Right," Morgan agreed. For the first time that day, Winthrop North took a long, hard look at me.

"Would you excuse us please, Doctor?" Gallagher said. "We have some business to discuss here."

"Five minutes, Mr. McKenzie." Around the tee I could see people I had known as a child, friends of my father's, people I'd played golf with all through my childhood at the Mesa Country Club.

"Well, what's the verdict, Paul?" asked Gallagher.

Paul Butler exuded venom, but still he announced, "I'll agree to it."

"Fine. Now I guess it's up to Dan."

The managing partner waited on Morgan's decision.

"One condition, Paul."

"What is it?"

"I want an associate on this one."

"When has there ever been a time when you couldn't find any number of associates eager to help you?"

"That's not what I mean. I want somebody who's mine.

I don't want to have to go around sheepishly begging partners to cut people free. I want somebody who works for me
and only me. I want it so, that if somebody else wants to use
that associate, they have to come and ask me. And I want it
so they think twice before coming round, and when they do
come round, they do it with their hats in their hands."

"I'm sure we can arrange that."

"Who's available?" Morgan demanded. "I'll need somebody today. Right now."

They began to talk about possibilities. Chet Johnson was
busy working for Gallagher. Ronnie Talbot was in a trial
with Walter Smith. "What about Ann Hastings?"

"No way." Morgan belched emphatically.

I looked over to where Winthrop North sat alone with
his glass of milk. I watched him for a long moment, then
felt the words come up and out of my mouth. "I'd like to
do it," I offered tentatively. It became as quiet as when we
learned that Travis Eddington was dead. "I'll do it," I declared, a little more forcefully.

"Can't do it, Doug," Morgan finally responded. "I need
someone now. We'll want to talk to witnesses. We may be
in front of a judge on a bail hearing this afternoon. I'm sure
we're going to need some research."

"I understand. That's okay. I'll do it."

He measured me in disbelief. "Hey," he stated flatly,
"you're going to win this thing."

"If there's a trial, would you let me ask some questions?
You know . . . of a witness?"

"Yes," he promised.

"Would you tell me how to do it?"

"Yes."

"I'd like to do it. If you'll let me."

"I'll be dipped in shit," Tom Gallagher said.

Morgan lit a cigarette and watched Winthrop North finish his glass of milk. "You think you could find this witness for me, this Juan Menchaka?"

"Yes," I assured him.

A stern gaze came at me across the old patio table. "One
thing."

"Yes?"

"I'm sure there'll be a witness for you. But that's only if we decide to take this case. And then it's only if we decide to take this case to trial."

"I understand."

"Doug, we can never make a decision based on the fact that you walked off this golf course."

"I know," I said. My God, was I doing it again? Not two hours before, I'd been planning my telephone call to the hiring partner in San Francisco. Now I was telling Daniel Morgan that I would abscond from the state amateur golf championship with him. Was I losing my mind? I looked back to Winthrop North, with Morgan's nasty pronouncement about his professional competence still ringing in my ears. "I'd like to do it," I said once more. Morgan closed his eyes and rubbed them. He smoked his cigarette. He finished his coffee.

My spikes clicked on the concrete as I followed the three law partners down the sidewalk to the parking lot.

2   "GET IN TOM'S CAR," Morgan ordered as I was putting my clubs in my trunk.

       "But I've got mine here," I said.

"We'll send a runner for it. Get in the car. Now! Let's go." I followed orders. "How about kicking it in the ass, Tom?" Morgan said.

Gallagher put the pedal down, and gravel sprayed, and in seconds the big Eldorado convertible was going seventy miles an hour on Williams Field Road with me in the backseat looking around for cops, knowing that drunk as Gallagher still was, we might never get out of jail, even if we did have with us the grand master of habeas corpus.

Suddenly Morgan yelled, "Stop!" and Gallagher hit the brakes. Morgan jumped out and hurried across a vacant lot to a little gas and grocery market. He came back carrying three cups of steaming coffee with plastic covers. He had a carton of Camel cigarettes. As we started again, he retrieved a pack of French cigarettes, Gauloises, from his sock. He looked at the package contemptuously, crumpled it up, and threw it into the road. He lit one of the Camels and inhaled a deep, luxurious drag, and the smoke came out through his nose and rose up to where it exploded in the wind created by the speed of the car. He took the lid off his coffee and turned around to me with his arm over the seat back.

"Okay, tell me again, where do we find Juan Menchaka?"

"Turn left on Elliot Road," I instructed Gallagher.

"Is he a Mexican?" Morgan asked.

"No. Basque. He came here from Idaho."

"You know him?"

"Yes."

"Very well?"

"Yes. He's my friend."

Morgan asked how that was, and I explained. I told him how each spring the herders would drive the sheep up the trail because they couldn't stand the heat of summer in the valley, how they would take them to the White Mountains above McNary, how the sheep would graze all the way up the trail and then graze all summer in the mountains until the time when the herders would drive them back down to the valley. "One summer when I was in high school, I went on the trail with them. Juan took care of me. My father wouldn't have let me go if Juan weren't in charge. He didn't trust the herders. But he trusted Juan."

"I didn't know they did that," Morgan said.

"Hell, Danny," Gallagher yelled at him through the wind. "We've litigated those grazing rights for Ferris."

"It's only the ewes, though," I informed him.

"What?"

"They can only drive the ewes up the trail. They have to take the rams up later, by truck. Their feet are too tender to make the drive."

We drove on past cotton field after cotton field. The bolls had broken wide open, and the white cotton puffed out. They would defoliate it soon, and then they would bring in the machines. In other fields hay was being baled. It was hot. Even in the wind of the convertible, it was very hot, and I could feel the sweat soak into my knit golf shirt, not just under my arms but down my back and around my belly. As I wilted with the heat, Morgan came to life. He kept turning in his seat, asking me questions. His eyes seemed to change color as they moved. "Any reason that woman might have had to kill him?" he asked me. "Other than maybe some kind of inheritance?"

"Not that I know of," I responded.

"What kind of a guy was Travis?"

"I don't know. I never knew him very well." I watched Morgan blowing smoke up into the wind. "I think he was a disappointment to his father," I added.

"Why do you say that?"

"Because that's what my father told my mother," I said. "I guess Ferris must have said something to my father. That's really about all I know."

I tried to remember Travis. I hadn't seen him in many years, and I realized that I couldn't remember much, only a dark-complexioned boy who was five years older than I, who by the time he was in high school had a heavy beard and seemed remote and lonely. I did have one vivid memory of him. Once, after I was in high school and he was out and working on the ranch, he tuned my car for me, my '51 Ford. When he finished, he said, "Hey, Doug, if you want me to, I'll chop and channel this car for you. And put cutouts on it. Then you could get it lacquered and get rolled and pleated upholstery." After that he smiled something akin to a leer and said, "Then maybe you could get some girls." That was all I could remember of him as we drove on through his father's fields on this day.

I saw a man I recognized walking up the road wearing knee-high rubber boots and carrying a shovel over his shoulder. "Why don't you stop, Tom," I suggested.

Tom pulled over, and Raymond Valenzuela came up to the car. "Hey, Doug, long time no see."

"What's happening, Ramón?"

"Same old shit. Irrigatin' cotton fields."

"You know where Juan Menchaka is?"

"The big corral." He pointed. "You hear about Travis?" he asked.

As Gallagher was pulling away, Morgan motioned him to stop. "You know anything about what happened?" he asked Raymond.

"Nope. Just that Travis went and got himself shot and killed is all I heard."

We drove on, across sections with roads I'd known all my life. Elliot, Guadalupe, Baseline, Alma School. We crossed the land of my childhood, the land where, from time to time, when something deep in my father's soul would scream, "That boy must learn to work," I would buck hay or irrigate or load crop dusters or herd sheep. (I even picked cotton there, but that was way back, before the big machines, back when the Eddingtons were just rich, before my father helped to make them wealthy.)

"So is your friend Juan Menchaka the kind of guy who can be pushed around?" Morgan asked.

"What do you mean?"

"Do you think a lawyer can put words in his mouth?"

"No," I said. "He may be a little nervous, but he's not going to let anyone put words in his mouth."

"The girl, Miranda, you know her?"

"Not very well. I mean, I've seen her. I know who she is. I just know she's had emotional problems."

"Funny," Morgan said. "I feel I know Ferris Eddington pretty well, but I don't think I ever met Travis."

"Oh, yes you did," Gallagher said. "When the firm had the ranch, before we sold it. Travis came up one weekend. Ferris had him along the time he brought that Angus bull up."

"Yes, that's right," Morgan remembered.

We came to the sheep, pen after pen and pasture after pasture. Occasionally among them you could spot a goat with a bell around its neck. As we approached the big corral, I could see Juan down the entry road standing with a group of men. "We should park out here," I told Gallagher.

Across the road stood the house where it had happened, a small, square, wood-frame house with a tin roof. Yellow police tape crossed the door and the window, and a deputy sheriff sat on the narrow front porch. Besides the yellow tape, the only thing that distinguished the sad little building was a redwood flower box that hung on wires beneath the front window. Brightly colored flowers, snapdragons, filled the box.

We headed up the short path to the corral. Two dogs greeted us. They ran around our feet and, with noses to our ankles, herded us over against the fence.

"What the hell?" Morgan exclaimed.

"It's instinct," I told him. "This is what they're born to do. They'll make sure we get there."

Darting around us, the dogs herded us on down the path. At the corral, half a dozen men spoke in Spanish, all the time drawing patterns in the dirt with their boots. They looked up as we approached, and the smallest of them came toward us. He wore a khaki shirt with the sleeves rolled up showing the stringy muscles of his forearms, which were nearly black from so many days in the Arizona sun. A leather apron that was dark and soft from years of work and the lanolin of many sheep covered his old, faded Levi's, which were rolled up at the bottoms. And he wore World War II combat boots like he always had, the kind he could still occasionally find in army-surplus stores if he looked hard enough. No matter where we went that summer I spent with him, if we passed an army-surplus store he'd insist we stop so he could look for those old-style boots, which were already becoming scarce. They laced up to where there was a leather flap that buckled around the top of his ankle. And he wore the same old felt hat with the years of sweat soaked through it. When he saw that I was there, he turned and gave a couple of quick orders in Spanish, and the other men dispersed.

"Hi, Juan."

Before he let go of my hand, he put his arm around me. "I hear you're a full-grown lawyer now."

"That's what they tell me."

"That's good."

I felt a little guilty that I hadn't been out to see him, but he didn't say anything about that. He just patted me and said, "I'm proud of you."

"Juan, this is Dan Morgan, and this is Tom Gallagher. They're with the law firm."

Shyly he shook both their hands, carefully looking them up and down without speaking.

"It's good to meet you," Morgan said.

"I get the feeling you are here to talk about what happened this morning," he said.

"We are, Juan. Ferris wants the firm to defend Rita."

"What?"

I nodded.

"Ferris will pay you to defend that woman?"

"I believe he intends to," I said.

"Why?"

"We don't know," I told him. "We're supposed to meet with him in a little while. But so far we haven't talked to him."

"Will you talk to us, Juan?" Morgan asked.

"Any reason I shouldn't?" Juan inquired of me.

I looked at Morgan, who said, "No," and I turned to Juan and said, "No."

"You all want some coffee?"

Juan led us to a small campfire. He picked up an old camp coffeepot and poured coffee into four tin cups. I knew there would be eggshells in the bottom of the pot to coagulate the grounds. I also knew there would be green chile and beans in the Dutch oven that sat in the fire by the coffeepot. I almost asked Juan if I could have a bowl. After all, I hadn't even gotten a full bite of my cheeseburger. But I saw from Morgan's expression that he was not there for a second attempt at lunch, and I followed as Juan led him to where he'd been when it all happened.

"I was here," Juan said. It was at a point in the far corner of the field next to the corral, the corner nearest the house. "I had a ewe that had been . . ." He thought a second, and said, "Well, you don't want me to waste your time with that. I had a sick sheep. That's why I was out here earlier than I usually am. I saw them ride up."

"Rita and her daughter?" Morgan asked.

"Yes. Rita and Miranda. They rode two of those quarter horses that Ferris bought from Tom Finley." Juan looked at me, seeming to think I would remember. "Good horses," he told Morgan. "They tied them there, right next to the gate." He pointed. "Then they walked to the house."

"How old is Miranda?"

"I'm not certain. Maybe twelve."

"Did you see the gun?" Morgan asked.

"No. I'm sure it was in Rita's purse. She carried a purse."

"How do you know the girl wasn't carrying it?"

Juan snapped around and measured Morgan with immense suspicion. He looked across the field, then back to Morgan. He turned and stared at me and tightened his jaw, and for a moment I was pretty sure he wasn't going to talk to us anymore. When words finally came again, Juan directed them at me. "That little girl didn't shoot her father."

"But," said Morgan, "I thought you couldn't see who did it."

"That's right," said Juan. "But that child did not shoot him. She wouldn't have."

Morgan watched him, and in time he asked the question he had asked before: "How are you sure Miranda wasn't carrying the gun?"

"Because it wasn't in her hand, and if it had been in a pocket, I would have seen a bulge. Hell, I don't think either one of them could have gotten it into a pocket. They wear those pants so damned tight."

Morgan turned toward the house. "I guess," he mused, "the gun could already have been in there. Couldn't it have been in the house before they went in?"

Juan turned to Morgan, oblivious to the question. "You're not going to try to lay this off on that little girl, are you?"

Morgan walked away from us, back along the fence toward the corral. He stopped, bent down and pulled his cigarettes from his sock. He lit one and watched the smoke drift up as he leaned against the fence. He watched the deputy sheriff stand up and stretch. After a few more drags, he dropped the cigarette, turned his shoe on it, and came back to us.

"If the girl didn't handle the gun," Morgan theorized, "fingerprints should prove it. Or were they wearing gloves?"

"No," Juan said. "Neither of them wore gloves, but I

don't think fingerprints are going to show anybody anything, and I can tell you for sure that the gun wasn't in the house ahead of time."

"How's that?" asked Morgan.

"Because both Rita and Miranda had been shooting the gun before they got here. They'd been practicing shooting at beer bottles."

"How do you know that?"

" 'Cause Robert and Johnny Camacho saw them."

"How is it you were looking at them so closely that you can be sure the girl didn't carry the gun?"

"I don't know. I just had that ewe up on my apron, and I was watching them." With his gaze still on Juan, Morgan turned his head a couple of degrees. "Rita is a good-looking woman," Juan finally said. That seemed to satisfy Morgan, and Juan went on to describe how he'd seen them go into the house and close the door. "I had no idea why they were there," he said. "I didn't know Travis was inside. I thought the irrigators were still using that place. I'd seen Travis around, but I figured he was just there to talk to the irrigators."

"Then what happened?"

"I heard the shots, six of them. I put the sheep down, and I stood up. I was shaking."

"Were the shots all together, or were they spaced out?" Morgan queried.

Once again Juan stared at Morgan suspiciously. "Only one person shot that gun," he said. Juan had figured out where Morgan was going before I had. "All the shots were one right after the other. Rapid succession. So close together that the gun could never have changed hands."

"What happened then?"

"They came outside."

"How long after the shots?"

"I don't know. Some time. A minute. Maybe two."

"Did they ever see you, Juan?"

"I'm sure they didn't see me before they went in the house. I was kneeling down here behind the fence. But I was standing up when Rita came out. She saw me then."

"Then what happened?"

"Rita dropped the gun. She dropped it in the dirt right beside the steps."

By the time he was finished, Juan had told us about how Miranda had followed her mother out onto the porch, how they had both sat down, how he'd gone to them. He described looking through the door and seeing Travis's hand, which he recognized. He grimaced when he talked about going through the door. "I knew he was dead without getting close." He described how he tried to talk to both of them and how neither said a word, how they just looked straight ahead. Finally he told us about going back into the house to use the telephone.

We walked across the road toward the house. Standing by the gate, Morgan made him tell it all again. And as Juan told the story a second time, I stared at the bright flowers under the window.

The deputy sheriff who sat on the porch recognized Morgan. "Hey, Dan, how are you?"

"Not bad, Phil. Any chance we can get in there and have a look around?"

"Nope."

"Can you tell me where they took the body?"

"PML."

When we returned to the campfire, Juan reported that earlier the police had swarmed the place, that they'd talked to him before we got there, that the Camacho brothers had come and told everyone about the target practice with the beer bottles. He informed Morgan that a lawyer, a prosecutor, had already talked to him.

"Really."

"Yes."

"What was his name?"

"Hauser," Juan said.

Morgan turned to Gallagher. "Who is he?" Gallagher shrugged. "Whoever he is, he gets up early," Morgan said.

Juan turned to me. "I have something I want to show you, Douglas." He went to his pickup and brought back a long, aluminum tube that had a cap on the end. He unscrewed the cap and drew out a fly rod. He jointed the two sections. "Graphite," he announced proudly. "Space age. This is the best thing man has ever invented. Are you still tying flies the way I taught you?"

"I do sometimes, just so I don't forget, but I never get to fish anymore."

The interview ended with Travis Eddington lying cold in the postmortem lab, while the four of us took turns casting a magic fly rod with a golden line shooting back and forth in fast, tight loops above a dusty flock of sheep.

3   THE ELDORADO SWUNG through the white gate and onto the long gravel driveway that led to the office where my father had all but lived and ultimately had died. "I heard the other day that Ferris is feeding twenty thousand head of cattle here now," Gallagher said. Along both sides of the driveway ran freshly painted white wooden fences. Beyond the white fences, steel and concrete feeding pens full of cattle, Herefords and Anguses, extended into the distance. Two trucks drove up and down the alleys between the pens spreading feed the length of concrete troughs where cattle had their heads stuck through the steel bars to eat. The driveway encircled the office, an aging two-story wood-frame building with a porch that ran all the way around. The building, as did the fence, showed a new coat of white paint. Behind the office to either side stood tall, open steel barns protecting great stacks of baled hay. Between the barns a small corral enclosed a number of horses, some Thoroughbreds, some quarter horses.

A lone Cadillac Sedan DeVille sat by the office building. Across the driveway from the car, a multigated cutting pen led to squeeze chutes and alleys that allowed cows to be sent out in many directions. Inside the pen, Ferris Eddington sat astride a big buckskin quarter horse. "Look at that!" Morgan exclaimed. "That horse must be seventeen hands high." The horse had cornered a group of steers with black hides and white faces. Nervously the horse stalked back and forth in front of the steers, his head swinging low to keep the animals in a group, occasionally forcing one steer away from the rest. A man on foot stood in a corner of the pen. By moving his head, Ferris Eddington would signal which gate the man was to send each steer through.

Did it seem strange that Ferris Eddington would be working cattle on the day his only son was killed? As we sat in Gallagher's convertible watching him work, my mind faded back to an event from my childhood. One evening when I was barely old enough to drive a car, my father asked me to go out to the ranch office to pick up some papers from his desk. I drove there and, using my father's key, let myself in. As I headed for my father's office, I heard the sound of someone sobbing. Quietly I sneaked around a corner to where I could see into Ferris Eddington's office, and to my astonishment I saw him there, the owner of the biggest cattle operation in Arizona, elbows on his desk and head in his hands, crying like a baby.

Late that night my mother told me that before he married Eleanor, the icy invalid whom I had always known as Mrs. Eddington, Ferris Eddington had married a young girl, a short-order waitress from Tucson, where he and my father had lived as fraternity brothers. When Ferris Eddington brought the uneducated working girl home, his father, old John Eddington, refused to let her in the house. Within a week, at the peril of disinheritance, old John's son acceded to an annulment. The father gave the girl some money, quite a bit, and sent her on her way. On the day I'd caught Ferris Eddington in tears, he had learned, my mother told me, that the girl, by then a middle-aged woman, had died, somewhere in California. Later I learned that Ferris Eddington did not come to work for three days after that. Apart from those three days and an occasional business trip, usually with my father to the stock show in Denver each year, there had never been a day after he graduated from the University of Arizona that Ferris Eddington did not swing onto his favorite horse and work his cattle.

So did it seem strange that he was up on that big buckskin the day Travis died? Maybe not.

Ferris Eddington saw us standing by the pen and waved to the man on foot that it was finished, then reined his horse around. Turning to glance over his shoulder, he yelled, "Oh, Tomás, call down tomorrow morning and tell them to send those Herefords up from the border. We have room for them now." He reached down from his saddle to open the gate, but Morgan took three quick steps and opened it for him. Outside the pen, Ferris Eddington dismounted. He stood ramrod straight, all six feet four inches. His hair had thinned since I'd last seen him. He was seventy years old, the same age my father would have been had his heart not blown apart five years before in the office across the way from where we stood.

He was my father's friend as well as his employer. At least I think he was my father's friend, my mother's suspicions to the contrary notwithstanding. A trophy case graces the main hallway of Chandler Union High School. In that case is a photograph of a state champion football team, with Ferris Eddington and Bill McKenzie standing beside each other in leather helmets. There is also a trophy with their names on it for the State Debating Championship.

"Hello, Tom."

"Ferris, I can't tell you how sorry I am."

"And you, Danny. Thank you for coming."

"What can I say, Ferris?" Morgan shook his head gravely.

Apart from a few more wrinkles and the thinner hair, Ferris Eddington had not changed much since I'd seen him last at my father's funeral. His large, finely shaped head still featured intelligent eyes, widely set above prominent cheekbones. His long, straight nose led down toward a chiseled chin. Not a bit of fat showed, and he looked still to be very fit. He wore a heavily starched oxford shirt, the kind he'd always worn, and the boots he'd had made in Texas. And there were the long, square, aristocratic fingers and the big diamond ring. Suddenly, as I watched him extend his hand to me, I realized I was not sure how to address the man to whom I was no doubt indebted for my job. I remembered that my father had always made sure I called him "Mr."

"It's good to see you, Mr. Eddington." I shook his hand.

"It's Ferris, Douglas," he said with a tired smile.

"I'm really sorry about Travis."

Without speaking he patted me on the back, and with his arm still around my shoulder and the reins in his other hand, he led me to where he would unsaddle his horse. Gallagher and Morgan followed. The procession moved slowly.

"Is your mother still in San Diego?"

"Yes. She's still teaching."

"You tell her to come and see me the next time she's home, will you?"

"Yes, sir," I promised.

After Ferris Eddington had groomed his horse and as the four of us were walking back toward the office building, Morgan said, "That's sure as hell a big quarter horse, Ferris."

"He's a good cutting horse," said the owner.

"I remember when you used to come up to Wickenburg, when the firm first bought that ranch, so we could all play at being cowboys," Morgan continued. "You'll probably never know how much we learned from you about how to run it."

"I think you all learned a lot about cattle and sheep law from having that place. And when I see what you're billing me for your time lately, I thank God you learned it on your own time and not mine."

Morgan and Gallagher laughed, but not very loudly.

We all climbed the steps and walked across the porch and into the office. The big clock still hung on the knotty pine wall. The Union Pacific calendar hung near the clock, as it always had. The rolltop desk looked the same, with the tickets for the truck scale stacked the way they'd always been. I stopped and looked into the office that had been my father's. The last time I'd been in there, my father sat behind the desk. Ferris Eddington came up behind me. "Your father would have been very proud of you, Douglas." He ushered us into his own office. "Well," he announced, "I'm going to have a drink. Can I get anyone else one?"

"I'll just have a cup of coffee, if you have some," Morgan said.

"Tom?"

"Scotch."

"Would you like something, Douglas?"

"If you have coffee, I'd like a cup."

When Ferris Eddington finally sat down, he looked at Morgan and Gallagher closely. If the way they appeared that afternoon bothered him, he didn't let it show. "I want her defended," he said.

"Why, Ferris?" Morgan demanded. "Why in hell would you want to help her now?"

Ferris Eddington stared out the window and sipped his whiskey. Turning back to us, he raised his index finger as if to emphasize what he was about to say. But then he said nothing. He reached for the silver cigarette box on the desk and drew out a Chesterfield. He lit the cigarette, took another sip of whiskey, and again he looked out the window. "My reasons are my own," Ferris Eddington said at last. "We'll just have to leave it there. This family owes that girl something. I want her to get a fair trial. I want her defended."

Morgan stared across the desk for a long moment. "Those sure were good-looking steers, Ferris," he finally said.

"Yes, we're getting those Angus Hereford cross-breds better every year. Will you defend her, Danny?"

"There are ethical implications. It's considered improper for a lawyer to be paid by one person to defend another person in a criminal case, unless you have the informed and intelligent consent of the defendant."

"I don't understand that."

"There's too great a potential for conflicts of interest. After all, Ferris, everybody's saying she killed your son. It wouldn't surprise anyone if you might want to help her into the gas chamber."

"But that's not what I want," Ferris Eddington protested. "I want her defended. I want her defended just as well as she can be. That's why I want you to do it, Danny."

"You could have no say in the defense whatsoever," Morgan said. "No matter how much you're paying us."

"So agreed. Just bill me for everything at your standard rates."

"I won't do it unless the child has representation."

"I'll take care of that as well. Can you find someone to represent her?"

"Yes," Morgan assured him.

"I can't imagine that anyone would suggest that Miranda shot him."

"Why not?" Morgan asked harshly. "I hear she has had some pretty serious problems."

"That's true," our employer conceded.

The sun dropped toward the horizon, and the light in the old paneled office began to go down as the two men talked about Miranda and her mother.

"They had Miranda at the Menninger Clinic in Kansas for a long time," Ferris Eddington informed us.

"What was wrong with her?" Morgan asked.

"I don't know. I only know that she had severe bouts of depression."

"How long has she been home?"

"Just through the summer. She was supposed to start school last month, but Rita decided to hold her out and look for a special school."

"How has she been?" Morgan asked.

"She seemed very normal right up until she was held out of school. Since then she's been moping around like she just lost her best friend."

"Where did Rita come from?" Morgan asked.

"Rita's mother came to work for me almost twenty years ago. She came down from Winslow and brought Rita with her. That was after her husband, a railroad man, had walked out on them. Travis got to know Rita here on the ranch. She was a good wife. I'm sure of that."

"Why would she kill him, Ferris?"

"I have no idea. You'll have to ask her. They told me that they took her to the county jail in Phoenix."

At that, we took our leave and walked across the old porch and down the steps to the car. "He sure as hell doesn't seem very upset," Tom Gallagher said.

4 WE DROVE WEST toward Phoenix through fields of recently harvested melons. Again I sat in the backseat and felt the wind that earlier had blown so hot mercifully begin to cool.

"You know," Gallagher yelled through the wind, "this land might well have been Frank Menendez's."

"What?" Dan Morgan yelled back.

"Yeah. Frank's father owned all these sections once. He ran his sheep here during the winters."

"I didn't know that."

"He sold it to old John Eddington in 1920."

"Why did he sell it?"

"He had to. He needed money to send Frank to Harvard."

"I'll be damned," Morgan said. "Frank never told me that."

"He won't talk about it. He still thinks old John cheated his father. I only know because once I had to do a title search for Ferris. I think Frank and Ferris are both still bitter about it."

"Huh?"

"Neither one got what he wanted. The deal left old John so strapped for cash that he couldn't send Ferris to law school. And losing the land meant Frank Menendez would never become rich."

5   AS WE DROVE up Washington Street toward the
    city, I asked Morgan if he really thought the girl
    could have done it.

"What do I know?" he said, staring straight ahead at the fiery sunset. "She was there. She was in that little house when it happened." He turned around to me, throwing his arm over his seat back. "One thing is sure. We aren't being paid to perpetuate myths about sugar and spice. You understand that, don't you?" I nodded. "You know, Doug, we might find out that it was definitely not the daughter who did it. But even if we do find that out, it certainly won't be our job to prove it. We may just want to leave it looking like she did it."

"I know. I understand how the adversary system works. It sounds like if someone proves Miranda didn't do it, that would prove Rita did. I mean, it looks like one of them must have done it."

"You don't think Travis could have shot himself six times?" Morgan asked, chuckling at his small joke.

"Maybe Rita shot him in self-defense, or maybe she was temporarily insane."

Morgan returned to the sunset. "Maybe," he pondered. "Maybe. But wouldn't things go a whole lot easier if it turns out the little girl did it?"

Gallagher pulled onto the ramp that ran down to the base-ment entrance of the county jail. "I'm going on to the of-fice," he told us, smiling. "Butler is supposed to have a partnership meeting set up to discuss some origination of business. You guys will have to walk over when you're fin-ished with Rita." Morgan thanked him for the ride, and we stepped out in front of the single steel door that was set in the concrete wall. There was a small Plexiglas window just to the side of the door. Above it there was steel mesh that appeared to cover a radio speaker. Morgan flashed his state bar identification in front of the window. A voice came through the speaker. "Hello, Dan."

"Hi, Albert."

A buzzer sounded, and the steel door swung open. We slid inside, and I flinched when the door slammed shut be-hind us.

"I think you've booked a woman named Rita Eddington. I need to talk to her."

Albert sat behind a large double pane of glass on a swivel chair surrounded by gray steel desks and a telephone switchboard. He wore the beige-and-brown uniform of the Maricopa County Sheriff's Department. "She's here. Cap-tain wants to speak with you first, though."

Another buzzer went off, and the steel door to our right opened. "Come on in, Dan," said the captain. "Can I talk to you for a minute?"

We followed the captain of the jail, a bulky man with a crew cut, whose name was Ed Brady. "Are you going to represent this Eddington woman, Dan?"

"We're here to talk to her about it."

"They're bringing her down for you."

A short concrete ramp took us into a larger room. Across the far side ran a curtain of heavy steel mesh, and behind the steel mesh sat a number of uniformed officers process-ing papers.

"Did they bring her daughter here, too, Ed? Her name's Miranda."

"She was here. That's what I wanted to talk to you about."

In the middle of the room there was a steel bench bolted to the floor. A tattooed man sat shackled to the bench, and a deputy sheriff stood near him with a shotgun, the muzzle very close to the man's head. At the far end of the room, three prisoners sat on another steel bench. They all wore blue dungarees and white T-shirts that had MARICOPA COUNTY JAIL sloppily stenciled across the front. Ed Brady climbed another small ramp that took us to a set of steel bars that crashed open as we approached. As the doors closed behind us, one of the men on the bench whispered, "Hey, that's Daniel Morgan." I don't believe that Morgan heard him. We came to a small cubicle office with a gray steel desk.

"It was the damnedest thing I've ever seen, Danny. Sit down. Please. Hell, she's only about twelve years old. I didn't know what to do with her. I called juvenile. Nobody's there. I called the juvenile detention center. On Sunday nobody knows what's going on over there. So I finally put her in one of those brand-new cells in the women's side. We haven't started to use them. So I knew she would be away from the general population. I wanted to keep her away from the rest of the prisoners while I figured out what to do with her. A little while later, a matron calls over. The little girl is not in the cell, she tells me. Now, I know goddamned good and well that no twelve-year-old kid's going to escape from that new wing, especially when I've got a matron sitting by the door. Anyway, to make a long story short, I go over there. We find the girl curled up in a little ball under the bunk that they just welded in yesterday. She doesn't move. She doesn't talk. Then we try—gently, Dan, we were real gentle—we try to pull her out. She doesn't budge. She's got one of her arms wrapped around a bar, you know, into the next cell and back. That's when we realize that something's funny. The girl is stiff, Dan."

"What do you mean, 'stiff'?"

"I mean stiff. Like dead. Like we sort of tried to straighten out her leg, and it wouldn't move at all. And it was more than her just trying to muscle it against us. It was like rigor mortis. But she was warm, and we found a pulse."

"What did you do?"

"I called the county hospital. They sent an intern over from the emergency room. He looks at her, feels her pulse, and calls a psychiatrist at the state hospital, a guy named McDavid. McDavid shows up, takes one look at her, and says the only way we're going to get her out from under the bunk without hurting her is to cut her out with a torch. He said it might have been different if he had a certain medicine and could have given her a shot. But he didn't have any."

"What did you do?"

"I had a cutting torch sent up, and we cut the cell apart. We finally wound up sliding her up over the top of what was left of the bar she'd wrapped her arm around. Carried her out like a little statue of a sleeping girl. Just as stiff as if she was made out of clay."

"What did you do with her?"

"McDavid called an ambulance, and they took her out to the state hospital. We never even processed her. Screw 'em. They want that little girl in jail, they can take her to Mesa." Morgan stared at the jail captain, not speaking. "Now listen, Dan. We never hurt that child, and that's the truth. I was just hoping it would be you coming down here today. If it was any different than I just said, you know I'd tell you about it. Now make Ferris Eddington understand that we didn't do a goddamned thing to her. Please. I don't need no more lawsuits saying I abused somebody, especially her. I get enough of those from the slime we cater to day by day."

Ed Brady stopped and waited for Morgan to give him comfort. Morgan lit a cigarette. He blew a smoke ring in my direction. With his thumb and forefinger, he squeezed the bridge of his nose. "Will you talk to Ferris Eddington for me, Dan?" Ed Brady asked nervously.

"What? Oh, yes. I'll talk to him, Ed. I think it'll be okay."

"Thanks. I'll get your woman over here."

Morgan asked if there was any way that we could talk to Rita in a room, instead of through a window by telephone.

"Sure. It's Sunday. Come on, I'll take you upstairs."

6 WE SAT IN an unfinished room. Pieces of crumbling mortar lay around the edges of the floor where it had fallen from the newly laid-up concrete block. Everything was gray: the new walls, the new steel table, the new chairs, all bolted into the new gray concrete floor. Light came from windows around the tops of the walls, and the room had a fresh, cool feel. We waited without talking, Morgan deep in his own thoughts. Finally the door opened, and Rita Eddington entered the room, eased through the door by a large, uniformed matron. Morgan and I stood up.

Earlier Morgan had asked me what Rita Eddington was like. When I told him she was beautiful, he frowned, shook his head, and gently rebuked me. *"No,"* he had said. *"I mean, what's she like? Would she kill him?"* Now, as Morgan gazed at Rita, I enjoyed the small delight that comes with vindication. Morgan stared, and for a moment, I swear, he could not speak.

Her lively red hair rested loosely on top of her head, as if it had been hot and she wanted it up and away from her neck. Wisps fell softly around her high cheekbones and the vibrant pink skin of her long neck. The ginger tendrils framed almond-shaped turquoise eyes that tilted upward, giving her a slightly feline quality. Her nose was perfectly straight, her lips full, and her teeth gleamed white. My mother had always referred to her as a strawberry blonde. My father had called her a Gibson girl. "That's how they made 'em in the good old days," he told me. ·

The matron led her to the table, and Rita looked nervously around the room, until she fixed on me. "Doug?"

"Hi, Rita."

"What are you doing here?"

"I work for him."

Morgan took a step forward, and Rita turned to him. He held out his hand.

"My name is Dan Morgan."

"Oh," Rita answered, showing recognition. "Yes, I know."

"You do?"

"Yes. You and my husband and my husband's father were branding calves one day." Morgan looked at her quizzically. "Up in Wickenburg," she reminded him. "My husband pointed you out to me that day, and he told me who you were. I remember you."

While they talked, I stared at Rita. I hadn't seen her in years. She was tall, almost as tall as Morgan. She wore a jail dress, a simple gray shift. The dress flared open where the bottom button was missing. I stared at her long, sculptured legs and perfectly turned ankles. It occurred to me, as I gawked, that I could not remember ever having seen her legs. Surely she'd worn dresses to school, but I couldn't remember her in anything except Levi's and cowboy boots. This day she wore shower shoes, flip-flops. They revealed her high, elegant arches, her beautifully formed toes, and an exquisite scarlet pedicure. Rita lowered herself into one of the chairs. She sat straight up, her legs apart like a man.

"Your husband's father asked that we come and talk to you," Morgan advised.

"Yes."

She pulled her thick hair out of its high ponytail, absently running her fingers through it before knotting it on top of her head again. Morgan suddenly became self-conscious. "I'm sorry for the way I look," he said. "I've been out of town, and I didn't want to take time to clean up before I came."

"You look fine to me. I'm used to being with men who work hard. Outside."

She put her hands on the table, and I could see a thin wedding band. I could see also that her hands were rough and cracked and brown from the sun. The rest of her body was pale and smooth. But her hands seemed the very reflection of years of hard work. A single dissonant note in otherwise-unrelenting femininity. I looked down at her silky feet under the table. They could have been made of porcelain. The red polish gleamed. I wondered if anyone else had ever pulled Justin boots off feet that looked like hers.

Morgan turned to the matron. "Georgia, we need to be alone."

"Sure, Danny," the woman said. *Does every law-enforcement officer in Arizona know Dan Morgan?* The woman left the room, and Morgan and I sat down across from Rita.

Before Morgan could ask a question, Rita spoke up. "Do you know where my daughter is?"

"She was here, but she became very upset. They took her to the state hospital."

"How upset?"

"Very."

"Could she move?"

"Apparently not."

"That's bad."

"Yes," said Morgan. "It sounded bad."

"There's a place called Camelback Hospital," she told him.

"I'm aware of it."

"Miranda has been there before. They can help her some." Then, after a pause, "And it's nice. You know. It's pretty. And it's comfortable. My husband's father can make sure they take her there."

"I'll talk to him," Morgan promised.

He then went on to tell her that Ferris Eddington wanted to pay him to defend her. Morgan explained his reservations. He told her he had Ferris Eddington's assurance that he wanted no say in the way the case was handled, that he would stay out of things entirely. "Do you want me to represent you? You may want to take some time before you decide."

She met his gaze directly. "Yes. I want you."

"You trust Ferris Eddington, then?"

"I trust you," she said. "I know who you are."

"We'll still need to get formal approval from the firm," Morgan continued. "That should be routine."

"I understand." Unconsciously she ran her hands up through her hair again, pulling the elastic tight.

"The firm will also insist that you formally consent to our being paid by Ferris."

"I understand the position you're in. I'll be happy to sign anything necessary to protect you."

"Now," said Morgan, "I don't want you to tell me what happened this morning. We'll talk about that later. But I do want you to tell me if you *know* what happened."

She looked at him searchingly for a moment and then said, "Yes, of course I do."

"Mrs. Eddington, they will no doubt charge you with—"

"It would probably be better if you called me Rita."

"With the murder of your husband. I need to know if you feel that you are in such a condition that, if you are charged, you will be able to understand the proceedings."

"You want to know if I'm competent to stand trial."

"That's right."

"I am."

"I can probably have you out of jail within an hour, but I'd like time to think about whether that's in your best interest. Do you think you can stand a night in this place?"

"I'm fine," she said. "For as long as you think I should stay here, I can handle it."

"Have you told anybody what happened in that house this morning?"

"No. No one."

"Are you sure?"

"Yes, I'm sure. They asked me if I wanted to talk about it, and I said no."

"What did they do then?"

"They left me alone."

"Good. That's what they were supposed to do. Now I'm going to tell you something, okay?"

"Yes."

"You do not talk about this case with anybody but me. Do you understand?"

"Yes."

"Nobody! Okay?"

"I understand."

"Not even Doug here."

She nodded.

"If anybody asks you about what happened—or about you, or your background, or anything—you tell them to get hold of me, and you remember and tell me about it. Okay?"

"I will."

"Do you know if Miranda said anything to anyone about what happened?"

"I don't think so. I don't think she was in a condition to speak."

"We'll talk at length later," Morgan said.

Rita nodded, and Morgan excused himself to go out and find the matron. As I sat looking at Rita across the table, I couldn't think of anything to say to her. But then I didn't need to. She did the talking.

"I didn't kill Travis, Doug."

"Rita, I don't think you're supposed to talk about it with anyone but Dan."

"Well, I didn't kill him. I just wanted you to know that."

7　WE HAD DINNER at the Arizona Club that night, sitting first in the crimson chairs that used to be at the east end of the bar and looking out at the city and the lights that spread toward Camelback Mountain and Scottsdale. Twenty-five floors below us, I could see the demolition equipment that stood ready to tear down the pawnshops and Harry Wilson's bar for a new city park and, beyond that, the Luhrs Building and the bright spots where some of the lights were still on in our office.

"I liked this place better when it was over there above the office," Morgan said. "You could get a room up there when you needed one."

"My father was a member then," I told him. I thought back to the old Arizona Club at the top of the Luhrs Building. I pictured the big arched windows and the crystal chandeliers in the dining room. I remembered the card room one floor below and the sleeping rooms where sometimes my father would stay when he played poker too late.

Morgan drank a beer as he reminisced. By then he looked quite normal. Scrubbed, even. He had taken a shower at the office. His hair was combed. He wore a fresh shirt and jacket, barely wrinkled by the suitcase he'd brought from Europe. His eyes were clear. Only the scars on his cheeks and the cigarette dangling from his lips reminded me of how he'd looked before. He'd seemed very happy ever since Paul Butler had told him about the murder.

We made small talk as he drank his beer and I sipped a glass of wine. He told me he'd found my résumé in his office. "Let me ask you something," he said, eyeing my glass. "How'd you ever wind up at Brigham Young? Somehow you don't look like the Mormon missionary type to me."

"I actually went to Arizona State first," I informed him. "I played on the golf team."

"Why'd you transfer?"

"It's a little embarrassing."

"Go ahead."

"After two years my grade-point average merged with my handicap. At that number I wouldn't have graduated."

"Sounds like good golf."

"I played thirty-six holes a day. At night I drank beer at the Sigma Chi house."

"So why BYU?"

"My mother came from a Mormon pioneer family. My grandmother had enough sons who were Mormon bishops that they were able to arrange for my redemption."

"And what about your father, old Bill? Wasn't that what Tom said his name was?"

"I don't think he ever set foot in a church in his life."

"Were you redeemed?"

"Well, at least as far as my grades were concerned I was. Say, Dan, are we just having a drink, or is this turning into some kind of interview?"

Morgan's cheek bulged from where he'd put his tongue. He chuckled without opening his mouth. "From there you went into the navy?"

"Right."

"What did you do in the navy?"

"I was a line officer aboard an amphibious aircraft carrier."

"An LPH?" he asked.

"How'd you know that?"

"Landing platform helicopter, right?"

"Yeah, that's right."

"Which one?"

"USS *Princeton*."

"Watch a lot of marines die, did you?"

I stared at him, stunned. "How do you know all this?"

"Oh," he said, "I know a fellow, a marine lieutenant, who's riding an LPH right now."

"Who is he?"

"Just a guy I know."

"What ship?"

"The *Iwo Jima*."

He knows some guy on the Iwo Jima, *and suddenly he's an expert on obscure naval history?* "I didn't think anybody paid attention to the amphibious navy," I said.

"I know a little bit about the Marine Corps. You came back to Arizona for law school?"

"Yes," I said, "but that was after I was kind of a ski bum for a couple of years."

"And you were the editor-in-chief of the *Law Review*. And then you clerked for the Ninth Circuit."

"Yep."

"Whew." He sort of whistled sideways. "Tell me this, Doug. Why in hell did you pass up that Brobeck firm to come down here?"

"You want the truth?"

"Yes."

"The judge I clerked for in San Francisco told me that you were the best trial lawyer he'd ever seen."

Morgan put his beer on the table and slowly leaned back in his chair. "Shit," he expelled slowly. He laughed. "Jesus Christ." He shook his head from side to side and laughed a little louder. "Shit."

"Well? Aren't you that good?"

He laughed again. "Let me tell you this," Morgan said. "If someday you decide you got bad advice, I just hope you remember you can't go goddamned blaming me." He picked up his beer and drained it, then stood up. "Anyway, Doug, it looks like we've got ourselves a murder case. We'd better eat. We'll be losing a few pounds before it's over."

"Wait. Can I ask you something?"

"Shoot."

"Is the reason Paul Butler was so eager to get me down for an interview, then offered me an inflated salary and a promise that I could work with you—was it that Ferris Eddington told him he had to hire me?"

"That's what Gallagher told me a few minutes ago."

I turned away.

"But, Doug?"

"Yeah?"

"Don't ever get the idea that you needed an assist in getting into this firm. Shit, I still don't know what the hell you're doing here."

"Thank you," I said.

We moved into the dining room. A waiter came and said, "Chef won't light nothin' but the grill. Not enough people." I looked around. Morgan and I were the only people in the dining room that Sunday night.

"Since we're here on Eddington money, we should probably have beef or lamb anyway," Morgan said, and we both ordered steaks.

"I have another question," I said as we waited.

"Go ahead."

"I took this course in trial practice in law school," I told him. "The professor said you should find out everything your client can tell you right off the bat. You know, so there won't be any surprises. So you won't be embarrassed. But you told Rita you didn't want her to tell you what happened."

"That's right," he said.

"I was wondering why."

He lit a cigarette and considered my question. "Did that guy tell you that it's unethical for a lawyer to elicit testimony from a witness when he knows that testimony to be perjured?"

"No. They told us that in the ethics course."

"Well, where would we be if I asked Rita what happened and she blurted out that she shot him? Six times? Deliberately and with premeditation?"

"We would know what happened," I told him.

"That's right. And later, if she decided she wanted to tell a different story, we wouldn't be able to represent her, would we? We'd have to go to the court and ask to be relieved."

"But she shouldn't be telling lies."

"Maybe not," he said as he raised his glass to his lips. After a sip of the beer and a long drag on his cigarette, he said, "Maybe not," again. Then he said, "But it's not our job to go around passing that judgment, is it?" He became very serious, almost grave. "I'm going to tell you something, Doug. And what I'm going to tell you is important to me. Never have I had a witness testify to something I knew to be a lie. Never!" He hit the table with his finger as he said "Never" for the second time. "But I believe this, by God: A human being has a right to try to save his own life. And if my client wants to do that, far be it from me to take his money just to foul him up. Do you hear what I'm saying?"

"Yes."

"Maybe you're right. Maybe Rita shouldn't lie. But, god-damn it, they shouldn't take people and put them in gas chambers and kill them either!" He whispered that, but so fierce was the whisper he could have been yelling. He rocked back in his chair, and after that he spoke quietly. "So we'll just let Rita's story cure a little, if you catch my drift. You got any problem with that? Or would you rather take the chance of later hearing her say something that you know to be a lie?"

"I guess what we don't know can't hurt us."

"Sometimes it works out that way."

Our steaks came, and I ordered another glass of wine. Morgan hardly ate at all. Mostly he sat looking out the window, thinking as he smoked and drank his beer. After I finished my steak, I stared with him in silence out at the lights that sparkled in the clear, dry air.

Finally he said, "If it turns out that the little girl handled that gun—you know, if the gun has her fingerprints on it, as well as her mother's—how are they going to have any direct evidence of who actually shot him?"

"I don't know," I said.

"I don't either. I've been wondering about that all day," he said. "I think they may not have a case." He took another drink of his beer. "Let me ask you something else," he said. "If the objective evidence yields the possibility that either one of them could have killed him, would it be to Rita's advantage to have anybody hear what the girl has to say about it?"

"It would," I told him, "if Miranda confessed that she, instead of Rita, did it."

"Yes, that's right." There was just the beginning curl of an ironic smile.

"You could cross-examine her on it."

He looked directly at me, as if about to make some great pronouncement. "There ain't no such thing as Perry Mason, Doug."

"*Miranda* might help," I offered, "if Rita claims she killed him in self-defense."

"True," Morgan agreed. "But we sure wouldn't want that child to testify that her mother simply murdered him, would we?"

"That would hurt."

"You know what's wrong with that kid, don't you?"

"No. I don't," I confessed.

"She's either in a fugue state or she's catatonic. You can bet on it. And you know something? Sometimes people don't come out of those things for a long time." He blew smoke upward and stared at the ceiling. He tapped his fingers on the table as he thought. "I want you to do two things for me," he said ultimately.

"Okay."

"I want you to go out to Tempe, to the university library, and copy any articles you can find on catatonia and on fugue states. You got that?"

"Yes."

"Then, as soon as you can, I want you to bring me up to date on the right to speedy trial. All the cases in Arizona in the last five years. The U.S. Supreme Court, too. And any other jurisdictions that seem to have written anything important. Also, I know somebody's supposed to be drafting new federal legislation on speedy trial. Get whatever commentary they've developed so far."

I told him that I would do it as soon as I could.

"I'll be damned," he said, seemingly dismayed.

"What is it?" I asked.

"It's this," he said. "Delay is always to the advantage of the defendant in a criminal case. If they can't get your client into court, they can't get him into prison. That's the way I've always looked at it. Hell, that's why they're working on this new Federal Speedy Trial Act. And sometimes delay means you win. Witnesses die. People forget. Delay can only help. But this thing may be a first for me."

"What do you mean?" I asked him.

"We may want to get this woman tried before that little girl wakes up."

8   AFTER DINNER I went back to the firm library, then walked to Morgan's office with copies of all the recent cases I could find on the right to a speedy trial. As I reached the door, I heard the sound of someone snoring softly, and when I peeked inside, I saw that Morgan was on his sofa, wrapped in a blanket, asleep. Funny, I thought. He'd told me he was going home. I closed the door.

In the morning, when I stepped out of the elevator and into the firm lobby, I stopped and looked around the worn old room, all bathed in morning light. I saw the scarred oak moldings and the deep leather furniture that had long before begun to crack and the bookshelves that appeared to have been placed there when the library overflowed. I walked past the portrait of Geronimo. I glanced out through the window with the chicken wire, the one that overlooked the parking garage. Josephine, who'd been there longer than the furniture, sat at her reception desk in front of the brass plaque with the raised letters that said BUTLER & ME-NENDEZ. The aged receptionist had been assigned to me as a secretary because she was Dan Morgan's secretary and because I was eventually supposed to work with him. Well, my working with Morgan had come to pass, and somehow the decaying offices looked better today.

"Good morning, Douglas." Josephine was as bright and

cheery as the flowered dress she wore. "Danny wants to see you in his office."

When I got there, he sat at his desk speaking to a man who sat across from him. I saw a shaving kit on the credenza behind him. "Come in, Doug. Come in. I want you to meet somebody. This is Pete Medina. Pete's a private investigator."

A well-muscled man in cowboy boots and a stylish straw cowboy hat rose.

"Doug McKenzie," I said.

"Doug's the young guy I told you about, Pete."

"Glad to meet you," Medina said to me. To Morgan he said, "I'll get on it, Danny."

"Find out everything you can about all of them, especially the girl named Miranda. And find out why Travis was living out in that irrigator's shack instead of at home."

"I got it." Medina moved toward the door.

"One other thing," Morgan instructed.

"Yeah?"

"Get a list of the current jury panel and find out what you can about those people."

"I got that, too," Pete Medina said, giving Morgan a small, knowing smile.

"Nothing that's going to get us embarrassed, Pete," Morgan cautioned. "Just real quiet. See what you can learn."

"I know the rules, Danny. I'll be a good boy." Pete Medina slid out of the office.

"I got the cases you wanted," I reported. "And a bunch of articles on catatonia and fugue states that I found out at the university." I put it all on his desk.

"Looks like your friend Menchaka was right," Morgan said, thumbing casually through the cases.

"What do you mean?"

"Haven't you read the morning paper?" He smiled, shoving the front section of the *Arizona Republic* across his desk.

The Eddington case had not made the headlines, which had been taken by Israel and Egypt and battle in the Sinai. But there, on the front page, below an article about Archibald Cox and his plans to testify to the Ervin committee about the "Saturday Night Massacre," I saw what Morgan wanted me to read.

HOMICIDE IN PROMINENT RANCHING FAMILY

I skimmed the story. It told of the death. It described what Juan Menchaka had seen and reported that both Travis Eddington's wife and daughter had been taken into custody. "Sources late last evening disclosed that Mrs. Eddington will be represented by Phoenix defense lawyers Daniel Morgan and Douglas McKenzie." I looked up. "They called me a defense lawyer."

"How about that?" Morgan said.

"How did they get our names?"

"I don't know. Maybe the jail matron. Let it be a lesson to you, though. Whatever you say from now on may wind up in the newspaper—or on television. So you be careful."

"I will," I promised.

"You made the front page of the sports section, too."

"What?"

"You're a celebrity, Doug."

"Oh. About the match. I'd forgotten. What did it say?"

"It said that half-assed pathologist got a lucky break."

Morgan came around the desk and pointed to a portion that was farther along in the Eddington story. It reported that two brothers, Robert and Johnny Camacho, had seen both Mrs. Eddington and her daughter taking target practice with a revolver within a short time before the fatal shooting. "That gun's likely got both their fingerprints on it," Morgan said. "And it doesn't really matter whether it does or not. We know now that they both fired it." I nodded. He ran his tongue around his square white teeth. "So how are they going to prove it was Rita who pulled the trigger?" he demanded.

"Maybe she had a motive. They can put in motive evidence, can't they?"

"Maybe Miranda had a motive."

"Rita was carrying the gun when it was over."

"Maybe she took it away from Miranda."

"Rita was carrying it in her purse when they went into the house."

"You just can't believe that little girl could have done it, can you, Doug?" He asked the question in a sort of patronizing way, as if he were demanding my confession to some fatal naïveté.

"I guess I can't believe that either one did it," I finally confessed.

Morgan butted out his cigarette and tapped his fingers on his desk. One of the firm's partners, Lloyd Burton, walked into the room. "You wanted to see me, Dan?"

"Yeah, Lloyd. You did the estate planning for Travis Eddington, didn't you?"

"Yes, for the entire family."

"How much does Rita Eddington stand to gain from Travis's death?"

A good question, I thought.

"Nothing."

"Oh, come on."

"It's true. Not one red cent. Everything out there is owned by the corporations or by Ferris individually. Ferris is the sole shareholder in all the corporations. You can ask Frank. He's the one who actually set it up."

"Why?"

"Ferris didn't trust Travis. Travis didn't even own the pickup he drove. We would tell Ferris that he should put certain things in Travis's name for tax reasons. He wouldn't do it, though. Travis didn't have a pot to pee in."

Morgan clicked his teeth together. "Did Rita know that?"

"You bet she did. She and Travis sat right in my office as Ferris and Frank told them. If she was going to kill him for his money, she should have waited till Ferris died."

"Thank you, Lloyd." As Lloyd Burton left us, Morgan stood up and strode around his office. He pointed at me triumphantly. "Well, there's motive number one. Gone. Got any more, Doug?"

"Well, he moved out of the house for some reason."

Morgan went to the window and looked down to the street, giving no attention to my latest observation. "You've got your car here, right?" he asked, suddenly changing the subject.

"Yes."

"Let's go find this prosecutor, this Hauser."

Shortly we were walking across the rotunda of the state capitol, across the Great Seal of Arizona, and up the stairs to the offices of the attorney general.

"Hello, Penny," Morgan said.

"Hey, Dan. What brings you all the way out here?"

"I want to talk to somebody named Maximilian Hauser."

The pretty receptionist reached for the telephone. She relayed the request, then turned back to us. "He wants to know if you have an appointment."

"No. I just thought he might see me for a minute."

Penny returned to the phone. A moment later she pulled it away, put her hand over the mouthpiece, and looked at the receiver with hostility. "He says you should make an appointment."

Morgan reached down and retrieved his cigarettes. "Ask him if we can have a look at the sheriff's report in the Eddington matter." She asked, then she said that we could not. "What the hell is this? You've got an open-file policy."

"Not anymore," Penny advised. "Things have changed around here. Hauser says you'll have to file a motion."

Morgan lit a cigarette and looked up the hallway. "Come on," he said to me.

"You can't go back there, Dan," Penny warned apologetically. "We've got security people now."

Morgan took a couple of long drags on the cigarette. "Let's get the hell out of here." In another fifteen minutes, we were walking into the Maricopa County Sheriff's office. "The sheriff's a Democrat," Morgan said.

"Is that important?"

"You bet it is."

"Hey, Dan, do you know everybody in Phoenix?" I asked.

"What do you mean?"

"Well, so far you've known the deputy sheriff out at the ranch and Albert at the jail and Captain Brady and the matron and Penny, and now it sounds like you know the sheriff himself."

He squinted at me curiously and thought about my question. "You know," he said, "Phoenix has gotten to be a big city, and I certainly don't know many of the newcomers. But this world you and I are working in is very small. And I've been in it for a long time. You get to know people. And you learn that you'd better treat them well. Now, let's go see the sheriff."

In the brightly lit office, we stood at a tall counter. On the other side, there were many steel desks. Men and women in uniforms typed and took telephone calls. Morgan yelled across the room, "Hey, Doreen, is Buck in?"

A woman with an ample bosom and a lot of burgundy-colored hair piled high on her head picked up a telephone. "Tell the sheriff that Dan Morgan wants to see him." The woman came to the counter. "Hello, Danny."

"How you been, Doreen?"

Doreen had prominent cheekbones and a square nose. "Pretty good. I'm a grandmother now."

"Impossible."

"It's true. It happened yesterday."

"Congratulations," he told her. "This is Doug McKenzie."

"So tell me, Danny," Doreen said, without the slightest turn in my direction, "are you and me ever going to get together?"

"Come on back, Danny!" hollered a stocky man with bushy eyebrows, and Morgan and I deserted Doreen to follow Buck Sussman, the county sheriff, down the hall.

"I'll bet that Doreen could burn a weekend down," Morgan speculated.

"Don't even think about it, Danny."

Once we were in his office the sheriff said, "I got a pretty good idea of why you're here. You want a little ex parte discovery in the Eddington case. Right?"

"You got the reports yet?"

"I do. I just read them. But I can't let you have them."

"Why not?"

"Because the attorney general's office gave me specific instructions not to."

"What?"

"Some new guy named Hauser. He called this morning. He was real serious. Nasty. And I can't afford to get in a fight with those guys."

"Why did the AG's office take this case away from the county attorney, Buck?"

"How do I know?" Sussman said. "Publicity, probably. It's a good way for a guy who comes out from Chicago to make a name for himself. I hear this guy is a professional prosecutor. What a fucking plum fell into his lap. A hell of a case, and it winds up against you. Big news coverage. He'll be famous when he convicts her. He's supposed to be good, too, and I can tell you he's going to be tough to deal with."

"Goddamn it, Buck, I need to see those reports."

"You'll get them anyway, won't you?"

"It'll take time. He's going to make me file a motion. I need them now. I need to know something. I've got to make a decision."

I moved over to a wall that was covered with photographs. There were pictures of the sheriff's posse all lined up on horseback and of hunting trips. One picture showed the sheriff with his arm around Carl Hayden, when he was senator. Another had him with Barry Goldwater and Lyndon Johnson the day they both spoke at Carl Hayden's funeral. In one of the pictures, I recognized Dan Morgan. The sheriff was in that picture also, as were a number of other men, all standing in a line at the edge of a cotton field. Both Morgan and the sheriff were very young then. Morgan had a crew cut, and his thick, dark hair was brushed until it stood straight up.

It was there, as I stared at that picture, the picture in which Morgan looked almost like a college boy, that I first saw it. The tattoo. Morgan didn't have his cigarettes in his sock the day the picture had been taken. He had them rolled up in the sleeve of his T-shirt, rolled up so the package held on top of his shoulder. And below the cigarettes the tattoo, the world with an anchor shoved through it. The symbol of the United States Marine Corps. He carried a Thompson submachine gun in the picture. All of them who had happily posed for the photograph carried guns.

"That was the day we busted the Morales brothers." The sheriff had come up behind me. I glanced back over to his desk, where Morgan was rapidly turning the pages of a thick document. "We caught 'em with more marijuana than this state had ever seen. Those were the days when only crazy people and saxophone players smoked that shit. And those were the days when Dan Morgan worked the right side of the street."

"What was he doing?" I asked.

"He was a deputy county attorney. He was the only attorney who ever had the balls to come out on an arrest with us. He'd tell us what we could do and what we couldn't do, so we didn't get some goddamned bleeding-heart judge suppressing our evidence. Danny got convictions for us. He was the best prosecutor this state ever had."

I looked back at the photograph. Apparently the man with the tattoo had earned some favors. And he was using one of them while his old friend gave me a tour of his office wall.

It didn't take Morgan long to read the report, and when he finished, the sheriff sat back down at his desk. Morgan smiled. "You can't put my woman's finger on the trigger."

"She was carrying the smoking gun when she came outside, Danny."

"Yes, but both sets of prints are on the weapon. None of the forensics gets Hauser there, and you know it."

"I think you're right," said Buck Sussman.

Morgan turned to me. "Let's go," he said with electricity, and I followed him out of the sheriff's office and back to the jail.

Once again we sat across the table from Rita Eddington in the unfinished room. "Rita, I'm going to ask you a question," Morgan said. "I want you to think about it. The whole question. Every word I say. I want you to be sure you understand what I'm asking. Then I want you to give me a simple answer. Yes or no. It's important. Nothing more than yes or no. Do you understand?"

"I understand."

"Did you kill your husband in self-defense?"

She took her time. Although she'd been quick to tell me the day before that she did not kill Travis at all, she thought about the question for a good long while. Her expression never changed, and she never took her eyes away from Morgan. She raised a callused hand and moved a delicate wisp of red hair away from the flawless skin of her face.

"No," she finally said.

"Thank you," Morgan said, standing and turning to the door. Soon we were in the courthouse coffee shop. Morgan stared vacantly at a steaming cup of coffee. Finally he stated flatly, "It better be that that little girl killed her father."

"What do you mean?" I asked.

"Otherwise we lose."

"Maybe Rita was insane," I ventured.

He loosened his tie. He blew on his coffee. "Oh, come on," he said.

"I guess there's certainly no way it was an accident."

He finished the cup and then scratched his head and stared at me for a while. "You know those cases on speedy trial?"

"Yes," I said.

"We have a hell of a lot better chance of getting her to trial quickly if they hold her in jail, don't we?"

"Yes," I said. "That's when the courts seem most concerned, when the defendant is not admitted to bail. Every one of those cases says that they can't just let someone rot in jail without a trial."

"Is there any way we want that child to be a witness at her mother's trial?"

"If Miranda shot him and will admit it, then I would think we'd want her."

Morgan laughed and lit a cigarette. "Unless we make some application for her release pending trial, we're going to look like hell on the record. It's going to be hard to argue for an accelerated trial setting on the basis that they haven't let her out of jail if she doesn't object to staying there."

"That makes sense."

"If that prosecutor, Hauser, is smart, he won't resist it. He won't take a chance of having to try her before that child wakes up and tells him what happened. But I'll bet he hasn't thought that far ahead. Not about the implications of bail anyway. And if he has, then he'll request that she be released himself. So I don't see that we have anything to lose by moving for her release, even if we really want her detained."

And so it was that we went to Rita Eddington's initial appearance intending to move for her release from the county jail and hoping against hope that our motion would be denied.

9   WE RETURNED TO the jail, to the room where the night before I'd seen the shabby prisoner who had sat shivering while a deputy held a shotgun to his temple. Now a small judicial bench occupied the room, and a court reporter sat behind his stenographic machine in front of the bench. To one side of the room, fifteen or twenty prisoners sat chained together wearing T-shirts and dungarees. An older man was putting on a robe.

"Afternoon, Judge," Morgan said.

The older man turned around. "Hello, Dan. Here for the Eddington woman, are you?"

"Yes, sir. We've got her."

"I'd just as soon take her first and spare you having to wait through all these men, but it looks like the State is going to be a little late. Somebody named Hauser insists we not go forward without him." So we waited, and the justice of the peace took the cases that sat all chained together. He would read complaints, advise the defendants of their rights, inquire whether each man understood the charges, ask if he could afford an attorney, discuss bail with the deputy county attorney who sat at a small desk in front of the bench. Mostly the JP would arrange for members of the public defender's office to talk to the men and set later hearings for consideration of bail. After a time the steel door to the room opened. A large man—he had to be six foot four—entered carrying a briefcase.

"Mr. Hauser?" the JP inquired.

"Yes, Your Honor, Maximilian Hauser representing the State of Arizona. I apologize for my tardiness." Maximilian Hauser had the look of a former football lineman who had fallen out of shape. He bulged under his coat, and his neck struggled at his shirt collar. His blond hair was cut shorter than was fashionable, and his face was very red.

"Are we ready to go ahead in the matter of State versus Eddington?"

"Yes, Your Honor. Ready on behalf of the State of Arizona."

"We're ready, Judge," Morgan announced.

"Then I'm going to ask that the room be cleared of everyone except counsel and that Mrs. Eddington be brought down." The JP leaned over the bench toward the chain of prisoners and explained that he would return to their cases as soon as he disposed of one matter involving a woman.

While the room was being cleared, Morgan introduced himself and me to Maximilian Hauser. "Yes. How are you?" Hauser said as he shook our hands without enthusiasm. Hauser's clothes were made for Chicago, not Arizona. He wore a gray three-button herringbone suit and thick-soled brogues that looked like they were constructed to withstand snow. He offered only one concession to his new home: He wore a bolo tie, a string of braided leather cinched up to his buttoned collar by a large piece of Indian-looking silver. It was the kind of tie so often seen on men who had moved to Arizona from somewhere east of the Mississippi River.

"What position will you take on her release?" Morgan asked.

"Well, just what do you think it ought to be, Mr. Morgan?"

"I was going to ask for OR," Morgan answered, unruffled.

"Then you will be disappointed in our position. I intend to oppose any release. Excuse me." Hauser pushed by to one of the desks set up for counsel and began to unpack his briefcase.

Suddenly two guards pulled Rita into the room. The JP inquired if she was indeed Rita Eddington, if the spelling of her name was correct, if she was represented by Mr. Morgan, and if she understood that she was charged by the attorney general of the State of Arizona with murder in the first degree. "Yes," she answered to each question.

"You should know that not only do you have a right to a lawyer, you have a right to remain silent. Anything you say may be used against you in court. Do you understand that?"

"Yes."

"You are presently incarcerated in the Maricopa County Jail. Is that correct?"

"Yes, sir."

"And we might add, if Your Honor please," Morgan said, rising, "that Mrs. Eddington should not be here. She is a lifelong resident of Arizona. She has family here. Her mother lives in Gilbert. Mrs. Eddington has a daughter to whom she is devoted and who is presently hospitalized here in Phoenix. Mrs. Eddington has never before been charged with, let alone convicted of, a crime more serious than a parking violation. I would remind the court that the only question before Your Honor is whether you may reasonably be assured that Mrs. Eddington will appear at further court proceedings. Your Honor, based upon the things I have just told you, we contend that there is no reason to even suspect that Mrs. Eddington will not make appearances in the future. But further, I would underscore the fact that at no time in this case has Mrs. Eddington attempted either to evade the authorities or to resist arrest. We hereby request that she be released on her own recognizance. I might add, Your Honor, that in the event you set a substantial bail, Mrs. Eddington will not be able to meet it." Morgan sat down.

"May I be heard?"

"Yes, Mr. Hauser."

Morgan whispered to me, "That court reporter got it all down, didn't he?"

"I think so," I told him.

"Lord," he continued as he stared at the man on the bench, "I hope old Clyde up there didn't hear a word I said. You just leave her where she is, Clyde," he said under his breath.

"I am constrained to observe," Maximilian Hauser boomed, "that the charge is that of first-degree murder. Therefore, as I am sure the court is aware, there is absolutely no presumption that the defendant is entitled to release. Moreover, the evidence against the defendant in this case is near conclusive."

Morgan jerked around and looked at Hauser suspiciously. He pulled out a fountain pen.

"Given these things, I am inclined not to dignify Mr. Morgan's request with a response. But there is one fact that I should bring to the court's attention and that I am sure Mr. Morgan will find interesting. We discovered this morning that the day before yesterday, Saturday, the defendant purchased two one-way airline tickets to Curaçao. One ticket was in her own name, the other in the name of her daughter, Miranda. Reservations were for noon yesterday, a time just hours after, as our evidence will ultimately show, Mrs. Eddington committed the cold-blooded murder of her husband. It will be of interest, I am sure, that there is no treaty of extradition between the United States and the Netherlands Antilles, of which Curaçao is an island. You see, Your Honor, the defendant has not only the disposition for but also the plans for flight. Not only does this evidence her guilt, it makes clear that she is not a candidate for bail. On behalf of the State of Arizona, I oppose her release under any circumstance."

"Before you sit down, Mr. Hauser, I have a question," the JP advised. "If you think Mrs. Eddington bought the tickets for the purpose of escape, why didn't she use them?"

"Your Honor, the defendant was seen by a man named Menchaka as she emerged from the house where, we will prove, she murdered Mr. Eddington. The defendant and Mr.

Menchaka knew each other. We assume that the defendant did not expect to see Mr. Menchaka there that morning. When she did, she realized that he would report the event and block her escape. She could not even attempt to shoot Mr. Menchaka; she had already emptied the gun into her husband. We would contend that she simply gave up."

The justice of the peace turned to Morgan. His air had lost all formality. "Danny, I can't let her out. Not in a case like this. You're gonna have to take it up with the Superior Court, if you want to go further with it."

"Thank you, Your Honor."

"Mrs. Eddington, to the charge of first-degree murder, how do you plead?"

"Not guilty, Your Honor."

"Mr. Hauser, does the State intend to proceed by information or to seek an indictment?"

"By information, Your Honor."

"Then we'll have to set the case for a preliminary hearing. Let's see, what's a convenient date?"

"Your Honor," Morgan said, "if Mr. Hauser is going to insist that Mrs. Eddington remain in jail, the hearing should be held as soon as possible."

"That makes sense, doesn't it?" The JP turned a page of a calendar. "Let's see. This is in Mesa, isn't it? How about Wednesday, day after tomorrow?"

"I have a conflict that day," Maximilian Hauser said.

"You'll need to resolve it, Mr. Hauser. Wednesday is the only day Judge Black handles preliminary hearings. If Mrs. Eddington is to stay in jail, you have to hold the hearing this week. Ten o'clock Wednesday, then, in Mesa."

I'm pretty sure that Dan Morgan hadn't fully made up his mind about how he would defend Rita Eddington when her initial appearance ended that afternoon. I say that because of what he said to Maximilian Hauser as we were walking out of the jail. "Your information will charge it in the first degree?" Dan asked him.

"That's right," Hauser said without slowing his pace.

"Does it make sense for me to talk to her about a plea?" Morgan asked.

Hauser stopped and turned on him. "Why should I even consider dealing when her conviction is going to follow as the night the day? If you want to plead her, you can plead her to the charge."

"Well, that makes it simple," said Morgan. Halfway across the patio between the jail and the courthouse, he finally slowed down. He turned to me with palpable heat. "Who does that fat bastard think he is, Shakespeare?"

10

IN A COURTROOM in what, back in those days, was the new superior court building, a trial stood in recess. Documents and photographs lay all around. A jury sat in the box, and a witness sat in the witness stand. All waited for the judge. Morgan walked to the rail and spoke across it to a man who pored over documents at counsel table. "Hey, Jake."

Jacob Asher came to the rail. I took note of his big nose and his five o'clock shadow and the way he was bent almost like a hunchback. He must have weighed 250 pounds, and he looked solid. He whispered to us in a deep, gravelly voice, "What do you say, Danny?" Morgan introduced me to him, then asked him what was going on. "I got a good case. A quad." I looked to the counsel table where a man in a wheelchair sat stock-still, apparently unable to move anything but his eyes. "That fuckin' jury over there is going to give me some money for this guy."

"I've got some business for you, Jake," Morgan said to him hurriedly, glancing at the empty bench.

"Let me guess," Asher said. "That little Eddington girl I read about in the paper."

"That's right."

"You're going to try to pin that murder on her, aren't you?"

"It could come to that. She's going to need a good lawyer. A guardian. And her grandpa pays his bills on time."

"What's old Ferris going to think of me?" Asher chuckled.

"I already talked to him. He wants me to select counsel for her. He won't have any say in what happens."

Asher looked at the floor. "Would you and I still be speaking to each other when this thing is over, Danny?"

"Yes."

"All rise." You could hear a quiet fluttering in the court-room as the judge strode up the steps to his bench.

"I'll do it," Asher said, and then he turned and stood at attention.

"She's in Camelback Hospital," Morgan whispered be-hind his back.

Morgan and I spent the rest of the day beside a two-and-a-half-ton GMC truck loaded with fresh-smelling bales of hay. We went through the better part of a twelve-pack of Coors with Robert and Johnny Camacho as we talked about what they'd seen the previous day, when Rita and Miranda Eddington had blown apart a number of beer bottles.

11 THAT EVENING THE firm held its monthly billing meeting. All the lawyers, twenty men and one woman, crowded around the big table in the main conference room so that one by one each could discuss the bills he was responsible for sending to clients. At first the room was noisy, but at five sharp Paul Butler struck his water glass with a pencil, and there was silence. Reverently (they seemed almost to be in prayer) each lawyer described the amount of time the firm had spent on given cases and what results had so far been achieved. Then the lawyer proposed an amount to be billed. Usually that amount was based upon the firm's standard hourly billing rates, and routinely it was approved by quiet nods of heads around the table.

Tom Gallagher had instructed me to act as billing attorney on an insurance-coverage case I'd worked for him. When my turn came, I announced that Gallagher and I together had $750 worth of time in the matter. "That's fair," Gallagher approved across the table. "Bill it."

Sometime later Ann Hastings recounted a zoning case she had successfully concluded for one of Paul Butler's real estate developers. She'd gotten the superior court to overrule the city building inspector's denial of a building permit for a penthouse restaurant on top of a newly built hotel. As she talked, I stared at her, at her thick, honey-blond hair pulled back into a loose bun, her oval face, the wide-set brown eyes, the fine nose, the full lips, which as she talked revealed her perfect, gleaming teeth. Ann was lovely. Not devastating the way Rita Eddington was, perhaps, but lovely in a way that made it impossible for you to separate her beauty from her intellect. And I guess I had it bad. Two weeks before, I had screwed up my courage. I'd gone to her office and stood on one foot and then the other until she looked up from the 1933 Securities Act. "I was wondering," I'd said.

"Yes?" she'd responded.

"I was wondering if you might like to have dinner with me—you know, maybe a little steak and grog sometime?"

"No."

She had gone back to her reading, and I had not spoken to her since.

"I have seventeen hundred dollars in time," Ann announced at the billing meeting. "I'd like to round it up to an even two thousand. It was a good result, and the client can certainly afford it."

She looked around the table and heard no objection. But as Ann was making the adjustment on her billing memorandum, we all heard Paul Butler. "Put another zero on it."

"What?"

"Put another zero on the end," Butler ordered.

Ann looked up. "That's twenty thousand dollars, Paul."

"Right."

"All I did was find that Florida decision and dictate a two-page brief. I spent most of my time waiting around at the city offices and sitting in court waiting for the case to be called. The city attorney didn't even resist."

"In the end the result will be worth many times more than twenty thousand dollars, and these clients like to pay well for good results." Ann Hastings wrote down the other zero. I saw Tom Gallagher look at Dan Morgan and shake his head.

The thing I really remember about that first billing meeting was the pleasure the senior partners took in announcing the amounts they would charge their clients.

Thousands upon thousands of dollars computed at standard hourly rates, most of the work not their own but that of other lawyers. And the pleasure came not just from bringing in money. It was much more. It had to do with the *ability* to bring it in. When Walter Smith was finished with a string of at least fifteen very healthy bills to various insurance companies, he took off his half glasses and looked at me. "Not bad, huh?" he said.

Dan Morgan's turn came around. "All I have is the Horace Apadaka matter," he said. I remembered the old Indian in the lobby. "I got the charges dismissed, but there's no way he can pay us. I have to write it off." A stiff silence followed as people shuffled their papers.

After the meeting we all walked to the Arizona Club for dinner. The night was soft and cool, and for the first time since I'd come home to Arizona, it felt good to be wearing a jacket. Except for a few drunken Indians in front of Harry Wilson's bar, the downtown was deserted. The only sounds came from our group, and I walked in the back of the pack and listened. Bets were being made on the Monday-night football game. In one quarter of the group, the question at hand was whether Gerald Ford was fit to be vice president of the United States. "He is not!" somebody yelled. "Don't ever forget he's the son of a bitch who tried to get William O. Douglas impeached." Others talked about ways to survive in a city that had such a lousy newspaper, and some newcomers to Arizona went on about how wonderful it was not to be looking forward to shoveling snow. I lagged behind, noticing how convivial they all seemed. I watched Ann Hastings shiver in the cool air and slide her arm through Lee Goodman's. I watched her narrow hips sway way up above her perfect ankles.

Then Dan Morgan came up from even farther behind and fell in beside me. "Have you read that stuff on catatonia?" he asked me.

"No. I just saw what the articles were about and copied them."

"Well, it's interesting. You know what a common cause of catatonic stupor is?"

"No," I responded. "I don't know anything about it."

"Violence," he whispered. "People fear an outbreak of violence in themselves, so they make themselves stiff like that so they can't injure themselves or other people. They call it 'splinting'. That kid could have gone that way after she shot her father. She may have been afraid of further violence."

"But we don't even know that she's catatonic," I said.

We walked on together until we reached Harry Wilson's bar. Morgan stopped at the door, and we were hit with the rich, rotten smell of stale beer and whatever else went on in there. Inside, I could see vague shadows of Indians moving around. An Indian woman staggered out through the door and moved by us on the way to the gutter, where she knelt down and made a retching sound.

"Want to stop for a beer?" Morgan asked me.

"I don't think I'd dare go inside."

"I once watched one Indian kill another Indian in there."

"Is that true?"

"Yep."

"What happened?" I asked.

"It was pretty ugly," Morgan said. "Guts strung all over the floor. You know, they're going to tear the place down tomorrow so they can build that park. Too bad. I'll miss it." He moved on.

The firm had the Arizona Club to itself that night, and by the time I got there, everyone had crowded around the bar, and they were all making a lot of noise. Pretty soon I realized that much of the noise was about me. Someone yelled, "Hey, McKenzie, is it true you gave up the state golf championship to work on a case with Morgan?" I felt awkward in that kind of light, and I squeezed in next to the bar for protection. After I got there, I saw that the bar-stool against which I'd pressed myself held Ann Hastings. "Sorry," I said, trying to give her some air.

"What'll you have?" the bartender asked.

"Let me see." I began to check out what was behind the bar.

"Would you like to share this wine with me, Doug? I

can't drink the whole bottle." I couldn't believe it. She'd spoken to me without being prompted. The first time. I looked up and saw her brown eyes.

"Just let me have a wineglass," I told the bartender as I continued to stare at Ann.

Then Ann Hastings asked me the same question I'd been met with when I walked in, but when she asked it, the tone held no irony, just curiosity. "Did you really walk away from that golf tournament to work on the Eddington case?"

"Yes."

She watched me as I poured myself a glass of her wine. "You ski, too," she said.

I said that I did ski, and she told me about how her father used to take her up to Flagstaff to ski when she was young. I told her about how I'd lived at Alta, Utah, for two years after I got out of the navy, and she said she'd always wanted to ski there. I was about to say something really stupid, like I'd be delighted to show her the place, when Tom Gallagher walked by. "Oh, Tom," Ann Hastings said, "I need to talk to you about that wrongful-death case that came in this morning." She touched my arm and said, "Doug, you finish the wine." Picking up her glass and falling in beside Gallagher, she disappeared into the dining room.

And that was it. I drank the wine. I ate a steak. I watched the Chicago Bears lose a football game on television. And I went home to my apartment.

12

THE NEXT MORNING Morgan opened a door of the credenza in back of his desk. Behind the door was a small refrigerator. "Want a beer?"

I looked at my watch. It was barely ten o'clock, but when I heard the tab come out of one can, I said, "Sure, what the hell."

"Where are you living, Doug?"

"At a place over on Third Street called the Kendall House."

"Do you know if there are any apartments available there?"

"They have a bunch of studios with lofts. That's what I have. I think those are all rented. But there's a penthouse, a two-bedroom apartment with a private patio. I think it's empty."

"That's a pretty nice apartment," Morgan said. He took a drink of beer and lit a cigarette.

"You know the place?"

"I used to own it," he said.

"You owned the Kendall House?"

"Yep. Owned it till Judge Baldwin gave it to one of my ex-wives. Then the IRS helped her sell it." Morgan smiled. "She forgot to pay some taxes."

"Was her name Frankie?" I asked.

"How'd you know that?"

"I saw her picture on the wall."

"Ah, shit." He exhaled.

I drank my beer, and it tasted good that early in the day.

"Listen, Doug, do you have your car here?"

"Yes."

"Would you take me over there to see if I can rent that apartment?"

We found the manager, and he told us the penthouse was available. The manager was a little drunk, but still he was concerned about cleaning deposits, bad checks, pets, and children.

Morgan reached into his pocket. Then, taking a cigarette from his mouth, he squinted and asked, "Would you like it in pounds, francs, or traveler's checks?"

The manager pawed through the different-colored bills and finally said, "Those blue things will do."

Morgan signed the checks, then the rental contract. Then he asked me for one more favor. "Will you drive me out to my house? It's really my wife's house, but it's in my name. I need to get some things and my car." We headed for Paradise Valley. When we passed the Biltmore, Morgan sighed. "Boy, we used to have some parties in that place." We turned at the Camelback Inn. Somewhere on one of the winding roads past the east end of the Paradise Valley Country Club, in a place I could never have found by myself, we came to the Morgan house. A driveway circled in front through rock and cacti. The house appeared small and simple. Finished with desert-toned stucco, it looked to be built of Mexican adobe, the real thing, not cement imitation. The style was Spanish, with log beams protruding through the top of the flat wall.

Morgan opened the hand-carved front door, and the house became large. We dropped down a number of steps to the highly rubbed hardwood floor of a long living room. The ceiling was now high. Large oil paintings hung on each of two walls. I recognized the artists. Orozco had painted one, and Siqueiros the other. Small paintings, street scenes of Vera Cruz, covered a third wall. In one corner a large, round Spanish fireplace projected into the room. The chimney rose to the ceiling like one-quarter of an Indian tepee. At the other end of the room, a staircase curved to a loft where a huge carved table was surrounded by books and paintings. One whole side of the room was glass. It looked down onto a garden and a square swimming pool. I could see that the bottom of the pool was a mosaic. Beyond the pool, across the rock and the saguaro cacti and the broad valley below, were the mountains. I turned, looking all around the room—at the white plaster, the gleaming wood, the bright oils of the paintings, the books, the grand piano that bore the name Knabe. I thought it was one of the most beautiful houses I'd ever seen.

"I never liked this place," said Morgan, who was now going through mail that sat on a desk by the window.

"Why not?"

"I don't know. I just never did."

I moved to the piano, upon which rested a number of gold- and silver-framed photographs, and what was becoming my photo tour of Daniel Morgan's life continued. There was a recent portrait of Morgan and beside it one of a handsome woman. The woman's dark hair was taken straight back into a bun. She might have looked severe, had it not been for something soft in her wide eyes. In one of the photographs, Dan Morgan and the woman, both in suits, stood before the entire Supreme Court of Arizona. Justice Levi Udall presided.

"That's the day I married Katherine." Morgan had moved to the piano. "Two Roman Catholics being married by a Mormon."

"They convened the whole court just to marry you?"

"No. It's just that I invited them, and they showed up. I was surprised that anyone besides Udall came. He had agreed to perform the ceremony. I didn't think the rest of them liked me." Morgan walked toward the kitchen.

"She's beautiful," I said.

"Do you think so?"

Through the open door came the hiss of two beer cans being opened. Morgan returned and gave one to me. "I'm going to get some things," he said. "Have a look around if you want to."

I examined the other photographs on the piano. There were a number of Katherine. In one that had to be recent, she stood with a girl who wore a cap and gown. I figured it must be her daughter, who, I'd been told, had graduated from law school. In other pictures there was Katherine as a girl. She swam. She rode a horse. She went to college. In one, when she was even younger, she stood with two men in front of what I knew to be Langdell Hall at the Harvard Law School. Finally there was a picture of Katherine in an elegant restaurant sitting between Dan Morgan and another man. The other man was a Mexican. He was big, much larger than Morgan. His hair was black, except for a classic touch of gray at the temples. His face was dark and aquiline. He was not handsome. Still, there was something that made me stop. The man sat behind a bottle of Dom Pérignon champagne, his big, hairy hand wrapped around the stem of a graceful flute. He smiled, and there was gaiety among the three of them.

I noticed that apart from this photograph and the one of the wedding, and the recent portrait, there were no other photos of Morgan on the piano. None when he was young, none carrying a gun, none exposing his tattoo.

I went up the curving stairway to the library. On one wall was framed the front page of the *New York Times* edition that reported the Supreme Court's decision in *Martinez v. The Warden of the Arizona State Prison*. And there were the books. The works of the great novelists, the great historians, the great philosophers. Then in one corner I saw three small volumes. One was a book of poetry called *Dark Songs* by Katherine Lawrence Peck. The two others were by Frank Menendez. One was *A History of the Arizona Sheep Man*. The other was *Arizona v. California: The Struggle for the Colorado River*.

I heard Morgan below me, and I walked back down the staircase. "My car still runs," he said. "I'll see you back at the office. I'm going to haul some things down to that apartment."

"Do you need any help?"

"No."

"Hey, Dan."

"Yeah?"

"Who are these people?" I was pointing to the picture of the two men with Katherine in front of Langdell Hall.

"That's John Lawrence, Katherine's father. He taught at Harvard Law School. And that's her brother. He went to school there."

"And him?" I pointed to the Mexican, the man with Morgan and Katherine and the champagne.

"That's Frank Menendez." Morgan seemed surprised that I didn't recognize the firm's founding father. He stared at the picture for a while. Then he turned away slowly, and for the first time that day there was sadness in his voice. "That was in Washington, D.C. It was the night after I argued *Martinez.*"

13

MORGAN TOLD ME that Hauser would call only one witness, the deputy sheriff who supervised the investigation. Under Arizona's new Rules of Criminal Procedure, the court could take hearsay evidence at the preliminary hearing. One witness could describe what other prospective witnesses would testify to at trial. The investigating officer could simply repeat what he'd been told by people he'd interviewed or whose reports he'd read.

"That's what I'd do," Morgan said. "That way he'll eliminate any chance we have to cross-examine his real witnesses and tie them down to a story on the record. I'm afraid it's going to be simple for him. Fifteen minutes and she's bound over for trial. Under the old rules, when they had to call all their important witnesses, you had a great chance for discovery. You could explore the prosecution's entire case. It was like taking depositions in a civil case. Not now. Now they can call one cop, who tells a JP why he believes your client's guilty, and you go to trial. So don't expect much today, Doug. It'll be a grubby little courtroom with nobody there but us, and it won't take long."

Contrary to Morgan's prediction, the Mesa justice of the peace courtroom was quite large and well appointed, with wood and carpet and earth tones, and the gallery was crawling with newspeople. As we entered, Morgan saw

Maximilian Hauser, and he put his arm in front of me and backed me against the wall next to the door. Hauser seemed to be talking to all of the reporters at the same time, waxing eloquent about the evidence they would hear, delivering an animated description of what the case was about and how he was going to prove it. Morgan nudged me with his elbow and nodded in the direction of the gallery. I saw Juan Menchaka, who smiled and raised his hand in a small salute. Robert and Johnny Camacho sat next to Juan. Gazing at Hauser, Morgan asked, "Do you think this douchebag is going to put his whole case on this morning?"

"I don't know. I don't know anything about this stuff."

Some of the newspeople saw that Morgan had come into the room, and as a group they moved in his direction. One of them asked him something. I didn't hear the question, only Morgan's answer. "Well, Sally," Morgan said in a voice so loud everyone in the room could hear. "I guess we're here to see if Mr. Hauser really has a case or if he's just been blindly listening to some overeager young policemen. I suppose that's about the least he should be expected to show us." As he said it, Morgan was looking directly at Hauser, and after he said it, the rest of us in the room shuffled uneasily in the hostile silence that lay between the two men. Then we heard the rattling of chains. Rita Eddington, in her simple jail dress, her hands in cuffs and her legs in shackles, was in the room.

The justice of the peace, like "old Clyde" whom we'd been before earlier in the week, was not a lawyer. And he was anxious about the proceeding. He sought to clarify his role early.

"As I understand it, gentlemen, the only question is whether the evidence the State presents here today establishes probable cause to believe that Mrs. Eddington committed murder. And the State does not have to prove to me that she did commit murder. If I conclude that simple probable cause exists, as I understand it, I am obliged to hold her to answer the State's charges in the superior court. Just like any other preliminary hearing." He looked nervously from Hauser to Morgan and back again.

"That is the law," Max Hauser said without rising.

"That's correct, if it please the court," Morgan said as he went to his feet.

We sat in the building that years before, while I was growing up, had been the public library in Mesa. The city had converted it to a large courtroom with adjacent offices. Where once I'd sat in the small library reading about Clarence Darrow, I was now at a counsel table beside a woman charged with murder in the first degree.

"You may call your first witness, Mr. Hauser."

"Do you suppose the sheriff can take these handcuffs off Mrs. Eddington?" Morgan pleaded.

"Get them off her," ordered the judge.

"The State calls Mr. Juan Menchaka," Max Hauser announced.

Juan wore an old shiny-in-the-seat blue serge suit and a khaki work shirt with a brown-and-black-plaid wool tie. He trudged to the stand, and he raised his right hand, and he said, "Yes, I will tell the truth." Juan told Judge Black exactly what he'd told Dan Morgan the Sunday before. They rode to the house. They went inside. The shots were fired. They came outside, and Rita dropped the gun. Juan pointed to large blown-up photographs of the house where it had happened and of the corral and the field where he had stood. He went over diagrams of the road and the walkway to the house. He identified the revolver Rita had dropped in the dirt.

When he finished questioning Juan, Hauser turned to Morgan with a satisfied expression. "Your witness, Counselor." We knew no more than we had when we walked into the courtroom.

Morgan rose to cross-examine. As he was about to speak, Juan's eyes narrowed. He had the same look he'd given Morgan when, on the previous Sunday, he said to him, "You're not going to try to lay this off on that little girl, are you?" Morgan turned and stared at me for a moment. He looked back to Juan. Finally he turned to the bench absently, as if his mind were miles away. "I have no questions, if the court please."

"Call John Camacho, Your Honor," Hauser said. Johnny sauntered to the stand and was sworn. "Mr. Camacho, were you working on the Eddington ranch early Sunday morning?" Hauser asked.

"Yes, sir."

"And what were you doing?"

"Me and Robert—he's my brother—we was bucking hay."

"Bucking hay?"

"Throwing bales onto a Jimmy deuce and a half."

"A Jimmy deuce and a half?"

"It's a GMC truck, Mr. Hauser," the judge interrupted. "Two and a half tons."

"Thank you, Your Honor. Now, Mr. Camacho, did anything out of the ordinary happen that morning?"

"I guess so."

"And what was that?"

"Mrs. Eddington, Travis Eddington's wife, her and her daughter came up the road."

"On horseback?"

Johnny shook his head.

"You need to answer out loud, sir," advised the judge.

"Oh. Yes. They rode horses."

"Then what happened?"

"They stopped and got off and picked up some beer bottles and put them on a stump. Then they took turns shooting at them with a pistol."

"And Mrs. Eddington forced her daughter to shoot the gun, did she not?"

"Objection! It's leading, and it lacks foundation."

"No, she didn't make the girl shoot it," Johnny blurted, before the judge could rule on Morgan's objection.

"Objection withdrawn."

Rita leaned toward Morgan. "What's he saying?" she whispered. "What's going on?"

"Hauser thinks you made Miranda shoot the gun in order to put her fingerprints on it," Morgan replied. "He wants it to look like you were creating a defense."

"That's nonsense. That's not true."

Morgan put his finger to his lips, signaling she should

be quiet. "I know," he whispered. "I was just hoping Hauser wouldn't learn that today."

Maximilian Hauser lifted a document from his table. "But Mr. Camacho," he pressed, "wasn't there a time that you said that Rita Eddington made Miranda shoot at the beer bottles?"

"I know what you're talking about," Johnny answered. "You're talking about what it says in that police report. But that's not what I meant."

"You know about a police report in this case, Mr. Camacho?" Hauser asked with marked surprise.

Johnny, sensing that he'd let some cat out of some bag, flushed and sneaked an apologetic look toward our table. "Yes, sir," he said to Hauser.

"And how is it, sir, that you know something about a police report?"

"Mr. Morgan told me about it."

"Mr. Morgan has seen a police report on this case?" Hauser jerked his eyes toward our table.

"Yes, sir. He told me he seen it." Dan Morgan faced Max Hauser with a dirty grin.

"Mr. Camacho, did you or did you not tell Officer Duane Hamblin that Rita Eddington appeared to make her daughter shoot at the beer bottles?"

"I object!" Morgan yelled, scrambling to his feet. "It's immaterial, Your Honor, and besides, he's trying to impeach his own witness."

"I usually hear everything in these proceedings. You go ahead, Mr. Hauser."

"Didn't you say that Mrs. Eddington made her daughter shoot the gun, Mr. Camacho?"

Morgan whispered to me, "What the hell kind of a ruling was that?"

Johnny answered, "Yes, sir." Then he added, "But it's not like that policeman wrote it."

Hauser paused nervously. "Why don't you explain?" he finally ordered.

"At first Miranda was shooting at some blackbirds that was sitting on a power line. She hit one. She killed it. Mrs.

Eddington made her stop that. She made her shoot at the beer bottles. She wouldn't let her shoot the birds. But the way you was saying it, you make it sound like Miranda didn't want to shoot the gun at all and Mrs. Eddington made her do it. And that's not true. Miranda wanted to shoot the gun. That cop you was talking about just didn't write down everything I told him."

Morgan cleared his throat loudly and laughed. "I was hoping you'd save that one for the jury, Max."

"Wait a minute," the judge said to Johnny. "You say this little girl was able to shoot a blackbird off a power line with a handgun?"

"Yes, sir," Johnny confirmed.

"How far away from her was the bird?"

"From the girl, sir?"

"Yes. From the girl."

"I'm not sure. Quite a ways."

"And you're sure she hit it?"

"Yes, sir. It blew feathers all over, and the bird hit the ground."

"Wouldn't mind taking that girl hunting," mused the judge. "I'm sorry, Mr. Hauser. Didn't mean to interrupt."

"No further questions," said the prosecutor, deflated.

Hauser went on through the morning, next questioning the gunsmith from Peterson Brothers' Sporting Goods, who had sold Rita a Smith & Wesson .38-caliber revolver the week before, then a ballistics expert who established that the same revolver had fired the six pieces of lead that were now held in a plastic bag marked "Exhibit Four." He examined a fingerprint man and an expert who specialized in paraffin testing. Toward noon Duane Hamblin, the deputy sheriff who had supervised the investigation, took the stand. Duane Hamblin brought photographs—pictures of the inside of the house and of Travis Eddington's corpse.

"Do you think you can stand to look at those things?" Morgan asked Rita when he first saw that the deputy sheriff had them with him.

"Yes."

When Hauser said, "I ask that Plaintiff's Exhibits Eight

through Thirty-two be received in evidence," the judge asked, "Any objection, Mr. Morgan?"

"I haven't seen them yet, Your Honor."

The judge made Hauser give the pictures to him, and Morgan spread them out in neat rows on the table in front of Rita and me. Rita looked at him, then looked at the pictures, very carefully. Morgan watched her, and after a while he whispered, "Do you have them in mind?" Rita nodded, and Morgan gathered the pictures into a neat stack.

"No objection, if it please the court."

"The photographs are received in evidence," said the judge.

For having expounded so vigorously on the advantages of being able to take discovery when the prosecution called live witnesses at a preliminary hearing, Morgan didn't cross-examine one witness until Hauser turned Duane Hamblin over. Then he asked a few questions. Somewhat reluctantly, Hamblin conceded that what we'd heard in court that day substantially constituted all the evidence he'd gathered; they had no direct evidence that Rita, instead of Miranda, had pulled the trigger. Only circumstances. Any evidence of motive? Not so far. Morgan asked him to describe what they found when they searched the house, and the deputy described a number of items of Travis's clothing.

"Did you see any articles of clothing in the house that did not appear to you to belong to Travis Eddington?"

"Yes, sir."

"How many?"

"One."

"Describe it, please."

"It was a piece of women's lingerie. It was sort of like a short slip. It was peach-colored, and it was lacy, and it had snaps that made a crotch."

"A teddy?" Morgan asked.

Duane Hamblin, who was blond and wholesome and looked younger than his years, said, "I don't know what a teddy is, sir."

"What size was this piece of lingerie?"

"I don't know," said the deputy.

But then the witness moved his mouth, almost articulating a second thought. "Yes, Mr. Hamblin?" Morgan said.

"It's just that, now that I think of it, I think it was kind of large."

"Large enough to fit Travis Eddington?"

"Possibly," the deputy allowed.

I could hear whispering in the gallery.

"Do you have it here today?" Morgan continued.

"No, sir."

"What did you do with it?"

"I just threw it in the evidence box. It's in Phoenix, in the evidence room."

Max Hauser called his last witness, Robert Wallace, the county medical examiner, to ask just two questions: "Did you perform the autopsy of one Travis Bowie Eddington? And, if you did, can you tell us what caused his death?"

"I did perform the autopsy, and death resulted from two of the six bullets that are in the plastic bag marked Plaintiff's Exhibit Two."

"Nothing further."

Morgan jumped to his feet. "Dr. Wallace, you cannot render an opinion with respect to *who* shot Travis Eddington, can you?"

"It is my opinion that Rita Eddington shot him."

"Oh?"

"In this case I read the investigative reports. I read the statement of a man named Juan Menchaka, who, I understand, testified earlier. Given what Mr. Menchaka reported, I concluded that either Rita Eddington or her daughter, Miranda, had to have killed Mr. Eddington. There simply appeared to be no other person who could have done it. That is, if Mr. Menchaka is to be believed."

"And that's what I'm getting at, Doctor. As between Rita Eddington and Miranda Eddington, you can't tell us which of them did the shooting."

"Indeed I can. Given the fact that Mr. Menchaka saw Rita Eddington carrying the gun—"

"Doctor, is this opinion based upon the tests you did and the autopsy you performed as medical examiner?"

"No, it is not."

"Indeed, any opinion you have with respect to which of the two women pulled the trigger is based upon what Juan Menchaka said he saw. Isn't that correct?"

The doctor thought on that one for a while. "I suppose that's correct. The circumstantial evidence convinces me that Mrs. Eddington killed her husband."

"I appreciate that, Doctor. But just so we're all clear, and I hope you understand that I mean no disrespect by this, the expertise you bring us as a board-certified forensic pathologist and as an experienced medical examiner cannot, in and of itself, assist us in determining which one of those two shot Travis Eddington. Isn't that correct?"

It took him a long time to answer, but finally the medical examiner said, "Yes, that is correct."

"Now, Doctor, you've testified as an expert witness many times in many different courts, have you not?"

"I have."

"And you are generally aware of the rules of court, are you not?"

"Yes, I suppose I am."

"Especially the rules of evidence dealing with the admissibility of expert opinions?"

"I suppose."

"And wouldn't you agree with me, Doctor, that if we were in the superior court today, before a jury, it would be improper to offer your opinion that Mrs. Eddington shot her husband?"

"Objection."

"Overruled."

"Yes, I suppose that's right," the doctor finally acknowledged. "My opinion, since it is not based upon my expertise, should be accorded no more weight than that of Mr. Menchaka or Officer Hamblin or anyone else aware of all the circumstances."

"And isn't it true that no expert of any kind is going to tell us which of the two women killed Mr. Eddington?"

"Counselor, it is my understanding that one of them was a young girl," said the medical examiner.

"Have it your way, Doctor. But you tell me, is an expert going to be able to come into court and render an expert opinion about which one of them did it?"

"No. Not in my opinion. Not as I understand the rules of evidence."

"There are things you can help us with, aren't there, Dr. Wallace?" Morgan said.

"I'm not sure I understand what you're getting at."

"Well, for instance, Travis Eddington had been drinking just before he died, had he not?"

"Yes."

"His blood alcohol level was point two four?"

"That's right," said the doctor.

"He was drunk."

"Yes."

Morgan went on to what the witness could tell about the angles at which the bullets that hit Travis entered his body, and after lengthy explanations, which I never did understand, Morgan asked, "Did you confer with people from ballistics about these matters?"

"Yes," said the medical examiner.

"Were you able to make a judgment, from all of this, about where Mr. Eddington was sitting when he was first hit?"

"I believe I can."

"Show us, please." Morgan was handing him one of the photographs.

The doctor pointed.

"And, Dr. Wallace, do you have an opinion of where the person who shot him was standing at the time that person first fired the gun?"

"Yes."

Again the doctor pointed at the picture.

"Do you think, sir, that you can fairly describe for us the path Mr. Eddington moved in, as he moved from here on the sofa to this place on the floor where he finally came to rest?" Morgan was passing pictures in front of the doctor.

"I think I can. Yes."

"Your Honor, I wonder if I might have Mr. McKenzie come around here."

"You may."

Morgan moved me to a small sofa he had prearranged to have the bailiff bring in from the hallway outside the courtroom.

"Now, if I may, Doctor," Morgan said, "I would ask you to come down here and, using Mr. McKenzie as a model, show us what happened."

Suddenly the doctor was pushing me to the far side of the sofa, over near where he told us they'd found an empty whiskey bottle. Then he pulled me forward just a little.

"It's my opinion," the doctor said, "that the first bullet that hit him was the one that pierced the aorta. That one entered here, to the left of the sternum above the number-four rib." He pushed hard on my chest. "That makes me believe that Mr. Eddington was bent forward at the time he was first hit." The doctor pulled me a bit more toward him. "He was probably trying to get up. Like this." More pulling.

I became aware then, as the medical examiner perched me in the position where Travis had first been shot, that Morgan had silently moved Rita from her chair at the table around to a spot from where she could study everything that was going on.

"Now, Doctor, where was the person who shot Travis Eddington when that first shot was fired?" Morgan asked.

"Here." The doctor moved to a place in front of me.

It was not the doctor, however, at whom I was looking. It was Rita. And Rita was looking at me. She stood just behind the doctor and to his right. Our eyes met, and they locked. Suddenly the theatrics of the little role I'd been made to play seemed very far away. I no longer heard what the medical examiner was saying. I was aware of nothing but Rita Eddington's eyes and the scared and furtive look that came into them as I stared at her. She killed him. I knew it from the way she looked at me as I sat teetering, as Travis had, when the first bullet she shot ripped through his chest and tore that big artery away from his heart. And not only did I know it, she knew I did. An irrational tremor shot through me as I realized that her hand was not two feet from the gun that lay on the court clerk's table, the one marked "Exhibit One." Another small tremor came, this one not so irrational, when I sensed Maximilian Hauser's eyes on me. I realized that he'd been watching Rita and me as we looked at each other.

I felt the medical examiner pulling me even farther forward, and then I was moving, as if falling, to the floor. The last thing I saw before my face hit the carpet was one of Rita Eddington's jail-slippered feet with its elegant arch and its sparkling, pedicured toes.

"Come around here, Rita," I heard Morgan whisper. "I want you to be able to see this."

After that, while my face ground into the carpet, Morgan asked question after question about each of the bullets that had been pumped into Travis's back, questions about how the person who'd fired those bullets would have had to move around the body as she did it.

When it was over, after Hauser had said he had no more witnesses and Morgan announced he had no rebuttal, the justice of the peace said, "Argument, gentlemen?"

Hauser rose and with great confidence announced, "On behalf of the State, I'll submit the matter on the testimony."

"Mr. Morgan?" said Judge Black.

"No one saw which one of them did it, Judge. And they don't have any forensic evidence to prove which one did it. They don't have a case." Morgan sat down.

"You know what troubles me?" the justice of the peace asked. "If this woman wanted to kill her husband, why would she go out there on a horse? Why didn't she take a real fast car, so she could make a getaway? What do you have to say about that, Mr. Hauser?"

"Sir, I simply can't answer that."

The judge looked around the courtroom, obviously perplexed. "There's much to what Mr. Morgan says, Mr. Hauser."

"But, Your Honor—"

"The court will be in recess for fifteen minutes while I think about it." The room began to hum. Reporters lit cigarettes. Someone found a coffeepot and brought cups to Morgan and me.

"Let's go outside, Doug," Morgan suggested. "I want a cigarette, and I don't want this judge to see me smoking it in his courtroom. I think he's a Mormon." We emerged into the bright sunlight. "My God," Morgan muttered. "If he buys that crap I just spewed in there and refuses to bind her over, we're in trouble."

"They can start again, right?" I asked.

"That's right. Just as soon as that kid wakes up and says, 'Mama did it,' they can refile. Christ, maybe I should have just conceded there was probable cause. But if I did, Hauser could make us eat that record if we ever did get to a good motion to dismiss. Goddamn it, I can't believe he didn't just rule. I had no idea he'd take it seriously." Morgan smoked nervously, pacing up and down the sidewalk along a row of sour orange trees. He came back and stood beside me and drank his coffee.

"Hauser didn't call the travel agent," I said.

"What?"

"He didn't call the guy Rita was supposed to have bought the one-way airline tickets from."

"Hmm," said Morgan. "That's right. You think something's fishy?"

"I don't know. I just noticed that he didn't call him."

"You think Travis was jacking off into that teddy?"

"It sounded to me like he must have been wearing it."

Suddenly my attention was drawn to McDonald Street, where a black hearse slid from the driveway of Meldrum's Mortuary and lumbered north. It was not the hearse, however, that caught my attention. It was the black Cadillac limousine that followed the hearse, the one where, through the smoky windows in the back, I could make out the sober visage of Ferris Eddington staring stonily ahead. Morgan followed my gaze as I snapped my head northward toward the hearse. I couldn't see through the windows of that car.

I could only imagine the gleaming box inside, the box that held the strange, dark-complexioned man who I knew would never again do things with large-size lingerie.

"Jesus," Morgan whispered.

I stood there with my head near the tree leaves and watched the procession of cars that followed the hearse and the limousine. I saw many friends of my mother's and my father's and many people with whom I'd gone through school. I stood quietly as the cars came out through the mortuary driveway and glided by me. Then I had a strange feeling, and instinctively I turned around and faced the courthouse. There, behind the glare coming from the corner window, I made out the lovely face of Rita Eddington. She was staring at the single file of cars, much the way I had been. Morgan turned toward the window.

"Christ" was what he said this time. After that, neither of us said anything. We just stood there staring at our client, who was difficult to see, because of the glare.

After Rita moved out of sight, Morgan spoke to me. "Hauser has something he didn't put on in there."

"What?" I said.

"He has something that isn't in any of those reports, something he's saving for trial."

"How do you know?" I asked.

"I don't know. It's just a feeling. But I'm sure he's got something he isn't letting on about. A surprise for us."

As Morgan brooded after some instinct for undisclosed evidence, Max Hauser came out of the courthouse and descended upon us. "Mr. Morgan, I want to know where you obtained the report that the Camacho gentleman spoke about."

"Well, Mr. Hauser, I'm not going to tell you."

"I regard your surreptitious acquisition as highly improper."

"Do you, now?"

"I believe it's unethical."

Morgan stopped in mid-drag on his cigarette. A flume of half-inhaled smoke escaped from his open mouth. He took another drag and turned away.

"What do you have to say?" Hauser demanded.

Morgan turned back. "That you're about to get knocked on your ass, fat man. That's what I have to say. And when that happens, maybe I will have done something improper. But as for my having that report, maybe you ought to go read the canons before you shoot off your goddamned mouth. Now get outta my way."

When the justice of the peace returned to the bench, he spoke quickly. "Mr. Morgan, I believe there is much to what you say. Nevertheless, I am going to order Mrs. Eddington held to answer the State's charges. And I am going to tell you why. We know that one of these two women killed Mr. Eddington. I agree that the evidence against Mrs. Eddington is not as strong as it could be. Still, she was, as they say, caught with the smoking gun. I heard no real evidence that the daughter did it. Therefore, if I look at just the evidence before me, I have to say that it was more probable that it was Mrs. Eddington who did it than her daughter. In my judgment that adds up to probable cause. It is therefore the order of the court that the defendant be held to answer in the superior court."

Morgan stood quickly to tell the justice of the peace that he understood the order. As the courtroom began to clear, Morgan bent toward me. "That's the first time I've ever been relieved to have a client bound over."

14 THE WOMAN AT the desk raised her head
and nodded at us.

"File it!" Morgan commanded. "Quick!"

I hurried through the door into the bustling office of the court administrator and handed the woman the document I had prepared at Morgan's order: "Defendant's Motion for Setting of Accelerated Trial Date."

"It'll be Henry? Is that right, Tami?" Morgan queried anxiously from behind me, seeking to tie down that which had already been arranged.

"You got it, Danny," Tami said.

The small, efficient woman stamped a number on my motion. Then, with a fountain pen, she wrote the letter *P* after the number.

"Judge Penrod," she confirmed. "Do you have a courtesy copy for him, or do I need to make up a file right now?"

Was it wrong? What we did that afternoon? Did it somehow lack propriety? "There ain't no law against it." That was how Dan Morgan had addressed such delicate questions the day we walked into the courthouse with the heavy prose of which I was so proud. "And it isn't mentioned in the canons either," he added. "All we're doing is seeking out a little information."

And that was all we did. Just obtained a little intelligence. We'd walked up to one of Morgan's old friends (one whose son Morgan had once walked away from a possession-of-marijuana charge) and asked her to let us know when Judge Henry Penrod's name appeared for assignment of emergency matters. Then we sat on the cold concrete bench across from her office door for two hours sipping tepid coffee, watching lawyers hand her motions for expedited relief, and waiting for her signal that the judge of choice's number had come up.

Once he saw that she had stamped my motion with a *P*, Morgan borrowed Tami Hirata's telephone. He called the judge's secretary to get a time, then dialed the office of the attorney general. "Penny? It's Dan Morgan. Tell Maximilian Hauser that the Eddington case has been assigned to Judge Penrod and that at five-thirty the judge will hear argument on the motion we served earlier today. I'm sure Hauser will want to have someone there."

Morgan hung up without waiting for a response, and at five-thirty Morgan, Hauser, and I sat in the office of the Honorable Henry Penrod in the old courthouse on Washington Street. The judge gave no attention to Hauser's anemic complaint about lack of time to prepare a response. Head down, chewing an unlit cigar, he pored over my pleadings through his narrow reading glasses.

As the judge read, I took stock of his office. In places the plaster had cracked, and one of the venetian blinds that covered a window looking out on Washington Street had come loose. The carpet was worn almost through in spots, and all in all the room had the same shabby gentility as the offices of Butler and Menendez. One difference, though: Western oil paintings covered the walls. Morgan had told me about the paintings. He told me that before going on the bench Henry Penrod had made a fortune trying plaintiffs' personal-injury cases and that a good piece of his estate hung in his chambers. I studied a big Remington cattle drive on the wall behind the judge's desk. And, also as the judge read, Morgan fingered a heavy bronze sculpture of a mountain lion attacking a buffalo. Even Hauser examined part of the collection, turning the pages of a novel by Louis L'Amour that had been on the small coffee table.

In time Judge Penrod looked up from my memorandum and moved his glasses down his nose so he could peer over the tops at us. He pulled the cigar from his mouth. I thought he was going to speak to Morgan, but before the words came, he moved his hand up and began to scratch his big, square head, which was covered with thick, gray crew-cut hair that stood straight up. Still scratching, he opened his mouth a little wider and laughed silently. Then the judge looked around the room. He examined his collection of paintings. He stared at the bronze. As we all hung there waiting to hear what he had to say, he looked out the window to the street below. He put his cigar back into his mouth and chewed on it. "You want me to set trial in a first-degree-murder case at my earliest convenience?" he asked with pronounced incredulity. Morgan moved his head forward in one silent nod. "Unlike you, Danny."

"Your Honor, my client is in jail. They won't let her out. She has a clear constitutional right to have her day in court as quickly as is reasonable." In those three sentences, Morgan presented the contents of my ten-page memorandum.

"Yeah," said the judge. "I read it." He turned the cigar over in his mouth and lit it. Taking that as a signal, Morgan produced a cigarette from his sock. He fired his lighter and moved his head back away from the smoke.

"Tell me something, Danny," said the judge. "Didn't I read that your client has a daughter who's laid up in some kind of a coma?"

Morgan exhaled a deep draft of smoke and a sober "That's right, Your Honor."

"Wasn't that child the only eyewitness to what happened?"

"No."

I was surprised and looked at Morgan, wondering if someone had come up with a phantom witness.

"Who else was there?"

"My client was there, Judge."

"Oh, yes," Henry Penrod said. He chewed his cigar and sat in a cloud of blue smoke. "And I guess she's going to tell us her daughter pulled the trigger. Right?"

"You know I can't tell you that, Henry."

"At any rate, you want your woman tried before the child wakes up to testify against her. Right?"

"We don't know when the little girl may wake up, Your Honor. We don't know for sure if she will wake up. All I know for certain is that I don't want my client rotting in that stinking county jail until that day may or may not come. And the law makes it clear she does not have to."

There came a time during the long moment that followed when I realized that the judge was smiling at Morgan in a way suggesting some deep understanding between the two lawyers who'd been around that old courthouse for so many years. Hauser saw it. He flushed as he looked first from the judge to Morgan, then back to the judge.

"So what do you have to say about all this—is it Mr. Hauser?"

"Yes, Your Honor. It's Maximilian Hauser."

"Well, what's your position, Mr. Hauser?"

"I'm not sure you should be on the case, sir."

"What?"

"I mean, sir, that we have not even filed our information yet. We conducted the preliminary hearing only this morning. I don't know how the case got assigned to you."

"My number came up on the emergency-motion calendar, and the court administrator assigned the case to me. That's the way we do things around here. Of course, if you don't think I should preside over this case, you certainly have a right to file an affidavit of bias and prejudice."

"No, Your Honor. That's certainly not what I had reference to. Of course—"

"So do you want this trial delayed until the little girl can testify for you?"

"Yes, Your Honor."

Morgan elbowed me and winked.

"Well, when is she going to wake up?" asked the judge.

"We don't know, sir," Hauser said.

"Was anyone able to talk to the child after the shooting?" the judge probed.

"No, sir."

"Then no one knows what she would say if you called her."

"No, Your Honor, but I am confident that we know what she saw."

"I take it, then, that you feel you have a case, even without the child's testimony."

Hauser remained quiet for a moment, thinking.

"I mean," said the judge, "you certainly would not have filed charges against this woman without having your proof at least substantially in line."

"No, Your Honor, that's right. We can proceed without Miranda Eddington. I just feel that it would be better to have all the testimony of every material witness."

"I'll tell you what, Mr. Hauser. Why don't we let Mrs. Eddington out of jail and wait a while to see whether we might not have your little girl's testimony?"

"Your Honor, Mrs. Eddington is a flight risk. We proffered strong evidence to that effect before the justice of the peace."

Again Henry Penrod looked perplexed and shook his head. "You continue to oppose release?"

"I must, Your Honor."

"Do you want a further bail hearing, Dan?"

"No, Your Honor, I just want a trial."

"And I'll bet you're going to tell me that the woman could not make bail anyway."

"She doesn't have a cent, Judge."

"And under the circumstances I suppose there is no way Ferris Eddington is going to do anything for her." Very quickly Morgan shoved his cigarette into his mouth.

At one point, while he was grinding his cigar to a juicy pulp, the judge shook his head and laughed another noiseless laugh. Under his breath he whispered, "Ah, shit." He opened a calendar. "Given the law before me," Henry Penrod announced, "I am not going to simply let that woman sit in jail indefinitely." He perused the calendar. "I have a products case against a pharmaceutical company set for the Monday after Thanksgiving. These Los Angeles lawyers tell me it's going to go six months, which seems outrageous to me, but that's what they say. We're going to have to try this one before that. How long is it going to take you to put on your case in chief, Mr. Hauser?"

In the end, Hauser and Morgan agreed that the murder case could be tried in a week. "Doesn't sound to me like you've got a lot of evidence. You're sure you want to go ahead on this basis, Mr. Hauser?"

"Yes, Your Honor."

"We'll start on Monday, November nineteenth. We'll worry about Thanksgiving when we get there. That gives you-all three weeks to get it ready. Good luck." Once again the judge shook his head incredulously. When we got up to leave, he came around from behind his desk. "Why do I have a feeling, Mr. McKenzie," he asked me, "that it was you who wrote the brief I just read?"

"He did, Judge," Morgan acknowledged.

"Well, it was a lawyerlike job," the judge told me. "You may consider your motion granted."

For the first time, I noticed that he had just a touch of a soft southern accent, and I remembered Morgan telling me that, long before, he had come to Arizona from Arkansas. I was still puffed up from his small compliment as the judge ushered us out of his chambers.

In the hallway Morgan and I waited as Hauser descended the curved staircase and moved out of earshot. "That son of a bitch has a surprise for us," Morgan said once again.

15   MORGAN INSISTED ON taking me to the Arizona Club for a drink that evening to celebrate Henry Penrod's granting my motion. He bought me a bottle of Dom Pérignon.

"So what did you think of Henry?" he asked as he poured his beer into a glass.

"I liked him," I said.

Then I saw that a tall woman on spike heels had walked up to our table. The woman sat down, uninvited. "So you're back," she said to Morgan.

"How's it going?" Morgan said, obviously pleased to see the woman.

"Not bad. How was Europe?"

"It was okay." Morgan reached over and patted her knee, then said, "Pauline Adair, this is Doug McKenzie."

At that moment it crossed my mind that Pauline Adair might have been Dan Morgan's sister. It wasn't so much that she looked like him, although she did appear close in age, and her wild black hair appeared as uncontrollable as his. It was more in the way she put her cigarette into her mouth, gripping it between her teeth and squinting from the smoke, then shifted the can of beer she was carrying to her left hand and extended her right.

"How do you do," she said in a low, breathy voice. I shook her hand.

She and Morgan chatted for a time. He asked how her law practice was going, and she told him she was handling a few criminal cases and a lot of divorces. While they talked, I sipped my champagne and watched them. I concluded that they'd known each other a long time and liked each other very much.

"I've been looking for you, Danny," Pauline Adair finally said. "That's why I came by this place. I thought I might catch you here. I'd called the house a few times, but you weren't in."

"I moved out."

"Oh," she said very slowly, stretching the word out.

"Right," said Morgan. "So why have you been looking for me?"

Suddenly she became serious, taking her time before speaking. "There's something I think I should tell you," she finally said.

"What?" he asked, now palpably suspicious.

"That Eddington girl you're representing?"

"Yes."

"Be careful of her."

"You know her?" he asked with marked surprise.

"I've met her."

"Bullshit."

"No. It's true. And it's very important that you never tell anyone I told you about it. I just figure there may come a time when you need to know."

She rose abruptly, and as quickly as she had appeared, she was gone. Morgan stared after her for a few seconds, then stood up. "I'll see you in the morning, Doug." He followed Pauline Adair toward the elevator, leaving me with no clue about what I'd just witnessed.

I sat alone at the table, finishing what was left of the champagne. Then I ate in the dining room by myself. Afterward I went to a movie at the Palms Theater, and after that I walked across Central Avenue and had a beer in the bar at Durant's.

When I drove back to the Kendall House, I hoped Morgan would be there, hoped that he would tell me what Pauline Adair's ominous warning was all about, but the lights in his penthouse were out. The night had a chill, and I put on a sweater. I got a can of beer from my refrigerator and found a chair near the swimming pool, which was little used that late in the year.

In time I heard the gate that led up the back stairs to Morgan's apartment. I stood up, thinking I could catch him and see if he'd like a beer, but as I stood, I heard a woman's voice. The woman sounded a little drunk. I stopped and listened to footsteps recede up the back stairs in the dark. Only the woman talked at first, and I couldn't make out what she said, but finally I heard Morgan's voice, easy, cheery, and clear. "You don't say," I heard him tell her. Then the door clicked behind them.

16

MORGAN SLAMMED A coffee mug onto my desk, and I jerked up from what I'd been reading. He dropped into the chair across from me. "The girl killed him."

"What?" I said.

He flipped open his lighter and lit a cigarette. "Miranda is the one who killed Travis."

"How do you know?" I asked.

"I just spent the morning with Rita, and she told me what happened."

"What happened?"

"The girl killed him. Did you read those articles on catatonia?"

"Yes," I said.

"Did they tell you anything?"

"Just what you said once before. It's often a reaction to a person's fear of his own potential for violence."

"Well, I'll tell you one thing. Miranda Eddington learned that she had the potential for violence that morning. She learned that real well."

"And you think she's doing what they call splinting."

"That's right," Morgan said. "She's got herself all splinted up, so she can't kill anybody else. Or so she can't kill herself."

"Did you ask Rita about those one-way airplane tickets to Curaçao?"

"Yeah. She told me it wasn't how Hauser represented it to the justice of the peace. She said the travel agent suggested the Netherlands Antilles because of some big promotion that was coming. He made the tickets one-way so she could take advantage of the deal when she paid the fare to come home. Some crap about credits that I didn't understand. According to Rita, the agent was just trying to save her some money. Pete Medina's on his way to Mesa to talk to the guy. If Rita's story checks out, it'll just confirm my worst suspicion."

"What's that?" I asked.

"That that shithead Hauser isn't to be trusted." He moved toward my telephone. "I've got to call Jake Asher," he mumbled, "if I can figure out how to work Butler's latest gadget."

"Just push the buttons and a speaker will come on."

Morgan pushed, and in a moment we heard a gravelly rasp. "Asher."

"Jake, it's Dan."

"You sound like you're in some kind of a tunnel."

"You're on a speaker. And Doug McKenzie is in here."

"So what can I do for you, Danny?"

"I hear you got some money for that quadriplegic."

"I did you guys one hell of a favor."

"How's that?" Morgan asked him.

"From now on, State Farm's gonna send *all* their work to Gallagher. I don't think we'll be seeing those half-baked hacks they hired for this one anymore. I stung those tight-ass sonsabitches this time, Danny." Asher's growl turned to laughter.

"Jake, you know the Eddington girl?"

"How did I guess that you weren't just calling to say nice things about money?"

"Jake, I'm going to have to take a shot at her." There was nothing unfriendly in it; he could have been saying, *"Guard your queen."*

"Her mother's gonna say she killed him?"

"I'd appreciate it if you wouldn't pass that on to this guy named Hauser. I just wanted to be up front with you."

"Are you gonna try to prove Travis Eddington was fucking his daughter?"

"You know I can't tell you that," Morgan said. "But I need to see her medical records, Jake."

"Think she was telling those shrinks that Travis was playing nasty, do you?"

"I just need to see them, Jake."

"Danny?"

"Yeah."

"You remember when you promised we'd be speaking to each other when this thing is over?"

"Yeah."

"I'm asking you to remember that promise."

"What are you saying?"

"I'm saying I'm going to have to see you guys in court. And if you want to save that McKenzie kid some unnecessary research, the statute is 13 A.R.S. 1802. It says you can't get information from a physician without the consent of the patient, and you ain't gettin' this patient's consent as long as I'm her guardian. If you want the case, McKenzie, it's *State v. Shaw,* and if you can't find it, call me. I'll get you the citation."

"Jake, can you tell us what her condition is?"

"It's the same. She hasn't changed since they took her out of the jail."

"What's their diagnosis?"

"You'll have to go to court for that one, too."

———

Procedurally it was surprisingly easy. I simply had Dr. Conrad Hardy, Miranda Eddington's treating psychiatrist at Camelback Hospital, served with a subpoena duces tecum asking for all Miranda's medical records, those we were sure Camelback had necessarily gathered from all the institutions to which Miranda had been committed. I attached a copy to a motion asking that we be allowed to take Dr. Hardy's deposition, since Jacob Asher would not let him talk to us, and we therefore had a right to discovery under the Arizona Rules of Criminal Procedure. Two days later Dr. Hardy sat on the witness stand in Henry Penrod's courtroom with a court reporter right below him poised to take down everything the doctor could be made to say and ready to mark every document he could be made to deliver. As I say, procedurally it was not difficult. It was when we made it around to the merits of the motion that the sledding got tough.

"State your name, please," Morgan said to the doctor.

"Objection!" Jacob Asher yelled in a low, rough tone. Then without preface, much less leave of court, Asher bent at his table and read from the statute with such husky force that he was not to be interrupted: " 'A physician or surgeon shall not be examined as a witness, without consent of his patient, as to any information acquired in attending the patient which was necessary to enable him to prescribe or act for the patient.' " Asher looked up from his volume of the code. "That's the law, Henry. You know it. I know it. And Daniel knows it."

"He is not asking for acquired information, Jacob," Judge Penrod said in his soft southern accent. "He's only asking for the doctor's name."

"I don't care, Judge. The only reason he's got us here is to get at what this little girl told her doctors, and he'll have to admit that if you inquire. I want a continuing objection to everything he asks."

Morgan did manage to get the doctor's name on the record, but that was about all. Jake Asher took up a position on the worn linoleum in the center of the courtroom and announced that his was the duty to protect a fragile child of tender years who was not there to defend herself. Then he virtually ground the proceeding to a halt with a series of rhetorical questions about how far toward the demented Morgan and McKenzie's zeal for their client would carry their collective imagination. "You know what they're trying to do, don't you, Henry?"

"Yes, Jacob. Though I do not know the details, I have a fair idea of their direction."

"Well, one thing is clear as a bell." Asher raised one of his broken fingers that had healed as badly as his shoulder and looked much like a claw. "The law," he said, "has a wise and ancient concern that we all make full and frank disclosure to those ministering to our medical needs without fear that later some lawyer is going to shove our secrets up our backsides. And the law forbids these lawyers from enlisting this little girl's physicians in what indeed may turn out to be a foul crusade."

"Dan," Henry Penrod said at length, "I'm not going to let you have those records, and I'm not going to let you examine any doctors about them."

"But, Your Honor—"

"Would you like me to continue the trial date in order that you may have the testimony of the child?"

"No, Your Honor. But I would like to ask Dr. Hardy for something that I believe is outside your ruling."

"Put your question."

"Doctor, have you made a diagnosis in Miranda Eddington's case?"

Before Jake Asher could say anything, the judge raised a hand and said, "Your objection is overruled."

"Yes, I have," said the doctor.

"What is your diagnosis?"

"Objection!" barked Asher.

"Sustained."

17

WHEN WE RETURNED from court Josephine told Morgan he needed to go to Tom Gallagher's office. I followed him down the hall.

"What is it, Tom?" Morgan asked.

"It's bad news," Gallagher said as he picked up a piece of paper and handed it to Morgan.

Morgan read. "Oh, Jesus," he said, and he crumpled into a chair and let his head drop.

"There's not a goddamned thing you can do, Danny. You did everything you could. More than you could."

Morgan wadded up the paper and angrily threw it at the wall. It landed at my feet, and I picked it up and straightened it out. It was a court order, a denial of certiorari. The United States Supreme Court had refused to review a case involving a man named Tyrone Roebuck. Morgan, his head in his hands, exhaled audibly. I silently lowered myself into one of Gallagher's chairs. "They set aside the stay of execution," Gallagher said. "They're going to do it Monday morning."

"We've got to do something," Morgan whispered, wild-eyed.

"There's nothing to do," Gallagher said very calmly. "It's over. You've exhausted all his remedies, as the lawyers say, both state and federal. You spent more of yourself on that guy than you ever should have." Gallagher paused. "I'm sorry."

Morgan turned toward an empty corner and ground his teeth.

"Dan," Gallagher said.

"Yeah?"

"Roebuck called."

Morgan closed his eyes.

"He wants you to attend the execution."

18   "FUCK HIM!" THE voice was hoarse and weak, yet possessed of great authority. It was Frank Menendez's voice. He had summoned us—Dan Morgan, Ann Hastings, and me. I was the new associate he had never seen and the son of Bill McKenzie; he just wanted to "eyeball" me. He wanted Ann because she was beautiful and he, by God, just wanted to look at her for a while. As for Morgan, the son he never had, no explanation was needed. I do believe, however, that the real reason Frank Menendez called us to his side that evening was so that he could say to Morgan the two words I just recited above.

When we arrived, Sue Menendez opened the heavy mahogany door to the thick-walled stucco house on Encanto Circle and led us down the dark hallway toward the library. The house smelled strongly of cigar smoke. "He's asked for you every day, Danny, but he's been so awfully sick."

Sue Menendez's husband, the man my father had so admired, lay in an overstuffed leather chair with his bare feet on a matching ottoman. He directed us to three chairs that had been placed around him. At first I couldn't look at him. Not only was his cancer-ravaged body cadaverous, but the fly of his pajamas buckled slightly and exposed him. He both shocked and embarrassed me. Feigning profound interest in his library, I looked around at the books and the

primitive Mexican objets d'art and his treasured Diego
Rivera oil painting. I even made a study of the ancient ar-
moire that served as a liquor cabinet. But in time I heard
his thin voice coming in my direction. "I understand you're
Bill McKenzie's son."

"Yes, sir." Then I had to look at what remained of him.

"I knew your father."

"Yes, sir. He spoke of you many times."

Not once did Ann turn away from him. And when he
said that she was beautiful and that he just wanted to look
at her, she stood up and stepped past his bony feet and the
spot where his fly was open, and she kissed him. "Thank
you, Frank."

"Will you have a drink?" Sue Menendez asked me.

"The tequila," her husband whispered. He looked at me
and smiled. "It's the best I have."

She poured two fingers of the clear liquid into a squat
glass and placed a lime beside it. "There's salt here," she
said, pointing. I regarded the glass with dread.

"You got any beer, Sue?" Morgan asked.

"And for you, Ann?"

"A glass of wine, if you have some open."

Frank Menendez nodded toward a wooden humidor on
the table next to his chair. "Would either of you like one?"
Morgan reached for his sock and his cigarettes. I bent forward and took a cigar. Sue Menendez placed a very small
shot of the tequila on the table beside her husband. She
picked up an ashtray that had two of the big cigars in it.
Each had been smoked down only about an inch. She re-
placed the ashtray with a clean one. On the table a book of
Spanish poetry lay open.

I sipped the tequila. To my surprise it slid down smoothly,
and only after it ignited gently somewhere near my belt line
did I realize that it had just a subtle hint of the cactus. "I
didn't know they could make tequila this good," I said.

"They only make this kind for very special occasions,"
Frank Menendez informed me. He turned to Morgan. "You
aren't letting this Tyrone Roebuck business get you down,
are you, Danny?"

Morgan lit his cigarette and took a can of beer from Sue Menendez.

"You know what Gallagher told me on the phone this morning?" Frank Menendez asked. With effort he shifted in his chair, waiting for an answer that did not come. I lit the cigar, and it provided an experience similar to that of the tequila. I don't know where he got them, although I did once hear that he'd been personally acquainted with Fidel Castro. "Tom told me you were planning to go down to watch the execution and that you had asked him to go with you. He said that he was goddamned if he was going to do it and that he's been telling you that you shouldn't go either."

"I have to go. Roebuck asked me."

"What business does that bastard have asking you? What's he trying to do, reprove you for not saving his worthless ass? Does he figure that since you didn't succeed, you should face the punishment of watching him go?"

Frank Menendez had begun to shake. His wife walked to him. She patted his shoulder.

"Calm down, Frank."

He looked up into his wife's eyes. "Well, goddamn it, Sue, what does he think he's doing? This is absurd."

"I'm the only person he's got in this world," Morgan said.

"And you know why that is? It's because he's scum. It's because he's an animal." Morgan stuffed his cigarette into his beer can. "Danny, you know how I feel about capital punishment. You know how many courts I've been in to argue against it. You know how much I dearly hoped I'd live to see it end. I know to a moral certainty that it is wrong. But I know something else, too. The reason it's wrong is not that people like Tyrone Roebuck don't deserve it."

"I don't believe that."

Frank Menendez struggled to sit up and propped himself on an elbow. He closed his eyes and twisted his head in pain. When he opened his eyes, his voice became stronger. "He's guilty, Danny. He raped her, and he tortured her, and he put a shotgun in her vagina, and he pulled the trigger. And he took more from you than he deserved to take."

"He needs me."

"Fuck him!"

Cigar smoke hung in the air. One of Bach's Three Part Inventions played in the background. And we all sat without speaking. I drank my tequila and smoked my cigar uncomfortably as Frank Menendez slowly lay back in his leather chair. Finally Frank Menendez spoke again. "Why in hell does Ferris Eddington want to pay us to defend the woman who killed Travis?"

"She didn't do it, Frank. Her daughter did."

"How do you know that?"

"She told me."

"And you believe her?"

"Yes, I believe her," Morgan said.

Frank Menendez stared at Morgan for a time. Then he turned to me. "I liked your father very much," he said, his voice fading to a bare whisper.

Sue Menendez abruptly ushered us out of the library.

When we dropped Ann at her place on North Central Avenue, I had to get out of Morgan's Ford in order to let her by. I hesitated then, and when she opened the door to her town house and turned on the light, I could see a little bit of the inside. It was pastel and cool, and there was a low table with a decanter of some kind of liquor. She turned and caught me looking before she closed the door. "Good night, Doug."

"Good night, Ann."

At the Kendall House, I headed for my apartment. "Doug," Morgan said after me. I turned back. "Would you be willing to go down to that thing with me?"

"What thing?"

"That business in Florence."

It finally registered. "Oh, God," I said. "You mean the execution?"

"Yeah."

19 GALLAGHER RELENTED. ONCE he knew that Morgan's mind would not be changed, he acceded to his old friend's plea and told him that he would stand by him at the dreaded hour in Florence. Unfortunately, that did not get me off the hook. Huge steel gates slammed behind us, locking us in a high-walled concrete pen. Morgan and Gallagher looked straight ahead. I looked up at the windless blue sky, and I saw my breath. I saw the guards with rifles walking around the cat-walk above us. Then steel gates in front opened, and Gallagher and Morgan stepped through. I hesitated, then took three quick steps and listened to those gates crash closed behind me.

Prisoners lined the yard we had stepped into. Some stood, some leaned against the wall of a low building, some sat on the ground. The prisoners wore blue dungarees and gave the impression of unkempt sailors. I learned later that they should not have been there that morning. Because emotions were known to run high on days of execution, every man was supposed to have been locked down in a cell at the peril of riot. But that morning, because of a mixup in time, a group of prisoners had been allowed to go outside. And those men watched us as we entered their domain. The collective gaze they cast upon the three of us in our blue suits and starched white shirts and silk ties confirmed a "heightened state of the blood." Tom Gallagher moved next to me and whispered so only I could hear, "What in God's name are we doing here?"

A uniformed guard approached us and said, "This way, gentlemen." We fell in behind him and began to walk across the yard, keeping a large cell block on our left and the low building on our right. One of the prisoners sitting not far from us pointed at Dan Morgan and spoke to the man next to him. The other man then looked at Morgan, and both of them stood up. I felt the gravel crunch under my shoes. As we walked, more prisoners stood, and others already standing came to attention. The hostility I had seen in their eyes evaporated, and as Morgan passed, I believe that every one of them nodded his respect. It could almost have been a military parade. Morgan followed the guard, seemingly unaware of the homage being paid.

Past the low building, we veered right, and there were more buildings, and beyond those, in the very corner of the prison, there was a small concrete-block structure. "Death house," Gallagher whispered gravely. Morgan slowed down. We all slowed, even the guard, and then, as we walked, we seemed to be in slow motion. We crept toward the little building, the guard seeming to pull us along. Morgan looked pale. He was even whiter than when we stepped out of Gallagher's Cadillac minutes before. He'd seemed all right that morning when he called once again to make sure I was up. He'd seemed fine when we ate breakfast at Apache Junction. He talked about a pro football game he'd watched on television the day before. And the whole trip down in Gallagher's convertible had been quite pleasant, just a beautiful ride through daybreak across the desert. Not once had one of us mentioned why we were going to Florence. But now, as I looked at Morgan, I realized that he must have been thinking about nothing else for days. Now he was drained. He stopped and stared at the little building, and for a minute I thought he was going to turn back. But then he walked on, and Gallagher and I walked on with him.

The door opened, and a man in a business suit came out. "Good morning, Mr. Morgan."

"Good morning, Warden," Morgan answered dryly.

"Mr. Gallagher?"

Tom shook the warden's hand.

"Mr. McKenzie?"

"Yes, sir," I said nervously, and the warden shook hands with me.

Then he turned to the guard. "Clear this yard," he ordered. "I want every prisoner in his cell and every cell locked. I want every guard at his station and every one of them armed. When it's buttoned up, bring Roebuck down. I'll be in my office, waiting in case the governor calls."

The two men went their separate ways, and Morgan, Gallagher, and I ducked into the ugly little building.

Inside, everything was a pale green color, the same green as a school blackboard, the color that is supposed to soothe. I remember the color, and I remember that the room seemed very open and airy. In the middle, roped off as if on display in a museum, stood a small hexagonal steel housing that looked something like a space capsule. A number of newsmen stood near the rope. They all knew Morgan, and they all seemed eager to speak to him. Morgan did talk to them, seeming all the while quite composed.

The gas chamber had windows all around. Within it was a single steel seat that had a belt attached and looked like something you might see on a carnival ride. While Morgan talked to the newsmen, Gallagher and I both looked at the gas chamber. "How does the damned thing work?" Gallagher asked a guard who was standing by the rope. The guard took us to the other end of the room, where we could get a better view through the door of the chamber. In a practiced monotone, he explained that a bucketlike container hanging under the seat had been filled with acid. A cyanide pellet was suspended just above it. He pointed to a guard near a door at the far wall. That guard stood by a lever, which was next to a telephone. At nine o'clock the warden would call on that telephone. Either he would say that the governor had called the whole thing off or he would order that the guard pull the lever and cause the pellet to drop. The only question then would be how long the man sealed in the chamber could hold his breath.

The door beyond the gas chamber opened, and a big black man surrounded by three guards and a priest came into the room. The black man wore white cotton pants and a white cotton shirt. He wore high-topped black shoes. Chains shackled both his hands and his feet. His eyes went everywhere, all around the room, as if to see where he could run. He spotted the chamber, and I heard him take in breath. He began to shake. Then the black man saw Dan Morgan. He whispered to a guard, and they let him hobble across the room to his lawyer. Morgan tried to speak but seemed unable to. Tyrone Roebuck spoke first. "Mr. Morgan," he said, "I just . . ."

"I told you to call me Dan," Morgan said.

"I just . . . Dan . . . I just wanted to thank you. You the only person ever gave a damn about me." Everyone moved back from Morgan and his client, even the guards. I strained to hear what Morgan would say, but he said nothing. Then I looked closely at him and saw tears running down his cheeks. Tyrone Roebuck spoke again. "Now, come on," he said. "You don't want to do that. You done your best. You're a good man . . . Dan."

The guards came forward. They gently prodded Roebuck toward the chamber. Morgan's tears kept coming. I wished I could get away; I felt that our being there might embarrass him. Gallagher created the excuse. "Jesus Christ, did you see this?" He turned me toward the wall behind us. A series of photographs hung all along the wall. Gallagher steered me over to where we could look at them closely. They were pictures of people who had been executed in Arizona. The newer ones were just prison photographs, the kind you might see in the post office, and I assumed that those were of the men who had been gassed. The older photographs showed men actually hanging in the gallows. Most of the men had bags over their heads. Some did not. One's tongue stuck out. Rope tied like hangmen's nooses framed the pictures of the hanging men. In the midst of the hanging pictures, there was a portrait of a woman, an old tintype photograph. The woman looked stark and severe, as if she could have been one of my Mormon ancestors.

"Do you suppose they didn't want to show a picture of a woman hanging?" I mused.

"No," Gallagher said. "I know what happened there. Let's see. What was that woman's name?" He snapped his fingers, trying to remember. "Ah, hell," he said, "I forget her name. She was the only woman they ever hanged in Arizona. When she hit the end of the rope, her head came off. There wouldn't have been anything left to take a picture of."

"It would be something, wouldn't it," I whispered, "if those were the actual nooses they used to hang those guys."

Gallagher said, "Look," and pointed, and I saw dried flesh and old hair ground into some of the ropes.

I turned around. Tyrone Roebuck sat in the gas chamber with the door closed. A clock hung on the wall above the telephone next to the lever. It showed exactly two minutes until nine. I looked at Morgan. There were no longer tears.

"Is there any chance the governor might stop this?" I asked Gallagher.

"That asshole?" he answered.

Gallagher walked over and stood beside Morgan, and I watched the clock. Fifteen seconds passed. A haunting question came to me: Could I watch this? I had watched one man die before. I mean, actually die. Expire. He was a black man, too, a marine who'd been shot all to pieces and brought back by helicopter to the ship. He lay on the hangar deck, at a place they called triage. I figured, if the marine was going to die, I was going to watch, if for no other reason than to be able to say I had once witnessed the great event. Having remembered, I guessed I could watch Tyrone Roebuck go.

A minute had passed. I looked at Morgan and Gallagher standing together. Gallagher put an arm around Morgan's shoulder. Now some color had drained from Gallagher's face. When there were thirty seconds left, I began to wonder whether the phone might ring early. *Maybe the gov-*

ernor will call. I watched the clock tick down. The phone rang, and the guard picked it up to hear the warden's order. Tyrone Roebuck jerked straight up. He looked at the guard, but the guard did not look at him. He only pulled the lever. Roebuck looked at Morgan. He waved a sort of half salute. Morgan saluted. Roebuck leaned back and took a breath, first through his nose, then deeply through his mouth.

I cannot tell any more about Tyrone Roebuck. That's because I turned away. I couldn't watch. I stared at the pale green wall until I heard an awful sound, and when I turned back, Dan Morgan was vomiting on the green linoleum floor. And Gallagher was yelling at me.

"Help me get him out of here!"

20 GALLAGHER STARTED THE CAR and began to pull out of the prison parking lot. I sat in the backseat, in my usual position. Morgan, in front, put his feet on the dashboard and his head between his knees. Gallagher gave a look of displeasure but held his tongue. Suddenly Morgan drew his legs back and, with a loud groan that sounded like an animal, blasted both feet through the windshield.

Gallagher slammed on the brakes. "Jesus, God, Danny!"

Morgan turned to me and, wild-eyed, yelled, "We cannot let that fat-ass kraut motherfucker convict Rita Eddington!"

We drove back through Chandler, Gallagher having much trouble seeing through the shattered windshield. Not a word was spoken until we were approaching the Baseline Tavern, and then Morgan said, "Pull in, I want to get a drink."

I looked at my watch and saw that it was barely eleven o'clock. Gallagher glanced at Morgan, seeming even more concerned than he'd been about the windshield. Still, he spun the big car into the gravel parking lot. We caught the pungent smell of stale beer as we walked through the front door, and we took the booth next to the jukebox. The only other patrons were a slightly tipsy couple in a corner booth who were lost in themselves. The man and woman wore western shirts that had been cut from the same piece of cloth, and they had on matching cowboy boots.

Gallagher ordered a cup of coffee. I said, "I'll have a beer." Then, for the first time since I'd known him, Dan Morgan ordered something other than a can of Coors. "Give me a bourbon, Hank," he told the bartender.

The drinks came. I took a long pull on my beer, then realized I'd finished half the schooner in one gulp. Gallagher sipped his coffee, and Morgan stared at the bourbon in front of him, which sat on ice in a short, heavy glass. He was reaching for his drink, and Gallagher was looking as anxious as he had when the pellet dropped under Tyrone Roebuck, when I heard a door slam. I glanced across all the empty steel-based tables to where a man had just come out of the restroom. He was a marine, and it was instantly clear that he was drunk. It was not that his hair was disheveled. It was too short to be. And it was not that he was out of uniform in any way. His tie was two-blocked, and everything was pressed and in line, even his cap, which was folded neatly over his belt. It was his eyes that betrayed his condition, the glaze over them, and the way he walked, as if he were trying to maintain his balance in a heavy sea. He was gloriously, pathetically drunk. The marine staggered a little ways toward the bar, where I saw the drink he'd last been working on, then his legs gave out, and he sat down in the middle of the floor. He wore sergeant stripes.

Morgan looked at the young marine. Then he looked at the drink he'd been reaching for. And again he looked at the marine.

"God Almighty." The bartender sighed. "This guy." The bartender walked around from behind the bar and bent over the marine. "Come on, fella, you gotta get out of here." The marine breathed a long whisper that seemed a refusal. Then he mumbled something about not being able to get up. A waitress tried to cajole him into moving along but had no more success than the bartender. "Call the cops," the bartender said to her.

Morgan stood up and said, "Wait a minute, Hank," and

he walked over to the young man on the floor and bent over him. "If you are fucking well really a marine," Morgan said, "you can fucking well get up off this fucking barroom floor and fucking walk out of here." The sergeant stood straight up and marched out the front door into the sunlight, and Morgan, as he followed, picked up his bourbon and poured it over an undernourished Boston fern sitting on the cigarette machine, a plant that certainly had no place in the Baseline Tavern anyway.

21   WHEN WE GOT BACK to the office that afternoon, after we'd driven the marine to his uncle's house in Chandler, I found a phone message on my desk asking that I call Sue Menendez. I dialed the number.

"Oh, yes, Mr. McKenzie. Thank you so much for calling. My husband would like to talk to you."

There was a long moment while she somehow got the phone to him, and then I heard his voice, which sounded stronger than it had before. "Douglas," he said, "I wondered if you would mind having a cup of tea with me."

"No, sir," I said, "of course I wouldn't mind." I paused, then asked, "When should I come?"

"How about right now?"

———

He was in a solarium at the back of the house, and he was sitting up at a table, looking much better than he had the evening I met him. There was an electric typewriter on the table, with books spread all around it, and there were letters stacked in envelopes. Sue Menendez brought a pot of tea, poured us both a cup, then left. There was a bottle of that same tequila on the table, and Frank Menendez poured some into his tea. He didn't offer me any this time. "I hear you helped Danny watch them execute Tyrone Roebuck this morning," he said.

"Yes, I did."

"How did it go?" he asked.

Now, how do you answer a question like that? I almost said "Pretty good" but thought better of it and found myself describing what happened in all the detail I could remember. I even told him about Morgan throwing up on the floor. I could sense, as I told that part, that it hurt him.

He nodded. "You think Dan is going to be all right?"

I told him I guessed he would be. I told him about the Baseline Tavern and the marine and the bourbon and the Boston fern.

He said, "I'll be damned." Then he said, "Listen, Douglas, the reason I asked you to come is that I wanted to talk to you about this Eddington case."

"Yes, sir."

"Why in God's name does Ferris want that girl defended?"

"Dan asked him that," I said, and I told Frank Menendez about our meeting out at the ranch offices the day of the killing.

"Well, what did Ferris say?"

"He said his family owed her something. He just said he wanted her defended. That was all."

Frank Menendez considered what I'd said, and he took a drink of the tea and looked around the sunny room and listened to the music that had come on the radio. "That's beautiful, isn't it?" he said. "Do you recognize it?"

"I think it's Schubert. I think it's the *Trout* Quintet."

He raised his tea toward me and nodded approvingly. "Tell me, where did this Rita come from?"

"I think she's from Winslow originally, but she went to high school in Mesa."

"She and Travis went to high school together?"

"Yes."

"What were they like together?"

"I don't know. I never saw them together. I didn't even know they were going out until they got married."

"Wouldn't you have been aware of who Travis Eddington's girlfriend was? I know your family was close to his."

"You would have thought so," I said. "But I didn't even realize he had a girlfriend."

Again he labored to drink his tea, and after a time he asked if I knew how Ferris Eddington felt about Travis's marrying Rita.

"No," I told him.

He must have seen something in me that I didn't know I'd shown. "Go ahead," he said. "You were going to tell me something."

"Oh," I said. "I was just thinking. I remember that my father was disturbed by the marriage. I think it actually upset him. I remember I once caught him talking to my mother about it. When I came into the room, they quit talking, but I remember there was something funny about Travis's marrying her, something my father didn't think was right."

"Would it have been that Ferris disapproved?"

"No. My father would have been open about that. Everyone on the ranch would have been talking about that. Besides . . ."

"Besides . . . what?"

"I was just thinking that Mr. Eddington always really seemed to like Rita. He was always very nice to her. It always seemed to me that he treated her more like family than he did Travis."

For a long time, Frank Menendez just listened to the Schubert and drank his tea. At certain passages he hummed along with the music. He was so thin and so sick, yet he seemed to be very happy. It was as if I weren't there, as if I were just a file he was reading, an incomplete package of materials from which he was trying to figure out what a case was about. I drank my tea and watched the afternoon shadows come across the courtyard outside the big windows.

"What does Rita Eddington look like?" he finally asked me.

I told him. I told him how tall she was, how pretty. I described her hair and her eyes. I explained how nice she'd always been to me.

"Did you know that Travis wanted to sell the ranch?"

"No," I said.

"It's true. He wanted to subdivide it into a big housing development. Ferris was reluctant. I think Ferris had dreams of his grandchildren working the place."

"That seems unlikely now," I said.

"Doesn't it?" said Frank Menendez. "I was just wondering if Travis's wanting to sell the ranch could make Rita want to kill him."

"Dan's sure she didn't kill him," I said. I then told him about how Morgan had gone to the jail and how Rita had told him it was Miranda who'd done it.

"You really believe that?" Frank Menendez asked me.

"I don't know. It's possible, I guess."

"Yes," he said, "anything is possible." Then he seemed to think out loud. "I suppose," he said, "if Ferris had let Travis develop the ranch, Travis would have gotten some kind of control of the Eddington fortune. Perhaps Rita found that possibility threatening. Perhaps she felt she had more to gain from Ferris than from Travis. You tell me Ferris always treated her kindly." I didn't respond. "Yes," he said. "Perhaps she somehow saw a fortune slipping away."

He began to look very tired. Sue Menendez came into the room. She watched her husband worriedly, then said to me, "I think maybe you should go now, Mr. McKenzie."

"Yes," I said. "I understand." I stood up.

"Wait, Douglas," Frank Menendez said. "Would you do something for me?"

"Yes."

"Would you see if you can find me a picture of Rita Eddington?"

I told him that I would, and he invited me for dinner the next evening.

22   DR. GIDEON EPSTEIN wore his shirt unbuttoned almost to his navel, and he wore gold chains around his neck and many rings on his fingers. He wore expensive bell-bottom trousers that were very much in the fashion of the day. Below his trousers were soft Italian leather boots with raised heels. His black hair was very curly, and I believe he'd had a permanent. Dr. Epstein brought us his expertise from his offices in Los Angeles.

"Assuming that what you have is catatonia, it's generally regarded as a form of schizophrenia," the psychiatrist lectured us. "It takes a number of forms. The stuporous form is the most common. That's your Eddington girl, you say? You say she's quite stiff?"

"Stiff and rigid was what they said at the jail," Morgan advised.

"To be very rigid is not common. Usually your stuporous catatonic would be described more as having a waxy flexibility. You can often change a catatonic's posture as you would mold wax or clay. If a person stays perfectly rigid very long, his muscles will tend to atrophy."

"I don't think that has happened to her," Morgan reasoned. "Jake Asher, the lawyer I mentioned, says her condition hasn't changed."

"More than likely, then, she's only rigid when she knows someone is paying attention to her."

"You mean she can turn this on and off?"

"Not in the sense that she's malingering," the doctor said. "But I'll almost guarantee you she can't stay in that same posture all the time. For instance, she has to eat, doesn't she?"

"That hadn't occurred to me," Morgan said.

"Sometimes you have to force-feed them. I've even seen cases where they had to be fed intravenously. But ordinarily they'll eat. It's usually when no one can see them. They'll gobble up anything that's around."

We sat for the better part of two hours while Dr. Epstein discussed Miranda Eddington's condition and the terrible emotional trauma that could have caused it. At the end of the interview, he agreed to testify for the defense.

"Consider yourself retained."

"There is one thing, Dan," Epstein said as he rose to leave. "What we're talking about here assumes the girl is catatonic. I really need to know her physical condition. I understand your problems with the judge, but if I could have a good eyewitness description of her, it might save me being surprised on cross-examination."

"We did our best, Gideon," Morgan said apologetically.

"It could be important," the expert said. "It could be critical."

Josephine arranged for a taxi to take the doctor to the airport. After he left, Morgan sank into his chair. "Remind me to make sure we pay him before the verdict comes in. The last time we used him, he learned we'd won before he sent us his statement, and I know he padded hell out of the bill."

"Will a jury like all that gold he wears?" I asked.

"Don't worry about that," Morgan reassured me. "Gideon Epstein knows better than to step in front of an Arizona jury looking the way he did today."

23   I DROVE TO the old house in Mesa, the one
     I'd grown up in, to look for a picture of Rita
     Eddington for Frank Menendez. I knew I
could find an old high-school yearbook, but I thought there
might be other photographs. I remembered some snapshots
of the Eddingtons that my mother had kept.

The last time I'd been in that house was when I lived
there during law school. That was after my father died and
my mother moved to California. I wondered how long the
place would be there; my mother was negotiating a sale to
a group of doctors who planned to tear it down and build a
clinic. I looked around—at the grand piano, the paintings,
my mother's books, her marble coffee table, and her gilt-
framed mirror, all preserved by a patina of dust.

Always before, when I'd gone home after being away,
the house had been filled with memories of my childhood. Afternoons coming home from school or from playing golf. Relatives—uncles and aunts and cousins—come
down from Navajo County to the warmth of the valley. My
grandmother. I would remember the parties my mother had
given, often with Ferris Eddington in attendance. Once, I'd
heard, Frank Menendez had been there, but I'd been too
young to meet him then. Sometimes the old house would
cause me to think of my brother who'd died. But now, as
I stood there alone, looking around the living room in the

dim light and the dust, all those things were eclipsed by the memory of when I lived there through law school, of coming home in the night dead tired, drinking beer out of quart bottles in order to sleep and get some fleeting reassurance that I wouldn't fail. I remembered Christmases destroyed in each of those three years by frantic study for final exams. It had been my introduction to pressure, my learning the meaning of angst. And as I stood there that evening, I didn't like the recollection.

I walked quickly to the small study where my mother had kept her photo albums. I turned pages, and finally I found a picture that would serve, one taken on the White River above McNary at Sheep's Crossing. My father and mother were in the picture, as were Ferris Eddington and Travis. So was Rita. They all stood on the bridge that crossed the river. I noticed that Rita stood closer to Ferris than to Travis. The picture had been taken in 1959. I could tell because Ferris Eddington's 1959 Cadillac sat in the background next to the river. He bought a new Cadillac every year; some years my father bought his used ones. The picture of Rita was clear and showed the color of her hair and her eyes, and she did not look much different than when we visited her in jail. Confident that I had what Frank Menendez wanted, I headed west toward Phoenix.

Sue Menendez led me to a table set with crystal and silver and flowers. Frank Menendez already sat at the head of the table. "We'll eat shortly, Mr. McKenzie," she said. "Let me get you a drink. What will you have?"

"Is there any of that tequila left?"

"Sit down, Douglas," Frank Menendez said. "Do you have a picture of Rita Eddington for me?"

"Yes, sir." I handed him the photograph.

Sue Menendez brought my drink and excused herself to see to dinner. I sipped tequila quietly and watched Frank Menendez study the picture I'd brought him. He seemed thinner than he had the day before, and he looked a little weaker. Still, his eyes were clear and bright.

"This what she looks like?" he finally asked.

"Yes. It's a good likeness."

"That looks like Sheep's Crossing," he said.

"Yes, it is."

"There used to be good fishing there, years ago."

"It's not too good anymore," I said. "It's better over on the Black River. It isn't fished so heavily, and sometimes it has decent mayfly hatches."

He wasn't listening to me. He was just looking at the picture, seemingly carried away to some other time.

"Did I ever tell you that I liked your father?" he said at last.

"Yes, sir."

"I liked your mother, too. I was once a guest in her home. That would have been when you were very small."

"Yes, sir."

"I've never seen this girl," Frank Menendez said. "I wasn't invited to her and Travis's wedding. I always wondered why." Sue Menendez carried a spinach salad into the room and placed it on the table. "Did you ever wonder, Sue, why Ferris didn't invite us to his son's wedding?"

"Oh, I don't know," she said. "I suppose I did. That's been a long time ago, though."

She left the room. When she returned the next time, she brought a platter bearing a rack of lamb. Then she brought a plate of fancy vegetables and an even fancier bottle of French wine. Montrachet. She poured the wine into my glass and into hers. Into her husband's glass, she poured a finger of the tequila. Then she looked at us and said, "Dinner, gentlemen."

With some effort Frank Menendez raised his glass. "We eat lamb this evening in honor of Ferris Eddington." He sipped the tequila. "So tell me, Sue, why does Ferris Eddington want to pay to have the woman who murdered his son defended by the best criminal lawyer in America?"

"I don't know, Frank."

"You assume," I interjected, "that she murdered him. Dan says he's convinced she didn't."

He turned back and again he studied the picture I'd

brought him. Frank Menendez didn't eat. He drank the tequila, and he stared at the photograph. I had no idea what
he saw in it or why he'd wanted me to get it for him. When
we finished dinner, Sue Menendez brought a bottle of co-
gnac to the table and poured some into two snifters. Frank
Menendez lit one of his cigars.

"You tell Danny to come and see me. You tell him I
want to talk to him about this case. Okay?"

"I will," I promised.

Frank Menendez turned to his wife. "When you wondered about why we weren't invited to the Eddington wedding," he asked her, "what answer did you come up with?"

"None. I don't know why they didn't invite us."

"May I keep the photograph, Douglas?"

I told him by all means, and he slipped it into a pocket of
his silk robe. When he moved, I could see that he wore slip-
pers, black velvet pumps, with his initials monogrammed
on the toes. He may have been emaciated but still, I
thought, he had style. I remembered the picture of him and
Morgan and Katherine and how he'd worn a tuxedo.

He puffed his cigar, and he drank his brandy, and suddenly the evening was over and I was driving my Mustang
back to the Kendall House having no idea why I'd been
there. I doubted that I would ever see Frank Menendez
again. I knew, though, that I felt somehow advantaged by
his demand that I visit. At least I'd seen him, and it didn't
matter that he was not the powerful presence he'd been in
the Washington picture, wearing the tuxedo with his hand
wrapped around the flute of champagne. I had talked to
him, and I had seen wild curiosity, enigmatic, maybe even
demented, but still alive and intelligent and vital. As I
drove in the cool night, I wondered what it was he'd seen in
that photograph.

24

ONCE AGAIN DAN Morgan and I sat in the Eddington Ranch office, and Morgan said, "I need to ask you something, Ferris." Ferris Eddington nodded. "Do you know anything about Travis abusing Miranda?"

Ferris Eddington closed his eyes. "No, Danny, but I assume you have found out that he did." Silence from Morgan. "I see." Ferris Eddington took a cigarette from the silver case that sat on his desk. He lit it with the matching lighter and inhaled pensively. "Does Rita say Miranda shot him?"

"I can't tell you that," said Morgan.

"Well, I guess she did, or you wouldn't have asked me what you just asked me. In answer to your question, no, I did not know that Travis had abused the child."

"Ferris, I need to know what you know," Morgan told him. "Anything that would cause you to suspect that Travis abused the girl."

"We certainly knew that something was amiss," Ferris Eddington acknowledged. "The child was so disturbed. We had her from one institution to another since she was seven years old. Something had to cause it. I wondered, but I suppose I never allowed myself to suspect that Travis had done such a thing." Ferris Eddington stood up and walked to the other side of his office. "When you say 'abused,' you do mean something sexual, don't you, Danny?"

"Yes."

"No. I never allowed myself to suspect it."

Now it was Morgan who lit a cigarette, and as he expelled his typically large draft of smoke, he looked around the office.

"Would you like something to drink, Dan?" Ferris Eddington asked.

"A cup of coffee."

"Douglas?"

"Yes, sir."

Morgan watched him leave, then turned to me. "So what do you think? Is he telling me the truth?"

"I don't know," I said. "I wasn't even thinking about that. I don't know any reason to think otherwise."

"Neither do I," Morgan agreed as he stood up and paced around the office. "Old Ferris sure didn't waste any money decorating this place, did he?"

For the first time, I noticed how spartan Ferris Eddington's office was. Badly finished knotty pine walls, government-issue desk, black metal file cabinet. Someone had hung photographs of several prizewinning bulls randomly on two walls. A photograph of Ferris Eddington shaking hands with Harry Truman sat on the desk. The floor was bare pine.

Ferris Eddington returned with an ornate silver pot of coffee, which he poured into three paper cups. "Here's cream and sugar, if you take it."

"Ferris," Morgan said, "what would you think if Rita did say that Miranda killed Travis?"

"Are you asking me whether I would believe her?"

"Yes."

"Yes. I would believe her."

Morgan looked at me and gave the slightest nod. "I need to ask you one other thing," he said.

"Yes," said Ferris Eddington.

"Would you be willing to testify to Rita's good character?"

Ferris Eddington took a long drag from his cigarette and butted it out in a silver ashtray.

"Yes, I would. Certainly."

"It's dangerous to put a defendant's character into issue in a criminal case," Morgan said.

"Oh?" said Ferris Eddington.

"Yes. If I call you as a character witness, and the prosecution has any kind of dirt on Rita, no matter how inadmissible it is, they can use it to cross-examine you. They can use it to show how little you really know about her character. You understand what I'm saying?"

"I understand. And I am sure there is nothing for you to be afraid of."

"How sure?"

"Very sure."

As we headed back down Baseline Road through recently picked cotton fields into the glare of the western sun, Morgan suddenly seemed to get cold feet. "Did I screw this one up, Doug?"

"What?"

"I think I may have really fucked up."

"Why?" I asked.

"Rita is telling the truth, and Ferris knows it. Somehow he, by God, knows it. For Christ's sake, that little girl is going to wake up and confess. What the hell was I thinking of when I pushed this thing to trial without that child?"

"You were thinking that when she comes to, Miranda will probably say that Rita did it."

"Well, maybe I ought to move for a continuance. Henry Penrod would give it to us and admit Rita to bail. Maybe I ought to do that."

I stared at the blazing sunset, and Morgan remained silent as we thundered across the valley under his great cloud of second thoughts.

25 THAT NIGHT, AS was becoming our habit, Dan Morgan and I sat in the Arizona Club's dining room. I expected more talk about the possibility of a continuance, but that didn't come. Indeed, Morgan never raised the subject again, and that night he and I just drank beer and ate and talked about his theories of trial strategy. At least Morgan talked. I mostly listened.

"I don't know that there's a reason to cross-examine any of their witnesses," he said, chewing on a bite of steak and studying me over his glass. "We have to concede that one of them killed him, and once we're there, nothing those guys can say is going to hurt us any more than we're already hurt."

"I think that's right."

"Then why the hell should I keep any of them on the stand any longer than I have to? Don't we want to make their case seem as short as possible?"

It made sense to me, and I said so. I realized as I did, though, that I had no idea what I was talking about. I'd never seen a trial, only some artificial exercises in law school, and, more than that, I'd never even once tried to imagine what this case would be like as it spun out before a jury.

"Yeah," Morgan said. "Anything we do to lengthen their case will just make it seem like they have more than they really have. I'm not going to let that happen."

The decision's having been made, he ordered another beer. He joked with the waiter, and for a moment I thought he'd put the case aside. The beer was taking effect, and he seemed very happy. But the moment didn't last. Within seconds he was talking about the case again.

"All we've really got is Rita," he said. "That psychiatric crap is just window dressing, just something the jury can hang an acquittal on if they want to. If they believe Rita, we win. If they don't believe her, we lose. It's as simple as that." Then, after a while, he said, "Goddamn it, I've got to spend some time with her. I've got to get her ready." I didn't say anything, for it was plain he was talking to himself and he didn't want to hear from me. "I want to finish her direct examination at five o'clock on Friday afternoon," he said. "I want what she says to soak into the jury's head over the weekend. That'll give Hauser a full two days to prepare to cross-examine her, but I figure if he has anything to impeach her, he already has it, and another weekend isn't going to give him anything he doesn't have already. What do you think?"

"I guess," I said, "it could be important that people have time to think about what she says right after she says it."

"I really believe that, Doug. Whatever people hear, if they can think about it before it's challenged, they tend to believe it. And the longer something goes unchallenged, the harder it is to persuade people it isn't true."

"I don't know anything about cross-examination," I told Morgan.

"Rule One," he said in a loud voice, with his eyes flashing: "You never ask a question when you don't know what the answer will be. If you never remember anything else, you remember that. That's Rule One of direct examination, too. It's just that it's a hell of a lot harder to follow the rule on cross, since the witnesses are usually hostile and they don't want to answer questions the way you want them to. You've got to be ready to force them to answer the way you know they should. Either that or you've got to be ready to show they aren't telling the truth." He stared at me as if to make sure I was taking it in.

"I have a feeling it's easier to say it than to do it," I offered.

"You're goddamned right it is. To do it well is the hardest thing I know."

"How did you learn?"

"Frank taught me, more than anybody. I went to work for the county attorney's office when I got out of law school. In those days, in that office, they just threw you into court the first day. I lost the first two cases I prosecuted, a rape case and a real brutal assault. Same lawyer defended both of them. Old Angus McBride. He was a slimy, unethical bastard. You couldn't help liking him, but he was a dirty son of a bitch. He called the same doctor as an expert witness in each case. I can't remember the guy's name, but he was worse than old Angus. He was the whore of Babylon, and he ran over me like a panzer division. And there wasn't a thing I could do."

Morgan paused and took a breath. "And let me tell you, there is not a shittier feeling in this world than standing in the middle of a courtroom watching your case fall apart because some witness is telling what you know are bald-faced lies and you can't do a thing to prove to the other people in the room that he's lying." He stopped to assess where he was in the telling of his story. "Anyway," he continued, "one day Frank Menendez saw me get butchered. I told him how embarrassed I was, and he told me to come to his office. He gave me some books about cross-examination. I didn't learn much from them. I learned more from what he told me."

"What did he tell you?"

"A lot—the things that lawyers who try cases learn after a while."

Morgan told me about what he'd learned from other lawyers and from judges, too. He explained the difference between direct and cross-examination. "You can lead them on cross. You can ask questions that not only suggest the answer but demand it. And that's all you do. You make them answer the question the way you want them to. You don't let them get away from you."

He told me about what you do so as not to let them get away. He talked about breaking up questions so each is simple and admits only yes or no for an answer. He went on and on about controlling the witness, about keeping the ring in his nose and keeping a short rope on the ring. He explained how you could point out all manner of incompetence and bias and prejudice and interest and corruption, how you could force admission of prior misconduct. "You're trying to persuade a judge or a jury that the witness doesn't know what he's talking about or, worse, that he's flat out lying." He finished his beer and ordered us both another. Then he became pensive. "You know something, though?" he said. "Just about every witness who takes the stand in any courtroom lies."

"Oh, come on," I said.

"No, it's true. I didn't used to believe it. Now I do. You see, the stakes are so high. It's a contest. Everybody wants to win—somebody always does. And somebody always loses. Nobody in this country ever wants to lose anything, so teams gang up, and they cheat and lie."

I stared at him incredulously.

"I'll give you an example. You remember that medical examiner who testified at Rita's preliminary hearing?"

"Yes. Dr. Wallace."

"Can you recall when I tried to get him to concede that his autopsy didn't tend to show whether it was Rita or Miranda who shot Travis?"

"Yes. He was offensive. He kept trying to argue Hauser's case for him. And he knew that was against the rules."

"You're goddamned right he did. The woman is accused of first-degree murder. She could wind up in the gas chamber. Could there be a more important time for a witness to be forthright and fair?" Morgan leaned toward me as if he really wanted an answer to that question, but before I could give it, he said, "And that little fucker pulled that kind of shit."

Suddenly he spun around and looked across the dining room. "Hey, Mason. Bring us another round."

He threw back half that next beer, before returning to

the subject of our medical examiner. "Hey, what can you do? It wasn't even really a lie. It was just a small push of the rules. You can't try to impeach a little bastard like that. You don't have any ammo, and anyway, if you try it, people don't like it. They think you're beating up on him. Probably doesn't hurt you anyway. But it's important to keep them in line." He had begun to ramble, but still I was spellbound. "It's the ones like him, though, the ones who have letters behind their names, you have to be ready for. M.D., Ph.D., CPA—they get paid for telling lies, and they practice at it, and they get damned good."

"What's Rule Two?" I asked.

"Huh?" he said. Then he hit the table and pointed at me. "Never, never, goddamn it, ask the question 'Why?' "

"Why?" I asked.

"Because the son of a bitch will tell you why. You don't want a hostile witness to have a chance to explain his way out of the box you get him in. You never say 'Why?' You never say, 'Explain.' You never say, 'Tell me your reasons for saying that.' " As he spoke, he affected a shrill twang and an effeminate swing to his head. "You never say, 'Well, Mr. Witness, if you couldn't see the fight, how can you be so sure my client bit off his ear?' " I stared. "He'll give you the same answer every time, Doug. 'Well,' he'll say, 'I saw him spit it out.' "

"Ugh," I said. Then I laughed.

"It's an old joke, Doug. But doesn't it make the point?"

"I think I'm beginning to get the idea," I told him. "What's Rule Three?"

"Do not ask that one question too many. When you've got the witness where you want him, sit down and shut up."

"What's Rule Four?"

Morgan turned once again to our waiter. "Bring us another beer, will you, Mason." He looked back at me. "What did you say?"

"Rule Four?"

"Oh. Yeah. Don't let them repeat what they said on direct. It only makes everybody remember it."

"And Rule Five?"

"Be brief. It's the only way to make points with any emphasis."

I sat enthralled as he told me stories of witnesses he'd let get away and savored the recounting of witnesses he'd disemboweled. "I'll tell you this, though, Doug. The best trial lawyer I ever saw was Frank Menendez." He pounded the table with both hands. "We have to get out of here. I'm getting drunk."

"Wait."

"What?"

"I once heard that you compiled something like a manual on cross-examination."

"That's true."

"Why don't you publish it?"

"Because I don't want the day to come that I have to watch every prosecutor in this town use what's in there on my own witnesses."

"May I read it?"

At that one he looked at me for a good long time. "Maybe," he finally said. "Someday."

26 SOMETIME IN THE middle of the night, I became aware of an insistent banging at the door of my apartment. I stumbled down from my loft, opened the door, and in the dark on the other side I made out the glow of a cigarette, and from behind the glow I heard the flat Arizona drawl that was Dan Morgan's voice. "Get your clothes on. We're going somewhere."

I didn't question him. I just got dressed and walked groggily to his car. When I was finally fully awake, I realized we were headed east on Camelback Road. "Where are we going?" I asked.

"I've got to see that girl," he said.

"What?"

"I have to see Miranda Eddington."

It took a minute to register. "You can't do that," I told him.

"Who says I can't?"

"Jake Asher . . . the judge . . . that doctor, whatever his name was."

"Hardy," Morgan instructed me on the doctor's name. "They just said we couldn't see her medical charts; they didn't say we couldn't have a look at her."

"Did you ask them if you could see her?"

"No," he said.

"You're going to break into that hospital," I said to him. "Aren't you?"

Morgan turned from the wheel and stared at me, and in the night, only partly lit by the moon, all I could see were his eyes. At first I sensed hostility, but then I knew that what I saw were nerves. Maybe he was as scared as I'd just become. "Yes," he said, and turned back to watch the road.

"Why?"

"Because I'm going to call Gideon Epstein to testify about Miranda Eddington's catatonia, and since he will never have seen her, I'm going to have to construct hypothetical questions based on assumptions about her present condition. And I don't want Max Hauser to be able to call witnesses afterward who can testify that the assumptions I ask Gideon to rely on are unreliable. I have to be able to describe her to him, Doug. In a way that will stick."

"That's what he was talking about when he was here. When he said he needed a description of Miranda."

"That's right," Morgan said.

He drove on, and I was left to try to figure out exactly what he'd told me—to think about that, and about how long it would take them to bring us before the board of governors of the bar when they caught us in the act of breaking and entering, and about why he needed me along. *Is he so scared that he needs the moral support only a conspiracy can provide?* Whatever it was, I wanted nothing to do with it, and there was a shaky moment when I was about to ask him to stop and let me out, but then I looked at him again, and the moonlight showed the scars on his cheeks and the fierce resolve in his eyes, and I could not speak. I stayed on for the ride.

I'd never seen Camelback Hospital, and all I knew was that it was where rich people who fancied themselves depressed or anxious or confused or drunk went to recover in comfort. I remember that I expected some sort of luxurious retreat, probably majestic, at least charming, with elegant grounds where the affluent people from the East could stroll and take the exquisite air of the desert. I guess

I was looking for the Biltmore or the Camelback Inn. Camelback Hospital, however, was an unremarkable one-story cement-block building in the middle of a subdivision. There were grapefruit trees around it, and though it was night, an American flag still flew in front. There was a plate-glass window along one side, showing what appeared from a distance to be a dimly lit lobby. It seemed very clean and efficient inside, and I could see what looked like certificates hanging on one wall. I saw all this from across the hospital's parking lot as Morgan drove slowly along Thirty-fourth Street staring intently through the shadows of the grapefruit trees.

One thing distinguished the building: Behind it, Camelback Mountain rose steeply like a huge guardian, like Gibraltar, and as Morgan slowly circled the place, the moon lit the mountain so it was clearly visible. It seemed for an instant that the mountain had thrown the moon up, like a military flare, to illuminate the land it protected, the scene of Morgan's intended operation.

"If they catch us, will they disbar us?"

"They aren't going to catch us."

"How do you know that?"

"Pete Medina checked the place out. There's just one guard, and the nurses only make night rounds at midnight and four o'clock. Now, let's get over there."

Before I knew it, he had parked the car in the shadows at the north side of the parking lot and we were headed east, moving low and fast. Morgan stopped abruptly at a hedge of oleander bushes, parted the leaves, and looked through. We could see the area behind the building. Wings at the ends extended at angles to the east toward the mountain, and within the perimeter created by these wings there was a large lawn. On the other side lay a swimming pool, a shuffleboard court, a net for volleyball and tennis courts. Beyond all this was a fence, against which a man in uniform leaned and stared at the mountain.

"She's in room fifteen," Morgan whispered very softly.

"How do you know?"

"Pete told me."

"Where's room fifteen?" I asked, barely breathing.

"I think it's over there. We need to get past that wall before the guard turns around."

"There'll be others," I said. "Nurses, interns, people like that."

"No. The care isn't that intensive. Let's go."

We plunged through the hedge and moved in low and close along the building where there was a sign that said dining room—dietary services. I heard something, and I felt myself jump.

"Dan, there's somebody over there."

"It's only a cat, goddamn it. Let's go."

"What if they have a nurse with her? Or another guard?"

"They don't."

"How do you know?"

"Trust me. I know. Now, let's go."

We crossed behind the building from the north to the south wing, where wooden doors with numbers faced onto a sidewalk the way they do in old-time motels. Before we got to them, there was a glass door that had the word RECORDS painted on it. Morgan stopped and stared at the word. He put his hand against the glass as if to shield his eyes from some nonexistent glare, and then he moved his eyes close to look through. He scanned the room that lay behind the glass door, no doubt looking for the cabinets that held the patients' records, particularly the cabinet marked "E."

"Please, for God's sake," I said, "don't even think about it."

I finally exhaled when at last he moved on toward the wooden doors with the numbers. We came to room 15, and Morgan turned to me and gave me an instruction. Though his voice was barely audible, the tone was intense in the extreme. "If this kid wakes up," he whispered, "it's a fifty-yard dash through those oleander bushes. You got it?"

"Yes," I said.

"Just as hard as you can go. Okay?"

"Right."

Then he produced a plastic credit card and, just as they

do in the movies, slipped it between the door and the jamb, and I stood by wondering how long it would take him to hot-wire a Ford. The door moved, and a sliver of light came from behind it.

"The light's on in there," I said.

"Yeah," said Morgan.

He pushed the door and slid inside. I hesitated from the same conditioned clutch that always comes when I'm about to go into a hospital room, the fear of the unknown, the specter of what the person I'm about to see may look like. The moment passed, and I followed Daniel Morgan into Miranda Eddington's hospital room. As I said, the light was on, and it lit a small, cheery room lined with wood paneling. There were twin beds, and my gaze first fell on the bed that was not used. I looked at the chenille bedspread for some time, carefully examining the narrow, salmon-colored ridges that ran its length. Then I looked at the carpet and noted the subtle warm tones in its rough weave. I glanced at the simple wooden chest of drawers at the end of the bed, and at last I brought myself to look at the other bed, the one that was in use.

In it lay Miranda. And there'd been nothing to be nervous about. She looked just as she had the last time I'd seen her, a pretty young girl with hair a darker red than and not quite as lustrous as her mother's. She lay on top of her sheets in a pink flannel nightgown, and she seemed to be at peace. Her blue eyes were open and fixed steadily on the wall across from her bed. Morgan had said he had to see her. Well, we'd seen her, and I was ready to head for the oleander bushes.

"Hello, Miranda," Morgan said. There was no response. Morgan passed his hand before her eyes. Nothing, not even a blink. "Can you talk to me, Miranda?" he asked. Her lips moved, but not to speak. They actually seemed to tighten. It appeared that she pressed her jaws together more tightly.

Morgan moved down the bed and took one of her feet in his hand, and with what looked to be some exertion, he moved her leg. When he managed to make it move about six inches, he let go, and the leg stayed exactly where he left it, suspended several inches above the bed. Morgan returned to me and whispered, "Doug, I want you to do something."

"What?"

"I want you to go over there and move her leg back the way it was before I moved it. Then you come back so I can ask you a question. You understand?"

"Yes."

"Now, you do it. Quick."

I took Miranda's foot, as Morgan had, and pushed. For an instant it seemed that she pushed back. I pushed a little harder, and her leg moved back to where it had been before Morgan had disturbed it. It felt much like moving a plastic doll's leg, one attached to the body with a ball joint. When I released her foot, Miranda's posture remained exactly as I left it, and I walked back to Morgan's side.

"Now I want you to think about this," he whispered. "Okay?"

"Yes," I told him.

"Could what you felt be described as a waxy flexibility?"

I thought. Then I said, "Yes, that's exactly what it felt like. That's a perfect description."

"Let's get the hell out of here." Seconds later we were back through the oleander bushes, and minutes after that we were roaring west on Camelback Road, and I was looking backward through the rear window with exhilarating relief at the absence of headlights behind us.

27 ON SATURDAY AFTERNOON I drove to Mesa to visit my grandmother. I sat in the sunny kitchen of the small bungalow her children (she had twelve of them) had built her in a grove of grapefruit trees when the winters in Navajo County had become too much for her, and she stood at the counter looking square and solid in a simple print dress, her white hair pulled back into a bun. She tossed flour onto her bread board and threw down a ball of wheat-colored dough, which she began to knead. "I got a letter from your mother today."

"Oh? Is she all right?"

"She says she is. She surely likes California. She loves that place she's living in."

I watched her strong hands work. The left one, my mother once told me, could knock a child who said the wrong thing clear across a kitchen. I'd always been careful never to say the wrong thing. She lifted the dough, dusted the board, and slammed the ball back down, punching, poking, rolling. I caught the rich smell of the loaves that were already in the oven. On the table I saw a newspaper article she had cut from the *Arizona Republic*. I reached over and drew it to me. It was the article on the Eddington case, the one with my name in it.

She put the dough she'd been working into a pan, then

put the pan in a corner to let it rise. She pulled two loaves from the oven, sliced off a piece, covered it with butter and honey, and put it on a plate. She set the plate in front of me and sat down. I took a bite and began to chew. She reached up and unhooked her wire-rimmed spectacles from her ears, untangling them from where they caught in her thick hair. She looked down at the newspaper article.

"Douglas?"

I swallowed. "Yes, Grandma?"

"How can a lawyer defend a person when he knows that person is guilty of a horrible crime?"

I burped out something about constitutional rights. "It's an adversary system, Grandma. Defense lawyers protect people from overaggressive prosecutions. They hold the government to its proof. They make sure innocent people aren't convicted."

Belle Pratt, daughter of both the Utah and the Arizona pioneers, wrapped the wire back around her ears and settled her glasses on the bridge of her nose. She watched me as I devoured the product of her strong hands. "Pshaw," she said.

28 IN THE DAYS that followed, I saw little of Dan Morgan. Routinely he went to the jail to prepare Rita to testify. Not once did he take me with him. Sometimes he met with Pete Medina, the private investigator. On the rare occasion when I sat in, nothing came of the meeting; Medina never found anything of interest on any member of the Eddington family. During that time I did what Morgan told me to do. I prepared proposed jury instructions. (He made me redraft the one on reasonable doubt at least five times, but at last he said he liked it and that he thought the judge would use it.) I prepared a trial brief, which contained support, such as existed, for our right to present evidence about catatonic stupor and to put on testimony of Gideon Epstein that killing her father could well have driven Miranda Eddington to her present condition. I also prepared a memorandum to support a motion for a directed verdict, which Morgan would argue at the end of the prosecution's case. I never did find a case just like the one we were to defend, but I found a couple of decisions from other jurisdictions that bore out an argument, at least by analogy, that the evidence was not sufficient to support a verdict. If Morgan could convince the court, it would mean dismissal. "No chance," Morgan told me. "I'll yell and I'll scream. I'll make a record. But this thing is going to the jury, and we might as well be prepared for it."

One day, as the trial approached, Morgan asked me to go down the hall with him to Walter Smith's office. He told me he trusted the elder civil trial lawyer's judgment when it came to picking juries. We sat on Walter's sofa and watched him across his big desk as he stuffed his pipe with rich English tobacco. He lit it, then he tamped it out with a pipe nail and relit it, filling his office with acrid-smelling smoke.

"Walter," Morgan asked, "is it true that the worse pipe tobacco smells, the better it tastes?"

"I'm afraid that's the case."

"Then that stuff must taste pretty good. It smells like sheep shit."

"It's the Turkish latakia in the blend, Daniel. The Turks cure it by spreading it over nets suspended above sheep pens, so it absorbs the rising nitrogen."

"Oh, for Christ's sake." Morgan pulled a cigarette from his sock. "So what kind of jurors do I want in the Eddington case?"

Walter Smith tapped the bit of his pipe on his teeth and rubbed a hand through what was left of his red hair. "If Rita Eddington's testimony is that the daughter killed him, women aren't going to accept it. They just won't have it. I'm afraid they'll see her as Medea—a spectacle akin to the female of the species devouring her young. I'd go hard at the women in voir dire. I'd try to force them to admit their true feelings—do my best to develop challenges for cause. And that's where I'd use my peremptories, on the women."

"That's about what I've been thinking," Morgan said.

In the end I went with Morgan to Goldwater's when he took Ann Hastings there to help him buy dresses for Rita Eddington. That was after Morgan had told Rita that we needed to go to her house to pick up some dresses for her to wear during the trial and Rita had told him that she didn't own a dress. "Strange," he had said to me.

"I can't remember her ever wearing one," I told him.

"All she said was that she didn't get off the ranch very often."

"You want to know what I think is strange, Dan?"

"What?"

"She has a perfect pedicure, but her feet never show. She always wears boots."

Strange or not, we went out with Ann to buy Rita some dresses. "I want them to be pretty," Morgan said as the three of us walked into Goldwater's.

That was when Ann Hastings blessed us with her feelings about our little expedition. "It seems such a cliché," she said. "It's like a cartoon from the *New Yorker*. You know. The beautiful defendant on the stand with her all-American long-stemmed legs crossed in front of an all-male jury."

And Morgan responded with his own sentiments. "When it comes to a jury trial, Ann, you can take your goddamned good taste and shove it. And if you don't believe that, you can go ask your big hero Walter Smith if it isn't true." There was malice in Morgan's tone, and it caused me to back up into a rack of brassieres and watch the two of them as they stared at each other with heat. "Listen, goddamn it," he went on, "you'd better understand that the process we're about to go through has very little to do with law, and very much to do with theater. And I'm not talking about your oh-so-refined Mr. Ibsen and Mr. Chekhov."

At first Ann looked as surprised as I felt. But then it passed. "Well, I'm not going to be part of that process, am I?" she said. "All I'm in for is to do a little shopping." I watched her turn and walk with a certain lilt in her step toward the endless racks of dresses.

Ann came out of the fitting room modeling a dress she'd selected for Rita. It was very tailored and put me in mind of the elegant suit she'd been wearing when we arrived. Her lustrous blond hair was drawn back in a bun, and I was thinking how beautiful she looked.

"No, goddamn it," Morgan barked. "I want hard-ons in that jury box."

Ann didn't flinch. She didn't blush. She just gazed at him with a level stare, and in a most ironic voice she said, "You don't like it."

"It isn't pretty, Ann. It's sophisticated, but not pretty."

Ann picked another dress and modeled that one, but

Morgan still wasn't satisfied. She picked another. And then another, and another. Always the reaction was the same.

At last Ann said, "Okay, Danny." She grabbed a dress off a rack some distance from where we'd been standing and headed for the fitting room. Then she came out. The dress was pale blue. It was knit, and it was very soft, and it clung to Ann in such a way that when she moved the way she was moving, I could tell she wore nothing under it, that she'd left her slip and her panties and her brassiere in the dressing room. She stopped and turned and stood in front of Morgan. Then she reached up and back to her hair and began to loosen it from whatever held the bun, and when she did that, I could see her nipples, which were erect. As her thick hair fell about her shoulders I could hear Morgan whisper, "Jesus."

"You want clichés, Danny, you got clichés."

"We'll take it!" Morgan yelled at the saleslady. "In a size eight." We took four more dresses before the afternoon was over, but none was quite like the blue knit. I was the one who forged Ferris Eddington's signature on the charge slip.

29 THE TRIAL STARTED on a Monday. A cold front had descended, and the early news had citrus growers lighting smudge pots all night long to keep the oranges from freezing on the trees. As Morgan and I walked up Washington Street, I could see my breath, so dense from the cold that it looked like his cigarette smoke. I shivered in my flannel suit. Morgan wore a lighter worsted suit, which was tailored stylishly and fit him to perfection. He looked good as he marched quickly and with determination. The roll of fat he'd brought home from France was now completely gone, and his hair was combed and in place. But it was not his tailoring or his barbering that drew my attention to the cut of Morgan's suit that morning. It was the rings of sweat that reached down the sides of his coat from under his arms. It seemed odd when it was so cold. I was nervous, too. But I didn't sweat. Morgan didn't show his nerves. Instead it was almost as if he were in a trance. He moved where he wanted to move and asked questions he wanted to ask and listened only to the parts of the answers he wanted to hear. He gave orders. He was not unpleasant, but he'd become like steel. And the sweat poured from him.

As we approached the steps of the courthouse, I remembered Frank Menendez's strict order that Morgan was to talk to him about the case, before trial. Morgan had not done so. I had reminded him three times, and though each time he promised he would see him, his reaction to my third reminder had been such that I didn't dare try a fourth. Now it was too late. We walked into the old brown building at the corner of Washington Street and First Avenue and up the stairs to the courtroom itself. It was big and open, and the lawyers' tables were side by side, with plenty of room between. The bench was high, and so was the witness stand, and everything was wood, and the morning light streamed in through venetian blinds. I liked the big room, and I was glad the trial was there. The other courtroom upstairs seemed cramped and misshapen by comparison, and those in the new Maricopa County Superior Courthouse on Jefferson Street seemed cold and small. They had no windows.

Rita Eddington, wearing one of the dresses we'd bought at Goldwater's, already sat in the courtroom when we arrived. She looked good in the dress, even better than Ann, if you were to put an objective point on it. She stood up and moved instinctively toward Morgan. Immediately she tripped, and I saw that her right ankle had been shackled to the table leg. Morgan caught her so that she didn't fall. He persuaded the deputy sheriff to unlock her, and he moved her to the table nearer the jury box.

After that, Morgan opened his briefcase and arranged his files and notebooks on that table. All his things were either black or dark brown. When he ordered them in neat rows on the table, they gave the impression of near-perfect order. In front of the chair nearest the jury box, he placed a thick black loose-leaf notebook. It contained, in organized sections, his notes for the entire trial, not only for his opening statement and examination of every witness, both cross and direct, but also his closing argument and points of law on certain questions of evidence. Morgan had told me he started preparation for trial by writing his closing argument first. He wanted always to know his case far enough ahead so he could do that. No surprises, he'd said.

When he finished arranging things, he drew from a pocket a brand-new pencil that had been sharpened to a razor point. He placed the pencil directly in front of his trial notebook, parallel to the front edge, with the lead pointing directly at the other table. After all this he gently touched Rita Eddington's arm. "Are you okay?" he asked.

"Yes."

"It won't last long, and I hope when it's over we can all just have a nice drink together. Okay?"

"Okay," she said, and then she put her hand on his.

"Let's sit down," Morgan commanded. And there we sat for about ten minutes as prospective jurors were led into the gallery behind us. We were sitting there, eyes straight ahead pursuant to Morgan's orders, when Max Hauser, accompanied by a couple of detectives and a junior lawyer carrying boxes of exhibits, came into the room. Morgan continued to stare straight ahead, refusing to acknowledge Hauser's presence, and Hauser went about his business seeming to be unperturbed by his adversary's silence. In time, though, Hauser cast an imperious gaze upon Morgan and then let his eyes move to the meticulously organized files and notebooks on our table. He blinked.

It took only one day to pick a jury, eleven men and one woman. "Henry Penrod isn't from California" was all Dan Morgan had to say when I expressed surprise at how quickly it had gone.

Dinner that first night was at Durant's. Morgan quietly pushed a trout from one side of his plate to the other. I had by then grown accustomed to his long silences; I'd figured out that they weren't some form of personal rejection, that he just had some need to think—no, brood—privately about the case. So I sat happily cutting a slice off a big T-bone, then looking around at all the red leather booths as I chewed.

"You remember that day you walked off the golf course?" he finally said to me.

"Of course I do."

"Remember I promised that you could question a witness in this case?"

"Yes."

"You can cross-examine Juan Menchaka. I think Hauser is going to call him first."

My steak caught in my throat and slowed me down when I tried to tell him that, his Arizona Club lecture notwithstanding, I didn't know how to cross-examine anyone, at least not when it counted, and Morgan just kept talking.

"This is all I want you to do. I want you to have him tell the jury very quickly that, given what he saw and heard, he didn't know whether it was Rita or Miranda who fired the gun. That's all. Just get him to concede that."

"I'm not sure, Dan. He's a pretty important witness. And I don't think he's going to want to do that. I could really screw this up."

"No you won't. He'll be forthright if it's you asking the questions. I'm not sure how he feels about me. I don't think he trusts me." I remembered the preliminary hearing, when Morgan had risen to cross-examine Juan and then had sat down without asking him any questions. "You talk to him in the morning, Doug. You make sure he'll do it. Then you establish just that one point and you sit down. I don't want you trying to gild any lilies."

I didn't get much sleep that night.

In the shadows at the end of the courthouse hall the next morning, Juan said, "Big case, huh?" and I said, "Yes," and sort of half whistled. Juan patted me on the shoulder and told me that I would do good. I asked him if they were going to call him as their first witness, and he said that was what they'd told him.

"I'll need to ask you one question."

Juan nodded, and I explained that it was our theory that Miranda had killed Travis. He tipped his head back and raised his eyebrows and made it abundantly clear that he was having none of it. There, in the uplifted eyebrows, was the same thing I'd seen the day Morgan had first talked to Juan at the sheep corral, the day Juan had said, "You're not going to try to lay this off on that little girl, are you?" Juan smiled an ironic smile that I'd seen many times before and said, "*Buena suerte.*"

I plowed ahead. "I just need to establish that if you only consider the things you saw that morning, you couldn't tell whether it was Rita or Miranda who pulled the trigger."

"And you're going to be asking the questions?"

"Yes."

He paused for a very long moment, still looking skeptical. "Rita carried the gun in."

"But," I said, "isn't it possible that Miranda got the gun away from Rita and shot him?"

"Rita was carrying the gun when she came out."

"She could have gotten it back."

"That little girl didn't kill her father, Douglas."

"But you don't know that for sure. Not from what you saw and heard that morning. Will you just admit that, Juan? When I ask you?"

He nodded, not speaking, and I hoped very much that the nod was in the affirmative. Then I heard Max Hauser's voice coming up the back staircase. Telling Juan I had to take a leak, I sneaked quickly around the corner out of sight. I was pacing back and forth in the hall, a little panicked, when I felt Morgan touch my arm.

"Are you scared?" he asked.

I meant to tell him that I wasn't, that I thought I had a pretty good handle on it, but those words didn't come out. "Scared shitless," I said. I started to tell him how unsure I was of what Juan would say on the witness stand.

"Come with me," he ordered, and he pulled me down the hallway and into the men's room. He locked the door and stood me against the wall next to a urinal. "I'm going to tell you something," he said, "something I've never told anybody except a couple of wives when we happened to be speaking to each other, and I don't know why I'm telling you." I stared at him, wondering what was going on. "I can't be involved in any case that's really important," he said, "without getting so scared it hurts. At least that's the way it is when it gets down to cutting nuts. Which is where we are right now."

"No kidding."

"So I'm scared. Look." He raised his arm. I could see
a ring of sweat that came all the way through the flannel
of his suit, the same ring that had been there the morning
before. "It embarrasses me," he said, "but that's the way it
is. I can't help it. It seems so silly, but there's something
about the whole thing. A trial like this one. The results
are so important. And that fat shithead is going to be out
there, all eager to make us look foolish." He stopped as if
some profound realization had come to him for the first
time. "You know," he said, "lawyers are pricks. They really
are. They teach it in every law school in this country. And
most of them can't do it. Try cases, I mean. The big cases.
They don't dare. If they have to stand up in a courtroom
on something important, they shit their pants. It isn't like
speaking to the Rotary. You just remember that, goddamn
it. No matter how scared you get. Most of the bastards out
there pulling down big money don't dare do it. Christ, for
the first year I tried cases, I threw up every morning before trial. This old courthouse doesn't have a john, men's
or women's, that I haven't puked in. It used to worry me.
That I'd get so scared. I thought something was wrong with
me, that maybe I was crazy. It doesn't bother me anymore,
though."

"Why not?" I asked him.

"Because I figured something out. The guys who don't
get scared don't get very good. So I live with it. Hell, I even
saw Frank Menendez throw up before a trial once." He said
that last part, about Frank Menendez, as if it constituted
conclusive empirical validation of his theory on fear and its
relation to quality of trial practice. "I guess what I'm trying
to tell you is that if I weren't sure you were up to this, you
wouldn't be in this courthouse. Now we'd better go."

I never had feared for my breakfast that morning, so I'm
not sure how much I needed Morgan's little locker-room
pep talk. Still, I did appreciate the thought. And now, as I
think back on it, I realize that in all the time I knew him,
that was the only time Dan Morgan ever told me how he really felt about anything. And I'm sure he never told anyone

else what he told me that nervous morning—anyone, that
is, but those two estranged women.

I didn't hear much of the opening statements I had so
looked forward to. I was too worried about questioning
Juan Menchaka. I did hear Hauser say something about circumstantial evidence being just as good as direct evidence,
as he promised to use circumstantial evidence to prove Rita
guilty beyond a reasonable doubt. Morgan, after much talk
about the presumption of innocence, summarized what Rita
would say. He also talked at some length about catatonia,
but it didn't really register.

I did hear very clearly, "You may call your first witness,
Mr. Hauser," and when the judge called it out, it was as
if a bell had been rung. Then Juan Menchaka, my friend
from so many years, wearing his shiny blue serge suit and
his brown twill shirt and his brown tie moved forward. He
hobbled toward the witness stand with a near-imperceptible
limp that I had never noticed before. When he settled in the
chair and put his left hand on the rail, the hand looked to
be the same color and as worn as the well-cured wood. He
raised his other hand and swore, in the name of God, to tell
the truth.

Juan related what had happened that terrible morning, how he'd seen Rita and Miranda ride up and go into
the house, then how he'd heard the report of pistol fire. So
little information, yet Max Hauser managed to draw it out
for forty-five minutes. He paused for effect as he asked
questions about Rita's purse and Miranda's Levi's, and his
dramatics left no doubt that Rita had carried the gun into
the house. He had Juan step down and look at a number of
blown-up photographs of the old house where the murder
had happened. The pictures, I remember, showed the flowers in the window box. Juan pointed to the spot where the
horses had been tied. He traced their path to the door and
told how Rita opened it. He described the shots.

"Then what happened?" Hauser asked.

"Rita walked out and dropped the gun."

"Mr. Menchaka, I show you what has been marked for
identification Plaintiff's Exhibit One." Such was Hauser's

flair that though dozens of people including himself had already checked the weapon, he asked Juan to inspect the gun to see that it wasn't loaded.

Juan handily flipped the cylinder out. "It's safe," he said.

"I ask that Plaintiff's Exhibit One be received in evidence, Your Honor," said Hauser.

"No objection."

Then, as the revolver circulated among the jury, Hauser asked, "What did you see next, Mr. Menchaka?"

"The blood," said Juan.

What a high point to end it on, I thought. But Hauser didn't stop. "Incidentally, Mr. Menchaka," he continued, "do you know whether, from the inside of this house, Rita Eddington would have been able to see you?" Hauser was pointing at one of the blow-ups.

I sat wondering why he would ask that question. Then I felt an explosive kick under the table and heard Morgan's harsh whisper. "Object!"

Without knowing how I got there, I was on my feet and my voice was out in the room. "I object!"

"The basis, Mr. McKenzie?" I heard the judge demand.

And there I stood, in front of Henry Penrod and in front of all those people, realizing I had no idea why I was standing, let alone why I'd opened my mouth. I looked at the man who was above me in the black robe while I tried to take a breath. Then, feeling the heat move to my face, I looked down at the table and found myself studying the grain. Eventually it registered that a yellow pad had been shoved into my line of vision. Without thinking, I read aloud what Morgan had written in his oversize, clear, bold hand. " 'It calls for speculation, Your Honor.' "

"Sustained." I was pretty sure that no one besides Morgan and me knew about the lightning that had just shot through my body and how much my knees were trembling.

Hauser announced he had no more questions for Juan Menchaka. I was still standing there, shaking and looking at Juan across the distance of that big room, when I heard the judge say, "Mr. McKenzie." I turned and gave him a vacant stare. "Since you are doing the objecting, I assume you will cross-examine."

And as soon as the judge had said it, my voice was out in the room once again. "Mr. Menchaka, given what you saw and heard that morning, you couldn't tell whether it was Rita Eddington or Miranda Eddington who fired the shots. Isn't that true?"

Without the slightest pause, Juan said, "That's right. Miranda could have killed him just as easy as Rita could have."

"Objection!" Hauser exploded. "And I ask that the jury be instructed to disregard that answer!"

I was stunned, but it was more by Juan's answer than by the force of Hauser's objection. I tried to calculate how much more Juan had given me than I'd asked for, just how much he'd said in support of the Morgan theory that he did not believe. I knew this much: Juan hadn't just honored our little deal that he'd nodded on by admitting to his own lack of knowledge, he'd told the jury Miranda might well have done it, and he'd told them so within minutes of Hauser's establishing how well he knew all the Eddingtons.

I remained silent as the judge looked from Juan to Hauser, then to the jury, and finally to the ceiling. I thought back to that night at the Arizona Club, the night when Morgan had gotten a little drunk and told me that everybody lies. *"There's just something about a trial. The stakes are so high. People take sides and team up."* I remembered our righteous indignation about the medical examiner who refused to concede Morgan's points at the preliminary hearing. Morgan may have been drunk then, I thought, but now I knew he'd been right. And I knew that even though Max Hauser had called him, Juan had become my witness. He had joined the team and shaded his testimony accordingly.

I tried to think how Max Hauser could cross-examine Juan's answer. Which of the areas Morgan had told me about could he explore? Bias, I thought. Yes. Bias. He should say, *"You are a friend of Mr. McKenzie's, aren't you, Mr. Menchaka? You took him up the sheep trail, didn't you? You taught him to fish and to tie flies? You treated*

him like the son you never had, because you liked him and
because his real father always saw to it that Ferris Edding-
ton treated you fairly and paid you on time? Is that not all
true, Mr. Menchaka?" And of course that was all true, and
because it was, my old friend had fudged the truth on what
was perhaps the most important thing he'd ever been asked
to say.

But Hauser didn't know those things. Neither did the
judge, and neither did the jury. Only I knew them. And
Morgan. Morgan knew them, too. For an instant I wondered whether he'd known what Juan would do. Then I
looked at him sitting at the table, his eyes aflame, not even
trying to hide a gloating smile. As I appraised his malig-
nant grin, I thought back to Chet Johnson's homey advice.
"He'll treat you like a mushroom," Chet had said. I looked
at the jury. They were all fixed on Juan. The young guy in
the front—his name was Caldwell—had stopped chewing
his gum. Mrs. Mendoza, the only woman left after Morgan
had exercised his strikes, moved her head, just slightly, very
slowly. And Guy Buckley, the crop duster, rocked back and
forth in his chair.

The judge struggled with Hauser's objection. In time the
prosecutor pleaded, "Your Honor, it's argumentative. It's
speculative. Mr. Menchaka offers an opinion on the ultimate issue. It invades the province of the jury."

For a moment I thought the judge was going to speak to
me, but finally he said that he would sustain the objection.
"Members of the jury, you are instructed to disregard the
witness's last answer." Feeling deflated, I sat down, and the
judge announced a recess.

In the hall I said rapidly, "God, Dan, I'm sorry. I just
didn't know what to say when he objected."

Morgan, his eyes still afire, was inhaling cigarette
smoke and laughing at the same time. "Are you kidding?"
he said. "It was beautiful." He slapped me on the shoulder.
"They heard it, didn't they?" Smoke was bursting from his
mouth and his nose both. "Goddamn it, it was beautiful. So
what if old Henry told them to disregard it? It'll just make
them remember it. Besides, what could you do? Hauser was

right. It was as inadmissible as it could be. It was awful. It was beautiful."

Then, as quickly as he had burst into his mood, Morgan turned sober, and I saw he was looking down the hall at Max Hauser, who was speaking to a squat young Mexican girl. Hauser spoke only a few words to the girl and then seemed to hurry her away down the staircase. He looked back up the hall at Morgan and me in a furtive way that made me think he hoped we'd not seen the girl.

Morgan said, "Oh, shit!"

"What?"

Just then Juan Menchaka came out of the courtroom, and Morgan said, "Would you please come with me, Juan?" Next he was leading Juan up the hall and through a door into the court reporter's office. I followed and found them looking out the window, down two floors to the street.

"Juan," Morgan said, "a girl is going to walk out onto the sidewalk. I want you to see if you know her." Under his breath Morgan whispered, "Goddamn it, I should have thought."

"That one?" asked Juan.

"Yes."

The girl who'd been talking to Hauser had walked to the curb in front of the courthouse and was about to get into a car that was waiting for her.

"Her name is Rosana Treviso."

"Is that her father in that car?"

"Yes."

"Does he work for Ferris?"

"Yes. He's an irrigator on the ranch."

"But he moved back to Mexico a few weeks ago. Right?"

"That's what I thought," said Juan. "That's what I heard."

Morgan grabbed my arm and said, "Come with me."

I didn't get a chance to say good-bye to Juan, for I was instantly trailing Morgan into another room off the hallway behind the courtroom. The bailiff sat in that room, and Morgan asked him if all the exhibits from the investigation were there. He said he thought so and produced a cardboard box. The box turned out to be empty, and the bailiff said, "They must be out in the courtroom."

"There was something else," Morgan said. "Something that isn't out there." For the first time since the trial started, his voice betrayed his nerves. Morgan hurried to the judge's chambers, and when I caught up to him, he was asking the judge for an extra ten minutes of recess. "I need it bad, Henry."

Suddenly I was hurrying to keep up with him down a back stairway, and then we were on a dead run out the rear service door, through a parking lot, over a low hedge, and through traffic across Jefferson Street. I actually heard tires skid. And then we were in the new courthouse, both breathing heavily as we ran up two or three flights of stairs. We burst into a big, warehouselike room, and Morgan was yelling as we went through the door, "Charlie, I need some exhibits!"

Charlie looked up from a large ledger. "Well, hell, Danny. How's it—"

"It's *State v. Eddington,* criminal number 73-956," Morgan managed to exhale as he bent over and fought for breath. The old man stumbled back through some large metal shelves that housed all sizes of boxes. In a moment he emerged with a cardboard box that was open, and he put the box on the counter in front of us. Morgan hesitated for an instant, and then we both looked inside. One pair of very old cowboy boots lay in the box. They had been Travis's. I'd seen him wear them before. I could see a frayed Justin label sewn inside the stovepipe of one boot. Draped lightly over the boots was the teddy, the peach-colored lingerie the deputy sheriff had described at the preliminary hearing. Morgan breathed a sigh of relief. He reached for the teddy. It was very sheer and looked delicate against the boots, which were caked with dried manure. Morgan turned the garment over so that we could read the label: SWITZER'S.

"You know where Switzer's is?" Morgan asked me.

"Sure, it's over next to Hanny's."

"Right. I want you to go over there right now and see what you can find out about this thing. Can we check this out, Charlie?"

"Yes," said the old man.

"You take it over there, Doug. You see if anyone can remember selling it to any Eddington or to a Mexican girl named Rosana Treviso."

As I was walking out with the teddy folded neatly in a bag, Morgan yelled at me, "Be damned careful with the evidence markings on that thing!"

I walked up to Adams Street, then to Switzer's. I saw across the street that they had finished construction of the new Adams Hotel. Inside the store I waited nervously as a large woman in a pale yellow sweater waited on two customers. At length the woman moved to me. Nobody would have called her pretty. Handsome, perhaps. Classy, in a rather sturdy way. A pair of narrow reading glasses hung against her ample chest, suspended by a gold chain. "May I help you?"

"I'm one of the lawyers in the Eddington murder case."

"Yes, I've read about it in the paper."

"I need to find out if anyone remembers selling a particular piece of lingerie."

"Yes." She sighed with a strange aura of resignation.

The woman's name was Laura Scott, and when I got her to the courthouse, I asked her to wait on the bench in the hall, and I went into the courtroom and tried to whisper to Morgan what I'd found out. He was listening to a witness and brushed me aside. Then he pushed me a yellow pad on which he'd scribbled *"Write it."* He read what I wrote down, then wrote below it: *"Go across street to clerk's office/Have subpoena issued in her name/Bring subpoena back and serve her/Do not let her get away!"*

Then Morgan wrote something else: *"Medical examiner."* I squinted to show I didn't know what he meant, and Morgan nodded toward the man who was in the witness stand. Dr. Wallace was there talking about entry wounds and exit wounds. He had a document open before him, which I recognized to be the autopsy report, and I heard him note that the aorta had been severed and the left lung had been pierced. One bullet had perforated the peritoneum, and one had lodged in the upper part of the leg. There was talk about rib levels and midaxillary lines. And before I could get out the door, Travis Eddington was dead.

That night, after I had served Mrs. Scott with her subpoena and after Morgan had extracted her promise to be in the office to talk to him at the crack of dawn, we drove to Mesa for dinner. Morgan had said he was tired of Arizona Club food. We ate at the El Charro restaurant, the one on Main Street. There were two El Charros in Mesa. The newer one on Country Club Drive near the house where I grew up had a fountain in the entrance and fancy tables and oil paintings on the walls. The old one wasn't so fancy. We sat in a booth by the jukebox, at a table covered with spotted linoleum framed with metal molding. In places the linoleum on the floor was worn through to the concrete. At the bar the people were all speaking Spanish. The bartender yelled a lot, and the beat-up jukebox filled the whole restaurant with mariachi music.

"This place may just have the best food in the world," Morgan opined. I told him I would not dispute that and ordered two green chili burros and a bottle of Coors.

Morgan hadn't spoken of Laura Scott nor her revelation since we left the courthouse. Indeed, he hadn't spoken one word as we drove from Phoenix. But then, sitting at the linoleum-covered table, after he'd finished near half a bottle of beer, he loosened up. "Now, tell me again what that woman told you."

"She said Travis Eddington bought that teddy for a Mexican girl who couldn't speak very good English."

"How did she know Travis?"

"She said his mother had brought him to Switzer's many times when she was shopping. When Travis was a little boy."

"What makes her think Travis was buying it for the Mexican girl? Maybe he was buying it for someone else? Maybe he was buying it for Rita."

"Not so," I said.

"Why?"

"Because once, when the girl didn't know Mrs. Scott was looking, Mrs. Scott saw her nuzzle up against Travis and kiss him, and he kissed her back. And it was the girl who picked out the teddy."

"Oh," said Morgan, and then he finished his beer. "So what was he doing with her, Doug? The Mexican girl?"

"I guess he was . . ." I was searching for a discreet word for the adventures of the son of the man who had provided my support for most of the years of my life.

"He was fucking her," said Morgan, sparing me from verbalizing my own conclusion. "He was shacked up with some irrigator's daughter. It was that girl who planted those flowers in that flower box. I should have known it, god-damn it. What in hell was I thinking? Did I think Travis Eddington had suddenly developed an acute interest in horticulture? That Travis suddenly got the feminine touch? We should've found that girl, Doug. *I* should've found her."

While Morgan stewed, I ate my two burros and sipped my beer and observed that it would have been tough to find her in the middle of Sonora.

"Well, Hauser sure as hell found her!"

I remained silent and then ordered another beer and another burro, this time a red one, and noticed that, notwithstanding Morgan's great promise that we would lose weight before the case was over, my belt seemed to be tightening. And I saw that, despite his readiness to give El Charro a five-star rating, he didn't eat. His enchiladas cooled as he sat and smoked and drank a cup of coffee and fretted about not having found the girl named Rosana Treviso.

"You know Hauser's going to have her coming at us, don't you?" Morgan said. I chewed and gave him an empty stare. "Didn't I tell you that son of a bitch had something we didn't know about? She's going to have her teeth bared, too. You know that, don't you?"

"Wasn't he supposed to provide us with something about her in discovery?"

"He was careful not to let anybody put anything about her in writing. That way he didn't have anything to deliver to us." I chewed on that along with the chili and the flour tortilla. "What in hell is that girl going to say, Doug?"

"I don't have the faintest idea."

"Well, I'll tell you one thing. It's going to be nasty." After that, time passed, and Morgan filled the place with smoke and drained a pot of coffee. "Tell me this, Doug," he said at last. "If we prove Rosana Treviso was in Switzer's with Travis, does that impeach Rosana or does it just give Rita a motive to kill him?"

"I don't know," I said.

"Neither do I," said Dan Morgan. "Let's get the hell out of here."

30   I GOT UP EARLY the next morning, and as I looked out the window to the east, I could see a slice of light, almost white, along the tops of the mountains. All else was black. By the time I had showered and dressed, the slice had become a band of dark orange and the mountains had turned deep purple, and palm trees stood against the orange light as black silhouettes. It was still and dark in the city, no wind, only absolute quiet. As I got into my car, I noticed that Morgan's Ford was already gone.

Soon I was sitting in the coffee shop in the basement of the Luhrs Building drinking coffee and eating an English muffin, trying to come fully awake. There my gaze fell on the front page of the *Arizona Republic*. I felt my eyes widen and my mouth open when, for the second time, I saw my name in the paper. In the bottom right corner, under "Eddington Murder Trial in Second Day," was a description of the first day of testimony. "Phoenix defense lawyer Douglas McKenzie," it called me once again. It didn't say "first-year associate." It didn't say "assistant to Phoenix defense lawyer Daniel Morgan." It didn't even say "second chair." "Yesterday morning," it reported, "under cross-examination by Phoenix defense lawyer Douglas McKenzie, key prosecution witness Juan Menchaka conceded that the defendant's daughter may likely have killed Travis Eddington, member of a locally prominent ranching family. Mr. Menchaka was the only eyewitness to the events of the morning of October 21 this year. . . ."

I thought about my ambiguous feelings toward Dan Morgan and his sneaky manipulations that had procured the concession made by the key prosecution witness. Then I thought about how many people would be reading the paper that morning. And as I read the article again, I pardoned Morgan on the spot, absolutely and forever.

An hour later we were back in the courtroom waiting, Morgan braced against the prospective appearance of Rosana Treviso, I savoring my newfound celebrity, and Rita Eddington seeming to sink quietly into depression. Somehow sure that she could provide potent impeachment, Morgan had hidden Laura Scott in the court reporter's room; he told me he did not want Rosana Treviso to see that we had her. And in this posture we waited for the double doors of the courtroom to admit the dreaded Mexican girl.

But the Mexican girl did not appear. Instead there came the ballistics expert, and for what seemed a never-ending hour Hauser used him to establish what everyone already knew, that Rita's gun had fired the bullets that had killed her husband. "No questions," said Morgan, and the ballistics man stepped down unscathed. Next the fingerprint expert came through the doors to instruct us on latent prints and known prints and ridges and swirls and furrows and points of comparison. Rita Eddington had handled the weapon, he told us all. Morgan did choose to cross-examine this witness. "You ascertained that Miranda Eddington also handled the revolver, did you not?"

"Yes. That is correct."

"Do you understand, sir, that the issue in this case is not whether these women fired that gun but which of the women fired it on a certain occasion?"

"Objection," said Hauser without rising.

"Sustained."

"Let me put it this way, Mr. Sullivan. The work you have done in this case does nothing to assist us in determining which of the women whose fingerprints you found on that gun shot Mr. Eddington, does it?"

"Objection."

"Overruled. You may answer that one, Mr. Sullivan."

"That is correct," said the witness. "I cannot tell you who shot Mr. Eddington."

"Then, why—can you tell us—are you here?"

"Objection!" Hauser yelled loudly. "Mr. Morgan must know how improper that is."

"Sustained," the judge said forcefully.

"Well, if I understand," Morgan pressed, before the other voices stopped ringing in the room, "you can't tell us any more than the ballistics man could. You know, the witness Mr. Hauser had on the stand for more than an hour just before you came in?"

"Objection!!" Hauser was now standing. And he was yelling, and he was reddening.

"Sustained. You know that's not proper, Mr. Morgan."

"I guess I do, Your Honor." Morgan was speaking to the judge, but he was looking right at the jury. "What I don't know, Judge, is why we're taking all this time on testimony that has nothing to do with the issues in this case."

"That's enough, Mr. Morgan," said Henry Penrod. The judge's voice was very low and calm, and I knew that he knew that my mentor had gone as far as he intended to go.

"That's all," said Morgan, measuring the jury. When he sat down at our table, Morgan winked at me. Then he turned, and once again he looked at the jury. I'm not certain, for I could see only the wild hair on the back of his head, but I'm fairly sure that Morgan winked at the jury. I say that because I saw two or three of the jurors smile back at him.

"Call John Camacho!" Max Hauser yelled, his voice still angry from the nasty exchange.

After that, mornings and afternoons passed by. Hauser slowly and elaborately put on the same case he'd presented at the preliminary hearing. He called the Camacho brothers and the man from Peterson Brothers who had sold Rita the gun, and the deputy sheriff who had reported the investigation, and the lab technician who had performed the paraffin tests, and all the rest of them. I remember that Johnny

Camacho said again that Miranda had shot at the blackbird on the wire and described how the bird had fallen to the ground dead.

And I remember how I clutched a little each time a witness stepped down and how I drew a breath of relief each time the next witness was not Rosana Treviso. I clutched again when we were walking back to the office one evening and Morgan asked me, "What in hell is that Mexican girl gonna say?"

"I don't know," I told him.

"You know he's got to be saving her for last," Morgan said, fretting. "She's damned well going to be potent. Rita's never heard of her. She has no idea who she is."

The next morning Hauser called the travel agent. His name was Jordan Pomeroy.

"Mr. Pomeroy, I'm showing you two documents that have been marked for identification Plaintiff's Exhibits Fifteen and Sixteen, respectively. Do you recognize them?"

"Yes, sir."

"What are they, please?"

"They are two airplane tickets I sold to Rita Eddington. One for her and one for her daughter."

"Were they for a flight to the island of Curaçao in the Caribbean on the afternoon of October twenty-first?"

"Yes."

"Are they one-way tickets, Mr. Pomeroy?"

"Yes, they are."

"I offer Exhibits Fifteen and Sixteen in evidence, Your Honor."

"No objection."

"They're received."

"No further questions."

Morgan stood and moved around in front of our table. "Mr. Pomeroy, whose idea was it that Mrs. Eddington go to Curaçao?"

"I guess that probably would have been mine."

"Will you explain that to the jury, please?"

Jordan Pomeroy described a special deal being offered by the Netherlands Antilles in an effort to increase tourism.

Mrs. Eddington, he told the jury, had said she wanted to have a small getaway with her daughter. Mr. Pomeroy had been able to arrange one at a bargain price. It simply required that Mrs. Eddington purchase return tickets in Curaçao once she had arrived on that island.

"Mr. Pomeroy, what if someone were to suggest that Mrs. Eddington was running away to the Caribbean, planning never to come home? How would that square with your dealings when you sold her those tickets?"

"That, sir, would be ridiculous."

Morgan stared into the jury box, making sure they got it. Then he turned to the bench. "May I have a moment, Your Honor?"

"Yes."

Morgan walked to the other table, bent toward the man who had called the witness, and, with his face right in Hauser's, whispered so softly that only Hauser and I could hear him. "If this guy is the basis for your keeping her in jail all this time, Max, you fucking well better have something potent for redirect."

Morgan straightened and turned to the bench. "No further questions, if it please the court." Then he turned back to Hauser and with a cold glare watched him rise. Hauser returned the same expression. His jaw moved in and out. He reddened. Without shifting his hateful gaze from Morgan's face, he announced, "I call Rosana Treviso."

"Mr. Pomeroy, you're excused," said the court.

I spun around, and there was a deputy sheriff easing the girl Juan Menchaka had identified for us through the courtroom doors. She was plain, short, and quite fat, and I felt a small shudder as I thought of the picture she would make in that teddy. As she moved closer to our table, I could see that her face had been badly scarred by acne. Also as she came closer, I could see that she was very scared.

With his hand cupped at his mouth so no one else could hear, Morgan bent over and whispered to me, "I want you to go out and get Mrs. Scott. Have her look in here. You make sure she can testify that this is the girl who was in the store that day." As I moved, he grabbed my arm. "Just barely crack that door. I don't want this girl seeing that woman."

By the time I cracked the door, Rosana Treviso was already on the stand, her right hand in the air. "That's the girl," Mrs. Scott said before I could ask her.

"Are you sure?"

"There's no question."

Then I cracked the door once more and made her look again. I opened the door a little wider, as wide as I dared. "Are you absolutely sure? Can you testify to it?"

"Yes. I told you," she said.

When I got back to my chair and had written Morgan a note that Mrs. Scott was good for what we wanted, Rosana Treviso was testifying. Her accent was heavy, her English quite broken, but there was no question that she could communicate. "I live now in Hermosillo," she was saying.

"And where did you live in September of last year?" Max Hauser asked.

"The ranch. The Eddington Ranch. My father work there."

"And were you employed on the ranch, Ms. Treviso?" She gave a vacant look. "Did you work there also?"

She brightened. "Yes. I help my father."

"What was your father's work?"

"Irrigator."

The longer I watched her, the stranger I thought the picture of Rosana in Switzer's picking out the teddy, which lay coiled within Morgan's briefcase. She was homely in the extreme. I couldn't tell how old she was, only that she had spent too many years working too hard. If there was such a thing as a peasant girl in Arizona that year, Rosana Treviso was that girl. I felt vague pity for her. Also, I wondered how Travis Eddington had seen something desirable there. And, as I thought about it, I realized that I never had really known the son of my father's employer at all. Somewhere blurred in my memory was a picture of a dark-skinned boy some years older than I, good-looking, strongly built, very lean. And he was rich. There was no question about that. At least his father was. I knew this much: If Travis Eddington had wanted to take a girl to Switzer's to buy her something soft and nice, he could have had his pick of almost any girl on the ranch. The daughters of the sheep men, the foremen. Beautiful Mexican girls who had black eyes that snapped and who could dance all night. I could not see one attractive feature as I looked at Rosana Treviso. Then I turned to Rita, whose skin was absolutely clear and whose strawberry blond hair was thick and full of life and whose eyes were turquoise and just a little watery. *What was wrong with Travis?* I wondered.

After a few more preliminaries, Rosana Treviso testified that she had once been to Travis and Rita's house. A pump, she said, on one of the wells had broken. Her father had been unable to get water, and he'd sent her to find Travis. She had gone to his front door, but there'd been no answer.

"What did you do then?" Hauser asked.

"I went in back."

"Why?"

"I heard voices."

"Was someone in back?"

The girl shook her head.

"You must answer with your mouth."

"Yes."

"Who was in back?"

"Mr. Eddington. Travis Eddington."

"Was there anyone else?"

She nodded, then caught herself and said, "Yes."

"Who, please?"

The girl raised her arm and pointed a stubby finger at Rita, and while she left her arm and finger extended in that mode of accusation, Rita stared at her. I watched Rita to see if I could judge some reaction, some surprise, some hostility, some fear. I saw nothing. If the turquoise eyes that rested on the Mexican girl showed anything, it was only a mild curiosity.

"May the record reflect that the witness has identified the defendant, Rita Eddington?"

"It may," said the judge.

"Ms. Treviso, did either Mr. or Mrs. Eddington see you while you were behind the house?"

"No."

"Did you hear either of them speak?"

Again the Mexican girl pointed at Rita.

"Mrs. Eddington spoke?" Hauser sought to confirm.

"Yes."

"Did Mrs. Eddington speak to Mr. Eddington?"

"Yes."

"Ms. Treviso, I want you to tell these people what Mrs. Eddington said to Mr. Eddington."

The witness turned nervously toward the jury. "She say this: She say, 'Don't you try touch me ever another time. I kill you.' "

Once again Mr. Caldwell stopped chewing his gum. Jurors looked at Rita, and something like a cold knife cut through me. Now it was I who wanted to kick Morgan into a position from which *he* could object. It hurt us. It had to be a bald-faced lie, and I wanted to jump to my feet and yell, but Morgan sat still, cold, as if nothing had happened. So did Rita.

It had scared Rosana Treviso, she went on to testify, when she heard Rita tell Travis she would kill him. Rosana had run back around to the front of the house and rung the bell until finally Travis had answered the door. Then Travis Eddington had gone with her to her father and had seen to it that the broken pump was repaired.

"No further questions," said Maximilian Hauser.

Morgan rose. I remembered the question he'd asked a few nights before, as I was swallowing my last bite of red chili: *Would use of the impeachment we had for Rosana Treviso establish a motive to kill for Rita Eddington?* I didn't know what Morgan would do, but I knew that he had fretted away many hours over his decision.

"What was your relationship with Travis Eddington?" he demanded.

The girl looked at Morgan suspiciously. "I do not understand."

"You saw Travis Eddington at times other than when you tell us he fixed the pump, didn't you?"

"I do not understand."

"You were very close, weren't you?"

This time Rosana Treviso did not speak. She just lifted a hand to show that she did not follow his drift.

"You and Travis. *Amor.*" And, pointing to his own chest, Morgan said, *"Su corazón. ¿Verdad?"*

The ugly girl screamed, "No! No! No!"

Hauser yelled, "Objection!"

The judge said, "I think we'd better keep it to the English language unless we get an interpreter in here."

I watched the jury. Most just looked a little startled, as though they'd heard something they should not have heard, but the crop duster named Guy Buckley glanced from the witness to Rita, then to Morgan, and shook his head. I read it to mean he was not going to believe that any man married to Rita Eddington would sleep with Rosana Treviso.

Morgan lifted his briefcase to the table. Rosana Treviso watched as he slowly opened it, never taking his eyes from her. He drew out the teddy like he was pulling out a sword, and the girl drew back in the witness chair. Morgan held the garment for a moment, then walked toward her. Rosana pulled back farther, and from the expression that came to her face, Morgan might well have been carrying a snake. The crop duster saw her move, and his eyes widened. Morgan veered to the court clerk's desk and dropped the teddy in front of the clerk. The clerk applied an exhibit sticker, and Morgan moved to where the witness sat and spread the peach-colored silk over the rail in front of her chair, making it look almost like a matador's formal cape spread out before an honored guest.

It was after Morgan had walked back to our table that I noticed something I had not before fully apprehended. The teddy was very large, just as the young deputy, Duane Hamblin, had testified earlier. It was large enough to fit the poor girl before whom it was spread. It was with palpable fear that the girl moved her gaze across the sheer, elegant object now known as Defendant's Exhibit One.

"That belongs to you, doesn't it, miss?" Morgan suggested softly.

"No!"

"Travis Eddington bought it for—"

"No! No!"

"Don't you remember going to a store called Switzer's—"

"Never. No!"

"On Adams Street—"

"No! No! No!"

"Just about three blocks over there?" Morgan was pointing.

Now the girl said nothing. She just stared at her adversary, crumpled, angry, and sad.

Morgan turned to the judge. "Your Honor, I have no more questions, but I ask leave to have one person enter the courtroom for just a moment."

The judge turned to Hauser, whose posture much resembled that of his witness. Hauser moved a limp hand to signify he had no objection.

"You go ahead, Mr. Morgan," said Henry Penrod.

"Get her," Morgan ordered.

I found Mrs. Scott and brought her into the courtroom, where we stood in the gallery near the small gate. If Rosana Treviso had reacted strongly to the teddy, she reacted even more strikingly to Mrs. Scott. Indeed, she gasped audibly when we walked into the room.

Morgan turned to us and shouted, "Madam, would you please look at this person!"

Mrs. Scott stared at the witness stand.

"Do you see her?"

"Yes."

"That's all, Your Honor."

"Redirect, Mr. Hauser?"

"No, Your Honor."

"Call your next witness."

"Your Honor, we have no other witnesses. We rest." Hauser collapsed into his chair.

31 THE JUDGE SENT the jury out so that Morgan could argue our motion for a directed verdict. Contrary to Morgan's promise to yell and scream, he took about one minute to make a perfunctory record. When Hauser began to rise, the judge lifted a hand to signal that he did not wish to hear from the prosecution. "I think you impeached that Treviso girl substantially, Mr. Morgan, but a reasonable man could believe her, and given what she said, this one's got to go to the jury. Let's get them back in here."

And before the judge could say anything else, Morgan announced, "I call Laura Scott, if the court please," and I knew then that the reason for his rush was his desire to finish his task of discrediting our Mexican girl before what she had said could lodge itself very deeply in the jury's collective memory.

Mrs. Scott told them what had happened. She told them how she'd known Travis Eddington since his mother had first brought him into the store years ago, when he was just a little boy. Then she told them how the Mexican girl who'd been on the stand earlier came into the store with Travis not long before the day of his death, and she described how Travis would show the girl certain items of lingerie and how the girl would reject them one by one until ultimately Travis showed the girl the teddy and she gave her approval.

She described how the girl, when she thought Mrs. Scott wasn't looking, nuzzled up against Travis and how at one of those times he had kissed her.

"Offer Defendant's Exhibit One in evidence," said Morgan.

"Mr. Hauser?"

"May I have a question on voir dire, Your Honor?"

"Yes."

Hauser looked at the witness with a contemptuous sneer. "How can you be so sure that is the garment you sold to Travis Eddington?"

"Because it has our label and it's the only one we ever carried in that large a size."

"Defendant's Exhibit One is received."

I heard a snicker in the jury box, and as I turned, I saw Guy Buckley, the crop duster, elbow his neighbor, Mr. Savoca. Both men smiled at each other. Others in the jury smiled also. Mrs. Mendoza gazed sternly at the witness.

"No further questions," said Morgan.

Hauser flushed but plowed on. "Mrs. Scott, when did you first hear that Travis Eddington had been killed?"

"I read about it in the paper the day after it happened," she responded.

"Then why didn't you come forward and tell the authorities about the incident you just described?"

Mrs. Scott stiffened.

"Well, Mrs. Scott, why did you wait until now to bless us with your story?" Hauser sneered. It seemed that he felt he could filter his own contempt for our witness into the jury box. "We're waiting, Mrs. Scott."

"I did not tell anyone because I admired his mother."

"And you think—"

"I would not have told anyone except that this young man came and found me."

"Now, wait a minute, Mrs. Scott—"

"I believe the witness has answered counsel's question, if it please the court," Morgan interrupted softly.

"I believe that she has, Mr. Hauser," said the judge.

"But, Your Honor—"

"Do you have another question? If you do, you may put it to the witness."

Hauser sat down, and we recessed for the evening.

"Well, what do you think?" Morgan asked me, after the courtroom had cleared and he and Rita and I were alone at the table.

"I don't think anyone is going to believe a thing that Treviso girl said. I mean, it was just too clear that she was lying. It was amazing. She just sat there and lied, and everybody knew she was lying." I turned to Rita. "I mean, you never said that, did you, Rita, about if he ever touched you, you'd kill him?"

Morgan instantly put his hand in front of our client's mouth. "Come on," he ordered abruptly. "Let's go get a drink."

————————

That night at dinner, Morgan talked about timing witnesses the next day. "I'd rather start with Rita and end with Rita. I know we can't do that, but it's important that we showcase her testimony." As he often did, he spoke more to himself than to me. Ultimately he reached some kind of a compromise with himself. "I'll get Gideon Epstein to fly in at noon. There's a flight from L.A. that arrives at twelve-thirty. That way I can beg Henry to let me take him out of order. I'll try to sandwich him between Rita in the morning and Rita in the afternoon. I'll put the other stuff on first thing in the morning. Real quick."

I chewed on a thick steak that was covered with white sauce and washed it down with heavy red wine. Morgan just poked at his dinner. This time it was an expensive one, for we were in a French restaurant in Scottsdale, called Etienne. Crystal sparkled, and candles flickered, and Bach played, and waiters lit Morgan's cigarettes. I listened intently, and Morgan talked on about how much he wanted to have Rita finish testifying right at close of court the next day, Friday, so that her un-cross-examined testimony could soak into the jury over the weekend.

"Do you really think that makes a difference?"

"You're goddamned right I do," said Morgan.

In the morning, consistent with his promise, Morgan made quick work of his preliminary witnesses. First he called the deputy sheriff who'd tried to pry Miranda from the jail cell. He was a stout man named Barrett who had heavily muscled arms but gave the impression of being very gentle as he described the dilemma he confronted that morning. "I didn't know what to do," he testified. "She would not move at all. She just laid there all wrapped around the bars. Then the psychiatrist came."

"And did he assist you, Mr. Barrett?"

"He said if we wanted her out of there, we'd have to cut the bars."

"What did you do then?"

"Captain called over to maintenance, and they sent a welder with a cutting torch."

"And did you cut the bars?"

"Yes. Anyway the welder did. I helped him. We were worried about burning the little girl."

"Let me ask you this, Mr. Barrett. Why didn't you just force her arms open enough so that you could pull her away from the bars?"

"I didn't dare try. She was so rigid I was afraid I might hurt her if I tried to bend her arms."

"What did she feel like?" Morgan asked.

"Absolutely stiff. Rigid. More than that, too. Like, if I tried to push one way, she pushed harder the other way."

"What happened after you got her out?"

"That psychiatrist called an ambulance, and when it came, we carried her out and put her in it."

The psychiatrist who had gone to the jail wasn't really a psychiatrist, at least not a full-fledged psychiatrist at that time. He had been in his first week as a psychiatric resident at the Arizona State Hospital. Still, he said, he knew a catatonic when he saw one, and the judge said Hauser's objection to his qualifications went to the weight, not the admissibility, of his opinion.

"Classic catatonic stupor. Just like out of a textbook," he told the jury.

"What did you do with her?" asked Morgan.

"I had her taken to the state hospital, and I attempted to arrange for her admission. They tried to find next of kin, and when they discovered that her mother was in jail and her father was not alive, they called her grandfather. The sheriff's people knew where to find him. The grandfather said that he wanted her taken to Camelback Hospital. At first Camelback said they didn't take cases that required such intensive care. Then they said they would take this girl. Apparently the grandfather is an influential man."

If there was any question about the admissibility of the young resident's opinion, there was none about that of our next witness, Dr. Conrad Hardy, Miranda's treating physician. The Harvard-educated, board-certified psychiatrist took the stand in Henry Penrod's courtroom once again. This time the judge softened a little, and he allowed Morgan to elicit not only a statement of the doctor's diagnosis but also a short description of Miranda's condition, at least so far as the information provided by the doctor was not based on his communications with his patient or his review of her records from other doctors. Miranda's lawyer, Jacob Asher, was in the courtroom again, raising the same objections he'd raised before. However, since there was a jury here now, he made himself quite unobtrusive. Out of deference to his old friend Morgan, he voiced his objections at the bench so that the jury could not hear his sentiments about what Morgan was trying to do to his client.

In spite of the judge's more liberal ruling, the doctor did not wish to testify about his patient, and when Morgan asked for his diagnosis of Miranda, Dr. Hardy balked.

"Can you not recall your diagnosis, Doctor?" Morgan said.

Dr. Hardy looked toward the judge. Before he could say a word, Morgan moved to the bench. "I ask that Dr. Hardy be declared a hostile witness and that I be allowed to ask leading questions on direct examination."

"I find Dr. Hardy sufficiently identified with interests adverse to the defendant as to be a hostile witness. You may treat this as cross-examination, Mr. Morgan."

"Miranda Eddington is in a catatonic stupor, is she not, Doctor?" Morgan pronounced authoritatively.

"Yes."

"That is her condition today?"

"Yes."

Morgan moved across the room and leaned against the jury box. "She lies in her bed in a rigid posture, does she not, Doctor?"

"Yes."

"She is mute and does not speak?"

"That is correct."

"She also displays what might be termed a distinct negativism. Isn't that correct, sir?"

Conrad Hardy tilted his head and measured Morgan suspiciously.

"Isn't that true, Doctor?" Morgan persisted. "Miranda Eddington presents a distinct negativism?"

"Yes, that's true."

"Tell the jury, please, what that means."

"If one attempts to cause her to do a given thing, she will often do exactly the opposite. For example, if one attempts to push her arm to the right, she will push it to the left. If she is asked to open her eyes, she will close them even tighter. That is what is meant by a so-called distinct negativism."

Now Morgan moved two steps and sat casually on our table. "Have you ever heard the term 'waxy flexibility' used to describe a person in a catatonic stupor, Doctor?"

"Yes."

"And in that state the person's arms or legs may be moved, yet there is such resistance as to create a feeling that the person is made of wax. Is that correct?"

"Yes, that's correct."

"And that phrase, 'waxy flexibility,' aptly describes Miranda Eddington's condition, at least part of the time, does it not?"

"That's correct."

"And Miranda's facial expression may generally be described as stony. Is that fair?"

"Yes. She has a stony facial expression."

"One last question, Doctor. How do you feed Miranda?"

"We leave her alone with food for just a few minutes. She eats, and then she resumes a position of immobility."

When Morgan sat down, Max Hauser said he had no questions. I watched the doctor walk from the courtroom, and I reflected upon the singular fact that Miranda's condition was a reality. It was there. It existed as a genuine event, and somehow it had to be explained.

"Call Rita Eddington," Morgan announced.

Here we go.

She shook as she stood up. She used my shoulder to steady herself before she walked toward the witness stand. She wore the pale blue dress that Ann had picked out. Unlike Ann, though, she wore a brassiere under it. Her strawberry blond hair fell loosely across her shoulders. As she neared the spot where she would raise her right hand, I saw something that struck me as odd, something just a little out of place in what was otherwise perfect femininity. Rita walked in a very straight way. Nothing moved back and forth. It was the walk of a working cowboy, absolutely direct. I'd never noticed that she walked this way before. I thought for an instant that she was just a little bowlegged, but when she stopped, just before she climbed into the witness stand, I saw that she was not. There was just the pretty turn of her calf and her ankle. That and the delicate shoes that showed the curve of arch and her toes, pedicured to perfection. I wondered how she managed the pedicure while she was in jail. She climbed the two steps and swore to tell the truth, then let her arms rest on the arms of the old wooden chair.

Morgan rose, moved to the end of our table nearest the jury, and leaned there, allowing his fingertips to brush the tabletop. "Did you kill your husband?"

"No. I didn't. I didn't kill Travis," Rita declared with great calm. She remained perfectly still and kept her eyes on Morgan without blinking. Sunlight poured through the windows on the south wall behind the jury. Venetian blinds broke the light, and it fell upon Rita in horizontal lines.

Clouds must have been moving above the courthouse, for when the broken light hit Rita, it seemed to play across her face.

That light made me think of a night long before. When I was in high school, there was a huge dance hall in Mesa, Arizona, called (imaginatively enough) the Mezona. As with so many of those places, the Mezona featured a ball covered with pieces of mirror suspended from the ceiling. When the ball turned, it caused flecks of light to move around the room. One night when I was sixteen years old, I leaned against a pillar in the middle of that old firetrap and watched the light from the turning ball chase across my high-school classmates as they pushed each other around the dance floor. I was too shy to ask a girl to dance, at least too shy to ask one that I would have wanted to dance with. In my hometown, if a teenage boy wanted success with the opposite sex, he'd better have played football, and not only that, he'd better have played in the backfield. (That is, unless he was a calf roper or a bull rider.) In those days I dwelled a lot on my own sorry state: a pudgy little kid addicted to junior golf, a game exquisitely designed to assure that no cheerleader ever crawled into the backseat of its number one acolyte's '51 Ford. As I leaned against the pillar, brooding, wondering whether I'd already been disqualified from ever finding romance, I heard my name. I turned to see Rita Toronto.

"Would you dance with me, Doug?" she asked.

"What?" I choked out.

"I was hoping you would dance with me."

I stood up straight and began to waltz the girl acknowledged to be the most beautiful in the senior class around the floor. I watched the light from the mirrored ball dance across her flawless face, and I knew that every boy in school was watching me. When, early on, I told Dan Morgan that Rita Eddington was about the nicest girl I'd ever known, I surely had, at the back of my mind, that night when she took away some of the pain of my sophomore year of high school. Now I watched the broken sunlight play across her lovely face in Henry Penrod's courtroom.

"Where did you first meet Travis Eddington?" Dan Morgan asked our client.

"It was on the Eddington Ranch, when my mother came to work there."

"How old were you then, Mrs. Eddington?"

"I was fourteen."

"Do you remember your first meeting?"

"Yes. It was the day we arrived. My mother and I were moving our things into the house that Mr. Eddington, Travis's father, had arranged for us. Travis rode up on his horse and introduced himself to us."

"What happened after he introduced himself?"

"I told him I thought his horse was beautiful. It was an Appaloosa gelding. He asked me if I would like to ride him. I told him I'd never been on a horse before. He reached down and said, 'Give me your hand.' Then he turned his foot out and said, 'Put your foot on mine.' Then he pulled me up behind him, and we rode all around the ranch. That was how I met him."

"How old was Travis?"

"He was seventeen."

"I take it you spent time with him after that?"

"He taught me to ride. Travis was a fine horseman. He gave me a horse. He was the handsomest boy I'd ever seen," Rita testified. She fell in love with Travis Eddington and bore his child. "Miranda was such a beautiful baby." They remodeled the old house, the one Travis's grandfather had lived in. They were very happy, until they realized that the beautiful child was not right.

"How old was Miranda when you learned that something was wrong?" Morgan asked.

"She was seven."

"How did the problem manifest itself?"

"She became wild. It wasn't like she became a bad girl. She was just wild. Uncontrollable. Reckless."

"Can you give the jury examples?"

Rita turned to the people in the box. "When Miranda was seven," she told them, "she learned to climb up on her grandfather's horse. It was a very large stallion. Before then Mr. Eddington was the only person who could ride him. But Miranda would ride him all over the ranch. Without tack. She could make him jump fences. When she was eight, she drove her father's pickup to Chandler to buy an ice cream cone. We felt we couldn't keep her locked in the house. But no matter how many times we told her not to do these kinds of things—no matter how many times we warned her that she could get hurt—she wouldn't stop. It wasn't that she was bad. She never hurt anyone. She was just uncontrollable in certain areas. When she was nine, she tried to ride one of her grandfather's prize Brahma bulls. These are just a few examples."

"Did she stay on for eight seconds?" Morgan inquired, smiling.

"No," Rita said soberly. "And she never tried that one again."

"What finally happened?"

"Later that year there was a bad incident, one where she did hurt someone. A boy at school, who was a year older than Miranda, struck one of her classmates. The boy was big for his age and a bit of a bully. Miranda went after the boy with a baseball bat. She hospitalized him. That was the first time she ever committed an act of violence."

"What happened then?"

"I didn't know what to do. Travis wouldn't even acknowledge that there was a serious problem. Finally I went to Mr. Eddington, Travis's father, who arranged for a psychiatrist to talk to her. After that day she was gone for two years."

"Where did she go?"

"First to the Mayo Clinic in Rochester, Minnesota. Then they placed her at the Menninger Clinic in Kansas. Then she came back. She was home a few months and had a complete breakdown. She spent about eight months at Camelback Hospital here in Phoenix, and after that they sent her back to Menninger."

"Were you able to visit her when she was in these institutions?"

"Travis never did. I did a few times, but they discouraged it."

"Can you describe her relationship with her father during the times she was home?"

"Well, up until last year, I thought Travis was just distant, but then . . ." The rest of the answer caught in her throat.

"Something happened?"

"Your Honor, I fail to see any relevance," Hauser objected.

Morgan ignored him, silently holding Rita's gaze.

"In light of Mr. Morgan's opening statement and the trial brief I've been provided, I'm going to allow some latitude," the judge ruled. "Don't overdo it, Mr. Morgan."

"What happened, Mrs. Eddington?"

Rita lowered her head into her hands.

"Did something happen last year?"

She straightened up, and staring at Morgan, she reached forward and gripped the rail.

"Did something happen?"

"Yes."

"What happened?"

Tears began to move down Rita's cheeks.

"It was in August," she said. "Late in August. It was still hot. I came home in the afternoon. It had been too hot to ride. I went into our living room. Miranda came running in from Travis's den. She didn't have clothes on. She was screaming."

"Did Miranda say anything?" asked Morgan.

Hauser rose halfway to his feet.

"Yes," Rita answered.

"Tell us what she said, please."

Hauser shot fully upright. "I object. That calls for the rankest hearsay, and Mr. Morgan knows it."

"I'll lay additional foundation, if the court please." The judge nodded, and Morgan went on. "You say Miranda was screaming?"

Rita took a tissue from the box beside her chair and dried her eyes. "Yes."

"Don't tell us what she said. Just tell us what she did, and describe her emotional state."

"She ran across the room, and she threw her arms

around my legs. She was sobbing and shaking. I asked her what happened."

"Now, I don't want you to answer the next question until the court has ruled on Mr. Hauser's objection," Morgan instructed. "Do you understand?"

"Yes."

"What did Miranda say happened?"

"Objection, hearsay."

Morgan turned to the bench. "Your Honor, to the extent it may call for hearsay, which I venture is questionable, it is plainly an excited utterance and thereby comes squarely within one of the classic exceptions to the hearsay rule."

"You may answer, Mrs. Eddington."

"She said that her daddy had put his thing inside her."

Morgan stood frozen in front of our table and let the seconds go by. The jury sat stone still. The only sound in the courtroom came from muted whispers in the gallery.

"Unless you feel you need to pursue this line, Mr. Morgan, now might be a good time for the noon recess."

Perfect timing. Let it soak in with Friday's clam chowder.

Gideon Epstein's flight from Los Angeles arrived at twelve-thirty. Morgan and I stood on the tarmac at Sky Harbor. The airplane parked some distance from the gate, and the passengers descended the stairway that had been rolled out. The small group walked in our direction. I searched, but I couldn't see Gideon Epstein among them. Just as I was becoming anxious, I saw that Morgan was shaking hands with someone, but not with the man we'd planned to pick up. Gone were the gold chains, the belled trousers, the soft Italian boots. Even the curly hair was missing. Before me stood a man in a gray flannel suit, and wing-tipped shoes, and a button-down shirt, and a regimental tie. His short hair was parted on the left, and his eyes were framed with horn-rims instead of the wire of the aviators. He carried a leather attaché case, and for all I saw before me, I could have been greeting a senior partner from Price, Waterhouse.

"Hello, McKenzie."

"Hello, Dr. Epstein."

In law school we learned how important it was to prepare witnesses. Hours were to be spent, sometimes days, sometimes even weeks. Preparation of Dr. Epstein took place in Morgan's Ford going from the airport back to the courthouse.

"Will there be evidence of chronic depression in the girl?" the witness asked.

"No," Morgan told him. "Remember, we tried to get her charts, but the court refused us. That order goes for the prosecution as well. We have nothing on her history, other than her mother's testimony that at the age of seven she became uncontrollably wild."

"Wild in what way?"

Morgan told him about Rita's testimony.

"Interesting," Epstein mused. "But no evidence of depression?"

"None," said Morgan.

"Good. I may need the absence of chronic depression when I'm cross-examined."

"Well, there hasn't been a word about it."

"And what should I expect of this Mr. Hauser?"

"You'd better watch yourself, Gideon. He's an aggressive son of a bitch, and he's not stupid."

That concluded the preparation. The doctor turned and looked back to me. He smiled and patted me on the knee. Well, I guess they'd done their dance before.

Henry Penrod granted leave to take the testimony of the doctor out of order, since he needed badly to get back to California. If Dr. Hardy's qualifications were impressive, Dr. Epstein's were overwhelming. Morgan took the better part of an hour establishing them: Johns Hopkins, residency in Europe, teaching positions at Harvard and Stanford, stints at Mayo Brothers and Menninger. He had written textbooks and served on presidential advisory committees. He had published more than three hundred articles on psychiatric disorders. Thirteen were articles on catatonia. And he had testified in state and federal court hundreds of times.

"Catatonia is generally regarded as a form of schizophrenia," our expert told us, after he listened to Morgan's hypothetical description of Miranda and testified that he agreed with Dr. Hardy's diagnosis of catatonic stupor.

"Is schizophrenia a psychosis?" asked Morgan.

"Yes."

"Does that mean a person with schizophrenia is insane?"

"Insanity is more a legal concept than a medical concept," said the doctor. "I can tell you, however, if you are speaking of the common notion of crazy, the schizophrenic would very likely fall into that category. You would especially think of the catatonic as crazy, whether in stupor or in the excited state."

"Do you know what causes a catatonic stupor?"

"The prevalent view is that stupor is most often caused by a recognition in the patient of a potential for violence within himself. The stuporous state is known to serve as a restraint against that violence. Often a catatonic stupor is referred to as a splinting of the total self. There is a well-known quotation in the literature of catatonia." The doctor carefully took off his horn-rimmed glasses, pulled out a pair of reading glasses, and began to open a book.

"Objection to the witness reading outside material," said Max Hauser.

"What is the text, Doctor?" the judge asked.

"It's *The Comprehensive Textbook of Psychiatry,* Your Honor. It's a fairly basic—"

"Yes," said the judge, "I'm familiar with it. I find that it is within the learned-treatise exception. You may rely on it, Doctor."

Gideon Epstein opened the book fully, balanced his reading glasses on his nose, and read to the jury: " 'Beneath the facade of immobility is a seething volcano of potential violence. That volcano can erupt at any moment as catatonic excitement, bringing in its wake homicide, suicide, self-mutilation, and generalized destructiveness.' "

The doctor closed the book and removed his glasses. Morgan stood still, allowing time for the testimony to settle in. I drifted back to the night Morgan and I had sneaked into Camelback Hospital, remembering how afraid I'd been that the administration might catch us. My fear had been misplaced. She had seemed so delicate, so doll-like, even as I pushed against her. *"If this kid wakes up, it's a fifty-yard dash through those oleander bushes,"* Morgan had said. Had he read *The Comprehensive Textbook of Psychiatry* before that night? Of course he had. I looked over to the stack of pictures of Travis Eddington's corpse.

When I caught my breath and returned my attention to Gideon Epstein, he was describing how an excited catatonic, if not treated properly with drugs or shock therapy, could finally die of exhaustion. By the time our expert was finished with his lecture, we all knew the difference between pernicious catatonia and periodic catatonia. We knew that catatonia could be treated with barbiturates. We knew that it usually had its onset between the ages of fifteen and twenty-five. We knew about negativism and mutism and posturing. We even knew about a gavage tube, the tool sometimes necessary to feed a catatonic. And, finally, we learned that of all the horrors embraced by the term "schizophrenia," catatonia at least stood the best chance of cure.

The jury seemed to hang on every word. So did the judge. Rita looked straight ahead during the entire testimony. At times her eyes welled, and the tears slowly moved down her cheeks.

"Doctor," Morgan said, "I want to ask you one last question, but before I do, I want you to assume two facts—the second of these facts is already in evidence; the first will be in evidence shortly. First, I want you to assume that a twelve-year-old girl fired six bullets into her father and thereby killed him. Second, I want you to assume that within an hour of that event, while she was locked by herself in a jail cell, that girl went into a catatonic stupor in which her arms were wrapped around the bars of the cell so rigidly that the bars had to be cut in order that she could be removed. Now, asking you to assume those things, I ask, do you have an opinion to a reasonable medical certainty whether the killing of her father would likely have led to her catatonic stupor?"

"Objection! That question calls for an answer to the ultimate issue in this case—that is, who killed Travis Eddington? That fact is for the jury to decide."

"Well, Mr. Hauser," Henry Penrod said slowly, in his soft southern drawl, "I don't believe that the doctor is being asked to testify to the fact. I think he's just being asked to assume it. And, as I understand it, Mrs. Eddington will testify to that fact, when she resumes the stand. Is that right, Mr. Morgan?"

"That's right, Your Honor."

"In that case," argued Hauser, "the doctor's opinion is irrelevant. If Miranda Eddington killed her father, she killed him. Whether that caused catatonia is immaterial."

"But," the judge reasoned aloud, "if the doctor can tell us that the catatonia likely would have followed from that event, doesn't it make the fact of that event more likely than it is in the absence of the doctor's opinion?" As he had when deciding other hard issues of law, the judge ran his hands through his short, brushy hair, letting his gaze wander all over the courtroom.

Hauser struggled for an answer to the judge's question. Before he could articulate one, the judge seemed to surrender to an unseen force inside his mind. "I am going to allow it," he said. "You may answer that question, Doctor."

"Do you have an opinion, Doctor?" Morgan asked.

"I do."

"And what is your opinion, please?"

"In all likelihood the killing of her father, if indeed she killed him, would have led to her catatonic state."

"You may cross-examine," Morgan said to Hauser, and then he turned to the jury, searching for a reaction. Every eye in the jury box remained fixed upon the psychiatrist.

Technically, Epstein had not rendered an opinion that Miranda had killed her father, only that if she had killed him, the killing probably caused her present state. I knew, though, that Morgan had taken his witness as far as any judge in any jurisdiction would ever have let him go. I knew that because I had written the brief.

Max Hauser rose aggressively. "There is a cause of catatonic stupor other than a fear of violence, isn't there, Doctor?" he said.

"Yes, that is true," Epstein conceded.

"Depression can result in catatonic stupor, can it not?"

"Yes, there are a number of reliable studies concluding that depression can result in stupor."

"Now, Dr. Epstein," Hauser announced, "it is I who would ask you to make a certain assumption. I would ask you to assume that a twelve-year-old child watched her mother fire six bullets into her father and thereby kill him. Could that not be a cause of depression?"

"I would certainly expect it to be. Yes."

Hauser looked down at his notes.

"In fairness to your case, Mr. Hauser," Epstein continued softly, "I should note that there is also another cause of catatonia."

Hauser's head snapped up. "Oh?"

"Yes," the doctor explained. "A fair body of research suggests that an imbalance of nitrogen in the brain can cause stupor."

"And that is a possible cause of Miranda Eddington's condition, is it not?"

"Is the girl's name Miranda Eddington?" Gideon Epstein asked.

"Yes, it is," said Hauser.

"Then yes, nitrogen imbalance is a possible cause of Miranda Eddington's stupor."

Morgan wrote a note on a legal pad and pushed it toward me. *Do you remember that there comes a time in cross when you should sit down and shut up?* Recalling his Arizona Club lecture, I nodded.

Hauser returned to his notes, perhaps looking for a bigger weapon. While he flipped the pages of a yellow pad, Gideon Epstein continued to speak. "Nitrogen imbalance is a possibility, but in my opinion it is a very, very remote possibility, inasmuch as—"

"But it's a possibility, isn't it?" Hauser barked.

The witness became quiet, and Morgan spoke softly. "Your Honor, if it please the court, Dr. Epstein should be allowed to explain his answer if he feels it requires explanation."

"Do you think that answer requires explanation, Doctor?" the judge asked.

"In fairness, it probably does," replied the doctor. There was something almost ecclesiastical in his tone.

"You go ahead, then."

"I was just going to say that the probability of such a coincidence—that is, the following of such a violent act by a completely unrelated chemical imbalance, all simply as a matter of chance—seems to me so remote as to require rejection."

Hauser returned to his notes, trying to get back to where he'd been. Once again the witness's pleasant voice filled the void.

"I rejected the notion of depression-induced stupor for a slightly different reason."

Hauser looked up with the unmistakable expression of a student jolted out of a daydream to answer a question he hadn't heard.

Epstein continued unabated. "You posit the possibility of catatonia caused by acute depression, which is to say depression brought on by an immediate and very traumatic event, yet in my experience I have never seen that happen. Instead it has always been chronic long-term depression that has slowly brought a patient to catatonia. And the literature, I know, is quite consistent with that experience. Do you have evidence that Miranda Eddington suffered from chronic depression?"

The witness and the jury waited silently for an answer.

"I'll ask the questions, thank you, Doctor," said Hauser. Gideon Epstein raised his hands as if to say he was only trying to help. "With respect to violence, Doctor, isn't it likely that a girl who watched her mother kill her father would feel certain violent impulses toward her mother?"

"Yes," Epstein conceded. "That is likely." Hauser turned to the jury, confidence flourishing. "But," the doctor continued, "I concluded that it was not such an impulse that caused catatonia in this case."

Hauser moved one step toward the witness stand. Seconds passed. I became aware of people behind me in the gallery. Fidgeting, rustling paper, a muffled sneeze. The jury, though, remained riveted.

"Why?" Hauser finally asked.

Dan Morgan looked up to Henry Penrod, and Henry Penrod returned the gaze. The judge closed his eyes and slowly shook his head back and forth.

"I was told," said the doctor, "that the girl was locked in a jail cell. By that circumstance alone, she would have been restrained. Splinted, if you will. She would thus have been prevented from committing any act against her mother. So restrained, the only violence she could have found threatening would have been violence against herself. And if she had killed her own father, I would expect her to have powerful self-destructive impulses. The only sound reason I can see for the stupor is her fear of violence against herself."

Hauser spun toward the bench. "Your Honor, I move that answer be stricken as nonresponsive to the question."

"It was responsive. And, Mr. Hauser, it was you who asked the question."

Hauser turned back to the witness. "You're being paid for your testimony here, aren't you, Doctor?"

Gideon Epstein leaned forward, and for the first time that afternoon there was a hint of hostility in his voice. "No," said the doctor. "I am being compensated for my time. My expenses are also being taken care of."

Hauser sat down without meeting his co-counsel's eyes. "No further questions."

"We'll be in recess for fifteen minutes. Members of the jury, please remember the admonitions of the court."

In the hall Morgan was on fire and belching smoke. "I believe I just heard Hauser have you testify that Miranda must have done it," Morgan whispered to Gideon Epstein.

"I had a feeling the fellow was going to take it a bit too far. Say, Dan, do you think if I walked to your office, one of your girls could get me a taxi? I think I may be able to make that three-thirty flight to L.A."

We watched our witness descend the stairs. Morgan pulled me farther down the hall. His hands were shaking. "Didn't it come out that Miranda must have killed him?"

"That's what I heard," I said. "Not in so many words, but that's what he said. If Rita had done it, Miranda would have had no reason to go into her stupor."

Laughing, Morgan walked up the hall. He did an about-face and came back to me. "Old Henry would never have let me get that in, not in a million years. You talk about evidence that goes to the ultimate issue. You think that jury bought what Gideon was saying, or do they think he's some kind of a witch doctor?"

"I think they were interested," I said. "I think they were hanging on every word."

"I do, too. I think jurors are damned skeptical about shrinks. You know, the black arts and all that. But that god-damned stupor is real, and it's got to be explained, and I figure Gideon damn well explained it." Morgan looked at me more intently. "You really think they were listening?"

"Yes. I do."

"Goddamn it, I'd like this son of a bitch to end right now. I've got to get Rita back up there to tell them what happened, but I want it to be quick. I don't want to take two more hours." Morgan looked at his watch, then back at me. "You think they like her?"

"Yes."

"So do I. But I don't want her up there too long. Not after Gideon. I don't think we need her that bad. Christ, anything could happen. A few too many tears and she could turn them right off."

Morgan paced up and down the hall. He came back to where I was standing and butted out his cigarette on the floor. "I don't know about Ferris," he said.

"Oh," I said. "I forgot. He's sitting over there."

"Yeah. I know. He's ready to go on the stand if we want him to. I don't know, though. It's damned risky to call him. And I feel like we're there right now."

"I do, too."

"I can just feel it," he said. "But if I put her character in issue and fat Max has something on her, one little thing, it could destroy her." I watched him. He looked at the ceiling, then at the floor. Then he turned around. Finally he pulled his cigarettes from his sock. "So what do you think, Doug? Should I call him?"

"If Ferris Eddington gets up there and says anything in her behalf, it's the same as his saying that he's sure that she's not guilty. I mean, isn't it? I mean, a man doesn't testify for someone if he thinks that person may have killed his only son."

"You're learning," Morgan said. "But, I'm telling you that it's goddamned dangerous."

We both looked down the hall to where Ferris Eddington sat rigidly on the bench by the courtroom door. Morgan scrutinized him coldly, unconsciously picking a piece of tobacco off his tongue. Then, he was off again, pacing up and down the hall, filling it with smoke and muttering to himself, until the bailiff came and told us it was time to go back into the courtroom. When the jury-room door opened, Morgan went absolutely still. And when the jury filed in, he relaxed into his chair with the easy anticipation of a man about to enjoy a cocktail.

"Are we calling Mrs. Eddington back to the stand?" the judge asked.

Morgan bit into his lower lip. Then, and on the first occasion I ever heard a real tremor in his voice, my mentor tentatively announced, "If the defense may call one more witness out of order, I would call Mr. Ferris Eddington."

I heard whispers behind me in the gallery.

"Is he here?" asked the judge with surprise.

"Yes he is, Your Honor."

"Will you please ask Mr. Eddington to come in and be sworn," the judge said to his bailiff.

Ferris Eddington, ramrod straight, walked through the

door and across the room toward the witness stand. All the eyes in the courtroom followed him.

"Excellent. Above question."

That was how Ferris Eddington described Rita's character. He said the same thing and added "impeccable" when Morgan asked him about her reputation for truthfulness. That was after our character witness had answered Morgan's questions about himself, after he had described his terms in the state legislature, his work on the school board, his membership on the Board of Regents. It was after he'd talked about this committee and that committee, this hospital and that hospital, after talk of the National Cowboy Hall of Fame in Oklahoma City. It was after lunches with presidents and statesmen. And it was after the description of his great joy when his only son married the poor but lovely girl named Rita Toronto.

Morgan didn't take long, and it was plain that he was more interested in presenting Ferris Eddington's background to the jury than he was in dwelling on Rita's. It was enough that the gentleman who sat before the jury was willing to climb into that chair. All else, to use one of Morgan's phrases, was window dressing. So when Ferris Eddington said "excellent" and "above question" and "impeccable," Dan Morgan sat down. Then he fixed his gaze upon our tabletop, as he waited to hear whether his opponent had anything to destroy his client. From the corner of my eye, I saw Hauser begin to rise, and I turned and saw Morgan's fingertips flex and dig into the table. When he finally made it to his feet, Hauser just stared at Ferris Eddington. Our witness appeared absolutely calm and not the least unfriendly. Hauser, on the other hand, seemed to exude blind hatred. "No questions," Hauser finally said.

I could hear Morgan breathe. I looked at my watch. It was three forty-five, an hour and a half before the judge would recess for the weekend. I wondered whether Morgan would draw Rita's testimony out that long just so the jury could sleep on it for three nights, without the benefit of cross-examination. That question did not have to be answered.

"Gentlemen," the judge announced, "I see I have a small problem. I have just received a message that there are lawyers here who say they badly need to have me hear a motion for a temporary restraining order right now. This could go on for some time. I wonder whether we should recess for the weekend at this juncture."

"Your Honor," said Morgan, before Hauser could get to his feet, "if I could have just fifteen or twenty minutes, I could conclude with Mrs. Eddington. I would be happy to wait and do that later this afternoon." He had done what he could. At least he'd been able to telegraph to the judge that he wanted to finish up. I didn't know that he could do more, under what were looking like unfortunate circumstances. But Morgan didn't stop. "However, Your Honor, I don't know what would be the pleasure of the jury. I don't know if these gentlemen and Mrs. Mendoza would want to sit out another recess this afternoon."

"Well," said the judge, "why don't we just ask them? How about it, members of the jury? Do you think you can endure another late-afternoon recess?"

They all began to look at each other. Some shrugged. Guy Buckley, the crop duster, spoke. "Hell, I'd just as soon stay." Mr. Savoca expressed the same sentiment, and in a moment they all looked to be of the same mind.

"Mrs. Mendoza?" asked the judge.

"I'll stay, sir."

"Then it's settled. We will reconvene as soon as I can deal with this matter."

Once the jury was out of the room, Morgan was whispering to me gleefully, "Did you hear that? Did you see that? They're with her. They want to hear her. Goddamn it, Doug, I think we're going to win this case."

After that we sat on the hard bench in the hallway drinking coffee, Morgan smoking cigarettes. Reporters and media people and spectators filled the hallway. Occasionally a reporter would come up and say something to Morgan, a word of encouragement, an old reminiscence. A couple slapped him on the back, but most of the people respectfully kept their distance. Some wandered back into the courtroom to get an earful of equitable relief.

Sitting there with nothing to do, I began once again to notice how lovely the old courthouse was. The wood, the hand-painted beams, the Spanish tile, the brass around the elevators. There was the graceful curve of the staircase that led up to where we sat on the second floor. Then, all of a sudden, I saw Ann Hastings ascending the staircase, and then there was Tom Gallagher, and Chet Johnson, and Walter Smith. "Hell," Gallagher said. "If you guys aren't going to work, let's go have a drink."

"He's got a TRO going on in there," said Morgan, "but he's going to let us finish with Rita before he ends today."

"Can you get us a seat?" Walter Smith asked.

They asked how things were going, and Morgan told them about Gideon Epstein's testimony and about how the jury had voted to wait and hear Rita's testimony. He told them about how cleanly Ferris Eddington had gotten off the stand. "I've never had a case fall into place like this one," Morgan told them.

Then we all went into the courtroom to save seats so our little group could spend that hour on Friday, an hour they would ordinarily have spent with a convivial cocktail, listening to the last twenty minutes of Rita Eddington's story. There in the gallery we whispered, while near the bench much noise was being made about a D6 Caterpillar bulldozer, which stood running and ready to push down somebody's concrete wall.

———————

"I bought the gun on Friday," Rita testified. It was five-fifteen, and Morgan had another fifteen minutes to finish the job. "Travis had moved out of the house, and I was nervous about Miranda and me being there alone."

She told the jury how she'd decided to take Miranda on a vacation before they put her back in school. The travel agent had recommended Curaçao in the Netherlands Antilles. That was why she'd picked that spot. No, she had never

acquainted herself with the law of extradition of that jurisdiction. She would not have known how to.

"Why did you go to that house that morning?"

"I had to see Travis. I needed to tell him where we were
going and when we would be back."

"But you stopped on the way?"

"Yes."

"And you shot the gun?"

"It was early, and I was afraid Travis might still be
asleep. I hadn't shot the gun before. I felt I should learn to
use it; that's why I was carrying it in my purse. When I saw
some beer bottles along the side of the road, I decided to
try it."

"And Miranda fired the gun also?"

"Yes."

"Whose idea was it that she shoot the gun?"

"Well, she asked me if she could."

"How long were you there?"

"I'm not sure. Quite some time. We used up two boxes
of shells."

"And you have heard testimony here in court that
Miranda shot a bird that morning?"

"Yes. Yes, she did that."

Rita went on to testify that there came a time when she
thought Travis would be awake. If nothing else, the gun
should have awakened him. So she and Miranda rode on
to the house. And, just as Juan Menchaka had told it, they
walked to the front door and went in.

Travis was not asleep. Indeed, to Rita, it looked as if he
had not slept at all. "He was drunk," she testified.

"Where was the gun at this time?"

"It was in my purse."

Morgan asked Rita to step down to the large floor plan
of the house that Hauser had already put into evidence. He
had her stand before the jury and trace for them her move-
ments once she'd entered the house. Now there were no
tears. It was as if Gideon Epstein's testimony had taken the
tears out of her, and she told the jurors what happened that
morning in a matter-of-fact way.

"Travis was here on the sofa." Rita pointed to a photograph.

"Is that the sofa depicted in the photograph which is Plaintiff's Exhibit Four?"

"Yes."

"What was his demeanor?"

"He was all slurred and nasty, and he wouldn't talk to us."

"What did you do?"

"I tried to talk to him. I told him we were going on a trip. I told him he should move back to our house."

"Did he speak to you?"

"No. Just some profanity."

"What did you do then?"

"I went into the kitchen to see if there was a pot and some coffee. I thought maybe, if I made some coffee, I could get him to talk to us."

"What did you do with your purse when you went into the kitchen?"

"I left it in the living . . . the front room. On the floor."

"You would have walked out through this door?" Morgan was pointing at the floor plan.

"Yes."

"Did you find some coffee?"

"Yes. And a percolator. I made coffee. I mean, I put it on the stove."

"How long did it take you to do that?"

"I don't know. Just a few minutes."

"And during the time you were in the kitchen, where was Miranda?"

"She was in the front room with her father."

"The same room where you had left your purse with the gun."

"Yes."

"During that time did you hear either of them speak?"

"Travis said something. I couldn't make out what it was."

"And Miranda?"

"No, I don't think she spoke."

"Then what happened?"

"I walked back into the front room. Then I stopped."

"Did something cause you to stop?"

"Yes."

The jury, every member, leaned forward.

"What did you see?"

"Miranda had the gun. She had it pointed at her father."

"Where were you when you stopped?"

"Here," she said, pointing at the floor plan.

"By this desk?" Morgan asked, holding up a photograph that showed a desk with a telephone on it.

"Yes," she said.

"What was your reaction?"

"I was scared."

"Then what happened?"

"Miranda just stood there, pointing the gun. She looked like she was in another world. Travis was scared. He was very scared. He started talking to her. Things like 'That's okay, baby.' I didn't know what to do. Then I saw the telephone, the one on the desk. I remember that I picked it up. And I dialed 0. When the operator came on, I asked for the police. I don't know what I thought I could accomplish by doing that, but for some reason I did it."

"Then what happened?" Now a tear came. "Tell us what happened, Rita."

"She shot him. Miranda shot him. After the first or second shot, he tried to get up, but he could only stumble. He fell flat on his face. And Miranda kept shooting."

Morgan stood and watched as the tear found its way down her cheek. The courtroom was dead quiet, and I heard a silent drum pounding, and on the exactly proper beat, Morgan said, "What did you do then?"

"I put the telephone down. I must have hung it up. No one had answered."

"And then?"

"I took the gun. I walked outside."

"Did you drop the gun?"

"I don't know. I must have. It was in the dirt when Juan came."

"Juan?"

"Juan Menchaka."

"No further questions."

It had begun with Juan. So far as we were concerned, it had ended with Juan. Now all that remained was to wait out the weekend, listen through Hauser's cross-examination, and rest.

"If he doesn't learn something dirty about her between now and Monday morning," Morgan observed, "he sure as hell isn't going to hurt her."

———————

Our little company moved toward the First National Bank Building, and soon we were ensconced in the deep red chairs at the Arizona Club. Morgan had a beer. The rest of us each had some kind of cocktail. I remember that Ann Hastings sat next to Morgan and sipped a gimlet. "Not too good, is he?" Tom Gallagher asked of Morgan about Maximilian Hauser.

Morgan shook his head. "He decided he'd take Gideon Epstein head-on this afternoon, and he got a real lesson. It was pathetic. I felt bad for him, and I don't even like him."

Morgan savored his beer as though it were good wine. He made jokes with Ann and told them all about the trial, how everything had fallen into place. He laughed with his beer can in the air, and he told Walter Smith about things that had happened during the voir dire of the jury. Then he got up and headed to the bar to order us all another round, and for the first time in five days he didn't have a ring of sweat under his arms.

"Douglas," Walter Smith said. I bent over the table so I could hear him through the noise.

"Did you ever check with the phone company about the telephone call your woman said she made while the girl was holding the gun on Travis?"

"No," I reported. "I didn't know she tried to call until I heard her tell about it this afternoon."

"Did Morgan check?"

"I don't know. I don't think he did." I thought for a moment. "Why? The phone company wouldn't have a record of a call like that, would they?"

"I don't know," Walter said between puffs on his pipe. "It's something I might want to find out, though."

Morgan returned with a waiter and more drinks, and I made a mental note to mention the phone company to him, but it didn't seem the right moment then, while he was raising another can of beer to his lips. He laughed and told a couple of very dirty jokes. In time other lawyers from the firm joined us, and lawyers from other firms came by the table to wish us luck. And the scotch I had in my hand seemed quite wonderful.

Then Chet Johnson said, "Oh! I forgot something." He reached into his pocket and pulled out a telephone message slip, which he handed to me. "That woman said to make sure you call her, Doug. She says she wants to invite you to a party."

Someone at the table said, "Hey, hey, hey," and I looked down at the pink slip of paper to see the name of an old friend, one whose friendship I had neglected, I suppose, as much as I had neglected Juan Menchaka's.

I wandered through the back hall of the Arizona Club to the reading room, where I slid into one of the overstuffed chairs and dialed the telephone. When she answered, I could hear noise in the background; it sounded like a busy restaurant.

"Sidney, it's me," I said, "Doug."

"I wasn't even sure you were back!" came her familiar yell. "Now I'm seeing your name in the paper every day!" Before I could say anything, she went on. "And Rita! My God! It's all unbelievable! And you haven't seen my new house. Listen, Doug, Vernon and I are having a house-warming party tonight." I began to hear music in the background, and it came to me then that Sidney Ellsworth (Sidney Ellsworth Christensen since she'd married the son of a successful contractor), the daughter of my mother's best friend, the closest thing to a big sister I ever had, was a little bit drunk. "There are a lot of people here that you know. They're all asking about you. You have to come, Doug! Bring someone, if you want to."

I thought about Ann Hastings for a moment, but I said, "I don't have anybody to bring."

"Then just come!"

I looked at the drink in my hand, and it occurred to me then that Sidney Ellsworth Christensen wasn't the only one who was a little drunk that Friday evening, and I knew I had no business driving all the way to Mesa. I told myself I should get some dinner and go home to bed. Instead I asked Sidney, "Can I wear a blue suit?"

"That's perfect."

The new French Provincial house on the ninth fairway of the Mesa Country Club turned out to be massive, with a large library, and a nursery, and a garden court. Waiters in dinner jackets carried trays of champagne and hors d'oeuvres. Bartenders mixed drinks at either end of the house. A five-piece band played music from Sidney's and my high-school days. Never before had I seen such a party in Mesa, Arizona. I knew most of the guests, had gone to high school with many of them. They all wore cocktail dresses, or suits, or blazers with plaid trousers. There was much blown-dry hair. For all I saw there, Westchester County might have come to my hometown.

They took me in as the fair-haired boy come home—the new celebrity. I was Phoenix Defense Attorney Douglas McKenzie. Old friends told me how proud they were of me, how they'd always known I would make something of myself. I wandered around the big new house, quite amazed at what having my name in the paper had done for my local standing. And, of course, there was talk of my mentor.

"You have to tell me all about Daniel Morgan," Mildred Warren said. "I was once on a jury where he defended a man. He was the sexiest man I ever saw. I just loved him."

"Morgan or the defendant?"

"Oh." Mildred Warren poked me. "Morgan."

"What about the defendant?" I asked.

"He was guilty as sin, and we said so."

I drank whiskey and walked and talked among the people I'd known all my life. Most wanted to hear about how my mother was doing. Some told me how much they missed my father. When Jimmy Ikeda, one of my father's cronies from the country-club card room, began to get teary in remembrance of how fierce Bill McKenzie had been with good cards in a bridge game, I slipped out through French doors and stood by Sidney's wrought-iron fence, looking out across the golf course where I'd spent so many hours of my childhood. There was a moon, and I could see how the palms and the eucalyptus trees had grown since I'd last played there. I was standing by the fence, feeling the whiskey seep into my extremities, when I heard steps behind me and then heard the voice of the woman who had invited me. "I'll bet looking out there brings back memories for you," Sidney said.

"Yep."

"You look great," she told me.

"You do, too," I said. "But you look different for some reason."

"I'm getting old, Doug."

"Not you."

"Tell me something," she said. "Do you really believe that poor little girl killed Travis?" There it was again, the question that seemed continually to be asked. And when Sidney asked it, the question had almost as much skepticism as it had when Frank Menendez had asked it, but it wasn't rhetorical. I could tell she wanted an honest answer. I took a while to give one.

"Yes," I told her. "I guess I believe Miranda killed him."

"She was such a fragile child," Sidney mused.

"Little girls can do nasty things," I said.

"I heard what Rita said Travis did," Sidney told me.

"Yeah," I said.

"It's hard for me to believe. He never was like that."

"What was he like?"

"I can't remember. But he wasn't like that. He was a good guy . . . painfully shy, but a good guy."

"The evidence is pretty strong that Miranda did it. We think we're probably going to win."

"It's cold out here."

Sidney and I walked back through the French doors into the glittering light of the main room. We found ourselves in a circle of people who were talking about Rita Eddington.

"I swear, she was the prettiest girl I had ever seen," a woman named Rachael Roberts said. "But so lonely."

Music played in a farther room, and people danced. Through a big window of many panes, I could see other guests gathered around the swimming pool, where the light filtered up through the water.

"She was always nice."

"I liked her so very much."

"I'm goddamned if I ever knew what she saw in Travis Eddington."

"Are you kidding? Travis could buy and sell anybody in this town. Ten times over. No disrespect, Vernon."

"I think she's innocent."

"She lied in court today."

My gaze jumped across the circle to the last speaker, a woman I'd never seen before, somebody's matronly wife. She was plain and plump, and her hair was turning gray. She had a hard look, all rectitude. A great quiet had come over the circle, and it lasted until, for the first time, I joined the conversation. "What did you say?"

The woman looked directly at me and gave me a tight, humorless smile. "Rita Eddington lied in court today." She took a sip of champagne, watching me over the top of her glass. I felt something like a vacuum in my chest.

"What do you mean?" I demanded. The discussion of Rita Eddington had sharpened into a dialogue between the woman and me, with the other people in the room involuntarily cast as spectators. "What do you mean?" I asked again, this time with a frantic edge.

"She said she called the police that morning, but she didn't."

"How do you know that?" I asked, my heart beginning to pound as I remembered the question Walter Smith had asked me earlier that evening when Morgan had gone to the bar.

"I work at Mountain Bell. There was no call ever made." The woman seemed to soften, and she took a step in my direction. No doubt she sensed what was shooting through me.

"But how do you know that no call was made?" I asked.

"Because if she had called, it would have been logged. And it wasn't."

"How do you know it wasn't?"

"Because we looked it up this evening."

"Why?"

"That lawyer, the one for the state—"

"Hauser?"

"Yes. Hauser. He and a bunch of them came over." Now her tone changed completely. The telephone company had a policy, she explained gently, that whenever a party asked for the police, the operator was to stay on the line, listening to make sure a connection was completed. All such calls had to be logged. No call was logged the day Travis Eddington was killed.

"Isn't it possible," I asked, "that the operator who took Rita's call just neglected to log it?"

"They got hold of every operator who was on duty that shift. No one remembers a call. Mr. Hauser had them all subpoenaed for court Monday morning."

Johnnie Walker Black Label rocked out of my glass and broke like a wave on Sidney's white carpet. I tried to think of a less than completely graceless way to make my exit. I couldn't think. I turned and walked toward the front door. The next thing I knew, I was driving eighty miles an hour on McDowell Road, headed toward Phoenix.

Morgan had been so careful, so meticulous, in showing Rita everything the prosecution had, every single piece of evidence, so she would collide with nothing as she told her perfect story. He had slipped, however, when he failed to think of the telephone company. It hadn't taken Walter Smith long to catch him in his slip, and it hadn't taken Max Hauser any time to catch Rita in her lie. What I was unable to sort out was the extent to which it would hurt Rita's case. All I knew then was that it was bad, and I pushed harder on the accelerator.

I held my finger on Morgan's doorbell for a full two minutes. Nothing. I ran down to my apartment and called the Arizona Club.

"He was here."

"I know that!" I yelled. "Is he there now?"

"Nope. He left about an hour ago."

I knew I was not going to be able to sleep, and I decided to go to the office. I could do some research. I could try to find law to block Hauser's evidence that no telephone call had been made. I remembered a case I'd once read about beans in Boston. A defendant wanted to offer evidence that no one had complained about his beans before a plaintiff got food poisoning. According to the Massachusetts court, it was hearsay. Somehow that night—it was probably the whiskey, or maybe the adrenaline—that sounded like it might have been close. Or if it wasn't, maybe I could find something else to support an objection to all Hauser's telephone operators. That was how I was thinking when I walked into the office.

I didn't make it to the library. Down the hall I saw a light coming from Morgan's office. When I got to his door, I saw Morgan sitting back in his chair staring at the wall, motionless. He had a can of beer in his hand. A half-burned cigarette smoldered in his ashtray. I watched him for a moment as, trancelike, he stared straight ahead. "Dan."

He snapped around. "What the hell are you doing here?"

I told him.

"Let's go!"

Thirty minutes later my car was parked in front of the Mesa telephone office, and I was following Morgan through the front door. A security guard found the shift supervisor, a woman named Jeanne. "But I thought you were here earlier," Jeanne said.

"Those were lawyers for the other side of the case," Morgan told her.

"What side are you on?"

"We represent the defendant."

"You're Mrs. Eddington's lawyers?"

"Yes."

"And that man named Hauser, was he the prosecutor?"

"Yes."

"I didn't like him."

Jeanne let Morgan look at everything in that building he wanted to see. It did no good. We were in trouble, Morgan's charm and Jeanne's willingness notwithstanding.

"It's pretty clear, Mr. Morgan, she never made that call."

Morgan squinted at her through the smoke rising from his cigarette. "Is this the log for October of this year?"

"Yes. See, this is an entry I made on the fifth of the month."

Morgan turned the pages forward, then turned them back. There'd been entries on a number of days, but not on October 21, the day of Travis's death.

Exasperated, Morgan studied the woman. "Jeanne, she made that call. There has to be something to explain it. What could have happened?"

"I don't know. They told me they called everyone who could have been on that shift. You want to see the notes on those calls?"

After Morgan went through notes of the small survey Max Hauser had persuaded the company to perform, we all sat in a break room drinking from a pot of coffee Jeanne had made. Morgan rubbed his eyes. "You know how bad this is going to hurt us?" he asked me.

"I'm not sure," I said.

"Bad," Morgan said. "Really bad." He sipped his coffee. "Goddamn it, Jeanne, she made that call." He sighed.

Though I could never have expressed it to Morgan, I had come to a different conclusion. Rita had not made the call. That was what the incontrovertible records we'd been poring over established in no uncertain terms. And as we sat in the cramped little break room at the phone company, drinking coffee with the woman named Jeanne, I realized that not only had I come to a different conclusion, I had

come to my senses. Rita hadn't just lied about the telephone
call, she'd lied about the whole thing. Morgan had done his
best to create a fairy tale that would hold together, but the
small lie about the telephone call was nothing less than the
loose thread that, when pulled on Monday morning, would
bring it all apart. Miranda Eddington had not killed her father, and no matter how many cheap psychiatrists Morgan
procured at great expense, it could not be made otherwise.
Juan Menchaka knew that. Sidney Ellsworth knew it. Frank
Menendez knew it. I'm sure Walter Smith and even Tom
Gallagher knew it. And now I knew it. I'd known it since
the time of the preliminary hearing, really, when Morgan
had made me get on the floor of the courtroom and play
dead and I saw the expression on Rita Eddington's face as
she stood over me.

"I'm sorry," said Jeanne.

We drank her coffee, then got up to leave. Jeanne moved
to walk us to the door. Suddenly she inhaled sharply.

"What?" Morgan said.

"Oh. It was nothing."

"No," said Morgan. "You were going to say something.
What was it?"

"Well, I was just thinking. There was a girl who worked
here part-time until sometime this fall. A student, I think.
Occasionally she filled in for people. But she wasn't here
that morning. If she had been, there would have been a record of it, and she would have logged a call like that. See, I
was just thinking, but it's nothing."

"What was her name?"

Jeanne rubbed the back of her neck as if trying to mas-
sage the girl's name from her memory. "I can't remember."

"Come on, Jeanne," Morgan pleaded. "Remember."

*Oh, come on, Morgan. We've got Hauser and an army
of telephone operators to face Monday morning. Better to
spend our time on legalities that might get the evidence ex-
cluded than on some fatuous hope for a phantom witness.*

Jeanne went to a telephone and dialed. She told someone
named Amy that she was sorry to wake her in the middle
of the night. "You remember that part-time earlier this year,

the tall girl with freckles?" Jeanne paused. "Yes, that's it, the one who wanted to be an architect." Another pause. "That's right. Joanna. Her name was Joanna Barnes."

"Where can we find her?" Morgan asked before Jeanne had put down the receiver.

"I'll see," said Jeanne, and she hauled out another book. "All we show is a forwarding address in San Francisco." She wrote the address on a slip of paper and handed it to Morgan.

"Is there a telephone number?"

"No. But I can check that for you." Jeanne made another telephone call, this time asking for the number of Joanna Barnes. "San Francisco shows two J. Barneses. No Joanna. Both J's are unlisted."

"Can you find out what those numbers are for us, Jeanne?"

"Not without a court order."

As we were walking out, Morgan asked Jeanne if she would mind not telling anyone we'd been there. "I won't say a word," she promised in a conspiratorial whisper. "I want you to get her off. I heard what he was doing to his daughter."

Morgan turned the slip of paper with the address of a girl named Joanna Barnes in his hands as we drove through the dead of night toward Phoenix. "Not much to go on, is it?"

"Nothing, if you ask me," I told him.

We were past the Tovrea Castle before either of us spoke again, and I finally spoke only because the silence was weighing heavy on me. "What do you think?" I asked. Morgan didn't answer. He just stared up the middle of the street in what looked to be a stupor of resigned desperation. "You're not going catatonic on me, are you?" I said, trying to smile.

"I think I want you to go to San Francisco."

"What?"

"Turn left."

"What?"

"You heard me. Turn, goddamn it!" At the airport Morgan said, "Here." He handed me an American Express card and five hundred dollars in cash. "You can buy clean clothes and a toothbrush when you get there."

"You carry this kind of money?" I asked as I watched him put at least as much as he'd given me back in his pocket.

"I won it in a poker game at the Arizona Club. I thought my luck was going good till you showed up tonight. I'll take care of your car."

By the time the first plane took off for San Francisco, dawn was beginning to break. I sat cramped in a seat with too little legroom, my blue suit looking like it had been slept in, and I had the worst hangover I could remember. In my pocket I carried the last given address for some part-time telephone operator, together with the name of a private investigator Morgan thought had moved to San Francisco and the name of a lawyer he knew there.

To find her was one thing, and I might just pull that off. But to find her possessed of a memory of a single early-morning telephone call—a call made on a day she wasn't working, one that hadn't been logged as it would have been if it really had been made—that was what I was flying nearly a thousand miles for. It was a wild-goose chase, and it was one I wasn't in any condition to make.

Once again I began to think about what Rita had testified to. I wondered why Morgan hadn't thought of the phone company (he had to have known that Rita's testimony about the call was coming), and in time the answer presented itself to me with near-crystal clarity. He was afraid of the truth. Wasn't that it? Somewhere down deep he knew that Rita had been lying all along, just as he'd wished she would. She had conscripted him (or had he conscripted her?) as an ally in the filthy task of putting the blame for murder on a little girl who lay in great terror, innocent and helpless and unable to protect herself. Maybe Morgan was simply too decent to take up that kind of vile endeavor with full apprehension of the truth. And that was why he didn't check up on her story of the telephone call before he let her testify about it. Maybe it was something in the nature of a Freudian slip.

A stewardess offered me breakfast, but I took only the coffee. "Bad night?" she asked. I stared at her silently, and she moved on.

I got a car at the San Francisco airport, a Chevy convertible, and the girl who rented it to me recognized the Duncan Street address that the woman named Jeanne had written down. "It's up in Diamond Heights," she told me. "I think Castro Street runs into it." I knew the city from living there the year before, and I drove up Market Street past all the dirty-movie theaters and all the bums, then turned left on Castro Street and passed all the young men holding hands, and as the girl at the airport had said I would, I ran into Duncan Street. I found the number where Joanna Barnes had said she could be located. It was a small, modern house that had a view of the city skyline far in the distance. At ten o'clock on that Saturday morning, I knocked on the door and waited. There was not a sound, nor was there a rustle when I knocked and waited three or four more times. Two kindly-looking elderly women came walking by on the sidewalk. "Do you know who lives in this house?" I asked.

"Two men," one of the women said.

"Do you ever see a girl about twenty-eight years old here?"

Each of the women gave the other a knowing smile. "No." There was a small laugh. "We never see a girl in that house." So there I stood at the top of a hill on a quaint street on a perfect San Francisco morning that was cool but full of sun. My headache had diminished, but I was left with a great empty, washed-out feeling. Convinced that nobody was home at the Duncan Street address, I drove my rented car to West Portal, where I bought shaving cream, a razor, toothpaste, and a toothbrush. Then I drove up through St. Francis Wood, out past the zoo and around Lake Merced. Eventually I wound up cruising down the long driveway of the Olympic Country Club. Out there it was no longer sunny. A misty fog crawled across the fairways and through the cypress trees.

It was not until I had parked and wandered into the pro shop and there gotten a peep at myself in a mirror that I knew what shape I really was in. I looked worse than I thought, standing there by a rack of cashmere and alpaca, worse than Dan Morgan had looked that first time I met him at San Marcos. And I knew it was probably easier to get away with that look in Chandler, Arizona, than it was upon the spot where I then stood. It was with some trepidation that I approached the assistant pro behind the counter. "If I bought some clothes from you," I asked, "could I put them on in the locker room?"

"You can change right here," he said cordially. "We have a dressing room."

"I need a shower." I hoped that no matter how wrinkled it was, the Brooks Brothers suit would tell him that I was not out of a gutter in the Tenderloin.

The assistant pro looked me up and down. "Go ahead," he finally said. "I think it will be all right."

I found pants and a shirt and a sweater. I even had new socks and a pair of loafers when I presented Morgan's American Express Card. I showered and shaved, and then, wearing my new sweater that had embroidered on the chest the letter *O* with two wings sprouting from it, I walked around the golf course. Tired as I was, the walk seemed to take away a little of the pain.

To this day I believe the Lake Course at Olympic to be the most beautiful place I've ever seen. It turns, and it rolls, and it slips away in the fog. And at times that Saturday morning, while I was trying to walk off my hangover, the fog broke and rays of sun slanted down through the big old trees that seemed to arch almost all the way across the fairways and made it seem for a moment that the course was indoors. The slanting sunlight created the feeling of being in a cathedral. I glanced past the eighth green and around the clubhouse. I looked up to the terrace that overlooks the eighteenth green. I thought back to the day two partners from Brobeck, Phlegher and Harrison had taken me to lunch and had a table specially set on that very spot. The day they'd offered me a job. "All our lawyers are expected to maintain at least one club membership," the older one, the one with the wire-rimmed glasses and the bow tie, had said. "Many of our younger men seem to favor this place."

I began to think once again about what had brought me to San Francisco this time. I thought about the little lie Rita Eddington had told, the one that had occasioned my wild-goose chase, and I thought about the big lie she'd told. I considered the role of Dan Morgan in laying the ground-work for the big lie. Had he, in his zeal, suborned her per-jury? I dwelled upon my own small supporting part in our treacherous adventure. Juan Menchaka's shading of his tes-timony came back to me as I stood there alone watching the fog advance back through the lovely trees and across the green, green grass. And then I saw, in my mind's eye, the figure of Miranda Eddington lying frozen and helpless in her hospital room.

It was there, with the fog thickening upon that hallowed field of battle, that the ageless and overwhelming question finally presented itself to Douglas McKenzie: How can a lawyer defend a person when he knows in his heart that the person is guilty? The answer, if really an answer came, had nothing to do with the empty abstractions I'd tried to sell my grandmother Belle. If there was an answer, it was that Douglas McKenzie could not do it, that no matter how high-minded the rhetoric, no matter how noble the packag-ing, it was a dirty business, beneath the calling of any de-cent man.

I gazed upon the golf course, and with an ache some-where deep in my soul I asked myself why I hadn't stayed in the city where I stood and taken up my proper position among decent people who lived their lives in gracious ways.

My reverie broke as I remembered the silly and useless mission Morgan had sent me on. When I drove back, there was still no answer at the Duncan Street house, so I drove into the city and checked into a hotel, the Clift. I called the number of the private investigator that Morgan had given me. A message said the phone had been disconnected. I called the office of Morgan's lawyer acquaintance. Apparently it was not open on Saturday afternoon, and when I called information to try to find a home number, I was told it was unlisted. The Clift graciously found me a city directory, but it showed neither the address of Joanna Barnes nor that of the lawyer nor the investigator. I called Butler and Menendez. Morgan wasn't in, and I left a message about where things stood. Then I decided I would try to get an hour's sleep.

When I awoke, it was dark outside. My watch said eight o'clock. It said it was still Saturday, and I concluded that I'd slept six hours. And, once again wearing clothes that looked like I'd slept in them, I sped toward the house on Duncan Street. It had become cold, and a thick fog lay across Diamond Heights.

This time the lights were on. I would learn something anyway—probably that whoever had taken Joanna Barnes's forwarding address had written it down wrong, but at least that would be something. I rang the doorbell. I heard steps and an unnaturally high-pitched voice. "Come in. Come in. Come in." The door swung wide open, and a tall, handsome black man stood before me wearing nothing but a towel. "Sorry," he said. "I thought you were someone else." We stood and looked at each other, and I concluded that he spent a lot of time at the gym. "I suppose I should ask," he said theatrically. "May I help you?"

"I'm searching for a girl named Joanna Barnes."

The man looked me up and down suspiciously, making me feel awkward, and I found myself babbling on about why I needed to speak to her. I managed to get out a capsule version of the phone-call story.

"Oh, this is too much!" he exclaimed. "Jerry! Oh, Jerry, Paul Drake is here at the behest of Perry Mason."

The black man walked back inside the house, and a white man, equally good-looking, came to the door. He had clothes on, a starched red-and-white-checked shirt and starched khaki pants. No shoes. I told him the same story, slightly polished up by my recent recital.

"Come in," he said.

"Well, do you know her?" I asked as I followed him into a room boasting shiny hardwood floors and Persian rugs and antiques.

Jerry studied me coolly. "She's my sister."

The black man sashayed back through the room. This time he had pants on. "Isn't that the most camp story you have ever heard?"

"Shut up," Jerry snapped. "This is important."

"I need to talk to her," I said.

"I know. Would you like a drink, while I call her?"

"No. That's all right."

Jerry picked up a telephone and dialed it. "Joanna?" He handed me the phone, and for the third time in rapid succession I explained why I was in San Francisco.

"Yes. Yes, I remember that call."

"You're kidding!" I almost dropped the telephone.

"No, I remember it. It was about seven o'clock—"

"Six forty-five," I said.

"Yes. On October twenty-first. A woman said, 'Get me the police,' or 'I need the police,' or something like that. Then, when I was trying to make the connection, she said a name, a Spanish-sounding name."

"Miranda?" I said.

"Yes. That's it. Miranda. She said the name, and then she shouted, 'Don't!' Then I heard a lot of noise, and the line went dead."

"May I come and talk to you? Please!"

"I don't want you coming to my apartment," she said.

"Yes. I understand. Perhaps there's somewhere public I can meet you. It's very, very important."

"There's a bar called Henry Africa's," she said. "It's on Van Ness Avenue."

"I know where it is. I'll meet you there in twenty minutes."

I looked at Joanna Barnes's brother. "So she heard it," he deduced.

The black man sauntered back wearing a black cashmere sweater, black slacks, and black loafers. "*Ça va?*" he asked as he poured himself a drink.

"Yes," I said. "She heard it. I can't believe it."

As I was leaving, the black man spoke to me once again. "Counselor," he said, "may I tell you just one thing?"

"Sure," I said.

"That sweater. It doesn't get it. It really doesn't get it."

———————————

I sat waiting at Henry Africa's among the Boston ferns at an antique table under a Tiffany lamp. With my forefinger, I turned the ice in a glass of bourbon, and I listened to the piano player on the balcony as he moved through a lanquid rendition of the theme from *Dr. Zhivago*. The music matched my mood. I thought of the feelings I had let myself have about Morgan, especially those I'd indulged out on the golf course. I tried, not quite successfully, to chalk it up to an all-time monster hangover. A strongly built girl walked in.

"Good evening, Joanna," the piano player shouted with a voice that had more gravel in it than Jake Asher's.

"How goes it, Harry?" the girl asked.

She wore clothes that surely would have found approval at her brother's house. Soft leather boots under a heavy, straight skirt and a blouse with long, loose sleeves. In her auburn hair, she had tied a blue scarf that was the most beautiful piece of silk I'd ever seen. She had a ruddy complexion, freckles, and the look of the outdoors.

There was a waiter near, and Joanna Barnes ordered a Campari and soda, and then she walked to my table and said, "Mr. McKenzie?"

"Yes." I stood and put out my hand.

We both sat down.

"You met Jerry," she said.

"Yes."

"And Clarence?"

"Yes."

"I don't quite understand what this is all about," she said. "You said you were involved in a court case?"

"Yes," I told her. "A murder trial."

"Oh," she said, seemingly impressed. "What does it have to do with the call you mentioned?"

"A woman named Rita Eddington is on trial for the murder of her husband. Yesterday she testified that she called the police just before her husband was killed by another person."

"I still don't understand, but I can tell you there was a call like the one you described the morning of October twenty-first, if that's important."

"It *is* important. Tell me this: How can you remember the exact date?"

"It was my last day in Arizona. I left for here that afternoon. It was a Sunday."

"Ah!" I said. "That explains it."

"Explains what?"

"Why you didn't come to the police and report the call. There was a lot of local publicity about the case, but you wouldn't have heard about it or read about it in the papers here."

"I suppose I should have reported the call to someone, but I was kind of preoccupied, what with my move. And it all happened so fast."

"Why didn't you record the call in the log?" I asked her.

"What log?"

I began to explain the matter in earnest and in detail.

"I didn't know about any log," she said.

I explained the company's policy on holding until connection was made on calls to the police and then logging the call.

"I knew you were supposed to hold until a connection was made, but I didn't know anything about a log."

"The records at the office don't show you on duty that morning."

"I know. We didn't want them to."

"Why is that?" I asked.

She took a sip of her drink. "It's something I'd rather you keep to yourself. Is that possible?"

"I don't know."

She took another drink. "I'll just ask you not to say anything unless you absolutely have to."

"Okay," I said.

"I was filling in for a woman who was spending the night with someone she wasn't supposed to be with. You know what I mean?"

"I guess so," I said.

"I'd rather not give you her name. A hint of it and she'd be in real trouble."

"I know this is a little late to be asking," I said, "but is there any chance you could let me fly you to Phoenix tomorrow? You might save an innocent woman from being convicted of murder."

"Well, that certainly sounds romantic, doesn't it?"

"It's true," I said. "It really is true. And they still execute people down there."

"How do I know that you're on the level?" she asked. "That you're not some weirdo?"

"I can have you call people," I said. "I'm willing to run all over the city until we find a copy of the *Arizona Republic*. We could call any of the television stations. The case is on all the news." I was even reduced to reaching for my state bar card, the one that got me into the Maricopa County Jail.

"I'd have to clear it," she said, apparently accepting my only credential. I looked at her. "At work," she said.

"Oh. Of course."

"What if they say no?" she asked.

"Well," I said, "we'd probably have to move to delay the trial while we somehow got a subpoena issued through a California court."

"I'm sure they'll say it's okay."

"Will you come with me?"

"Yes. I'll go."

I swallowed and took a great deep breath. "Can I buy you another drink?"

"No. I'm at my limit."

"I need to check on plane reservations."

"Yes," she said.

"Will you wait here while I call?"

"Yes."

"Don't move."

"I won't."

I returned as quickly as I could, and to my enormous relief she was still there, stirring her ice with a swizzle stick. "The earliest I could get a flight was four o'clock tomorrow afternoon. I made you a reservation coming back at six-thirty Monday evening. Is that okay?"

"Yes."

I sat down. I yelled over to the bar, "I'll have another one, please. No. Wait a minute, you don't want another drink, right?"

"Why don't you just order me a club soda."

"And a club soda," I added. My hangover ended then and there. I looked at my watch. It was nine-thirty. I took a drink of the fresh bourbon and leaned back and spread out my arms. "I haven't eaten in two days," I said.

"There's a little place up on Polk Street where you can get a sandwich."

"I don't suppose you'd like a sandwich?"

"I'd have a cup of coffee with you," Joanna Barnes offered.

I polished off my drink and paid the check. I may have staggered just a little as we walked toward the door, but by the time we were walking up Polk Street, I was in control, blissfully braced by the whiskey against the San Francisco night air. At the café Joanna had a cup of coffee and a croissant. I had a four-egg omelette and a beer. She told me about growing up in upstate New York and how she'd studied architecture in New York City and in Europe, then gone to Scottsdale to live at the Frank Lloyd Wright Institute at Taliesen West. They didn't pay her enough to support her penchant for expensive clothing, though, and she'd sneaked over to Mesa to moonlight at the telephone company. "Finally I accepted a position with Skidmore, Owings and Merrill here in San Francisco," she told me.

I told Joanna about Dan Morgan. I even described how I'd walked off the golf course to help him in this case.

"Tell me about the woman you want me to testify for— Rita something?"

I recited the whole story—the killing, the trial, my relationship with the Eddingtons, even Sidney Ellsworth's party. I told her about my wild-goose chase to San Francisco. "I was convinced she'd lied and that Morgan had put her up to it. I've been feeling pretty bad about it. She's a fine person, and she has always been very kind to me."

"Well, if my hearing that telephone call means she didn't lie, she didn't lie," Joanna assured me.

I thought of how high my stock would rise at Butler and Menendez when I returned with this prize. I ordered another beer and wondered just how impressed Ann Hastings would be when I delivered this airtight proof that Dan Morgan had not sent a boy to San Francisco. "That is the loveliest scarf I've ever seen," I said across my omelette.

"Thank you."

"I know a woman who would look good in it." I was on my third beer then and coming truly to recognize the value of the hair of the dog.

"A mother? A sister? Someone else?" She smiled.

"A someone else."

"Uh-huh," she murmured. "What's she like?"

"She's beautiful. She's very intelligent. She's a very good lawyer."

"If you want me to, before we leave tomorrow, I'll take you to where I got the scarf."

I guess it was the beer, or more probably the bourbon I'd drunk before the beer, or maybe it was just a natural high from having found our savior in the form of this big, strapping girl. "Would you?" I asked Joanna Barnes.

I woke up in the elegant room at the Clift Hotel with another hangover. It was less virulent than the one the day before, and a cup of coffee was all I needed to get on top of it. I called Morgan's apartment, and this time he answered.

"Dan?"

"How you making out up there?"

"I've got her, and she remembers the call, and we'll be there at six o'clock."

"Jesus." I could hear him breathe. "I'll be at the airport for you."

Somehow I still could not believe I would have Joanna Barnes in Phoenix that evening. It was all too good to be true. In truth she hadn't been much more difficult to find than had Mrs. Scott at Switzer's. I picked up the telephone again. "I'm sorry to call you so early. I was just a little nervous about—"

"I cleared it with my boss," Joanna said. "I'm packing a bag. You can pick me up at two o'clock."

"Are you going to tell me where you live now?"

"I'm at 1134 Vallejo Street. It's near the top of Russian Hill."

I checked out of the Clift. I drove to North Beach and had some bacon and eggs at a little café off Washington Square, where I checked the *Chronicle* to see who led the final money standings on the PGA tour. I read all the gossip in Herb Caen's column, though it meant nothing to me. Then I read Charles McCabe's column, which I remember sang the praises of soap and a brush over canned shaving cream and touted some brand of English mustard. When I was finished, I still had two hours before I could pick up Joanna Barnes, so I drove to Sausalito and walked along the bay. I window-shopped and finally drank a beer on the terrace of a hotel that looked back across the bay to San Francisco. I sat happily gazing at the beautiful white city sitting above the blue water and beneath the clear blue sky. The only blemish on the morning was the little worry that Joanna Barnes might not be there when I went for her.

She wore a suit. She threw her small bag into the backseat of the convertible I'd rented, and asked, "Can we take down the top?" I headed down Broadway toward the freeway entrance. "Don't forget the scarf," she said.

"What?"

"I was going to take you to get the scarf."

"Oh," I said. "I did forget."

"You had a nice impulse last night. You shouldn't let those just go by. Do you want me to take you there?"

"Is there time?"

"We have lots of time. It's on Maiden Lane."

In ten minutes we were in a place full of slinky-looking women's clothes. The shop was round and had a graceful ramp that spiraled up to a second floor. "Mr. Wright designed this building," Joanna told me as we went in.

"What?"

"Frank Lloyd Wright."

Joanna looked for the scarf without success. Pretty soon a woman with a low voice and a heavy accent came to us. "Joanna, my dear." The two women exchanged pleasantries, and Joanna asked her about the scarf. "I think we have another," the woman said. "We had only two, if I am thinking of the right scarves. Helga brought two back from Singapore. They had come from China."

The woman led us toward the back, under the curved ramp, where she found the scarf locked in a small display case.

"Did you say there are only two?" I asked.

"Yes." She explained that they had been made in China of some kind of fancy silk. Two had been taken to Singapore, where the woman who owned the shop we were in had found them.

"Oh, buy it," Joanna urged. "That way I won't have to worry about seeing it on somebody in San Francisco."

"I'll take it," I said. Then I looked at the price. I thought I'd been able to mask my reaction, but both women spoke.

"Believe me," the saleswoman said, "it is worth every penny."

"The pain will be gone long before she stops enjoying it," Joanna added.

It was too late to go back. I handed the woman Dan Morgan's American Express card. "Can you gift-wrap it?"

An hour later I handed the same credit card to a woman at the airport to pay for Joanna Barnes's ticket. Two hours after that we landed in Phoenix. Morgan was waiting.

"I've heard all about you," Joanna said as she shook his hand.

"I've heard enough about you," Morgan said, "to be damned glad you're here."

We drove to the Adams Hotel, and after we had checked Joanna in, we all had a drink in the Old Bar. Morgan grilled her about the telephone call. Her story matched Rita's testimony flawlessly, except Joanna remembered more than Rita had. She recalled Rita shouting the name Miranda in a panicky voice. Morgan relaxed a little and bought us dinner at the restaurant in the hotel. We talked about things unrelated to the Eddington case. Mainly Morgan and Joanna talked about architecture. To my surprise, Morgan seemed to know a lot. *He must have had a case involving the subject. Or maybe his wife tutored him.* I heard names such as Mies and Le Corbu and Bauhaus and Fallingwater. He talked about Taliesin and the Imperial Hotel in Tokyo.

When we left Joanna at the hotel elevator with an appointment to meet us at the office in the morning, Morgan said, "Come with me, Doug," and I followed him back to the bar, where he ordered us another round. "Well, what do you think?"

"About what?" I asked.

"About what that girl proves."

"I think she proves that Rita's innocent."

He lit a cigarette. He inhaled and rubbed the smoke out of one of his eyes, then took another drag while smoke was still coming from his nose, and now he exhaled a protracted "Ah, shit" and a long train of smoke. He rubbed both eyes with his thumb and forefinger and let the smoke continue to pour out of him. He seemed very tired, and when he looked up, his eyes were red.

"Why?" I asked. "With this—I mean, with what Joanna says—don't you think Rita was telling the truth?"

"I *know* Rita was telling the truth. I've known that all along. I'm just not sure Joanna Barnes proves it."

"Why?" I said.

"Let me ask you this," Morgan said: "What if it had been Rita, not Miranda, who was holding the gun on Travis when Rita made that call?"

"I don't understand."

"Well, goddamn it, isn't it possible that Rita could have

killed him but that she made the telephone call to create a witness in her favor just before she pulled the trigger?"

"I never thought of that," I said. "I was so relieved when I realized she hadn't lied about making the telephone call. If anybody gets the idea she did that, then it looks . . ."

"Yeah," said Morgan. "It begins to look deliberate and premeditated and malicious."

"But you're not thinking about not using Joanna?"

"I'm not sure what I'm thinking," he said. "I left your car over in the Luhrs garage. I'll see you in the morning."

I don't know what Morgan did after he left the hotel that evening. I remember I went to sleep without hearing his car drive into the Kendall House, and I remember that his car was gone when I got up the next morning. But when I arrived at the office, he sat in the main conference room in a pressed suit and a starched shirt. Tom Gallagher and Walter Smith were there with him, and they were all in an intense conversation.

"I'm afraid of it, Walter," Morgan was saying. "I think that jury's with Rita, but it's possible they may not believe her. If they don't and I call this Barnes girl during my case, they may decide Rita made the call deliberately to set up a telephone operator as an unknowing accomplice. Then it's first-degree murder. No chance for second. No chance for manslaughter."

Walter Smith tapped his teeth with the bit of his pipe. Gently he chewed his lip and thought for a while. He took a couple of puffs of his heavy English tobacco and then a sip of coffee. "Bad theater," he finally said. "You call that girl to corroborate Rita and it may look contrived."

"That's what I'm afraid of," said Morgan.

"But," Walter continued, "if you save her—if you call her after Hauser has put on his evidence that no telephone call was made—I wouldn't think you'd have the problem. You'd simply be protecting Rita from incompetent evidence. Somehow it's better theater. Mr. Hauser will have played in your court and been made the fool."

"What if Hauser has somehow gotten wind of Joanna

Barnes?" Morgan said. "Then he isn't going to put on any evidence about the call. Then I lose Joanna Barnes as a witness."

"How's he going to get wind of your having found her?"

"I don't know, but anything can happen."

"Couldn't you call her after you see if Hauser calls someone from the phone company?" I asked, interrupting the two partners.

Morgan glared at me. "What the hell am I going to do? Rest? Then when Hauser says, 'No rebuttal,' I say, 'Whoops, Judge, I just forgot to call a witness who's so important we went all the way to San Francisco to find her'?"

It was pretty clear that Morgan didn't want me to answer that question. Walter Smith was kinder. "If it were someone with less experience," he told me, "the judge might let him do it. But Henry Penrod isn't going to let Dan Morgan get away with that kind of trick."

"Hell of a judgment call," Tom Gallagher interjected. "You put her on now and she may not be worth as much, may even hurt you. You wait and she could become dynamite, but you may lose the chance to use her."

Morgan looked at Walter Smith pleadingly. "I don't know what to do, Walter."

"I'm just glad I don't have to make the decision."

"Me, too," Tom Gallagher said.

"Thanks for coming in early," Morgan said to them, and they both left to go about their mundane tasks of a Monday morning while Morgan and I sat in the conference room alone. The decision weighed heavy, and though his shirt was starched and his suit pressed and his hair combed, he looked tired. "Ah, shit," he said. Then suddenly he became calm. "Fuck it," he said. "There's no way that son of a bitch knows we have her. We'll wait. We'll wait till he calls all his phone-company people, and then we'll shove Miss Barnes up his smug, fat ass." After that he didn't look so tired. "Do you want to take her testimony?" he asked me.

"What?"

"Do you want to question her?" I couldn't speak. He had caught me completely off guard. "Well, you're the one who discovered the problem at the phone company. You're the one who found her. And I promised you that day on the golf course that you could take the testimony of a witness."

"But you let me take Juan Menchaka."

"That didn't count," he said. "I still owe you one."

"She's too important. I could screw it up."

"She's too good," he said. "You won't get in trouble with her."

"I suppose," I said, "even if Hauser doesn't introduce the absence of the call, the judge might let me call her. I mean, like due to my lack of experience, I just forgot the first time."

"Don't count on it. But if you want to take her, you can. It's your choice."

"If we win, they'll say it was her testimony that won it for us."

"That's right. Yours would be the first face on the six o'clock news."

"I'll do it."

We spent the next hour getting ready, first Morgan and I going over the questions I would ask Joanna Barnes, then over and over the questions with Joanna as Morgan tutored me on when I could lead her and when I should not. When we were finished, I brought her to the courthouse and, nervously looking around to make sure nobody saw me take her in, hid her in the court reporter's office just as we'd hidden Mrs. Scott. I even locked the door so that no one could get in and see her. Then I sat at counsel table, waiting, trying to look calm.

When the jury finally filed in, when Rita had resumed the witness stand, when the hum of conversation in the gallery had subsided, the judge said, "Mr. Hauser, you may cross-examine."

"You did purchase Exhibit One," Hauser began, holding the murder weapon aloft.

Rita said, "Yes."

"You carried Exhibit One in your purse. Is that correct?"

"Yes."

"You carried it on the morning of October twenty-first?"

"Yes."

"You carried it as you approached the house in which your husband died, did you not?"

"Yes, I did."

"You carried the gun into the house?"

"Yes."

"And you pulled the gun from your purse."

"No. I did not do that."

"And you pointed it at your husband, didn't you, Mrs. Eddington?"

"No. I did not."

"You held it on him."

"That is not true."

"And you pulled the trigger."

"No!"

"You shot your husband six times."

"No!"

"And you watched him die."

"That is not true, Mr. Hauser."

"You never picked up that telephone, did you, Mrs. Eddington?"

"I did. I called."

"You remember that for sure?"

Rita looked at our adversary curiously. "Yes," she said, "I'm sure."

"How sure are you, Mrs. Eddington?"

Then Rita studied her antagonist, not with mild curiosity but with pronounced suspicion, while all the time I took comfort in Hauser's signal that he was bent upon falling into our trap.

"I made the call," Rita said. "I'm positive."

"No further questions," Hauser said.

And that was it. No stinging revelations. No burning embarrassments. No surprises. Only the prosecutor's benign argument of his theory of the case, all politely denied, and his precisely laid foundation for what he plainly expected to be demolition through the testimony of Mountain Bell

Telephone. One thing was clear. Morgan had spent a lot of time unnecessarily preparing Rita for a cross-examination that never really materialized. He said he had no redirect.

"Your Honor, the defense rests."

When Morgan said it, it was like a door had slammed shut, and only at that moment did I fully appreciate what he'd been going through. Only then, in the ominous, reverberating silence that followed, did it finally become clear to me, really clear, that our case was finished. It was over. If Max Hauser did not reopen the question of the telephone call, Joanna Barnes would not testify in *State of Arizona v. Rita Eddington*. And if she didn't testify, we would have wasted the only witness we had who made me know beyond doubt, any doubt, that Rita Eddington did not kill her husband. And Morgan had risked such sacrifice for just a touch of theater, for just a little drama.

"Rebuttal, Mr. Hauser?" said the judge.

Hauser rose slowly. I saw under the table that Morgan grabbed his knee hard to stop it from shaking. I wrapped my hands around a pencil until I realized I was about to break it. "Yes, Your Honor." The prosecutor turned with great confidence toward the jury. "The State calls Mrs. Esther Crockett of the Mountain Bell Telephone Company." There was a rustle in the courtroom, and I could hear my pencil click as I dropped it on the table. I watched a squarely built woman walk to the witness stand. The log, she testified, when Hauser put it before her, was kept in the ordinary course of the business of the telephone company, and it was the regular practice of the company to keep the log. The entries in the log were made at or near the time of the events they reflected, and the people who made the entries had reliable knowledge of the events they recorded. Hauser took his witness through these matters efficiently in his effort to move the log through the intricacies of the rule against hearsay.

"Now, Mrs. Crockett, if a person dialed a telephone operator in Mesa, Arizona, on October twenty-first of this year and asked to be connected with the police department, under the routine business practice of your company would that call be recorded in the log before you, which is marked Plaintiff's Exhibit Fourteen?"

"Yes."

"I offer Plaintiff's Exhibit Fourteen, if it please the court."

"No objection," said Morgan.

When he said he had no objection Morgan had before him a lengthy memorandum Ann Hastings had prepared while I was still searching for Joanna Barnes, which argued that even if it was within the business-records exception to the hearsay rule, the log was barred by the constitutional right to confrontation. Rita Eddington, the document pleaded eloquently, had a right to cross-examine everyone who was on duty at the telephone company that fateful morning. It was not enough that a bunch of phantom witnesses testified through an empty log. Everyone on duty should have been called. Of course, the problem had been that, if pressed, Hauser was in a position to call all those people.

"Did you say you had no objection, Mr. Morgan?" asked the judge with surprise.

"That's right, Your Honor," said Morgan as he turned Ann's memorandum upside down.

"Plaintiff's Exhibit Fourteen is received."

"Was there any report of such a telephone call logged that Sunday morning, Mrs. Crockett?"

"No sir. Apparently no such call was ever made."

There was a large rumble from behind us in the gallery. I glanced at the jury, and their collective expression resembled the look they'd all given Morgan that first day when, during voir dire, he told them Rita was going to place the blame for murder upon her only child. Heads began to turn toward the lovely woman who sat next to me, and Rita Eddington scribbled on a yellow pad: "I made that call."

Morgan put his hand on hers and smiled at her. "I know," he whispered.

Max Hauser turned to Morgan and smiled malignantly. "Your witness, Counselor."

"Ever hear of a woman named Joanna Barnes, Mrs. Crockett?" Morgan asked without getting up.

"Yes."

"She fill in for your operators at the telephone company every once in a while?"

"Yes. That's right."

"Nothing further, Your Honor."

That was apparently the first whiff Max Hauser got of what was about to come at him, and when he heard it, he stopped smiling.

"Your Honor," said Hauser, "I'm prepared to call every operator who was on duty during the time in question to testify that no call such as that described by Mrs. Eddington was received. I don't know whether Mr. Morgan . . ." He seemed to be searching for words.

"Your Honor," said Morgan, "I'll stipulate that none of the people Mr. Hauser has interviewed received the call Mrs. Eddington made that morning."

"Well," said the judge, "that would seem to save us some time. Members of the jury, you may take it as an established fact that none of the people interviewed by Mr. Hauser received the call that appears to have been placed in issue."

Both Guy Buckley, the crop duster, and Mrs. Mendoza smiled; they'd already gotten it.

"Further rebuttal, Mr. Hauser?"

"No, Your Honor." Hauser sat down, and where minutes before there had been the nasty smile, there was now a look of sick disorientation.

"You rest, then, Mr. Hauser?"

"What? Oh. Yes, the prosecution rests."

"Call her," Morgan ordered, loud enough so that the jury could hear.

"The defense calls Joanna Barnes, Your Honor." I wasn't even nervous as I said it. But suddenly I remembered that I was the only one who could find her where I had her tucked away in the court reporter's office.

"Oh. Your Honor, I need the court's indulgence." Henry Penrod nodded. I trotted out of the courtroom and up the hall. Suddenly my heart sank. *What if the door has locked both ways? I just wanted to lock people out of that office. What if I've locked her in? What if she needed to go to the restroom? What if she's in there with her legs crossed in agony? Or, worse, what if I can't get her out?*

I knocked tentatively, and the door opened. "Am I on?" she asked.

After she was sworn, I took her through a little background, how she'd come to Arizona, how she'd worked at Taliesin West, how she'd gotten a part-time job at Mountain Bell. I established that she'd been there on the morning of October 21 and that she'd left for San Francisco that day. "Did you receive a call that morning asking to be connected with the police?"

"Objection!" Hauser yelled. "That's leading."

I didn't expect it, and it made me jump, and I found myself looking all over the courtroom, grasping for something to say.

"Overruled."

"Your Honor, I think I have a right to lead on preliminary matters."

"I already overruled him, Mr. McKenzie. You may proceed."

"Did you receive such a call, Ms. Barnes?"

"Yes."

"Could you tell whether the caller was a man or a woman?"

"It was a woman."

"Tell us, please, everything you heard during that telephone call."

"Objection. That calls for rank hearsay."

That time I did not jump but instead looked directly at Max Hauser, who was very red, very nervous. "If the court please, I offer Mrs. Eddington's prior consistent statement to rebut the implication of a recent fabrication." I looked at Morgan, and he raised his eyebrows, acknowledging he was impressed.

"You may be right, Mr. McKenzie," I heard the judge saying, "but I think I'll let it come in, simply because Mr.

Hauser has placed the matter in issue. Also, it sounds to me like Ms. Barnes may well have been an eyewitness, or should I say an earwitness, to what happened that morning."

"That's right, too, Your Honor."

"Thank you, Mr. McKenzie," the judge drawled. "Now, you go ahead and examine your witness."

"Please tell what you heard on the telephone that morning, Ms. Barnes."

She turned to the jury. "It was a woman. Her voice was urgent. She sounded desperate. She said, 'Get me the police; I need the police.' Then I heard her say, 'Miranda, Miranda, don't, don't!' Then I heard a lot of noise, and the telephone went dead. I had not been able to make a connection with the police department."

"Did the noise sound like gunfire?"

"Objection."

"Yes, Mr. McKenzie, that is a bit leading. See if you can't rephrase it."

"What did the noise sound like?"

"I didn't think about it at the time. It didn't seem very loud. But looking back, I think it may have been a gun."

Joanna went on to tell them that the company procedure was to listen until a connection was made on all calls to the police, but she did not know that there was a log in which such calls were to be reported. And she finally told them that she hadn't come forward earlier because she didn't know of the case until I called her in San Francisco. I sat down, having fulfilled my promise not to ask her the embarrassing question, the one that would have gotten one of the women Max Hauser had no doubt interviewed into trouble.

Hauser now looked like a man with the wind knocked out of him. "May I have a moment, Your Honor?" The judge nodded his permission. When at last he began, Hauser said, "Miss Barnes, from what you heard, you could not tell how far from the telephone the thing that caused the noise you testified about was, could you?"

Has he hit upon the thing that made Morgan so ner-

vous? Will he try to argue that Rita could have made the call and shot Travis at the same time?

Joanna thought about Hauser's question. "Well," she said after some time, "if it was a gun, it must have been a fair distance from the phone, or I probably would have heard it more clearly."

"But you don't know that, do you?"

"I don't know it," she said, "but that's the way it sounded to me."

"No further questions."

It was over, save for closing arguments and the court's instructions to the jury. It was over, and Miranda Eddington had not awakened.

The jury went out at one-thirty that afternoon. Morgan and I drank beer from the little refrigerator in his office as we waited for their verdict. When the *Phoenix Gazette* arrived, I read the lead story: "Under examination by Phoenix defense attorney Douglas McKenzie, San Francisco architect Joanna Barnes testified . . ." I read the article three or four times. Morgan languished in his chair, drinking his beer and smoking one cigarette after another. When people came in to ask how it was going to come out, he said, "Who knows?" Once, after a long, introspective silence, he turned to me and said, "If they look at her when they file into the box, they've acquitted her. If they don't look at her, they've found her guilty." He crushed a cigarette. "It's one of the laws of nature." Later, while he was staring out the window, he said, "I hate waiting for a jury." The telephone rang at six o'clock on the dot. Morgan picked it up, then he looked at me, startled and a little frightened. "We've got a verdict."

When they filed in, eight of the jurors looked directly at Rita. After that the only surprise, so far as I was concerned, was the foreman (or I should probably say foreperson). It was Mrs. Mendoza, the only woman left after we'd run out of strikes. She handed the verdict to the clerk, and the clerk handed it to the judge. The judge looked at it and handed it back to the clerk to be read. "In the matter of State of Arizona versus Rita Eddington, we the jury, duly empaneled, find the defendant not guilty."

Rita put her forehead on Morgan's shoulder and said, "Thank you." Then she looked at me and squeezed my arm. "Douglas," she said, and she kissed me on the cheek.

After the judge finished making a thank-you speech to the jury, the courtroom exploded. Newspeople were running all over, and it was only then that I knew how many of them had been there. Some were slapping Morgan on the back and asking him for statements. Someone shook my hand and said, "Nice going." The judge slipped out through the door behind his bench. Guy Buckley, the crop duster, touched Rita's shoulder and smiled at her. Then I spotted Max Hauser and saw that he was glaring at Morgan with a look that was fierce and full of hatred. Morgan, I'm sure, did not see it. He was too distracted by the cacophony. Then I felt a hand on my shoulder. It was Juan Menchaka. "Ferris sent me," he said, "to make sure she has a way to get home."

When it was over, after both Morgan and I had had television cameras pointed at us and microphones shoved in our faces, Rita and Juan and Morgan and I walked through the cool evening air to the Arizona Club. Morgan ordered the drink he'd told Rita he wanted to have with her. It was champagne, Mumm's, and he raised his glass as if to propose a toast, but then he didn't say anything. He just put it down, and nursed his beer as the rest of us sipped the champagne. Looking back, I don't remember that one word was spoken at the table. We all just sat there until our glasses were empty, no one able to break the silence. Finally our failure at conversation made things awkward, and Rita asked Juan to take her home.

We walked with them to the elevator. Rita was wearing the blue dress that Ann had picked out at Goldwater's. As the elevator doors began to close upon them, I saw that Juan had grown very old. Rita raised her hand to us. She looked tired and drawn, but she was as overwhelmingly beautiful as ever.

32   "MAX HAUSER STEPPED on his dick!" Morgan crowed. "That's what happened."

Things had picked up since we put Rita on the elevator. There'd been a firm meeting that Monday evening at which a designer Paul Butler had hired to propose new offices made a presentation about carpet and wall coverings. Morgan and I skipped the meeting, electing to stay where we were. He bought me another bottle of champagne, this time a magnum, and we waited for the firm to appear at the Arizona Club for dinner. Eventually they came, not only to eat but also to pay their respects to Morgan and me. We gathered in the southeast dining room, where we could see the city lights and watch the airplanes taking off and landing in the night. When Ann Hastings arrived, she took a seat next to me and shared my magnum of champagne, and we watched Morgan regale the group with stories of Maximilian Hauser's improvidence.

Walter Smith toasted us eloquently, saying that perhaps the firm needed fancy new offices to house such skilled advocates. Cheers followed. Paul Butler even lifted a glass in Morgan's direction.

Morgan looked across the table at me and raised his can of beer. "To you, Doug. Rita Eddington owes you one. This year she truly has something to be thankful for." Only then did I realize that we'd finished the case in time for Thanksgiving. "Was it worth leaving the golf tournament?" Morgan asked.

"Yes."

"You should savor this one," he told me. "It isn't often that you save a person who's actually innocent."

I felt Ann Hastings's hand on my arm. "You should have seen Morgan after you called down to tell him you'd found that Joanna Barnes," she said, still touching me. "I thought he was going to explode."

"It was nothing," I said. "I just went to the address we'd been given."

"Well, you sure became a hero at this place."

I looked around the room at all the lawyers of Butler and Menendez. In the center was Morgan. No, not Morgan—Daniel Morgan; somehow I'd almost forgotten that was who he was. And as I watched him in the midst of all the gaiety, there was a moment when I almost shouted, "You're damned right it was worth leaving the golf tournament! Of course it was!" But I didn't do that. I just sat and sipped my wine and felt the adrenaline slip away. I could still feel the spot where Ann Hastings had been touching my arm long after she'd removed her hand.

In time I realized that Morgan had left the party, and then that Ann had left as well. Almost all of them had gone, except Walter Smith and Tom Gallagher and a small group that had started up a poker game. I watched them play for a while, then headed for the Kendall House, still feeling too good to want to go to bed but having nothing else to do. When I opened the door to my apartment, I saw the fancy box containing the scarf I'd bought for Ann in San Francisco. In the hurly-burly of the day, I had forgotten all about it. I picked up the box, turned it over a few times, then thought, *What the hell, she won't be in bed yet,* and I got back into my car and drove up North Central Avenue to her town house.

I rang the bell, and I heard movement inside. I felt a tremor as I realized what I was doing and then, as the door began to open, I heard a voice. The voice was not Ann's. Which is not to say, however, that the voice was unfamiliar.

"I told you to get the hell out of here," came the flat Arizona drawl. The door swung wide. I saw the tattoo. Then I saw the rest of him, stark naked. "Christ!" Morgan rattled. "I thought you were—"

I didn't hear the rest of it. Looking past him to an open staircase, I saw Ann Hastings descending into the muted light. Her pale blue robe had slipped open to the waist, and she was in the act of closing it.

I turned and ran for my car. I was headed east past Apache Junction with the accelerator on the floor when finally I started to think. Until then I had it vaguely in mind that I would just keep going, all the way to the Black River. I would fish. I would get there in time for the morning hatch, and the browns would be up off the bottom of the river, taking the insects. But around Apache Junction it occurred to me that it was winter and I couldn't get through the snow, and there would be no flies anyway. At last it dawned on me that I didn't even have a fly rod in the car. It also came to me that, once again, I was too drunk to be driving.

I stopped, then pulled slowly up to an all-night coffee shop. The hard-looking waitress and I were the only ones in the place. Under the harsh lights, her skin seemed tanned almost to leather. She read fashion magazines at the counter as I drank coffee and stared out at the black of the desert night and felt the sting of my embarrassment. When finally I drove back toward Phoenix, not quite sober but at least fairly lucid, I conceived a better plan. I would drive north to Utah; I would go skiing.

33 IN THE MORNING, drinking orange juice in the hope that it would wash the taste from my mouth, I had second thoughts about the little trip I'd planned with such care the night before. I couldn't, it seemed to me, just leave, not without telling someone at the office. But then I didn't have anyone to report to except Morgan, and I figured he wouldn't want to talk to me any more than I wanted to talk to him or Ann. The specter of running into them at the office crowded the edge of my mind—awkward glances, interminable elevator rides, the coffee lounge. I pushed it all back. *To hell with them. I'm outta here.*

I failed to make a clean getaway. As I was carrying my skis to the door, I looked up and saw Morgan and Ann in front of me. "Can we come in?"

"I guess so," I told him, and I put down the skis. They stepped inside and stood awkwardly until I told them to sit. "I have some coffee made," I said.

"Okay."

I got them coffee, and we sat looking at one another across a pair of scarred Head Deep Powders.

"Look, Doug, we didn't know it was you. I thought you were that goddamned Axel Stern. You know, when I told you to get out of there last night."

"Who's Axel Stern?"

"He's a guy who won't leave Ann alone. A doctor. A plastic surgeon."

"Well," I said, "you didn't seem exactly prepared to entertain, even if it was me."

He fumbled for a cigarette. I saw his eyes squint down. He grinned.

I looked at Ann. She was not smiling. "What a mess," she said.

"I was just bringing you a present that I'd forgotten to give you." I had said it before I thought about it.

"What present?" Ann said.

"I bought you something in San Francisco."

"Will you give it to me now?"

I found the package, and silently I handed it to her. I was beyond feeling silly anymore. When she pulled the vibrant blue silk from the orange tissue, she said it was the most beautiful scarf she'd ever seen, and I was sure she meant it. She ran her finger over it, lightly tracing its delicate hem. She wrapped it around her neck. It was as lovely as I thought it would be, back when I'd been drinking all the bourbon and the beer with the voluptuous architect who became my wonderful witness.

"It's beautiful," she said again. Then she got up and came over and kissed me. Right on the mouth. It was sort of a gentle, friendly kiss, but it was right on the mouth. I held on to her for a long second. I inhaled the rose perfume that had saturated the San Francisco boutique and, below that, the damp earth scent of jasmine. I could smell cigarette smoke in her hair.

"I bought it in San Francisco," I told Morgan as she sat back down. "I put it on your American Express card."

"That's fine," he told me.

"It cost a hundred and fifty dollars."

"For that?"

"There are only two of them in the world," I said.

"It's beautiful," Ann said to Morgan. "It's worth it. It really is. And thank you for it." She reached over and kissed Morgan, harder than she'd kissed me, and differently. Then it was over; I could talk to them.

"So you know our secret," Morgan said.

"I guess I do."

34   I THREW MY BOOTS and a duffel bag into the trunk of my Mustang, then took down the top, angled my skis and poles across the center console, and headed north. When I reached Flagstaff and the pine country, it became cold, so I stopped and put on my sheepskin coat, the one I'd bought in Hong Kong. I drove on across the Indian land with the car heater blasting up my legs, and I took the old road across Navajo Bridge toward Jacob Lake and Fredonia. At the bridge I stopped and dropped a rock. I counted to fifteen (it always took fifteen seconds) before I saw the splash in the Colorado River. By the time I hit Kanab, it was so cold I had to put up the car top. I pushed on through the little Mormon towns with the redbrick gabled houses that looked like my grandmother's. It was night when I reached the Salt Lake Valley, and as I passed the prison, it began to snow.

I turned east, and at the mouth of the Little Cottonwood Canyon the flakes became huge and fell straight down out of the black, windless sky. I stopped and put on chains. When I stood again, I held out my hand and watched as the snowflakes built up. The only sound came from the gurgling creek, which was not yet frozen this early in the year. I blew the weightless snow from my palm and headed up the canyon.

It snowed without wind for seven days, and for seven

days I skied through bottomless powder that rolled over my shoulders. Not once did they have to close the mountain. Each morning I awoke to the sound of 105 mm recoilless rifles, but they never brought down an avalanche.

I stayed at the Rustler Lodge, where five years before I'd been the assistant manager. I met a girl named Jane Bartholomew, who ran the reservation desk at the lodge. Before Alta she'd been a ski racer, a member of the National Development Team, and she knew how to wind up a pair of skis in deep snow. I liked her immediately; she looked a lot like Joanna Barnes. She was tall and ruddy, with freckles. She wore her hair in a single heavy braid that swung from side to side across her back as she skied. Every day I watched Jane's hair swing left and right as I followed her down runs with names like Gunsight and Stone Crusher and High Rustler.

One night after dinner, Jane and I walked down to the Alta Lodge on snow so cold we could hear it crack under our feet. She put her arm through mine and pressed against me as we descended the covered steps to the lodge. We made our way to the Sitzmark Bar and took a table at the window by the fireplace. For once that week, the clouds broke, and a moon lit the mountain. I leaned back in my chair and stared up toward the Baldy Chutes.

"You all right?" Jane asked.

"I think I'm tired. I think you've worn me out."

"Maybe you've been spending too much time in an office," she suggested.

"I helped try a case," I said. "It was a pretty important case." I was going to tell her about Dan Morgan and Rita Eddington and how I'd gone to San Francisco and found a witness who looked like her and who had won the case for us. But then I saw that Jane Bartholomew wasn't paying attention; she was staring over to the bar at a ski instructor who drank tequila shooters and spoke with an Australian accent.

I headed back to Phoenix in the morning.

35 ON MY RETURN from Utah, I stepped off the elevator wondering whether I would find work at Butler and Menendez what with *Eddington,* the only case I ever really worked on, having become a part of history. I figured I might go to Walter Smith and solicit work on one of his medical-malpractice cases, but in the back of my mind stood San Francisco.

"Douglas."

"Good morning, Josephine."

"You must call Jacob Asher," she said, without the slightest acknowledgment that I'd been away. "He says it's urgent. He says he's Miranda Eddington's guardian."

"He is," I said numbly, taking the slip with his number on it. In my office I sat down and dialed.

"Asher."

"It's Doug McKenzie, Mr. Asher. I'm returning your call."

"I thought I should let you guys know," he said, "Miranda Eddington has come to life."

"Oh, God," I heard myself say involuntarily.

"And," Jake Asher continued, "your man Hauser gave me what he euphemistically refers to as a courtesy call this morning."

"I don't understand."

"He wanted, he said, to do me the courtesy of telling me he may charge her."

"Charge her with what?"

"Who knows? Murder, maybe."

"You've got to be kidding."

"No. I'm not kidding. I'm very serious."

I sat quietly and felt the earpiece burn against the side of my head.

"And, McKenzie?"

"Yes."

"He says he may try to certify her for trial as an adult."

"Can he do that?"

"I don't know, McKenzie. You're the legal talent."

"It isn't fair!" I yelled.

Asher laughed bitterly. "You want to know what else he says?"

"What?!"

"He says you and Morgan proved she did it."

I didn't answer, just held the phone.

"Have Danny call me," Asher ordered. Then he hung up.

A moment later Tom Gallagher walked into my office, looking more grave than Jake Asher had sounded. He was wearing a black suit and a white shirt and a black tie. "Are you going over?" he asked me.

"Over where?"

"To the funeral."

"What funeral?" I asked. "I didn't know anything about any funeral."

"Mrs. Miller died."

"Who?" I said.

"Ada Miller? The woman who took Dan in when he was a little boy, when his father ran out on him?"

"I thought Dan grew up in your house. I thought he was like your adopted brother."

"He only came to live with us after he was in high school. First he was with Ada—Ada and Beth. Beth was Dan's first wife. You knew that, didn't you?"

"Yes."

"He moved in with us after he and Beth became a little too close for Mrs. Miller's comfort. That's when the priests at St. Mary's asked my father to look after him."

"I didn't know that."

"Well, Ada Miller died this week, and the funeral is this morning. Dan could probably use some support."

So it was that I wound up spending my first morning back at work sitting next to Ann Hastings in the back pew in the chapel of A. L. Moore's funeral home, watching a handful of people dressed in black wander in and sit randomly to stare at a gleaming black-and-bronze casket. When we arrived, Dan Morgan sat alone on the right side at the front of the chapel. Gallagher, because he also was to be a pallbearer, left me with Ann and moved forward to sit by Morgan. Two young men who looked to be in their early twenties sat on the left side of the room, and behind them a plump girl. One of the young men wore a marine dress uniform with lieutenant's bars.

"I think those are Dan's children," Ann whispered to me. "They had to bring the marine officer back from the Pacific. He's on a ship."

"Do you know the name of the ship?" I asked.

"I think it's called the *Iwo Jima.*"

"Morgan once told me he knew someone on the *Iwo Jima.*"

"Yes," said Ann. "His younger son."

"Why aren't they sitting with him?"

"They don't speak to him," she said.

"What?"

"They didn't like the way he treated their mother."

Then I saw Beth Morgan, the woman I knew from a photograph on the lounge wall, walk up the aisle. She sat by the girl, and the marine turned around in the pew and put his hand on her knee in a comforting gesture. As she sat there, Beth appeared calm and composed. In time Morgan turned toward his first wife. His face was drawn, and he looked much the way he had the morning they led Tyrone Roebuck to the gas chamber. Morgan and Beth gazed at each other across the room for a long time.

I didn't listen to the eulogy, but at one point I did hear the preacher say something about the departed's having taken into her home Daniel Morgan, who had thereafter risen to national prominence as a trial lawyer. When he said that, Morgan lowered his head even further. When it was over, Morgan and Gallagher and Beth's sons—Morgan's sons—and two men I'd never seen carried Beth's mother to a waiting hearse in the parking lot.

"Morgan paid a lot of money for that casket," Ann Hastings said to me as I watched it sliding into the black Cadillac.

After that, Ann and Gallagher and I stood on the asphalt in the sun and watched the two sons move away from Morgan without speaking. Morgan lit a cigarette, but he did not appear to enjoy it. I watched him standing there all alone, and then I saw Beth walk over to him. At first she just looked at him, but then she tried to put her arms around him, and as she did, Morgan flinched, seeming not to know what to do. I watched Morgan, and I shivered at the prospect of having to tell him what Jake Asher had told me earlier that day. I stood there wondering why Asher's call had so affected me. Then I began to feel anger rise as my thoughts shifted to Maximilian Hauser.

Later that day Josephine called to alert me that Morgan had returned from the cemetery, and I walked toward his office to do my duty and tell him about Jake Asher's call, but when I saw him with his head somewhere near his knees, I couldn't bring myself to it. I went instead to Tom Gallagher's office and told him what had happened. "Let's go tell him about it," Gallagher said.

Morgan stared out the window while Gallagher delivered the news. "So what the hell are we supposed to do?" Morgan said, still gazing vacantly to the east.

"Asher wants you to call him," I said, shoving the number across the desk.

With no change of expression, Morgan pushed the buttons on his phone. "Jake, I've got you on a speaker, and Tom Gallagher and Doug McKenzie are in here."

"McKenzie tell you what happened?"

"Yes."

"What are we going to do, Danny?"

"I guess you'd better get her a good criminal lawyer."

"That's why I called," Asher said. "Ferris Eddington wants you."

36   "I WANT YOU at this meeting," Morgan told me. "Ferris likes you, and there's probably going to be some explaining to do on why we can't represent the girl. Butler and Gallagher are going to be there to talk about the bill for the quarter."

At exactly ten o'clock, Josephine ushered Ferris Eddington and Jacob Asher into the conference room. "Gentlemen," Asher whispered. We all sat down, and Gallagher poured coffee around the table.

"Dan, I can't tell you how grateful I am for the work you and Douglas did."

"I'm glad we could do it, Ferris. It was a good case."

A quiet tension settled over the table, and Butler took advantage of the silence to push the firm's statement toward the client. "Ferris, we wanted to go over the bill for this quarter. You can see it includes Dan's and Douglas's time as well as all the time I had on the sale of those two sections down on the border. We also have a substantial advance for costs for investigators, our expert psychiatrist, and for travel. In my matter there are expenses for surveyors. We have also written the bill up some because of what was quite clearly a successful—"

The big hand with the diamond ring reached over and shoved the document to the side. "This is not what I came here to talk about," Ferris Eddington said. "I came to discuss how my granddaughter is to be protected. I am told we may have to have someone in court for her as early as next week. Will you represent her, Dan?"

"I can't do it, Ferris. I'm sorry."

"Why not?"

"How can I defend her?" Morgan reasoned. "In essence I already proved that the girl is guilty."

Ferris Eddington spread his arms wide on the table and leaned forward.

"Besides," Morgan pressed defensively, "I represented Rita. That creates a conflict of interest. Whoever defends Miranda may have to attack Rita."

"Well, it's my understanding that those sorts of conflicts can be resolved. Mr. Asher here is Miranda's legal guardian. He tells me that he will consent, on her behalf, to your representing her." Ferris Eddington turned to Asher for confirmation.

"That's right, Danny. It seems to me that if I'm really looking after her interests, I see that she gets the best lawyer she can get."

Morgan shook his head. "We represented Rita. We proved she didn't do it. What are we going to do now, turn around and try to prove she did?"

"I asked Ralph Daniels in Mesa about it," Ferris Eddington said. "Ralph said he thought, with proper consents, you could represent her." Ralph Daniels had practiced law in Mesa for as long as I could remember. When Dan Morgan heard the name, he rolled his eyes to the ceiling.

"Ralph drew this up, and Rita executed it," Ferris Eddington continued. He pulled a document from the inside pocket of his jacket and handed the paper to Morgan. I sneaked a glance over Morgan's shoulder.

"I, Rita Eddington, having been represented by the law firm of Butler and Menendez, through attorneys Daniel Morgan and Douglas McKenzie, being fully informed in the circumstances, hereby freely and voluntarily consent to said law firm and said attorneys representing my daughter,

Miranda Eddington, in any action that involves the death of Travis Eddington."

Still shaking his head, Morgan passed the document to Gallagher. As Gallagher read, I inspected the bill Paul Butler had tried to discuss, and found the bottom line. I hid my reaction from the man who was expected to pay it. *No wonder Butler's in the room,* I thought. I looked at Ferris Eddington, at the hard set of his jaw, at a coldness in his eyes that I'd never seen before—that I'd never looked for. He watched Gallagher read.

"Ferris, we do have a sizable statement for last quarter's work," Butler pleaded.

"I don't want to talk about it until we get this matter straightened out."

"Does that mean," Butler ventured tentatively, "that you don't intend to pay this bill unless Dan takes Miranda's case?"

Ferris Eddington said nothing.

Gallagher finished reading and looked at Morgan. "I don't know," he said.

"I don't like it," Morgan persisted.

"Well, think about it, Danny," Ferris Eddington ordered. "I have some business over at the Valley Bank. I'll be back in two hours for your answer. I need to know." He walked out of the room.

Gallagher stood up and went to the credenza. He came back with the coffeepot.

"Douglas," Butler said to me, "you may know him better than any of us does. What do you think he intends to do?"

"I think," I said, "he isn't going to pay us unless we defend Miranda."

"I think you're right," Butler said, giving me a hard look. "And we find it very unpleasant to have to sue a client for a fee." He traced his finger across the bill. "I see that you yourself, Douglas, have a fair amount of time here that might go uncompensated."

"I think this is a discussion for partners," said Gallagher.

Jake Asher and I took the suggestion. As we were walking out the door, I heard Morgan say again, "I don't like it, Paul."

Back in my office, I drank coffee and thought about the mess we were in. I reminded myself that they seemed to like me at the firm and that I could probably ride out an unpaid bill. Besides, there was always San Francisco. Ann Hastings appeared at the door. She asked me what was going on, and I told her. "Oh, God," she said. "If Eddington doesn't pay that bill, Morgan's dead in this firm."

Later I stood next to the conference-room door. I could hear raised voices. The only thing I could make out distinctly was an eruption from Morgan. "We've got some real ethical questions here. We ought to talk to Frank about them, goddamn it."

I returned to my office. I sat with my back to my desk, thinking about the situation, then heard Morgan easing himself into one of my chairs.

"So what do you think about all this?" he asked.

"We know that Miranda shot him. There's no question about that. If we were to defend her, we'd probably have only one defense—insanity. So, we wouldn't be taking a position inconsistent with our defense of Rita. And when you consider that we have consents from both Rita and Miranda, it seems to me that maybe we ought to be able to represent her."

"That's exactly what I've been thinking," Morgan declared. He stood up, and I followed him back to the conference room, where Gallagher and Paul Butler still sat in the same chairs as when I left. Ferris Eddington was at the head of the table. "We'll do it, Ferris," Morgan said.

"That's a great relief to me, Danny. Now, how much is that bill you wanted me to look at?"

"With our standard hourly rates rounded up slightly, because of a very successful result in Rita's case," Paul Butler reported, "it's three hundred fifty thousand dollars, Ferris."

Out of the same pocket from which he'd drawn Rita's consent, Ferris Eddington produced a checkbook and a fountain pen, and without looking at the bill, he filled in the check, signed it, and pushed it down the table. That left us to stare at one another silently, prepared to enter our appearance, once again, in a case called *State of Arizona v. Eddington*. There were to be times when Dan Morgan would ask how in hell it happened. Well, what I've just written is how it happened, as best I can remember.

37 "WHATEVER HAPPENS," MORGAN said, "we've got to stop Hauser from getting her certified as an adult. We've got to keep her in juvenile court."

"How do we do that?" I asked.

"That's for you to find out."

I started in the index to the Arizona Revised Statutes. I looked for some provision to certify a juvenile as an adult. Finding nothing, I read the table of contents and found no more. Then I read the entire juvenile code, and when it revealed nothing, I turned to criminal procedure. After that I looked under "children," then under "adults," then "certification." I think I'd read the Arizona Constitution and was well into the digest for the *Pacific Reporter* when my eyes finally blurred and I hung my head among the books spread across both tables that separated the stacks in the library.

"Screw it!" I slouched to the coffee lounge, where Morgan and Gallagher and Walter Smith were talking to a newly hired associate. I poured a cup of coffee.

"So what did you find out?" Morgan asked.

"Nothing," I confessed. "I can't find anything. I don't think there's anything on it."

"Oh, yes there is," Morgan said. "I've read some of that stuff before. I just can't remember where it is."

"Well, so far, I can't find it."

"Can't a child be certified to be prosecuted as an adult in Arizona?" Morgan asked Walter Smith.

"I don't know, and I don't care," said the civil litigator.

"A juvenile may be tried as an adult under certain circumstances." That came from the new associate, one Lester Pierce, and his voice was bold and authoritative. I knew that he'd just come from a judicial clerkship on the Supreme Court of the United States and that the firm felt lucky to get him, since he'd been first in his class at the University of Arizona Law School. Rumor had it that he wanted to work with Dan Morgan.

"Under what circumstances?" I demanded.

The new associate lifted his left hand and touched his forefinger in a motion calculated to check off circumstance number one. "First," he said. "There must be probable cause to believe that a crime was committed and that the juvenile was involved in its commission." Pierce looked at me to make sure that what he said had registered.

From my other side, I heard Morgan say, "Hauser has that one." I turned to him. "Well, she did kill her father," he reminded me.

"Second." Pierce touched his second finger. "There must be a finding that the juvenile is not amenable to treatment or rehabilitation as a delinquent child within the juvenile court."

"Your man Hauser has that one, too," Walter Smith opined, and when I looked at him, he said, "Hell, if Mayo Brothers and Menninger can't fix her, the Maricopa County Juvenile Court isn't going to do much."

"What's next?" Morgan asked.

"A finding that the safety or interest of the public requires that the child be transferred for criminal prosecution."

"He's probably got that one, too," Morgan lamented. "She did kill him. She's going to be viewed a threat to the public safety, and no judge is going to want to put her in with other children. Anything else, Pierce?"

"Yes. Before a juvenile may be prosecuted in superior court, it must be shown that said juvenile is not mentally ill."

"Aha!" Morgan belched. "We've got him! She's crazy as hell. That's why she's been at places like Menninger. That's why she was in that stupor. Hell, that's why she killed Travis. If you're right, Pierce, Hauser'll never get her into superior court. There's no way he can prove she's not mentally ill."

"And, of course," Lester Pierce continued, "superimposed on all this is the procedural requirement of notice and hearing. Due process, you know." The new associate blessed me with an enigmatic smile, one that suggested he hadn't been told of Douglas McKenzie's exploits before the Honorable Henry Penrod. "I'll be back," he announced. I knew he was going for something I should have found in the library, and by then I was sure that Pierce was brilliant. More than that, he possessed a certain élan that enabled him to pull off that virtuoso performance in front of Morgan and Gallagher and Walter Smith.

"Oh, sweet Christ," Tom Gallagher said, "we've got another goddamned walking encyclopedia. How long till Butler rotates off the hiring committee?"

"Two years," said Walter Smith.

"How in hell many more of these little geniuses is he going to recruit?"

Lester Pierce returned with a manuscript—a symposium, he told us—to be published in the *Arizona Law Review*. An entire volume to be devoted exclusively to juvenile law. "They sent it up to me to edit and cite-check," Pierce said proudly. He turned the dog-eared pages until he found the section he wanted, then handed it to me.

I scanned down until I came to a heading: "Requirements for Waiver." I read a little, then looked at Morgan. "You don't call it certification," I told him. "You call it waiver. The juvenile court waives its jurisdiction." Morgan nodded, and I read further. "It's based on a judicial interpretation of an ambiguous constitutional provision. No wonder I couldn't find it."

Morgan nodded again and pulled a cigarette from his sock. "What's it say about requirements before the juvenile court can waive its jurisdiction?" He lit the cigarette, and I read.

"It says exactly what Pierce just told us. Besides all those other things, the prosecution has to prove that the juvenile is not mentally ill."

"Well, Miranda Eddington is twelve years old, and she's nuts, and that's why that fat bastard ain't going to get her out of juvenile court." Morgan shook his head in a way that said the matter had been closed, that our problems had been put to rest, and he left the room.

I returned to the *Law Review* article, and when I came to a certain spot, I found myself reading aloud to Walter Smith: " 'Where competent evidence is adduced that a juvenile is committable to a mental institution, subjugation of the child to the adult criminal system does not serve the interests of either society or the juvenile.' " I looked up. "If to keep her from being prosecuted as an adult we have to prove she's committable to a mental institution, what will they do with her then, Walter?"

"I don't know, but my guess is they'd commit her to a mental institution. Doesn't that stand to reason?"

"The state hospital?"

"That would be my best guess."

"We could," I reasoned, "wind up having to keep her in the state hospital so that Max Hauser doesn't get a chance to put her in prison."

"And, my boy," said Walter Smith, "it hasn't been long since they called that place the insane asylum." He got up to leave, but before heading out, he looked down at me. "You know—snake pit."

38 THIS TIME WHEN Morgan and I went to Camelback Hospital to see Miranda Eddington, we walked right through the front door. Dr. Hardy—a very cordial Dr. Hardy—escorted us through the lemon yellow reception area, up a bright hall, through a door onto the patio, and in the direction of Miranda's room.

"You know, Doctor," Morgan remarked as we strolled freely, "this place is very nice. It's the first time I've ever been here." I noticed that despite the conspiratorial wink he gave me behind the doctor's back, he was not as upbeat as usual. He seemed sad. Not depressed, necessarily. Just a little sad, a little flat.

At Miranda's door the doctor told us we could talk to her as long as we liked. "I'll see that we get copies of all her records for you. We'll have them before you leave." And for the second time, Morgan and I slid into Miranda Eddington's hospital room.

She sat propped against pillows on the bed, bathed in the light from an open window. She wore a blue-checked western shirt, a pair of faded Levi's, and no shoes. Her bare feet looked fragile and aristocratic, like her mother's. Her red hair was darker than her mother's. Pulled back into a ponytail, as it was that morning, it drew attention to her cheekbones and her big eyes. She was, I thought, almost as pretty as Rita. A clear quality in her face suggested intelligence. When we entered the room, she was reading an issue of *Western Horseman*, and when she saw us, she lowered the magazine to her lap. "Hello, Doug."

"You remember me?"

"Yes," she said. "I remember when you helped me catch a fish."

It transported me back to a summer day not too many years before. I'd been at sheep camp, fishing with Juan Menchaka that summer, when Travis Eddington had brought his daughter up to the White Mountains for a few days. One afternoon Juan watched her as she chased a sheep around the corral. "I'll bet you we could hook that little girl to a trout," he speculated. As I stood in her hospital room, I remembered how we had been on a long, slow bend of Paradise Creek and how, when Miranda Eddington dropped the fly on the water, the trout's strike was so violent that it made her jump and set the hook involuntarily. And I remembered how she'd laughed and how I thought she might wet her pants as Juan gently coached her until she brought the little rainbow to the net. I hadn't thought of that day again until I watched her on her bed in Camelback Hospital, but as I watched, I remembered how the meadow where we fished ran to the ponderosa forest and how green it was from all the rain that summer and how blue the sky. But mainly I remembered a pretty little girl in a yellow jumper and a little trout darting through the gin-clear water. And I remembered how pleased Travis had been when his daughter caught the fish. I even remembered what he had said that summer day. "You know," he said, "I think she's having a good time, I really think she is." And I remembered that Travis's voice sort of cracked as he said it.

"It was a Light Cahill," Miranda said.

"Yes," I said. "The fly."

"Juan made it."

"That's right," I said. "Juan tied flies that caught fish."

Then our new client looked at the man beside me, and I said, "Miranda, this is Dan Morgan."

"He was with you the night you came to see me."

My chest tightened. "You remember that?" I asked.

"Yes."

"Do you know why we're here, Miranda?" Morgan asked her.

"Yes. Grandpa says I need a lawyer."

"And Doug and I are going to be your lawyers. Do you know that?"

"Yes."

"How do you feel these days?"

"Wonderful," she said. "I get to go home tomorrow."

"Is that good?" I asked her.

"It's great. Grandpa bought me a horse." She turned to a bedside table and picked up a photograph, which she proudly handed to me. It was a picture of a small, well-formed mare. "She's half Arabian and half quarter horse," Miranda said. "Do you like her?" Her eyes sparkled, the way they had the day she caught the trout. She seemed like nothing other than a pretty young girl who'd gotten a nice present.

"You need to talk to me, don't you?" she said to Morgan.

"Yes."

"It's okay."

"Miranda, do you remember the day your father died?"

"Yes."

"Do you remember what happened that day?"

"Yes."

"Can you tell us what happened?"

"Yes."

"What happened, Miranda?"

"Mama shot him."

39   LATER THAT DAY I sat at my desk thinking about what had happened, first the
shock, then how Morgan had stopped in his
tracks, suspended, with his eyes pointed in the direction of
the swimming pool. I thought of how when he shook it off,
he came back to her and explained that she should tell her
lawyers the truth, that we couldn't tell anyone else what she
said, that she had to tell it just the way it happened so that
her lawyers could take care of her. I pictured Miranda, just
as calm repeating the words as she had been the first time
she'd uttered them. "Mama shot him." I thought about how
Morgan simply walked out of the room, leaving me to tell
our new young client that we would come back and see her
later.

At my desk I had before me the records that Dr. Hardy
had copied for us. There were the charts of every examination and all treatment Miranda Eddington had ever received. I began to read, apprehensively at first, knowing
that I would see gruesome descriptions of terrible things
that Travis Eddington had done to his only child. I turned
page after page, but no such thing came up from the materials before me, not so much as a hint. I saw phrases like
these: "mother cold and remote," "father assumes more ac-
tive role in child rearing," "patient fears mother." I learned
that Miranda was "bipolar," sometimes "grandiose," some-

times "hypomanic." A drug called lithium had been considered. One note said, "Electroconvulsive therapy indicated." What I did not see was a portrait of a fiend in the form of Travis Eddington. In fact, the only thing I read of Travis that first afternoon, apart from his role in rearing Miranda, was a note that the patient's father seemed to be kind and caring.

As I read on into records of more recent observations, the diagnosis changed to that of possible schizophrenia. One doctor had considered the use of a drug called Thorazine. The records were difficult to read. My eyes grew tired, and I was grateful when Ann Hastings came into my office and I had an excuse to stop for a moment.

"I wanted to tell you," she said, "I'm going to cook dinner at Dan's apartment tonight. We'd like you to come, if you're not busy."

I hesitated, wondering how awkward the evening would be, but finally I said, "Sure."

"Great. Seven-thirty for cocktails. Tom Gallagher will be there, too."

"Morgan told Gallagher about the two of you?"

"Yes."

"This will be good," I told Ann. "I can tell Morgan what I'm finding in Miranda Eddington's medical records."

40 IT WAS NOT GOOD, however. Indeed, Ann's dinner party at Morgan's apartment ended in something shockingly near shambles, and as I look back, it stands in my mind as the event that marked the beginning of the bad times for Daniel Morgan, and for me. I say it marked the beginning knowing well that Ann's small party had hardly anything to do with causing the trouble. The cause of the bad times came, I suppose, the day Miranda Eddington woke up. Or, if not then, the day we heard her say the words "Mama shot him." But for me it will always be that intimate little dinner that seemed to launch the downward slide.

The evening began harmlessly enough. I walked into his apartment, and Morgan said, "Fix yourself a drink," and I fixed one. Then I listened as Morgan and Gallagher discussed the week in sport, moving from football to basketball and on to the future of spring training and the San Francisco Giants. When they'd exhausted the subject, I tried to edge in a word about Miranda's medical records, but Morgan would have none of it and directed the conversation to what it was like to be on Hotel Street in Honolulu in 1942. And when I tried to bring up such things as chronic depression and the medical use of the drug called lithium, Morgan wanted to talk about the comparative merits of the Continental as against the Cadillac. Finally he got

Gallagher going on why Watergate had happened to Richard Nixon. All this while Ann Hastings cooked four Cornish game hens, and we ate bacon-wrapped canapés.

Through it Morgan tried to look like he was having a good time. Once he put his hand on Ann's arm and, with a mouthful of hors d'oeuvres, said, "This stuff is really damned good."

We ate the game chickens, and at the end of the evening we all sat around the table, each with a drink. Morgan had his beer, the rest of us some fancy liqueur in snifters. It was then that the doorbell rang, and it was then that the trouble began. Morgan looked curiously at Ann. He put his beer on the table, walked around a corner to the door, and opened it.

"Hello, Danny," came a voice from outside. Ann Hastings gasped. "I went to the house," the voice said. "Then finally I had to call Josephine to find out where you'd gone."

"I'll call you in the morning, Katherine," Morgan whispered. "I'll be at the office. I'll come up to the house if you like."

"I'd like a drink, Danny."

"There are some people here," Morgan said. "I'll talk to you tomorrow."

"I'd like a drink, Danny," the voice insisted.

"This isn't a good time."

"I think it's a good time."

"No, Katherine. It really isn't." I heard a small shuffle, then a click. The door clicked again as Morgan locked it. He returned to the table and slid quietly into his chair without looking at any of us. I stared across my snifter, across the fresh flowers Ann had put on the table and through the glass of the sliding door that led onto the patio. Outside, it was too dark to see very much. There was a faint outline of a palm tree in the blue light from the swimming pool. That was all I could see as I stared into that distance, unable to look anywhere else.

Something moved across the patio. I blinked. *It might be a person,* I thought. Then something rocketed from the patio, tumbling through the air in my direction. Before I could recoil, I heard an explosion. I suddenly realized that the glass I'd been looking through was falling. In what seemed slow motion, individual shards descended to the carpet, settling around an overturned patio chair. The handsome woman whose picture I had seen before stepped carefully through what had been the door.

"I'll have that drink now, Danny."

Morgan put his hand to his forehead, then lowered his nose a little closer to the table.

Tom Gallagher stood up. "Still drinking martinis, Katherine?"

"That would do nicely, Tom. Thank you."

When Gallagher moved toward the tray with the bottles and the ice bucket, the handsome woman moved toward me. I almost tipped backward in my chair. She put her hand out. "We haven't met. I'm Katherine Morgan." I stood and coughed out my identity. "Hello, Ann," Katherine Morgan said quite pleasantly.

"Hello, Katherine."

Gallagher rattled the cold steel cocktail shaker. Morgan just sat looking at the marred surface of his table. He had managed to light a cigarette. After Gallagher handed the stemmed glass to Katherine, he asked Ann if she would like another drink.

"No thanks, Tom. Doug promised he would take me to a movie tonight, and I'm going to hold him to it."

As I say, that evening seemed to mark the beginning of times gone bad. I think back to the shattered glass on Morgan's ratty carpet and now, these many years later, I'm struck by how it resembled the bubble that had once been *State of Arizona v. Eddington*.

41   I TRIED TO TALK to Morgan about what I'd read in Miranda Eddington's medical records. "Tell you what I want you to do," he ordered brusquely. "I want you to go out and talk to her. She likes you. I want you to get her to tell you what really happened that morning. That is, if she actually remembers. I have a feeling she doesn't. I can read those goddamned records myself."

"She seemed pretty firm about what happened when we talked to her."

"You just go talk to her again. See if you can't get her to tell you the truth."

I moved toward the door.

"Doug," Morgan said.

"Yeah?" I answered.

"I don't know why you're so edgy. They haven't even charged her with anything. If we're lucky, they won't."

The hospital had sent Miranda home, so I drove out to the ranch to find her. I headed for the office, hoping Ferris Eddington might arrange for me to talk to Miranda, while at the same time avoiding Rita. I didn't have to go very far. As I pulled into the driveway, I could see both grandfather and granddaughter in the cutting corral. Miranda sat on the little mare whose picture she had shown me, and Ferris Eddington on his big quarter horse. Miranda sat and watched, fascinated, as her grandfather let his horse work back and forth, nosing Angus steers around. I parked at the office and walked across the truck scales toward the pen, and as I approached, I heard Miranda laugh, then scream, "Get him, Grandpa!" Ferris Eddington looked back and smiled at her. He moved one of the black steers to the corner of the pen, then turned his horse and tipped his hat to her.

Miranda saw me, shouted "Doug!" and trotted her little mare over to where I stood.

"Do you like her?" she asked me.

"She's beautiful," I said. "Does she have a name?"

"Belle," Miranda said, "and she can run."

"Belle? That's my grandmother's name," I told her. Miranda laughed. "You sure look good up there."

"Thanks," she said. Her eyes flashed as she sat straight up in her saddle in the morning sun, and I couldn't believe it was the same child I'd been reading about.

Ferris Eddington rode up. "Hello, Douglas."

"Good morning. I need to talk to Miranda, if that's all right."

"Well, I promised her that we would go for a ride this morning," he told me as he swung down off his horse. "Why don't you go for the ride? That way you can talk and I can work." He opened the gate, came out of the pen, and handed me the reins, which I took involuntarily. I looked up at the big buckskin just waiting to move his ears back.

"I'm not sure I can ride this horse," I said. "I didn't know quarter horses came this big."

"Oh, he's no problem," my employer said, patting the horse's neck. "He's just a big fine boy. You be good to Douglas, Zapata. We need him." I reached up and ran my hand across the horse's mane. "I'll bring your coat to the office," Ferris Eddington said. I took off my coat and tie, and I slipped a tasseled loafer into a stirrup that was a long way off the ground.

"If we do this often," Miranda said, "maybe Grandpa will let you use a pair of his boots. He has big feet, too." I liked her. I really liked her, I acknowledged, telling myself that I should remember why she needed a lawyer.

The oversize quarter horse rode so smoothly that when Miranda kicked Belle into a trot and Zapata followed, I could barely feel it, and when we began to gallop, I felt nothing but his easy power. We loped along the feeding pens where the Anguses and the Herefords had their heads shoved through the bars into the troughs, passed down the soft road at the end of a section of cotton that had been plowed under, and then we turned and ran the horses along a field that in a few months would begin to yield alfalfa. I was amazed at how well Miranda rode. She had a lot of her grandfather in her. When we slowed to a walk, I felt more comfortable, but only because I'd been a little nervous that Ferris Eddington might see me riding his horse that hard. The day was warm, and it felt good to be outside as I pulled up and rode in step beside Miranda. "Is your mother around today?" I asked.

"No," she said, looking at me and smiling. "She left right after her trial. She needed to get away."

For a moment I wondered how Ferris Eddington had gotten Rita's signature on that consent form if she had left town right after the trial. "Do you know where she went?" I asked.

"California, I think. That's what Grandpa said."

"Did you get to see her before she left?"

"No. She really had to get away, after what she'd been through." Miranda smiled as she told me this, and somehow she seemed wise beyond her years, so understanding of Rita's needs, so calm and serene. Once again I reminded myself that I was talking to a child who needed a lawyer, and I flashed back to what I'd read in those records. And it all seemed strange—the smile, the bright eyes, the understanding. She acted as if nothing had happened.

"It wouldn't have done much good for her to come and see me. Not in the condition I was in."

Suddenly I wanted to ask her what it had felt like to be in that condition. I thought better of it, though, sensing that it would be wiser to leave those matters to the experts. I did ask her how she felt. "Wonderful," she said. "Free. I don't like hospitals anymore. I like it here on the ranch."

Then she began to canter her horse one more time, and the single braid of her hair swung from side to side across her back, reminding me of Jane Bartholomew, the girl I'd met in Utah. We came to a barbed-wire fence that was gated across the road. Miranda kicked hard, and Belle broke into a full run. Suddenly horse and rider were above the wire of the gate. I gasped. Belle landed gracefully on the other side, and Miranda stopped and gently turned her around. She watched as I reined Zapata, dismounted, and opened the gate.

"Are you sure you should do that?" I asked as I walked the horse through.

"Oh, that's easy," she said. "No problem." She jumped two irrigation ditches before we finally stopped near an old grove of tamarack trees.

"Miranda, I need to go over with you exactly what happened the day your father died."

"You mean the day my mother shot him, don't you?"

"Yes, that day," I said. "Can you describe it all?"

Then, for the first time, she told me her version of the story I'd heard come from her mother's mouth. She confirmed that she and her mother had decided to ride to where her daddy was staying. She told me how her mother said they should practice shooting the pistol. She described how they'd set up the beer bottles.

"Do you remember shooting a bird that morning?" I asked her.

"Yes," she said. "A blackbird. I just shot in the direction." A distant look came into her face. "I didn't mean to hit it. I really didn't. It was an accident."

As we dismounted, she went on, telling me how they had pulled their horses up to the fence by the house, how they had walked into the house, how her daddy was in a bad way because of drinking whiskey.

"What happened then, Miranda, when you got into the house?"

"Mama said, 'I'll make some coffee,' and she went into the kitchen and started making coffee. Then she came back."

"Then what happened?"

"They were talking."

"Do you remember what they were saying?"

"Mama was trying to tell him how we were going on a trip."

"Yes?"

"Then Daddy said something to her, real loud, and she stopped talking."

"Then what happened?" I asked.

"He said it again." I looked at our young, beautiful client, waiting. "And Mama reached in her purse, and she pulled out the gun, and she shot him." I kept staring. "Then Juan came," she said. "And then they took us to the jail. And that's when I went like I was on the night when you came to see me."

"Do you remember what it was that he said to her?"

"I didn't understand it."

"But do you remember what it was?"

"I think so."

"What was it, Miranda?"

"He said, 'Rita, are you some kind of goddamned lesbo?' And Mama turned around. I don't think she was sure what he'd yelled at her. She said, 'What?' Then he said the *f* word. You know what I mean?" I said I knew. "You know? With 'ing' on the end?" I said I knew. "He said, 'Are you some kind of a *f*-wording lesbian?' And that's when she pulled out the gun and shot him."

The two horses moved dust around under the tamarack trees, and I stared out across two sections of pasture.

"Doug?"

I turned back to her.

"What's a lesbian?"

I tried to look perplexed and said, "I guess I'd better check it out."

That seemed to satisfy her. She stood there holding the reins as if nothing had happened. She was as bright and free and happy as she had been before she started to tell me the story.

Belle nuzzled her, and Miranda put her arms around the

horse's neck and squeezed it. "Have you ever seen anything this beautiful?" she asked.

"Miranda, do you remember your mother picking up the telephone that morning?"

She looked at me curiously, then said, "No, she didn't pick up the telephone. Why would she?"

"Are you sure of that?"

She thought a moment and said, "I'm sure." Then I asked her one more time, and she said, "I'm sure for sure. I would have seen it if she picked up the phone."

42 AT SIX O'CLOCK the following morning I turned on my television set only to see the news that the grand jury had indicted Miranda Eddington for first-degree murder. Maximilian Hauser, it was announced, would represent the State of Arizona, and he had filed a petition with the juvenile court asking that it waive its jurisdiction over the child. As the announcer outlined what had happened in Rita's case, the screen showed footage of the house where Travis Eddington had died, of the courthouse, and of Morgan and Rita and Juan Menchaka and me descending the steps, victorious. They must have surreptitiously sent a cameraman to the ranch, for there were even a few seconds of Miranda sitting on Belle. The mellow voice reported that the new charge came after Rita Eddington's defense team had proved that the daughter, not the mother, had committed the homicide. I choked when I heard it.

Morgan called me to his office late that afternoon. He wanted to know what Miranda had told me. As the daylight went down, I told him about my horseback ride. "So what do you think about it?" he asked, reaching for a can of beer.

"I don't know. She seems very sincere, very believable, but it bothers me that she's so sure that Rita never picked up the phone."

"Yeah?" he said. "Well, it bothers me, too. A lot. She can't be telling what happened. It's too damned clear that Rita did pick up that phone."

"So you think Miranda is lying," I said, unexpectedly defensive.

"I don't know that I'd call it lying. She may believe it. Hell, she's crazy. Maybe she hallucinated the story she told you."

"Dan?"

"Yeah?"

"You remember that woman named Pauline Adair who stopped to talk to you at the Arizona Club?"

"Yes."

"She's an old friend of yours, isn't she?"

"Yes."

"Is she gay?"

He sighed. "Queer as a three-dollar bill."

"When she said she knew Rita and that you should be careful with her, she was saying that Rita was gay, too. Wasn't she?"

"Probably. But that's bullshit."

"What makes you say that?"

"Trust me. It's bullshit."

"Well, Travis must have gotten wind of the possibility that Rita was a lesbian. Miranda doesn't even know what the word means. She couldn't have hallucinated that."

"The hell she doesn't know what that word means. The kids she's known in the places they've had her? You don't think they talk about that kind of stuff? Christ, the kids she's been exposed to are worse than I was when I was that age."

"She sure doesn't want to go back into a hospital. She says she doesn't like them anymore. She likes being free."

"Well, she'd better be prepared to go back into a hospital. Otherwise she's going to wind up in superior court. And if that happens, she'd better get prepared to go to prison. And let me tell you, Doug, they talk a lot about the possibility of being a lesbian down there."

"Are you sure they can convict her?" I recalled how

Morgan had been before, when we'd only first heard of Rita's case. I remembered him sitting on the patio at the San Marcos golf course, looking up at the eaves of the clubhouse. I could almost see his mind turn as he began to think that maybe they couldn't prove it. And then I thought about how, late that night, as we sat in the Arizona Club, he talked about how maybe, just maybe, if we could get Rita to trial before Miranda came out of the stupor, Max Hauser wouldn't have enough evidence to convict her. I remembered how he'd schemed and how his eyes had sparked electricity. I remembered how much fun it had been. No, not fun. More than that. And I wanted it back. Maybe, just maybe, if we could talk about it, scheme a little, work it out, maybe we could save Miranda. *And what if we can get her off? What if, in the end, we can get them both off? How will that play on the six o'clock news?* When I asked him if he was sure they could convict Miranda, I hoped that he would talk the way he had before, and I hoped his eyes would flash and that he would narrow them down like a fox and say, *"Well, Doug, it looks like we've got ourselves a murder case and we'd better get something to eat, because we're going to be losing a few pounds before this one's over."*

Morgan didn't say it, though. And his eyes did not flash. He just stared at me. "They know where Joanna Barnes is," he said. "We taught that fat bastard how to make his case." Then he stood up. "I've got to go. Tell Josephine I'll be at Pauline's office."

When I gave that news to our secretary, I asked if she knew why he was meeting Pauline Adair. "She's representing him in his divorce," Josephine answered.

———————————

I went back to my office and reread the *Law Review* comment about the waiver of juvenile court jurisdiction. Then I went into the library and read the cases that had been cited in the comment and some other cases I found on my own. When I was finished, I was convinced that the only way we could keep Miranda Eddington from being tried as an adult in superior court was to prove she was so mentally ill as to be committable to the state hospital. We could take our choice: the risk of state prison against the certainty of what Walter Smith had called the "snake pit." I dictated a short memorandum setting forth my conclusion and my reasons, and when Josephine typed it up, I left it on Morgan's desk.

43 MORGAN STUCK HIS head through my
door and said, "How about coming down to
my office?"

I followed. I could smell the cigar before we got there.

"You remember Doug McKenzie, Gideon."

Dr. Epstein put down a cup of coffee and stood up, extending his free hand. "Sure. From Rita's trial."

"It's good to see you, Doctor."

"You're to be congratulated on that case."

"Thank you."

He wore a double-breasted charcoal pin-striped suit that looked Italian. He had on Gucci shoes and a hand-painted silk tie. His hair was curly once again, and the cigar had a Cuban band.

"I asked Gideon to fly over to take a look at this case," Morgan said.

"And it appears you have a very interesting situation," said the doctor.

"What we've got, Gideon," said Morgan, "is a question of whether this girl is so mentally ill as to be committable. If she is, they can't get her out of juvenile court. Later we might reach the issue of whether she was insane when she shot him, but for now we just need to know whether we can prove she's committable."

"What's the standard for committing someone under Arizona law?"

Morgan read from the memo I'd left on his desk: " 'The question is whether, because of a psychological disorder, a person is likely to be dangerous to himself or to the person or property of others and is in need of supervision.' "

"That's certainly easier to meet than the typical definition of insanity," the doctor opined.

"Right," said Morgan. "We're still under *M'naghten* in Arizona, which will make things tough if we ever have to prove insanity in superior court."

"Isn't there some minimum-age requirement before you can try a child as an adult?" Epstein asked.

Morgan turned to me. "Not in Arizona," I told them. "In a number of states, there is. I know in New Jersey it's sixteen, and in Minnesota it's over fourteen. And, oh, yeah, in Illinois it's over thirteen."

"You have her charts now?" Epstein asked.

"All of them."

"Why don't you let me see them."

I carried all the records from my office to the conference room and left them there with the doctor. I assumed they would take him the better part of the day, since it had taken me three days to get through them. Then I went to the lawyers' lounge and poured myself a cup of coffee. That was when Tom Gallagher caught me.

"Sit down. I want to talk to you," he said. I sat down, and after he had taken a long noisy slurp from his cup, Gallagher said, "How do you think Dan is doing?"

"Fine," I said. "I guess."

He eyed me suspiciously. "Well. What is it?"

"What is what?" I asked.

"What is it that makes you qualify it with that 'I guess' crap?"

"I don't know," I said. "He just seems down. And he doesn't like this case. I don't think he does, anyway."

"Ann Hastings say anything to you about Katherine's entrance the other night?"

"No. She didn't talk about it."

He put his coffee cup on the table. "Come on, goddamn it, tell me what you know."

"I don't know anything. She didn't say anything. I'm sure it really upset her. She made me take her to a movie when we left, and then she didn't say anything. We sat through the whole movie, and she didn't say a word. And she didn't say much when I took her back to her car. I haven't seen her since."

"Well, it should have upset her. Don't you think?" I sat mute. "It should have just scared the shit out of her," he said. "Did you know Katherine's going to divorce him?"

"I heard he's gotten a lawyer. Does it matter, though?"

Gallagher gave me a sharp look.

"I mean, he'd already moved out of the house quite a while back."

"You ever been divorced?" Gallagher said.

Gideon Epstein popped his head around the door. "I think we can talk about these now, McKenzie."

"You read that stuff already?"

"Yes."

"I can't believe it," I informed him as we walked toward Morgan's office.

"There's a history of a lot of depression," the psychiatrist reported. "I think I could probably testify that suicide is a very real possibility. That would give you evidence that she's a danger to herself."

Morgan nodded.

"Too bad your prosecutor didn't have those records," Epstein continued. "He just might have made something of that depression theory he was trying to develop. Still, I don't believe that a twelve-year-old child is catatonic without a real need to splint an impulse to violence. And I can testify to that for you, Dan. There I would think you have a danger to self or to others." He stopped for a moment to let Morgan consider the things he'd told him. He lit another cigar and blew a smoke ring.

"Can you see her this afternoon?" Morgan asked.

The doctor looked at his watch. "I'm sorry, Dan. I've got a noon flight to San Diego. I have to go on the stand in federal court there at two o'clock." He pulled a leather-bound pocket calendar from inside his suit. "When's your hearing?" he asked.

"Next Thursday at two P.M."

"I can make it," Epstein said as he consulted his calendar. "I can get the early flight, and that would give me a chance to talk to the child before we go to court."

"Good," Morgan said. "Can you testify to a reasonable medical certainty that when she shot him she suffered from a psychological disorder?"

"No question."

It came to me that Gideon Epstein had already committed to deliver what we were paying him for—what Ferris Eddington was paying him for—and this without even having spoken to Miranda. And I knew that he didn't really want to see Miranda, that the only reason he needed to see her was to buttress himself against cross-examination. I said something then that I hadn't planned to say that morning, and somehow I felt a little foolish saying it.

"Miranda says she didn't shoot him."

Morgan glared at me as I tried to plow the ground he so obviously felt we had already been through. It was the doctor, however, who spoke. "Dan tells me that there was a telephone operator who heard the shooting."

"That's right," I said.

"He says the woman is unimpeachable."

"True," I conceded.

"And yet the child is adamant that her mother never picked up the telephone."

"I talked to Miranda again last night," I said. "I called her. She was even firmer about it."

"The mother testified about the phone call, even before you were aware that the telephone operator existed?"

"Yes, that's right," I acknowledged.

"Then how can you suggest that the mother wasn't telling the truth?" Epstein finally asked me.

"I didn't suggest it. I said that's what Miranda says."

"Sounds to me like they have a pretty strong case against the child," Epstein concluded.

"Yep," Morgan said. "And we're the ones who put it together for them."

"Well, maybe Rita won't be here to testify against her," I said. "She's gone. She went to California. Maybe she'll stay away, so they won't be able to get a subpoena served on her."

There. I had spit it out, what I'd been wanting to say all along. It had sounded innocuous enough. But I knew what lay beneath the surface, what it really signified. Rita, the woman Morgan had worked so hard to save, the woman Morgan believed in so much, the woman Morgan had proved innocent (and it was Morgan who proved it, not I, no matter what the newspaper said), that woman, Rita Eddington, was now our enemy. Only Rita Eddington could convict our client. She was the enemy, just as Miranda had been the enemy as we rushed to force a judgment before the child could come to and say what we feared she would say, before she could say the very thing she was saying now. And our best hope, at the time Dan Morgan and Gideon Epstein and I sat in Morgan's office that morning, was that Rita Eddington would just plain get lost. And at that moment, when I said Rita might stay away, I was wishing once again that Morgan would talk about it, that he would say something about the possibility that we could get that child off scot-free, the possibility that we could win. But once again he refused.

"You want to roll the dice, Doug?" he asked. "You want to risk her in superior court just on the possibility they won't get their witness? You want to take the chance of putting her in that women's prison?"

"Do you really think they would do that to her?"

"Weren't you with me down in Florence, goddamn it? Didn't you see what they did to that man? There's nothing they won't do. There are judges over there who would put her in that same gas chamber, then go to church and talk about it. You want to take that kind of chance?"

I didn't answer. I stared out the window toward Camelback Mountain. It was a while before I realized that Morgan and Gideon Epstein had gone.

44   IN 1964 AN Arizona juvenile court judge sent a fifteen-year-old boy to the Arizona Industrial School for the period of his minority for making an obscene telephone call, and the Arizona Supreme Court affirmed. When the boy's parents and their lawyer got to the United States Supreme Court, in a case now called *In re Gault,* a majority of five reversed. According to the Court, certain requirements of procedural due process had not been met. Notably, none of the justices questioned the juvenile court's decision to incarcerate a boy for that many years for one dirty phone call.

As I sat in the library reading *Gault,* I wondered what an Arizona juvenile judge would do to a twelve-year-old girl who had unloaded a revolver into her father. Not a pleasant matter to ponder on a Monday morning. Well, I wasn't reading *Gault* to see what kind of punishment Miranda might look forward to, anyway. I was looking to see what kind of protection she might expect, if left to the vagaries of the juvenile system.

Mr. Justice Fortas, writing for the majority, said a juvenile had a right to a lawyer. Miranda already had two of those. He said the juvenile was entitled to notice of the charges and could not be made to incriminate herself. That seemed to add nothing to what Miranda already enjoyed. Finally, said Justice Fortas, absent a valid confession, a juvenile court could not make a finding of delinquency unless it had heard sworn testimony subjected to the opportunity for cross-examination. There it was, what I had been looking for.

We might be able to keep Miranda in juvenile court and still require Max Hauser to produce Rita to give live testimony. And Rita would not want to see Miranda convicted. After all, she was her mother. If Rita would simply stay away, we would win. And even if she did show up, it would only be her word against Miranda's. We might still win. Of course, Hauser would no doubt bring Joanna Barnes back to corroborate Rita's testimony. Beyond all that, we might already have committed our young client to an institution from which she would be unlikely ever to return. I muddled along, and none of it added up. I rode the elevator down and walked around the block. I walked over to Tom's Tavern and ate a bowl of beef stew and watched a snooker game in the back room.

Late that afternoon Morgan came to the office, and I caught him behind his desk opening the day's mail.

"What can I do for you?" he said.

"I did some research," I told him.

"Oh?" he said absently.

"I found a case called *In re Gault.*"

"Uh-huh," he mumbled as he read a letter.

"It holds that even in juvenile court the state has to produce live witnesses and subject them to cross-examination."

"That's right." He looked up at me. "I'm familiar with *Gault.*"

"Well," I said, "Hauser'll have to get Rita here. They can't even get a finding of juvenile delinquency without her."

"But," said Morgan, "if we don't concede what happened, that she killed him, and show that she did it because she was mentally ill, they'll try her as an adult."

"Maybe we can just show she's mentally ill, not concede she killed him."

Morgan moved toward the door. "I've got to go."

As he was walking out, Gallagher appeared and asked, "Do you want to get a drink?"

"I can't," Morgan answered. "I'm having dinner with Katherine."

"Oh," Gallagher said.

"Yeah," said Morgan.

45

"HELLO."

"Dr. Hardy?"

"Yes."

"This is Douglas McKenzie. I'm one of the lawyers—"

"I know who you are."

"I was wondering if I might come and talk to you."

"Anytime."

Miranda Eddington said she had not killed her father. I believed her. I'd believed her when she first said it in her hospital room, and I still did. I didn't know why, given what she'd said about Rita's not making the telephone call Joanna Barnes had heard. But I did believe her, and I sickened with the thought of conceding that Miranda had done what Morgan was preparing to concede she had. So I'd reached for the telephone and dialed Camelback Hospital and asked for the doctor.

When I arrived at the hospital, Dr. Hardy got us both a cup of coffee and said, "Let's go out on the patio; it's too nice a day to be inside." We sat at a table near the volleyball net. I could see the mountain and the blue sky above it. The doctor's tweed jacket and bow tie made him look like a college professor. "All right, shoot," he said. "What is it?"

"May I ask you a question?" I said.

"Of course."

"Do you think Miranda Eddington killed her father?"

"No."

I shrank inside. "Why not?" I asked.

"Because she told me she didn't shoot him, and I believe her."

"But why do you believe her?"

"Because I believe she is an absolutely honest person. Why don't you believe her?"

"I didn't say I don't believe her."

"Well, you're here."

"Her mother said Miranda shot him?"

"Do you believe that?"

"I'm having profound doubts."

"Her mother had a very good reason to lie."

"I know," I acknowledged.

"Her mother wasn't a very good mother."

"I know," I said. "I read the records." Dr. Hardy sipped his coffee and watched me. "I heard once," I told him, "that her mother might have been homosexual."

"Well, I wouldn't know about that," the doctor said.

"Rita Eddington called for the police the morning of the shooting, and a telephone operator heard the shots. She corroborated Rita's testimony in spades."

"I know," Dr. Hardy said. "I read all about it in the paper."

"Miranda is adamant that her mother never picked up the telephone."

"Any reason to think the telephone operator lied?"

"No chance," I said. I explained how I'd gone to San Francisco to find her, right before the last day of trial. "She didn't even know about the trial until I told her about it. She had absolutely no reason to lie."

"So," said the doctor, "if Miranda is telling the truth, if Rita really killed him, she had to have made the call to create some kind of an alibi."

"We've talked about that possibility."

"And Rita would have been holding the gun on her husband when she made the call."

"Yes."

"Or holding it on Miranda."

"Yes," I said. "I guess that's possible."

"A pretty terrifying event for a little girl either way," the doctor suggested.

"No doubt about it," I said.

"Miranda could be blocking," said the doctor. "Or she could have just been so damned scared she didn't perceive exactly what her mother was doing."

"Ah." I sighed. "That could explain it."

"You say you read the girl's records," said the doctor. "Did you see anything in them suggesting a reason to kill her father?"

"No."

"She loved him."

"Why did she become catatonic?"

"I don't know. She had a long history of depression, all capped by watching her mother kill her father. I imagine that was the cause, but I don't know for sure. I know catatonia is said to be a form of schizophrenia, but I don't think it can be categorized that neatly. I believe it falls within a number of forms of mental illness, including the mood disorders."

"Can I tell you something, Doctor?"

"Surely."

"We had an expert, a psychiatrist named Epstein."

"Oh, yes. I'm acquainted with Gideon Epstein." Dr. Hardy chuckled sardonically.

"You sound like you don't think much of him."

"Go ahead. He was your expert. What's your point?"

"We were barred from obtaining Miranda's medical records."

"Yes. I know. I was at the hearing."

"Dr. Epstein was very concerned whether the prosecution had evidence of chronic depression. He gave an opinion that the recognition of violence in herself caused Miranda's stupor. A history of depression would have undermined his opinion. Since the prosecution had never seen the charts, Dr. Epstein was able to make it look like there was no record of depression. He really ran over the prosecutor on cross-examination."

"Well, Gideon's a professional witness. I shudder to think how much he was charging for that opinion. All I can tell you is that she did have a long history of depression, and it's my opinion that most probably the depression resulted in the stupor."

"So you were never worried that she might wake up and become violent?"

"No. We didn't even station a nurse in her room, either during the day or at night."

"She seems so happy now."

"She's high," the doctor said. "That's the other side of the depression. She's a manic-depressive. Do you know what that means?"

"Vaguely."

"She's being medicated, but she's still up, and it's being pushed by that horse her grandfather bought her. She'll swing back the other way." My face dropped. "It's treatable," Dr. Hardy said.

"What if she were committed to the state hospital? What would you think of that?"

"I think that would be one of the worst things that could happen to her. She doesn't need that kind of treatment. She can be taken care of at home, where she may just grow up to have a decent life. She has a nurse there at the ranch. You know that, don't you?"

"No. I didn't know that."

"It's not as if we just kicked her out of here. She's lucky. Her grandfather can afford quality treatment."

"If she's tried and convicted, she could go to prison."

"I can't help you there."

"Could she stand going through a trial?"

"Probably. With medication."

46

WHEN I LEFT THE HOSPITAL, I drove to the ranch. I found Ferris Eddington in his office talking to a fertilizer salesman. I asked if he knew where Miranda was, and he told me that she was in the far barn with a blacksmith. At the barn, Miranda was watching a small, wiry man, a farrier, who had one of her mare's forelegs tucked onto his thigh and was running a file across the bottom of the horse's hoof.

"Hi, Doug."

"How are you doing, Miranda?"

"Great," said the young client. "But we can't ride today." She pointed toward her horse's hoof.

"That's okay," I told her. "I just wanted to talk to you a little."

I asked her to walk with me, and we strolled to the corral near the office, where a mare was hovering over a young colt. "Those are Thoroughbreds," Miranda said. "Grandpa is going to race the colt. He says that it's got blood."

"Miranda, I have to ask you something."

"Okay."

I stammered, and the child looked at me curiously. "Go ahead. Ask."

"Miranda, do you know what men and women do in order to have babies?" I felt my face bloom scarlet.

"Sexual intercourse," she replied, unfazed.

"Yes."

"Yes. I know," she assured me.

"They touch each other."

"And take off their clothes," she added brightly.

"Yes," I said.

"Yes, I know about all that stuff."

I watched the colt try to get its mouth up under its mother's flank, then watched it gambol around the corral.

"Miranda . . ."

She cocked her head to one side and opened her eyes wider, and I noticed again that they were the same color as her mother's. "What is it, Doug?"

"Miranda, did your daddy ever try anything like that with you?"

Her mouth stretched wide, as if she'd tasted something bitter. "Of course not," she said without a pause. "Fathers don't do that." She turned abruptly and watched the colt. "Duane Perkins tried it."

"What?" I said.

"Duane wanted to take our clothes off and look at each other."

"Who's Duane?"

"Legrand Perkins's boy."

"How old is Duane?"

"My age."

"What did you tell him?"

"I said no. I told him that Methodist children don't do that. Mormons might. But Methodists do not."

I drove back to the Luhrs Building.

47 I WALKED INTO Morgan's office and just started talking. "Dr. Hardy says he believes Miranda when she says Rita killed Travis."

"Well, Dr. Hardy didn't sit through Rita's trial, did he?" Morgan continued balancing his checkbook without looking up.

"No, but he says that—"

The telephone rang. Morgan picked it up and looked at me coldly. "Hello. . . . Yes, Pauline." He put his hand over the receiver. "This is going to take some time," he whispered to me. "I'll come by when I'm through." I spent the rest of the day reading cases and waiting for Morgan. He never came.

The next morning I cornered him in the lawyers' lounge. "I went out and talked to Miranda again," I told him. He opened the top of the coffeemaker and pulled out a used filter.

"She says Travis never tried anything with her. Sexually, I mean."

He pushed past me, dripping coffee along the floor until he reached the garbage can. "Children never admit to those things," he said. He left without making a fresh pot, and I stood silent, certain that I'd chased him away.

After that the hours ticked by, and I waited for the moment when Gideon Epstein would return to tell us all that our beautiful young client should be locked up with a bunch of crazies. There came a time during one of those ticking hours when I lowered my head to my desk and whispered into the mahogany, *"She's innocent, and we're going to have destroyed her."*

I straightened up and walked to Morgan's office. Empty. I went to Tom Gallagher's.

"He's in trial—in Yuma," his secretary answered.

I moved toward Walter Smith's office, then turned back. I thought about it for a long time before I picked up the telephone. At least I tried to think about it. I drank a cup of coffee and gazed out the window until four airplanes had taken off and three had landed. I watched the cars below in the street. I walked around the office. In the end I watched one hand reach for the telephone and the other dial it. Then I listened to myself say, "Mrs. Menendez, this is Douglas McKenzie. I was wondering if I might come out and speak with your husband."

He didn't look much worse than he had the last time I'd seen him. He lay in his chair in the library with his long, thin legs stretched across the ottoman as they had been that first night, when I'd gone to his house with Morgan and Ann. He was smoking one of his big cigars. His eyes were still alive, and he was still quick to offer me a drink and a cigar. "Danny never came to see me," he said.

"I told him to. I told him more than once, but he was awfully busy."

"I was glad to see you won the case."

"Did you know that we represent the girl now, Rita's daughter?"

"I heard that, yes. Interesting situation, isn't it?" I was relieved that he didn't ask me about the propriety of getting into that situation.

"That's what I wanted to talk to you about," I said.

"Yes. I figured you came for more than a cigar." I stared at him in silence, unable to speak. "You've come to tell me something," he said. "So you go ahead and tell me." When

I remained silent, he said, "Are you going to tell me, or are we just going to sit here and listen to the music?"

"Will you promise never to tell Dan Morgan I came here?"

"I won't tell Danny you came. Now, you go ahead."

I told him everything. I started by describing what had happened at the trial, everything that Rita had said, and what Gideon Epstein had testified about. I told him about how I'd found Joanna Barnes. I even told him about the Mexican girl, Rosana Treviso.

"I know all that," he informed me. "I read it in the papers."

I told him what Miranda had said. And what Dr. Hardy had said. And what Miranda's records said and what they didn't say. Then I got to the reason I was there. "Dan won't even talk about it. I'm worried that he and that Gideon Epstein are just going to get her shoved in the state hospital, because Dan's afraid to have her tried for murder. And Epstein hasn't even talked to her. He refused to take the time. He already has his mind made up to do what he's being paid for."

When I finished pouring it out, Frank Menendez struggled to get the small shot glass of tequila to his mouth, and after he smelled it and wet his lips, he warmed and lit a new cigar. He smoked and thought, and in the quiet I felt a great relief. I felt cleaned out, almost light-headed. I drank the hot liquor, and I smoked the cigar, and I relaxed into his deep leather chair. There was a little guilt for having sneaked around behind Dan Morgan's back, but it was nothing compared with the relief.

"What your little girl says doesn't square with what your lady from San Francisco says," Frank Menendez observed.

"That's right. Dr. Hardy says Miranda may be doing what he calls blocking, or maybe she was so scared she didn't see Rita make the telephone call."

"You believe that, do you?" It was not a question. It was a challenge, and he made it in the voice he used when he'd asked Morgan if he really believed that the child had shot her father. My heart sank with the recognition that he, too, had concluded that Miranda was lying.

"I don't know," I said. "I don't know anything about psychiatry."

"I don't believe it," Frank Menendez said. "I don't believe that the girl would miss or forget that kind of a phone call, not if she remembers everything else that happened."

I felt something inside me go soft. "She's probably lying to me," I said.

"You don't really believe that, though, do you?"

"No," I said, "not really."

"And that's the reason you're here." I nodded. "The Barnes woman, the one you found in San Francisco, did I read that she'd been an architect at Taliesin?"

"Yes."

"Ever check that out?"

I looked up at him. "No," I said. "No. We never did."

"Did you check up on her at all?"

"No. Maybe we should have."

"Well, you were sort of on the wrong side of the case to want to do that, weren't you?"

"It all happened so fast."

"Right," he said. Then he looked around the room until he fixed on the telephone book.

"Would you mind getting that directory?" I did it. "Look up the number of Wesley Peters." I turned the pages.

"Would you dial it for me?" I dialed the number and cradled the receiver on his shoulder in a way that he could hold it. Then I sat down. "Wesley? Frank Menendez. How are you? . . . Ah hell, I'm doing fine. . . . No, no, I'm in the pink. It's amazing what they can do with medicine these days." He struggled to raise his glass in the fashion of a toast, and he winked at me. "Listen, Wesley, the reason I'm calling is to ask whether you ever had a woman named Jo-anna Barnes at Taliesin. . . . Yes, that's right, she did come to testify."

After that, Frank Menendez listened, occasionally saying "Yes" or "I see" or "That's interesting." Once he said,

"Do you know why she left in such a hurry?" Then he said, "Really?"

When he said good-bye, I jumped up and took the receiver from him. Then I sat down and waited.

"There's talk that your Miss Barnes was chased out of town by a jealous husband," he reported.

It took me a few seconds to figure out what he'd told me. "Oh, God," I said.

"What did you tell me Pauline Adair said about Rita Eddington?" Frank Menendez asked.

48 TWELVE HOURS LATER I stood in the rain on Vallejo Street in front of the apartment where, less than a month before, I had picked up Joanna Barnes to take her to the airport. My return to San Francisco hadn't been an exact repeat of my other trip. For one thing, I didn't have a monster hangover, even if I had downed more than one tequila after Frank Menendez told me what his old buddy had said about my star witness. And before that second trip, I had time to take a shower and pack a bag. But the way I'd been told to go was no less forceful than before. "You get the first plane you can to San Francisco," Frank Menendez had ordered, "and you find that woman, and you confront her, and you have a good witness with you who can watch exactly how she reacts."

"I don't know about this," I had said. "I don't know what Dan will think."

"I don't give a damn what Danny thinks. I'm still the senior partner in this firm. And I'm telling you to get your ass up there."

As I stood in the morning drizzle in front of Joanna Barnes's apartment, I had beside me a man named Blaine Larsen, a private investigator whose name Frank Menendez had given me. Somehow, since it was San Francisco, I had expected him to speak like Sam Spade and look like

Humphrey Bogart and drink at John's Grill. As it turned
out, he was a Mormon from Panguitch, Utah, who had
spent twenty years with the FBI and had seven children. He
didn't even have a trench coat, so his polyester suit was getting soaked through. We stared through the rain at the For
Rent sign in the window, and then we walked up three steps
and looked through the window at the gleaming floors that
were bare of furniture.

"Seems like she up and left," Blaine Larsen said.

"Ah, shit."

A Chinese woman trudged up the hill toward Jones
Street, using a newspaper to shield her head from the rain.
"You ever see the woman who lived here?" I shouted. The
Chinese woman walked on.

Blaine Larsen and I spent the next hour knocking fruit-
lessly on doors throughout the neighborhood. None of
the neighbors, most of whom were Chinese, knew her. A
couple of people remembered seeing a nice-looking young
woman come and go from the apartment, but no one saw
her move out. Eventually we stopped at the corner of Jones
and Green streets. I stared down the hill to the bay. Alca-
traz was barely visible through the rain.

"Maybe," Blaine Larsen offered, "we can get a lead
through the landlord. I took his number from the For Rent
sign." We found a telephone and called the number. No
luck. Joanna Barnes had simply abandoned the apartment
without returning the keys. She didn't even ask for her de-
posit back. We couldn't look for a bank account, since she'd
always paid her rent in cash.

We drove up to Duncan Street. When I knocked on Jerry
Barnes's door, Clarence opened it. He didn't recognize me
at first. I reminded him about Perry Mason. "Ah, yes," he
said, "the sartorial tour de force." The words were his, but
not the manner. All the cockiness and the elegance were
gone. "Come in," he said. Shoulders down, he turned and
led us into the house.

"I need to find Joanna Barnes," I said. "I wondered if I
might speak to her brother."

"He isn't here anymore."

"Can you tell me where he is?"

Clarence started to cry. "If I knew that, I'd go get him."

"How long has he been gone?"

"I don't know. I came back from New York a couple of weeks ago, and he wasn't here. All his things were gone." He looked at me pleadingly. "I can't find him," he whimpered.

"I'm sorry," I said.

"Do you have any idea where his sister might be?" Blaine Larsen asked.

"The last time I saw Jerry, he told me that Joanna had gotten a job on a big construction project overseas. I think it may have been in Saudi Arabia. Or was it Singapore? I can't remember."

At the airport I thanked Blaine Larsen for driving me around the city.

"I'll do the best I can to find them," he told me.

"It's important," I said. "It's really important. Especially Rita Eddington. She's got red hair—strawberry blond—and she's got turquoise eyes. And she's damned good-looking. I want to know if she's keeping company with Joanna Barnes."

I flew back to Phoenix, and I called Frank Menendez to make my report. I told him about our lack of success in finding either Joanna Barnes or her brother, and I told him that Blaine Larsen was after them. I also told him the one other thing I'd discovered. "I called the Skidmore firm. That's the big architecture firm she told me she'd gone to work for. Their personnel manager said he's never heard of her." When I hung up, I fell asleep exhausted.

49

THE RINGING TELEPHONE jerked me awake. I rolled over and searched for the clock—6:45 A.M. I groped for the receiver. "Hello."

"Get me the police; I need the police," came a thin whisper.

"What the hell!"

"Miranda, Miranda, don't, don't!"

Am I still asleep? Am I dreaming some strange, terrible dream? On the telephone I heard a bang, then another, then more, until there'd been six. I began to shake.

"Now, what did that sound like?" the thin voice demanded.

"Who the hell is this?"

"It's Menendez. Now tell me what that sounded like."

"Oh, hell." I exhaled, the world coming back into focus. "It sounded like a bang. It sounded like a car backfiring."

Sue Menendez was trembling as she opened the door. "I think it's finally gotten to his brain," she said as I followed her to the library. A light dusting of feathers covered the carpet, and I could see the back of the sofa where the stuffing had been blown out. A .38 revolver lay on the table by his chair. "When he made me get that gun," Sue Menendez whispered, "I thought he was going to end it."

"All right, Douglas, who fired the gun, Sue or me? We were the only ones in the room."

"I don't know," I said. "Should I know?" I actually suspected that Sue pulled the trigger, since he looked too weak to lift the gun, but I knew he wasn't after the well-reasoned law-school answer.

"And, if you were called as a witness to testify about what you heard, would you be willing to suggest how far the gun was from the telephone on account of what you heard?"

"No," I answered.

"Joanna Barnes was willing to do that." I saw beside the revolver a court reporter's transcript. He must have ordered Joanna Barnes's testimony. He'd read it to me over the phone. That was why it was so exact, so spooky.

"Yes," I said. "Yes. I remember that. It was on cross-examination."

"That's right. I'll read it to you." He picked up the transcript. "Mr. Hauser said, 'Miss Barnes, from what you heard, you could not tell how far from the telephone the thing that caused the noise you testified about was, could you?' She answered, 'Well, if it was a gun, it must have been a fair distance from the phone, or I probably would have heard it more clearly.'" Frank Menendez looked up from the transcript. "She really helped your case, Douglas."

"I know," I assured him. "She put the gun in Miranda's hands."

"That's right, she took advantage of the big, soft lob your Mr. Hauser tossed her. She knocked it out of the courthouse."

"He's not my Mr. Hauser," I said.

"Why did your Miss Barnes say that, Douglas? If she was just an independent witness, just a woman who hadn't thought enough of the call to report it to her superiors at the telephone company, let alone the police. How the hell does she come off, a month later, remembering this call well enough to bless the jury with her opinion that the sound was so muted that it must have been made some distance from the telephone? You say you couldn't testify to something like that. How the hell can she? Why would she take that kind of a shot at the prosecution?"

"I don't know," I said. "Maybe she had just sided up with us. I think she liked us." I thought about how Juan Menchaka had strained to help us just a little.

"Maybe," Frank Menendez allowed. "It happens." He worked himself into a more comfortable position. The exertion caused him to breathe harder. "But what she said was right on point. She had thought about it. And it was completely gratuitous."

"God," I said, "I still don't think she could have been in complicity with Rita."

"Why not?" he demanded, working to adjust his robe.

"She didn't even know about the trial."

"Didn't she?" he asked, placing his tongue in his cheek.

"No. I surprised her in San Francisco. If she were going to lie for Rita, she'd have let us know about herself earlier."

"Would she?" he asked, this time raising his eyebrows.

"Well, yes. Otherwise how were we going to find her?"

"Let me ask you this," Frank Menendez said. "Why didn't Danny find that woman earlier? Why didn't he have you check out Rita's story?"

"We didn't know it could be checked out. We didn't know about the telephone-company log."

"You say 'we,' Douglas," he observed. "Did you, yourself, know what Rita was going to say about that telephone call, before you heard it from the witness stand?"

"No. Dan never told me about it."

"Did Dan know about it?"

"I assumed he did. He was the one who talked to Rita. He prepared her to testify. He was at the jail with her every day, but he never let me go with him."

"He what?"

"He never let me go with him to interview Rita."

Frank Menendez very slowly lit a cigar, thinking, analyzing what I'd told him. He lay back in his chair and watched the smoke climb toward the ceiling. "Why didn't he have you sit in with him, as he prepared her?"

"I don't know. He just never let me go. I guess he thought my time was better spent in the library."

Frank Menendez gave me a very suspicious look, and I thought he was going to pursue the subject, but then he just struggled for a drink and thought some more about what I'd told him.

"If he knew about the call," he finally asked, "why the hell didn't he follow it up?"

"Maybe he just didn't think."

"People do not just fail to think," he lectured me. "Haven't you learned that yet? Isn't that what Dr. Freud teaches us? That you don't just forget things?"

"Something like that," I conceded. "I guess."

"Well, you know this much. Danny Morgan doesn't just forget to think about following up a story like that telephone call." His voice had fallen to a bare whisper, but when I tried to ask if I should let him rest, he wouldn't allow me to speak. "Perhaps," he mused quietly, echoing a thought I had once entertained, "Danny was afraid, unconsciously afraid to follow it up because he knew down deep she was lying, and he knew he would find out she never made the call."

"Or maybe," I interjected, "Rita never told him about the call before she testified, for fear we would find Joanna Barnes and discover things she didn't want us to know about her."

"A definite possibility," my new mentor acknowledged.

"But wait a minute." I realized I was being drawn into the old man's game. It was silly, this intrigue. Sitting in a richly appointed library, talking Sherlock Holmes, speculating about something too wild ever really to have happened. "If Joanna Barnes were going to lie for Rita," I said, "she would have had to come earlier. I didn't bring her back to Phoenix until Sunday afternoon. The trial ended Monday. If it hadn't been for my dragging her down here, she'd have missed the trial."

Frank Menendez pointed to a piece of paper on the

table near his chair. It looked like some kind of a computer printout. He nodded, and I picked it up. "It's from United Airlines," he said. "I have a friend who got it for me." It was a passenger list for a night flight—San Francisco to Phoenix—November 24, the night before I brought Joanna Barnes to Phoenix. I ran my eyes down the list: "BARNES, J." Assuming that was Joanna, if I hadn't gotten her on the phone that Saturday, she would have been on a flight to Phoenix that evening, instead of chatting with me on Polk Street.

"There's a telephone number beside the name," Frank Menendez said. "It's unlisted. You should have our San Francisco investigator check it out to see if that's your Barnes, J."

"There's no need," I said sheepishly. "I kept her number. I thought I might drop in on her again someday." I shook my head and let out an asinine laugh as I pulled out my wallet and compared the numbers. "It matches," I told Frank Menendez.

"Well, well," said the senior partner.

50 ELIAS BUTLER STRODE into Morgan's office. "Danny, Frank called me this afternoon. He said that you aren't returning his calls. He told me to tell you to get your ass over to his house this evening. You're supposed to go, too, McKenzie."

Elias Butler marched away, and Morgan exhaled a waft of smoke and rubbed his eyes. And later I sat in the Menendez library for the second time that day, listening to Bach fill the smoky room.

"You're a hard man to get hold of, Danny," Frank Menendez said.

"Frank, I'm sorry," Morgan said, looking like a scolded boy. "I really am. I was going to come before. I've really been busy."

"Katherine giving you a hard time?"

"Yes."

"I always liked Katherine."

"I know," Morgan said. "So did I."

"Well, since I couldn't get you, I've had Douglas over here a couple of times to tell me about the Eddington matter. Curiosity, you know." I flinched and tried to assess whether he had honored his promise to me. "Douglas tells me you're getting the girl certified committable to keep her from going to trial."

"That's right. I don't think they can get her out of juvenile court."

"They'll hospitalize her if you do that, won't they?"

"They probably will."

"You know how hard it is to get somebody out of a mental hospital when they've been through a commitment proceeding?"

"Yes, I know."

"What if the girl didn't kill him?"

"She did it, Frank." Morgan turned with a sharp look that accused me of playing my broken record to his senior partner.

"But what if she didn't?" Frank Menendez pressed.

"She killed him, Frank."

"But what if she didn't, goddamn it?" He strained, trying to get up to his elbows. "That's what I'm saying, Danny. I'm simply asking you to assume, for the sake of argument, that she didn't do it. And if she didn't, don't you think it inappropriate not to defend her?"

"The girl did it, and she is sick. She's nuts, Frank. And we are defending her. That's what I'm trying to do."

Frank Menendez relit his cigar and asked if I would mind refilling his small glass. After I put the cork back in the bottle, he smelled the liquor. He puffed on the cigar. He rested. "I believe that Rita lied to you, Danny, and to that jury."

"Rita didn't lie to me."

"I believe she did."

Morgan chafed in his chair. He lit another cigarette, and as Sue Menendez happened to walk through the room, he said, "What do you have to do to get another beer around here, Sue?"

She brought him a bottle. "Douglas?" she asked.

"I'm fine," I said.

"She didn't lie to me," Morgan reiterated.

"I think Rita is a lesbian, Danny."

"Bullshit," Morgan said.

"I think Travis finally realized that and called her on it."

Morgan got out of his chair and walked to the corner of the

room, where he leaned against a bookshelf. "That's why she killed him, Danny. Somehow he found her out, and for some reason that made her kill him."

"Come on, Frank." Morgan looked at the ceiling and blew a long contrail of smoke upward. "Come on," he said again.

He stared at me, trying to appear incredulous. But behind the mask, something was churning up. He began to tap his foot, and he moved the hand that held the cigarette to his mouth, but then he just tapped his lip with his thumb. A ring of sweat began to move down beneath his arm.

"I believe that the Barnes girl from San Francisco was Rita's lover, at least part of the time. I believe that is why she lied about the telephone call."

"What is this crap?" Morgan's gaze went all over the room. "What is this crap, Frank?" He turned to look up to the ceiling again. He took another drink of beer, and he jerked his eyes toward me. "What is this horseshit?"

I didn't speak. I didn't have to. He knew by my sober silence that I subscribed to what he'd just been told, and he also knew that I'd gone behind his back.

"Let me ask you this, Danny. Why didn't you check out that telephone-call story before you let her testify about it?"

Morgan blanched. This time he really looked like he'd been caught at something. And he did not answer.

"That was unlike you, Danny. Come on, tell me why you didn't follow it up."

"I didn't know about it, Frank. Not until she testified about it in court." The guilty look in his eyes seemed to beg my forgiveness as well as Frank Menendez's.

Frank Menendez struggled to take another sip of tequila. He took a little lime and salt with it. "When's the last time your own client truly surprised you from the witness stand?" he asked, wincing from the drink. Morgan didn't answer. "I make it about twenty years," Frank Menendez said. "So why did she hide that telephone business from you, Danny? I know it wasn't because you neglected to demand she tell you everything. Why'd she do that, goddamn it? You've been brooding about it for weeks now. Why did she do it?" Morgan had turned to stare at the ceiling again. "If she'd have told you about it, you'd have gone to the telephone company and checked for the call, wouldn't you?"

"Yes."

"And you'd have hired somebody to check Joanna Barnes out, wouldn't you?"

"Yes."

"What do you know about Miss Barnes?"

"Nothing. Ah, shit. She's an architect who worked part-time for the telephone company. That's all."

"Well, I know this," advised Frank Menendez. "She's a lesbian. She lied about working for that big-shot architecture firm in San Francisco. And she's recently hauled her ass out of her apartment without notice. And I know this, also, Danny. She was on her way to Phoenix when Douglas intercepted her and saved her paying her own airfare down." Morgan turned to me in shock. I nodded in affirmation of what he'd heard. "Now tell me, Danny," Frank Menendez said, "why didn't Rita Eddington tell you about that telephone call?"

Morgan stared at his mentor, wild-eyed. "That goddamned bitch!" The words erupted from somewhere deep inside him. Then his eyes went calm, suggesting he'd returned to his senses. "This is all absurd," he said. "This is crazy. I'm not going to listen to this silly shit, Frank. I've got more important things to do." Morgan walked out of the library and out of the house, and I heard his car start up and pull away, leaving me without a ride home.

As his wife was handing me the keys to his car, Frank Menendez ordered, "You get him to come back and talk to me."

I cornered Morgan in his office the next morning, and I talked to him without asking if I could. I talked so fast that he couldn't stop me. I confessed everything, even the trip to San Francisco. I told him how bad I'd been feeling about doing things behind his back. I told him that I would understand if he didn't want me working for him anymore. And finally I told him that he was supposed to go back and see Frank Menendez. Then I sat and watched him stare out the window without speaking for a full five minutes, and I began to think he'd slipped into a coma. Finally a secretary stuck her head into the office. "Mrs. Morgan is on the phone, Dan. She says she needs to talk to you." He blinked and looked up at her, his face blank. The secretary shifted uncomfortably in the doorway. "What do you want me to tell her, Dan?"

"Tell her to go fuck herself." He turned to me. "Let's go see him," he said. In the car Morgan said sadly, "You did the right thing." He stared silently at the road for the rest of the drive.

―――――――――――

"What are you going to do?" Frank Menendez asked in the sunny room off the kitchen.

"I don't know," Morgan answered.

"I know what I'd do," Frank Menendez said. "I'd waive her out of juvenile court and let the sonsabitches try to prove it."

"We'll look like hell."

"Why?"

"Because we already proved she's guilty."

"So what? Is it written somewhere that lawyers aren't supposed to argue both sides of an issue? I thought that was what we went to law school to learn to do. Now Mr. Hauser has to prove it. He'll have to produce those women. He won't be allowed to use the record you made. You have any question about that?"

"About what? That he'll have to produce live witnesses?"

"Yes."

"Of course he'll have to produce live witnesses."

"Well, there you go."

Morgan worked at his coffee. "I don't like it," he said.

"Well, I'm not going to sit here and lecture you on the adversary process, but you know for damned sure that little girl is entitled to every bit as good a defense as her mother was."

"I'm afraid of it," Morgan said.

"Why? Because you know those two women are going to be coming at you?"

Morgan took a deep breath. "Even if your theory is right, I'm the one who set it up so they could do it. I'm the one who put that little girl where she is right now. But I don't accept your theory, Frank. The reason she's there is that she killed her father, and the reason she killed him is that she is mentally ill—and because the bastard had it coming. And I don't want her going to prison." He stood up and slowly walked around the room. "I never should have taken this case, Frank. We never should have let Ferris push us into it. We did it without even going to the management committee. I should have come to you."

"That's water under the bridge now. You've got to do right by that child."

"If she's convicted of murder, it's a disaster."

"If she's committed to the state hospital, it's a disaster."

"Not as bad."

"She's innocent. A jury isn't going to convict her."

"You believe that? You really believe a jury isn't going to convict her?"

With awful effort, Frank Menendez leaned forward. "Danny, I believe that the Holy Ghost descends into the jury room and makes the people there do the right thing."

"Then tell me this, Frank. Could that be why Rita Eddington walked out of the courtroom a free woman?"

51

WE WENT OUT to the ranch—Dan Morgan, Jake Asher, and I. We found Miranda in the swimming pool at her grandfather's house. We watched as she pulled her little-girl's body from the pool, shivering in the afternoon chill, and slipped into a terry-cloth robe. Then we all sat down at a table with an umbrella. That was when Morgan explained the choices before us, when he told Miranda that unless we established that she was mentally ill and maybe that she should be in the state hospital, she would likely be put to trial as an adult and could face the possibility of going to prison. And that was when she spoke the words that made us see the light.

"I didn't kill Daddy," she said. "So I don't see why I should have to go to either the prison or the hospital. I just want to stay here."

I looked at Jake Asher, and he looked at me and nodded, and we both knew that the decision had been made. Dan Morgan was not so quick.

"But you don't understand, Miranda," he tried to explain. "If we—"

"I want Doug to decide."

I jerked around from where I'd turned to watch Belle graze at the far end of the lawn. "What?"

"I trust Doug," Miranda said, not taking her gaze from Morgan.

"What?" I said again. "Why do you trust me, Miranda?"

"Because when I was in that room and I couldn't move, you were the only one who came to see me."

I closed my eyes. "Dan went to see you, too," I said.

"I know. I trust him, too."

Morgan didn't close his eyes. He just turned slowly toward the pool.

"But I want you to decide," Miranda said as finally she turned and looked at me.

"I think," I said at last, "we should waive her out of juvenile court and let the sonsabitches try to prove it." Done.

That afternoon Dan Morgan telephoned Gideon Epstein in Los Angeles and told him that we would not be needing his services.

The next morning we drove out to the juvenile court and once again found ourselves in a room buzzing with journalists and television people.

Max Hauser got things started in his naturally aggressive way. "Your Honor, I would note for the record that Mr. Morgan has not filed the required response in opposition to our motion. It makes it very difficult to prepare for—"

"That's right, Your Honor," Morgan interrupted. "We filed no opposition, because we do not oppose the state's motion. We join in the request that this court waive its jurisdiction and that Miss Eddington be tried as an adult." An even greater buzz filled the back of the room, and then came the clatter of newsmen running for telephones.

With what appeared to be mild curiosity, the young judge ran his tongue across his teeth. "May I sign the order lodged by Mr. Hauser, then?"

"We ask that you do, Your Honor," said Morgan. Then Morgan turned to Hauser and spoke so loudly that everyone in the room could hear him. "You goddamned well better not lose this one, too. Right, Max?" The chatter in the room died instantly. "Thank you, Your Honor," Morgan said deferentially as he strode quickly toward the door with me following close behind.

Out in the hall, Morgan slowed his stride, then stopped and turned on me. "Well, you got your way," he said. While I stood off balance searching for something to say to him, he spoke again. "We goddamned well better not lose this one. Right, Doug?"

52 "DOUGLAS," JOSEPHINE SAID, "a girl left this for you." She handed me a document that bore the bold signature of Maximilian Hauser and the title "Notice of Hearing."

"Who the Christ is Eldon Phelps?" Dan Morgan yelled after I slid the paper across his desk.

"I know there was an Eldon Phelps who practiced law in Mesa when I was in high school," I told him. "He was a Mormon bishop."

"That goddamned son of a bitch."

The next thing I knew, Morgan and I were at the other end of the hall across the desk from Walter Smith, who sat in a thick cloud of foul-smelling smoke from his pipe.

"The bastard has managed to use some trumped-up crap about needing immediate approval of the juvenile court's action to get us assigned to some Mormon bishop from Mesa named Eldon Phelps," Morgan reported to the elder trial lawyer.

Walter Smith smiled and played the bit of his pipe across his teeth. "Sounds like he may have taken a page from your book, Daniel."

"I've never even heard of Eldon Phelps," Morgan snapped.

"I knew he'd been appointed," Walter Smith said. "I

haven't appeared before him yet. I don't think he's tried a case since he's been on the bench."

"Well, do you know anything about him?" demanded Morgan.

"Only that he's said to be devoutly religious."

"Oh, Christ, that's all we need." Morgan sighed as he bent over and pulled a cigarette from his sock.

"You can challenge him peremptorily now, you know," said Walter Smith. "All you need do is file a notice of change; you no longer have to file an affidavit of bias and prejudice. You just have to do it before your first appearance in front of him."

"I know," said Morgan. "I know." After that there was much talk about other judges to whom we might be randomly assigned in the event we should kick the novice Eldon Phelps off our case, judges long proven to be dangerous to defendants in criminal cases. Then there were telephone calls to a number of lawyers, none of whom knew anything about the new judge who had no track record.

Later I stood with Morgan in the hallway of the fifth floor of what was then the new courthouse, at a door with a bright new plaque that read JUDGE ELDON PHELPS. Morgan opened the door, and we both went into the small anteroom, where there were two more doors that swung into the courtroom. Morgan cracked one door just enough so that he could see in. Then, when he moved so that I could look, all I could see through the narrow crack was the bright light of the courtroom and a kindly-looking man up on the bench, in a black robe with thin hair brushed straight back and close against his head. I did manage to get the impression that he was being polite to whoever was talking to him from somewhere out of my line of sight.

In the elevator Morgan said, "What the hell can you tell from looking at somebody?" In the street he continued, "It would be malpractice to take a chance of getting some of the guys they've got sitting on that bench, and if we haul off and file a notice on this Phelps, they'll assign somebody else immediately, and it ain't going to be Henry Penrod."

I didn't fully appreciate what he was saying to me that day in the street, but now, with the years behind me, I could name those judges he was so afraid of, those who, as Morgan had once observed, would send a girl to the gas chamber, then talk about it at church. And it was with their specter in the front of Dan Morgan's mind on Jefferson Street that winter morning that it was decided the Honorable Eldon Phelps, whatever he turned out to be, would preside.

Within the hour we sat before the new judge, not as we had with Henry Penrod in old, worn, overstuffed chambers with oil paintings on the walls and novels on the tables but in the bright glare of the open courtroom. And how different was this courtroom from the one in which we had defended Rita Eddington. Gone was the spacious gallery. Missing was the ornate woodwork behind the bench. Absent was the brass trim and the hand-painted beams at the ceiling. And nowhere were there windows. We sat at a table near a jury box in the cramped room, which was covered with a brown veneer intended to pass for mahogany. The trim around the brown veneer was flat black, and the bench was small. The only concession to the decorative was the superior court seal on the wall behind the bench, that and the Arizona state flag. The man in the black robe with his thinning hair pasted backward peered down from the small bench and seemed perplexed. "I'm not sure, Counsel, that I understand our purpose here."

"Your Honor," Max Hauser said as he rose solicitously, "this is a matter of some sensitivity in that it involves charges against a juvenile, and we thought it best, before we began preparation for trial, to have this court approve the juvenile court's waiver of its jurisdiction. Simply as a formality, if Your Honor please."

"What bullshit," Dan Morgan whispered to me under his breath.

"But," said the judge, "from the minutes of the juvenile court, it appears that both sides requested that the defendant be tried in this court. Frankly I don't see the—"

"That's right, goddamn it," Morgan whispered to me. "Hauser's only doing this to get a judge he thinks he'll like.

How can the son of a bitch stand up there with a straight face?"

"Did you say something, Mr. Morgan?" the judge asked.

"No, Your Honor. Only consulting with my co-counsel." The new judge said no more, but his eyes lingered on Morgan, and they were devoid of warmth and full of deep suspicion.

As Max Hauser explained that it was only out of "an abundance of caution" that he sought this small confirmation of what had gone before, Morgan hastily scribbled a note to me: "If Hauser likes this guy so much, maybe we ought to file notice for a change of judge right now, before I let him take jurisdiction. If he signs that order, we're stuck with him."

I raised my hands to show I had no idea of what we should do. I looked up at the bench only to see that the thin-haired man from Mesa was giving us another cold stare. Dan Morgan chewed on the butt of his pencil as Max Hauser continued to try to explain why we were there.

"Perhaps it does make sense," the judge said at last. "Out of an abundance of caution, that is. Do you have any objection to my signing the order Mr. Hauser has prepared, Mr. Morgan?"

Morgan almost bit off the end of the pencil, but finally he said, "No, Your Honor, no objection."

"Perhaps," said Eldon Phelps, after he'd signed the order and thereby fixed himself as the one toward whom we would bow in the coming weeks, "this would be a convenient time to discuss scheduling. Do you intend to present any motions to suppress, Mr. Morgan?"

"Not at this time, Your Honor."

"Then, Your Honor," said Hauser, "I would ask that a trial date be set."

"How much time do you need, Mr. Morgan, to prepare for trial?"

"We are ready now, Your Honor."

I flinched. We needed time, at least so it seemed to me, to find out exactly what had gone on between Rita Eddington and Joanna Barnes.

"My client is of tender years," said Morgan. "This trial is going to be hard on her. She is innocent, and she has a right to a speedy trial in order that her innocence may be established. So I would ask, Your Honor, that you set the matter for trial as soon as possible."

I supposed he did not need to consult with me; as he had pressed to get Rita to trial before Miranda could come alive, now he pressed to get Miranda to trial before Rita could come home. Or, perhaps, before Max Hauser could find her.

"Innocent, Mr. Morgan?" I heard the judge ask. "As I have read the file, I have gotten the impression that you already proved she was guilty." The judge smiled, but it was apparent that he did not think what he'd said was funny. Morgan didn't respond. I could see his jaws tighten as he looked up at the bench, but he did not speak. Beyond where Morgan stood, I could see Max Hauser smile.

"Is three weeks acceptable—January second?" the judge asked after he'd blessed Morgan with a long stare confirming that the new judge from Mesa did not trust the veteran trial lawyer from Phoenix. "We'll arraign Miss Eddington on Monday morning at nine o'clock."

53 IN THE STREET, Morgan stopped short. He bent over and put his hands on his knees. Then he straightened back up and took a deep breath. "Where the hell does that son of a bitch come off prejudging that girl? We should have filed a notice on him. We should have kicked his ass off this case." He walked on, glowering straight ahead as our shadows lengthened on Jefferson Street. Then, in the elevator going up to the office, Morgan's anger seemed to drain away. "We're going to look like hell before this is all over. I don't like this goddamned case."

When we got off the elevator, I heard someone say, "Hello, McKenzie," and when I turned, I saw Pauline Adair standing in the lobby on a glistening pair of patent stiletto heels.

"Hello," I responded. "How's it going?"

Morgan just kept walking. Pauline Adair said, "Danny." He stopped. "I've got to talk to you about this stuff." She walked over and took his arm and said, "We have to sit down and get it all sorted out."

As Pauline spoke, I looked past her across the lobby to where the hallway began. Ann Hastings stood in the shadow, her long arms hanging loosely at her sides. At first I thought she was going to speak to Morgan, but then she just waved at me and gave a halfhearted smile. She turned and hurried down the hallway and out of sight. Morgan and Pauline Adair slowly moved across the lobby. I followed them.

"How much is your capital account in this firm?" Pauline inquired.

"I'm not sure," Morgan answered.

"My God, Danny. We've got to be able to sit down with her and show her these figures. Don't you even keep track of your capital account?"

"It's somewhere around eighty thousand dollars."

"I'll get hold of Paul Butler. He'll know what everybody's got, right to the penny."

"I don't want him involved. I'll figure it out."

"How much is that ugly Ford you're driving worth?"

"I don't know," Morgan said as they turned in to his office and closed the door.

54 TWO DAYS LATER I looked up from my desk to see Morgan putting down a cup of coffee. He slid into a chair and reached for a cigarette, then stared at me until he said, "You really believe she was lying, don't you?"

"Yes," I said without embellishment.

"That's a crock," he said. "You get some smart-ass comment from Wesley Peters that Joanna Barnes is a lesbian, a comment that nobody has followed up, one that's probably based on nothing but nasty gossip. Pauline says Rita's a lesbian. Well, I can tell you that's horseshit. Then you find out that Joanna has moved. From this you and Frank come up with some hideous conspiracy, and you act like you believe it."

"There's also that airplane reservation."

"Yeah," he said, "something a computer burped out. Let me ask you this, when you brought her down here, did you make a reservation in Joanna Barnes's name?"

I thought back. "Yes," I replied.

"Yeah? And did you make it before eleven o'clock that Saturday night?"

"Let's see," I said. "I called from Henry Africa's. That was maybe nine."

"And did you give them her telephone number?"

"I don't remember."

"You ought to remember something like that."

"I was a little drunk."

"Well, did you have her number by the time you called the airline?"

I paused, trying to remember. "Yeah, I think I did. Her brother had written it down for me."

"There you go," he said. "You probably gave it to the airline. They always ask for it. And they fouled up and placed an extra reservation for Saturday night in their computer. She never made that reservation. You did." He said this as if it should settle the matter of airline reservations, and I left it there, not telling him how his theory really struck me.

"She lied about working for Skidmore," I finally reminded him.

"How do you know she lied? Maybe some partner there had offered her a job without having told the personnel manager." I shook my head. "Or maybe," he continued, "someone had just encouraged her so much that she assumed she had a job there before she did." I didn't bother to respond. "Or maybe she just lied, goddamn it. Maybe she just couldn't bring herself to tell us she couldn't get a job. She sure as hell was telling the truth when she said she'd been at Taliesin."

"There's what Miranda says."

He lit his cigarette and blew smoke at the ceiling. He shook his head. Then he yelled, "Hey, Charlene!" and a secretary from the station at the corner came to the door. "Would you mind getting me another cup of coffee?" he said, pushing the cup at her. Then he smiled and added, "Just for old times' sake."

"You, too?" Charlene asked me.

When Charlene brought the coffee, Morgan took only one sip. "I know there's what Miranda says," he said, standing up. "But Miranda's the defendant." He walked out of my office.

After that, at the behest of Walter Smith, I turned the pages of a Supreme Court opinion that said the statute of limitations in a medical-negligence case does not begin to run until the plaintiff knows or reasonably should know that his doctor has committed malpractice.

55

WHEN I ARRIVED at my office the next morning, the telephone was ringing. I lifted it. "Douglas, it's Sue Menendez. My husband asked that I call to see if you can come and see him."

He looked bad, worse than he had before, thinner, more cadaverous, and he'd begun to turn a yellow color. Things were such that I found myself asking something I hadn't asked him before, something that had always seemed somehow inappropriate, almost impertinent. "How are you feeling?" I said.

"I'm a sick son of a bitch," he replied. "But don't you worry about that. You just tell me what's going on in our case."

I told him everything, even about Judge Phelps's distrust of Morgan.

"Danny isn't exactly a Mormon bishop's type," Frank Menendez observed.

"Dan still says he believes Rita was telling the truth. It's like I'm not even working on the case. I'm doing work for Walter Smith and Tom Gallagher. I don't know what's wrong with him, but he's changed. Maybe it's the divorce."

"Danny's a veteran of the divorce court," Frank Menendez reminded me.

"The change started when his first wife's mother died."

"That's grief, and a little guilt. You get over that fast."

"Well, there's something eating him, and I don't think it's anything I did."

Suddenly Frank Menendez altered course. "How did you feel the day that jury acquitted Rita?" he asked me.

"Very good," I said. "Great."

"How do you feel about getting Rita off now? I mean, now that you're representing the little girl?"

"Bad." I paused. "Well, at first I felt bad. I felt like we'd done in an innocent child. But now I have a feeling we can get Miranda acquitted, too."

"And wouldn't that be a coup?"

"Yes," I acknowledged.

"But you don't feel excited about it."

"No," I said. "It's not the same as when we were defending Rita. It isn't fun."

It was dark in the Menendez library, and the music was somber, Albinoni's Adagio, and we sat and listened to the music for a while without speaking.

"Something happened," I said.

"What happened?" he asked. I shifted uneasily. "You go ahead and tell me."

"I was just thinking."

"Go ahead."

"Once," I confessed with my head down, "when we needed to see Miranda, and Jake Asher wouldn't let us—when Dan needed to know for sure what she looked like in that catatonic stupor—you know?"

"I understand."

"We sneaked into Camelback Hospital and looked at her. In the middle of the night." Frank Menendez nodded gravely. "I didn't know it then, but Miranda was aware of us," I continued. "And now she remembers it. She believes we were there because we were concerned about her. She has no idea we were there so we could put the blame on her. At least I don't think she knows that. The other day she said she trusts Morgan and me, because we were the only ones who cared enough to go see her in the hospital. I can't get it out of my mind, and it makes me a little sick."

Frank Menendez nodded again. Then he said something that struck me as curiously out of place but which nonetheless I have never forgotten. "My father was a fine man who was very good to me," he said. "He loved me."

I listened to the music.

"Did Danny do his typical job in Rita's case?" he asked.

"I don't know what you mean."

"Did he figure out everything that happened and tell her about it before he let her tell him her story?"

It took me all the way back to Rita's preliminary hearing, when I'd watched Morgan interrogating the medical examiner in great detail, when I'd watched him place the photographs and diagrams in front of Rita so carefully, making sure she inspected them and understood what was in them. "Yes," I said. "He did that."

"Such that she could tell her big lie without any of the facts getting in her way?"

"Yes. I remember sort of thinking about what he was doing, right at the time he was doing it."

"If you feel a little sick, how do you think Danny feels?"

I said nothing.

"I'm the one who taught him to do that," Frank Menendez told me. "I don't think Danny ever told a client to commit perjury in his life." He closed his eyes. He laughed and shook his head. "Oh, Lord, I hope you win this case."

Sometime later Sue Menendez came into the room.

"I'd like a cup of tea, Sue," he said.

"Douglas, what can I get you?"

"A cup of tea would be fine," I told her.

She brought the tea, and we sipped it in silence. I don't know how much time passed before he spoke again, but when at last he did speak, he only whispered. "I've been thinking."

"What?" I said, leaning closer to him.

"I've been thinking that if Joanna Barnes knew Rita, and if she lied for her, she had to have talked to her while Rita was in jail."

"Why do you say that?"

"They had to get their stories straight."

"I assumed they planned it ahead of time. Before Rita went out to that house. Before she bought the gun."

"I don't think so," Frank Menendez said. "If she planned to kill him, I don't think Rita would have taken the child with her. She'd have had no way to know that Miranda would go into that stupor or whatever you call it. I don't think she'd have dared take a witness with her."

"Maybe she was trying to set Miranda up to frame her."

"I don't think so. That's too chancy. I'm pretty sure Travis just took her by surprise when he called her on her homosexuality. She shot him. Miranda's condition became just a coincidental place to put the blame."

"Killing him seems like a pretty severe reaction to his little discovery."

"Yes," said Frank Menendez. "There has to be something more. She had to be terribly afraid of being exposed. Still, I'll bet that's what happened. And if it is, your Barnes woman had to have visited her at the jail."

"I'll go check," I said.

"Yes," said Frank Menendez. "Yes. Do that."

56

ONCE AGAIN I stood at the tall counter in the sheriff's office. "I need to talk to the sheriff," I told a big woman whose belly rolled over her gun belt.

"Do you have an appointment?"

"No," I said, "but—"

"You'll have to have an appointment."

"I'm Douglas McKenzie."

"I don't care if you're the Queen of Sheba, son. You'll have to have an appointment."

"I work for . . ."

"Let him in! He's okay."

I turned to see Doreen, the burgundy-haired grandmother, waving at me. Moments later I was sitting by Buck Sussman's desk, and within minutes one of the deputies from the jail was there.

"Yeah," the deputy said. "One time. One time a woman came to see Mrs. Eddington. That was the only person who ever came to see her besides you and Dan Morgan. And Mr. Eddington."

"Mr. Eddington?"

"Ferris Eddington."

"Ferris Eddington came to see her?"

"All the time."

"How many times?"

"I don't know. A lot more than Dan Morgan. Almost every day. He'd stay for hours. He always came at night."

I looked at the sheriff, stunned.

"What did the woman look like?" I asked the jailer. "The woman who came to see Mrs. Eddington?"

"She was—"

"Wait a minute," I interrupted. "Did Ferris Eddington talk to her through the glass, or did he talk to her in that room?"

"I always let them use that room where you and Dan talked to her."

"Was the matron with them?"

"No," he answered defensively. "I knew Mrs. Eddington wasn't going to try to pull anything."

"Jesus Christ," Buck Sussman whispered. "You keep your mouth shut about this. Okay, Shorty?" Shorty nodded, cowed, and Sussman winked at me. "I don't do that for Republicans."

"What did the woman look like?" I asked again. "The one who came to see her."

"Damned good-looking," said Shorty.

"Can you describe her for me?"

"Shit. Let me think. I don't know." Shorty paused and rubbed his head. "I just remember she was really good-looking. Different from Mrs. Eddington, but damned near as good."

"Did she have sort of curly hair?"

"I can't remember."

"Did she wear the sort of clothes that come from a boutique?"

"Huh?"

"Did her clothes look expensive?"

Shorty gave me a blank look.

"Would you be able to recognize her again?"

"I'm not sure. Maybe."

"If I could find a picture of her, would you be able to recognize her?"

"I could at least take a look."

"Thanks, Shorty. I'll be back."

I parked my car on a gravel flat and walked to a terrace where there was a fountain in front of a building with large windows. The building was constructed of stone and concrete and wood and looked like it grew out of the rock on which it was built. For a few long seconds, I took in the grand panorama of the desert below as a young man lectured a group of people near the fountain.

"If you will notice the line of the roof, you will see that it follows the line of the mountain ridge behind the building. That was part of Mr. Wright's approach. And you will note also that the visible ends of the rafters are all cut on different angles. Mr. Wright did that to break the light, much as the angle of the rock you see on the ridge does the same thing."

"Amazing," a young woman said.

The group moved toward a breezeway that ran between sections of the building. I followed along and peered with the rest of them into a spacious living room and heard about the tradition set by Mr. and Mrs. Wright of evening clothes and cocktails before dinner. When the guide noticed my eavesdropping, he gave me an inquisitive smile. "Can I help you?"

"I'm trying to find some information about a woman named Joanna Barnes."

"Crazy Joanna?" He laughed. "Larry!" A redheaded man walked across the patio. "Larry, could you to talk to this gentleman about Crazy Joanna?"

"What do you mean, 'crazy'?" I said.

"Why are you interested in her?"

I didn't tell Larry the entire story, just that I was a lawyer and she might be a witness. Larry told me he had read about her testimony at Rita's trial.

"Actually, I came out here to see if someone might have a picture of her."

"I doubt that anybody here would be able to tell you a lot about her," Larry said. "She kept pretty much to herself. More than anyone I've ever known, to tell the truth. And I really don't know anything about her. I asked her to dinner once." He shrugged. "I struck out." Larry scratched his red head. "Oh, yes," he said. "She lived in her tent the entire time she was here. She never built a house. She lived alone."

"Are you an architect?" I asked.

"Yes. Let's go in here." I followed him into a large room that was full of drafting tables. There was an older woman in the room looking over some blueprints. "Did you ever know anything about Joanna Barnes?" Larry asked.

"I always kind of liked her," said the woman, "but I never got to know her."

"See, nobody really knew her," said Larry.

"I never thought she was a very good draftsman," the woman added.

I followed the architect around the room, enjoying the gentle breeze that was pulled through the open windows, surprised by how helpful he tried to be. He would ask people what they knew about Joanna. They would say they knew nothing. And at the end of half an hour, all I'd learned about the treasure I found in San Francisco was that she was sometimes called "Crazy Joanna," that she was seemingly uninterested in an aging architect with red hair and a potbelly, and that she was thought, in some circles, to be an inferior draftsman. Oh, yes, and she'd spent her nights in a tent alone under the starlit desert skies. We moved on, and eventually we came to a bulletin board. On the board there were many snapshots, pictures of people standing around various construction sites. My architect said, "Let's see," and he ran his finger around the photographs until he said, "Here's Joanna."

I looked closely at the photograph and recognized her standing beside my guide in a group of people lined up on a spiral staircase constructed of brass, connecting two floors of what was, judging from books in low shelves along the walls, a law office. "That's you," I said to Larry.

"Yes," he said. "Defeated. That was the day she shot me down. That was the day we completed that project. You may take the picture if you like."

"I heard once," I said, "that Joanna Barnes was a lesbian."

"May I take comfort in that explanation of my rejection?" he said, chuckling.

Late that afternoon I was back in the sheriff's office asking Buck Sussman if I could show my newly acquired picture to Shorty.

"You bet," said Sussman, examining Joanna appreciatively. "Let me ask you this, though. Is there a chance you'll ever have to call him as a witness to identify her?"

"It's possible, I guess."

"Then you don't want to just show that to him. You might weaken your identification. Give it to me. I'll show you what you want to do." The sheriff took the picture. "Becky!"

A blond woman in a sheriff's uniform stuck her head around the doorframe. "Yeah, Buck?"

"Do something for me, will you, Becky?"

"Sure."

"Blow this woman up to five by seven, then set up a photo spread, and get Shorty up here from the jail. I want to have him look at it."

To me Buck Sussman said, "The woman signed in under the name Julie Belasio." He showed me a sheet from a sign-in log.

"Is that her signature?"

"No. That's Albert's handwriting."

When Becky returned, she had enlarged the photograph and cropped it close around Joanna's head. She placed the picture on a table and surrounded it with a number of five-by-seven-inch photographs of other women.

"Are they all white women, Becky?" Sussman asked.

"No, Buck," she snapped tartly. "I've got her in here with a bunch of Eskimo midgets. Jesus." Becky looked at me. "I've only been doing this for fifteen years."

"Okay, let's have a look." Buck Sussman bent over the array of what Becky called "female Caucasians age about thirty."

"Not bad, Rebecca. Bring Shorty in." Soon the small

jailer appeared. "Okay, Shorty," said the sheriff, "see if you can find that woman who came to visit Rita Eddington in that bunch." The deputy shuffled through the pictures, then looked at each a second and a third time. "What about it, Shorty? Is she in there?"

"Shit, Buck, I can't tell."

"Well, try, goddamn it."

Shorty looked more closely. "If it's any of them, it's this one." He turned to Buck Sussman apologetically with Jo-anna Barnes's picture. "She was this good-looking, but I'm not sure if it's her."

57

I BELLIED UP to the bar in Durant's. Jack Durant himself was sitting with a buxom lady of about fifty-five. The woman had jet-black hair and a lot of makeup, and she sat very close to him.

"Buy this gentleman a drink!" the owner yelled at the bartender through the smoke and the noise. "And another one for the lady, as well." My bourbon arrived, and I tipped the short glass in the direction of my host. "Had to build this place!" he shouted at me. "I'd been kicked out of every other restaurant in Phoenix. Were you aware of that, my dear?"

"I believe you once mentioned that, Jack," the lady guest acknowledged.

After a while Mr. Durant escorted the woman to a booth in the back, and I crawled up onto a barstool. I nursed my drink and thought about Ferris Eddington and his daughter-in-law in that room with the fresh cement and without the matron. I pictured him going into the jail at night. I could see his big, erect frame marching down the shadowy ramp to the darkness near the entrance.

It was as I sat there at the bar in Durant's, drinking bourbon and imagining things, that I first realized I'd become nearsighted, that eventually I would have to wear glasses.

The front door opened, and a woman walked in alone. I could see that she was tall and willowy and well dressed, but I could not make her out well enough to tell what her face looked like. She walked toward my end of the bar. As she came nearer, I saw that it was Ann Hastings. "What are you doing here?" she asked, putting her hand on mine.

"Just having a drink," I said. "What about you?"

"I'm tired of watching television."

"You watch television?"

"Yes," she admitted.

"I didn't think you would," I told her.

"Well, there you go," she said. "I do."

The bartender came, and she ordered a can of Coors, and when he brought her the beer, she raised it. "Well," Ann said, "here's to better days. It seems like they weren't so long ago."

"I'll buy you dinner."

"That's the nicest thing I've heard in two weeks."

"I haven't seen you in two weeks," I said.

"I've been avoiding you."

"Why?" I asked.

"I don't know. But I have."

"Where's Morgan?"

She took a deep breath. "I don't know." She looked at me directly, eyes wide. She exhaled. "He won't see me."

"Why?"

"I think I make him feel bad about certain things he's done in his life."

"He won't see me either," I told her. "At least mostly he won't. I think it's sort of the same thing."

"You don't mean because of what he did with me?"

"No. Because of what he did with Rita Eddington."

"Oh," she said, visibly relieved. She raised her beer again. "Yes. The case has turned around, hasn't it? I've been thinking about it."

"And what do you think?" I asked.

"I think Morgan's chickens have come home to roost."

I laughed. "That's one way of putting it."

She turned to look across the bar, and I stirred my drink and stared at her near-perfect profile. "Can I ask you something, Ann?" I said.

"Yes."

"What do you see in him? In Morgan." She turned and stared straight at me. I rocked back. "I'm sorry," I said. "I had no business asking you that. You don't have to—"

"No, Doug, that's all right." She put her hand on mine for a second time. "It's just that I don't know how to answer you." She looked back across the bar. "What is it that *you* see in him?" she asked.

"What do you mean?"

"Well, it's pretty obvious that you have as big a crush on him as I do."

"What? Oh, come on." I watched her run her tongue across her gleaming teeth, saying nothing. "Ann," I said, "I can promise you I have no desire to get naked with Dan Morgan in my apartment."

"That's not what I mean," she said, turning back to me, "and I think you know it. So I'll ask you again. What do you see in him?"

"I'm not sure," I told her. "On the one hand, I'm repelled by him. Did you know that I was once a naval officer, Ann?" She nodded. "And now I'm reporting to a marine grunt. Hell, he's got that awful tattoo. Still, I can't help feeling some—I don't know—adventure. I think maybe it's because he seems so tough, yet he's so nice to people." I took a deep breath. "He's the kind of guy you want with you in a real rough bar. He has this energy. It's like he's always about to explode, but then he does very nice things for you. Like when he let me take Joanna Barnes's testimony."

Ann considered what I'd said. She drank some of her beer. Finally she nodded. "Dan is a very kind person. He really does care about people."

"The first time I saw him, he had this old Indian client, Horace Apadaka, who'd been farting in the firm lobby. They were going to court, and the old man was scared. Dan put his arm around him and tried to comfort him. I liked him for it." She smiled. "Or, hell," I said, "maybe it's just that he's some kind of a celebrity. Whatever, he surely knows his way around a courtroom."

"That he does," said Ann.

"He got the charges against Horace Apadaka dismissed."

Ann laughed. "I remember," she said.

"So what do you see in him, Ann?"

"Maybe the same thing you do," she said. "Besides, Doug, don't you know that women can't resist bad boys?"

"Are you being ironic?" I asked.

She stared at me. "I guess I hope I am," she said at last.

I finished my bourbon, and she drank her beer. Later, in a red leather booth, we both ate steaks and shared a Caesar salad. We didn't talk much, but it felt comfortable to be with her, and familiar. "It was so nice," Ann said. "You know, when you guys were defending Rita."

After dinner Ann took me to a place she liked on North Central and bought us coffee and cheesecake. As we were leaving, she asked if I wanted to follow her home for a drink. "You can even watch a little television with me," she promised.

I wanted very much to accept her invitation, but I said no. I guess I figured there were enough complications between Morgan and me. I drove back to the Kendall House.

58   FRANK MENENDEZ DIDN'T look as bad as he had the day before. His eyes were alive once again. "Goddamn it," he said. "Didn't I tell you she visited the jail?"

"I'm not sure it was Joanna Barnes," I cautioned. "I went out to Taliesin and found a picture of her, but the jailer couldn't identify her positively. He said it could have been Joanna, but he wasn't sure. Albert, the guy who signed her in couldn't even remember doing it."

"It was she," Frank Menendez said.

"The jailer told me something else, something I should probably tell you about."

"Yes?"

"Ferris Eddington visited Rita while she was in jail. All the time. At night. And the matron would leave them alone together for hours at a time." I waited for the scandalized reaction that would surely come. He only nodded, though, as if the news simply shored up what he suspected all along.

"We have to find Rita," he told me. "I don't know what the hell we do when we find her, but we must find her."

"That's a tall order. That Blaine Larsen, that investigator you referred me to in San Francisco, can't even find Joanna Barnes, and he's supposed to be really good. I don't know what we can do about Rita."

"Do this for me," he instructed. "You go to the ranch. You walk right up to Ferris. You tell him that I sent you. You tell him that I want to know where Rita is."

"But—"

"No buts! You just go tell him that. Then you come right back here and tell me what happens. Now, go!"

Two hours later I returned. "Did you find him?" came the fierce whisper down the hall the instant I walked through the front door.

"Yes."

"What happened?"

"I did what you told me to do," I reported, easing myself into the chair by his feet. "I told him that Frank Menendez wants to know where Rita is."

"What did he say?"

"Nothing. At least at first he said nothing."

"What did he do?"

"He cried," I said. "Tears started running down his face."

"Uh-huh," Frank Menendez said. "Did he ever say anything?"

"Finally he said that he didn't know. He said, 'I don't know where she is, Douglas.' Then he got out a handkerchief and tried to wipe his face."

"Then what did he do?"

"He got back on his horse, and he rode away."

"Sue?"

"Yes, Frank," she called from another room.

"Would you please bring me those pictures we were looking at?"

"I'll get them."

"Tell me, Douglas, did you ever know that Ferris Eddington was married once before—before he married Eleanor?"

"Yes," I said. "My mother told me that one time."

"The girl's name was Hattie Hunt."

"I didn't know her name."

"Ferris's father drove her away."

"Yes."

"She's dead now."

"Yes, I know. My mother said that Ferris took her death very hard."

"Yes," Frank Menendez confirmed. "Very hard."

Then Sue Menendez came into the library carrying a tray with tea and two photographs. One was the picture from the White Mountains that I'd brought from home, the one with Rita and Travis and Ferris Eddington and my parents at Sheep's Crossing. The other showed Frank Menendez, when he was very young, standing next to an equally young woman.

"That's you," I said, looking up.

"That's right," Sue Menendez said.

"You were beautiful." I fumbled, trying to catch my tongue. "I mean, you're still beautiful. . . ."

"That's all right, Douglas." She smiled gently. "Thank you."

"She is beautiful, isn't she?" Frank Menendez sighed, his eyes remaining on his statuesque wife. "Always has been."

I turned back to the picture. I saw a young Ferris Eddington. They all were very young, and they all stood by a Ford Model T. Then I looked at the girl beside the Eddington boy. "I'll be damned," I said.

"That tell you anything?" Frank Menendez asked.

"She looks just like Rita," I said, incredulously. "Almost exactly like Rita. Like Rita dressed up in old-fashioned clothes."

"Those jodhpurs and high-laced boots were all the rage," Sue Menendez remembered. Then she said, "The old black-and-white picture doesn't show it, but her color was the same as Rita's. Her hair and her beautiful eyes."

"The girl is Hattie Hunt," Frank Menendez said.

I looked up at him. "I had sort of figured that out."

"So what do you make of it?" he asked.

"Ferris is in love with Rita. And he has been for a long time."

"No question about it, and if Sue's arithmetic is sound,

Rita was about four months pregnant with Miranda when she and Travis got married."

"Does that mean anything?"

"I don't know, but I have a theory. Do you want to hear my theory, Douglas?"

"Yes, I do."

"I think that when Rita's mother first brought Rita to the ranch, Ferris was stunned by her resemblance to Hattie. And—"

"Ferris really did love Hattie, didn't he?" Sue Menendez's voice sounded like it was drifting into another part of the old adobe house. "We all liked Hattie. I really truly liked her. Ferris's father ought to have been—"

"And I think Rita was equally stunned by Ferris's wealth and power," Frank Menendez continued. "A potent chemistry developed, from which I believe our young client, Miranda Eddington, was brought into this world. Do you follow my drift, Douglas?"

"Yes, I believe I do." I leaned closer to him.

"They had a problem, however. There was no way, given how important appearances are to him, that Ferris Eddington was going to dump poor old pathetic Eleanor. But if Rita went away to have the baby, or to have an abortion, Ferris might have lost her. And from her perspective, if she went away, she might have lost her chance at all that Eddington money and all that Eddington land. I can't even guess which of them was more fearful of what the little problem they had created might cause. You may speculate on that one, Douglas. But I do have a pretty clear idea of the solution they settled on."

"I'm listening," I said.

"There was Travis. Marry her off to him. Keep it in the family. Travis had never had any success with the opposite sex anyway, and his father could rationalize it as being something the young man needed. I don't know how they made it happen, but apparently young Travis took to the beautiful girl the way a trout moves to the fly."

"Do you think that Rita was in love with Ferris Eddington?"

"Of course not. That was the real problem, the one she could never solve. She was homosexual. She might have been in love with his power, and his money, and his land. But with Ferris himself? No! And that may have made Travis's death inevitable."

"You've lost me," I said.

"I mean that by the time Travis figured out that there was something better to do with that little thing than pee through it, he'd probably become pretty demanding."

"Frank," his wife chastened him from the sofa.

"Oh, yes, Sue. Rita was able to put up with Ferris's old withered cock—"

"Frank!"

"At least she could as much as Ferris wanted to use it. But Travis was a young, strapping boy, and that was another story. And that other story led Travis to his suspicions, and when those suspicions ripened and he asked his wife if she was a lesbian, Rita knew she was in trouble deep." Frank Menendez paused and rested.

"Why," I asked, "would it mean such trouble? Because Travis would divorce her?"

"No. No. Travis was no threat. Travis was a pussy." He raised his hand to show his wife he wanted no more of her social training. "It was Ferris. If Travis ever told his father about his suspicions, one thing would have led to another, and Ferris would have found out what she was and what she'd been doing. And here, all these years, Ferris had believed she loved him. Truly. Passionately. She'd made him young again. You ever take a real close look at Eleanor Eddington, Douglas?"

"Yes," I said.

"And what would Ferris Eddington do if he found out that Rita was stepping out on him? With a woman?!"

"I don't know."

"Well, it wouldn't surprise me if he'd have killed her. And it wouldn't have surprised Rita either. And I know this much for a fact. She'd have played holy hell ever seeing a penny of Ferris's money. At a minimum he'd have kept the firm alive for years fighting to see that she didn't." Now

Frank Menendez was exhausted, but he managed to add his conclusion. "So," he said, "when Travis let her know he was wise to her, she panicked. And she killed him. And it all happened on the spur of the moment. She really didn't have time to think. Then enter your lovely witness from San Francisco with her little visit to the county jail. They could blame it on the child, who couldn't defend herself. What harm after all? Who knew that Maximilian Hauser wouldn't be able to take a joke?" Exhausted, Frank Menendez lay way back in his chair and listened to the music.

"If you're right," I said at length, "if she was after the Eddington Ranch all along, then she'll come back. She'll come back to testify against Miranda."

"Yes," Frank Menendez agreed. "She'll have to defend herself. If someone shows she murdered Travis, she'll be out in the cold. She'll have to find a way to do it with Ferris's blessing. But she'll be back. Both those greedy bitches will come to tell the story they concocted."

"Is there any way we could prove all this?"

"I don't know. But if we were even to try, we'd have to start with Ferris."

"And he's paying our bills," I observed.

"Yes," Frank Menendez said. "Nasty, isn't it?"

59 MORGAN AND I finally talked about the case. At least around it. A couple of days after I showed Joanna Barnes's picture to Shorty, I told Morgan what Frank Menendez had deduced. He raised his eyebrows in apparent skepticism. "I know that a woman once came to see her in jail, Dan." He said, "Big deal," and I told him it was Joanna Barnes. He said, "Bullshit, it was probably just a newspaperwoman trying to get a story." I said, "Ferris Eddington went to see her almost every day, and it was always at night, and they'd go in that room, and they'd be in there without a matron." That stopped him dead. He lit a cigarette off the one he'd been smoking. I told him, "Ferris wept when I asked where Rita was." All Morgan did after that was sip coffee, blow great wafts of smoke, and stare at me coldly.

The next day we sat by the Eddington swimming pool, and Morgan watched Miranda and made notes, as once again she told us what happened. She told the same story she'd told before. Exactly. I noted, though, that she did not ask Morgan if he knew what a lesbian was. I waited for it. But then, when she studiously avoided it, I knew that she'd figured out that it was a subject that made people (at least me) nervous.

When he was finished, after he'd gone over her story a second time and then a third time and had made his notes and told her how he would ask her questions in court, he said, "I need to talk about one more thing, Miranda. When someone who is a child has to testify in court, there is sometimes a question whether they can. There's a question whether they know about how you have to tell the truth." She nodded. "Do you know what perjury is, Miranda?"

"Yes."

"Tell me what it is."

"It's lying when you've taken an oath to tell the truth."

"Do you know that it's against the law?"

"Yes. It's a crime."

"Fine. I'll have to ask you these things in court before you testify. You say it just like you did here. Okay?"

She said she would, and Morgan and I got up to leave. "Mr. Morgan," Miranda said.

"Yes?"

"I'm not committing perjury."

In the car Morgan said, "She seems very bright."

"Yes," I said.

"Funny. People have been saying that Travis was kind of slow."

I stared at him for a moment, then said, "Dan, she isn't Travis's daughter."

He turned on me and kept looking for such a time that I was afraid he'd run off the road. "You want to get an enchilada?" he asked, finally returning his gaze to the highway.

At El Charro, I ordered two green chili burros and a bottle of beer. It all tasted good, and it felt good to be back in the same booth where once Morgan had discussed strategy with me. This time, however, talk of tactics didn't last long. "If we're lucky," Morgan predicted, "we'll never have to call her."

"How's that?" I asked.

"Rita won't show up, and we'll have a motion to dismiss."

"Don't count on it," I said.

"You know something?" Morgan said.

"What?"

"You're getting to be a pain in the ass."

60 "GODDAMN IT, PAULINE, tell us. It's important." This time Pauline Adair had come to the Menendez house with Dan Morgan and me. And this time there was no fancy tequila and there were no cigars. We had been ordered to appear, and for Morgan and Pauline the appearance was made under silent protest. "You said she's gay," Frank Menendez said. "Now you tell us what you know."

"I'm not going to tell you. I never should have said anything in the first place."

"It's bullshit, Frank," Morgan said. "I don't know how she got this hair up her ass, but it isn't true."

"How do you know it isn't true, Danny?"

"Trust me, it isn't true."

"What I told him is true. But I'm not going to tell you how I know. I can't tell you, Frank. I truly cannot tell you. I really don't much care at this point, but you all would do well to believe me."

Frank Menendez moved his gaze back and forth between the two of them. "Let's see," he said irritably. "You say she's gay, Pauline, and you say she's not, Danny, and neither one of you will tell me how you claim to know. What the hell is going on here?" The aged lawyer's unspoken suspicion suddenly became palpable. In shock I looked from Morgan to Pauline, then back, then back again.

Are you not, I asked myself, *the world's number one* pendejo? *College, the United States Navy, law school, a year hanging out with some pretty hip people in San Francisco. And, on top of that, two years as the assistant manager of a ski lodge. How in the world have I remained this naïve? How could it have taken me this long to figure it out? Morgan felt my time was better spent in the library? That's why he refused to let me be in that fresh-smelling room with him and Rita while he prepared her to testify? That same room where Ferris Eddington spent even more time with her than Morgan did. Come on, Douglas! And all the time he was seeing Ann.*

I stared at Morgan as he and Pauline sat silently in front of Frank Menendez. I thought back to a couple of nights before, when in that same library Morgan, thinking about Rita, had let fly with "that goddamned bitch!" Frank Menendez had speculated that Ferris Eddington might have killed Rita if ever he were made to know she was a lesbian. That possibility seemed less remote, as now it dawned on me that Morgan might have done the same thing.

But I still couldn't see the reason for Pauline Adair's fear, for her unwillingness to tell everything. After all, Pauline already seemed well out of the closet. I thought about it. I'd heard stories of powerful women in Phoenix, stories told in bare whispers. There'd always been talk about a high-placed judge, never married, whose name I should probably not write down. Maybe those women had something to do with Pauline's silence.

"I gotta go," Morgan announced abruptly. Once again I watched him storm down the hall toward Frank Menendez's front door.

"I'm in his car," Pauline Adair said, and she, too, was gone.

I stood up. Then I looked down at Frank Menendez, and I saw that he had turned a terrible color. He lay there, stretched across the chair and the ottoman, unable, I was sure, to move. His breath came short and weak. And for the first time since I'd known him, it truly came to me what I'd been watching all along. It had been as certain for Frank

Menendez as it had for Tyrone Roebuck. His eyes closed, and I realized that I couldn't hear him breathe. Sue Menendez came into the room. She stopped short, then backed up, and I watched her as she stood there against his books, staring down. She turned anxiously to me, then back down to him. "Frank?" she said, panicked.

"I just need a short word with Douglas," Frank Menendez whispered to his wife, and I could hear her breathe again. I lowered myself into a chair. "She'll come back. You know that, don't you, Douglas? Rita will come, and probably that other greedy bitch, too."

I nodded.

"You've got to get ready for them. You've got to take care of that little girl. Whatever you need to do, you've got to protect that child. You know that."

Again I nodded my head, and again I watched him close his eyes. Then I knew that it was time for me to go, and I got up from his chair, and I moved toward the door.

"Douglas."

"Yes?"

"Did I ever tell you that I liked your father?"

"Yes, sir," I said. Very slowly I walked out of his house.

61

WE SEARCHED FOR RITA. As the trial neared, even Morgan pitched in and hired two local investigators. He still paid lip service to his notion that "Douglas McKenzie and Frank Menendez have sat too long in Frank's library, drinking tequila and composing fiction." But when he spoke to Mr. Brooks and Mr. Pepcorn, he barked "Find her!" and he told them to disregard the expense. He even had me bring Blaine Larsen down from San Francisco to meet with them and report on his progress with Joanna Barnes.

"I can't believe it," Larsen said. "This Barnes woman seems to have fallen off the earth. I even sneaked some help from the FBI office up there. They couldn't find a thing. It's as if she never existed."

"Keep looking," Morgan ordered. "And keep looking for Rita Eddington. The two of them just may be jungled up together."

For me, Christmas 1973 never happened. The office put up a tree, and I received a card and a ski sweater from my mother, but for Dan Morgan and me the holiday did not exist. The days before trial slipped by, and we agonized over the absence of information about Rita. Blaine Larsen called from San Francisco to say that he'd exhausted all his leads on Joanna. And Ferris Eddington stayed away from the ranch even longer than he had when the woman named Hattie Hunt had died.

Because Maximilian Hauser had proceeded against Miranda by indictment instead of information, there'd been no preliminary hearing, and we had no real indication of how he planned to prove his case. Two days before trial, I called him to ask point-blank whether he was going to be able to produce Rita Eddington. I hoped he was looking for her as desperately as we were. His secretary insisted that he wasn't in, and, unsurprisingly, he didn't return my call. So the day before trial, New Year's Day, I drove to the state capitol and persuaded a guard to let me into the near-empty building. I strode straight back to Hauser's office.

He looked up from his desk. "Do you have an appointment?" he demanded.

"Do you have Rita?" I shot back.

"She's on our witness list, isn't she? I assume you got our witness list?"

"Can you produce her?"

"What rule do you know that requires me to reveal that to you?"

I stood planted in his doorway, glaring.

"If that's all you have," Hauser said, "I have quite a lot of work to do." I didn't move. "Do I need to call somebody, McKenzie?"

62 "WHY DON'T WE go down and steal a couple of Danny's beers," suggested Tom Gallagher, "and you can tell me all about it."

"Okay."

We slipped into Morgan's office, opened his little refrigerator, and pulled out two cans of Coors.

"Sit down."

I obeyed.

"Now, what happened?"

I told Gallagher about my visit to Hauser's office. Gallagher laughed.

"It isn't funny," I said.

"No?"

"No, it isn't. He's a very rude man," I said.

"Oh, yeah?"

"Yeah. And I think the only reason he's prosecuting Miranda is that he's pissed off at Morgan, on account of what Morgan did to him in Rita's trial. Morgan's rude to him, too. Hell, Morgan's even worse than Hauser. They're in this vile fight. And I'm sick of it."

"Is that it?"

"Yeah, that's it," I said.

"Drink your beer, Doug."

I did, and then I stood up to leave.

"You want to know something?" he asked.

"What?"

"You don't have to be an asshole to be a trial lawyer. That having been said, you never want to lose sight of the fact that you are part of the milieu."

63 THE NEXT MORNING Morgan, Miranda, and I sat at the table near the jury box in the nondescript courtroom of Eldon Phelps. Once again Morgan arranged his papers meticulously on the table, and again prospective jurors flowed into the gallery behind us. We waited, as we had before, for Maximilian Hauser. I looked at Miranda next to me as she stared innocently ahead. Morgan also stared straight ahead, unblinking. Max Hauser finally came into the room, and I looked around anxiously, expecting to see Rita Eddington close behind. Rita wasn't there. There was only Hauser putting down his briefcase, looking tired and all alone. Apparently, he would try this one by himself.

The bailiff opened the door and announced that the judge would see us in chambers. Unlike the courtroom, the judge's office had windows, small vertical slits of glass. You could not see out of them well, but at least they let in some light. And the office was large, almost as large as the courtroom.

"Well, gentlemen, do we have any matters to resolve before we pick a jury?" Eldon Phelps inquired.

"We have one matter," Hauser said.

"Sit down. Sit down." The judge waved a hand around the room, and we each found a chair. "Yes, Mr. Hauser?"

"There's the matter of voir dire of the jury, Your Honor.

The State would ask that you conduct it. That you ask the questions."

"Yes," the judge agreed, "I intend to do that." His answer came so quickly that it surprised even Hauser, who was cut short from a prepared argument.

"What?" I heard Morgan say loudly.

"Yes. I'll question the jurors, Mr. Morgan."

"That's improper, Judge."

"I'll be the judge of what's proper in my courtroom, Mr. Morgan."

"I mean, Your Honor, that isn't done. Not in this court. That's the way they handle it in federal court, but not in this court."

"That's the way things will be handled in my court, Mr. Morgan. I've had my experience with shrewd lawyers, who sway the jury before the opening statements are made. It isn't going to happen in my court."

Morgan bristled. "I want a court reporter."

"Yes, Mr. Morgan, you may have the convenience of the record," said the judge.

The court reporter arrived, and Morgan dictated a long objection. "That's all I have," he said.

Then the judge addressed him in an unexpectedly friendly tone. "I realize, Mr. Morgan," he said, "that you don't have to tell me this, but I wondered whether you would care to enlighten me as to any defense you may have."

Morgan stared at him, perplexed. He turned toward Hauser, then back to the judge. "First, if it please the court, I want to see him try to prove that my client is guilty." Morgan's arm stretched across the office toward Max Hauser.

"But I thought, Mr. Morgan," the judge said, "you had already proved that your client is guilty."

Morgan moved his hands from the arms of his chair to his knees. His grip tightened. I watched his jaw move in and out. "Not in this case, Judge. Not in this case."

"Aren't there questions about the propriety of your appearing in this case, Mr. Morgan?"

"We have concluded that there are not."

"Well, I notice that no party has moved for your disqualification, and far be it from me to second-guess the judgment of a firm as distinguished as yours. Shall we proceed?"

Eldon Phelps stood and reached for his robe. We all stood. The judge looked back to us. "But *I* have problems with it, Mr. Morgan. I have problems."

"I have one matter, on behalf of the defense," Morgan announced. The judge, one arm in his robe, turned. "I ask," Morgan continued, "that you instruct Mr. Hauser not to offer evidence of the prior trial or mention it in his opening statement, and I ask that you inquire, in private, of every prospective juror whether he or she was aware of the prior trial. In private, Your Honor. As you know from our trial brief, it is our position that no one can fairly serve who is aware of that proceeding or its result."

"Yes," Eldon Phelps acknowledged, with one arm still only halfway into the sleeve of his robe, "I recall you filed such a request. But I am not sure, just because a juror is aware of that matter, it necessarily implies said juror cannot be fair."

"Well, that matter certainly seems to have had its effect on you, Judge."

Eldon Phelps turned red, and then he moved to sit again, very slowly. Before the judge could put down his robe, Morgan whispered to me very softly so there was no chance of the judge hearing. "You think we've got enough to file an affidavit of bias and prejudice on this son of a bitch?"

"I don't know," I whispered back. "But he sure scares me."

At first the judge was unable to make words come. Finally he said, very slowly, "Now listen here, Mr.—"

Abruptly Morgan swung around. "I guess, Max, it's really your call. I suppose it's all just a question of how much error you want to invite."

"You listen to me!" yelled Eldon Phelps.

"We have yet to hear the State's position on the matter, if it please the court," said Morgan.

The judge sputtered, then turned to Hauser. "What is your position, Mr. Hauser?"

Hauser thought about the situation for a good long time. "Mr. Morgan may have a point, Your Honor," he finally conceded. And with that concession we commenced upon a procedure that drove the jury commissioner's office to bedlam with the steady demand that more and then more citizens be sent to Eldon Phelps's chambers, where, one by one, each privately detailed for us the extent to which the news coverage of our victory in Rita Eddington's defense had poisoned his or her respective well.

It was not pleasant; Eldon Phelps did not allow anyone but himself to ask a question, and we sat in the same chairs, squirming, for two days, until he'd managed to assemble twelve people who were either sufficiently illiterate or sufficiently new to the state of Arizona as to be unaware of what had gone before. When it was over, we had six men and six women gazing across the rail of the jury box, hands raised, promising to do their duty. Looking back, I realize that I do not remember the names of those people. I can still name the jurors from Rita's trial: There was Guy Buckley, the crop duster, and Anthony Savoca, who wore elevator shoes, and Mrs. Mendoza, and all the others. But I can't remember anything about those twelve people who were left when Eldon Phelps got through with his voir dire. No. I do remember this: They were decent-looking men and women, and they appeared to be earnest in the desire to do the right thing.

When Max Hauser rose to make his opening statement, I sat on the edge of my seat, waiting to hear him promise the jury that Rita would appear. He didn't make that promise. He delivered a mercifully short narrative of what he claimed had happened. "We will prove beyond a reasonable doubt that the defendant killed her father," he finally said. "Further, we will prove that she killed her father with premeditation and deliberation and with malice aforethought. In other words, ladies and gentlemen of the jury, we will prove that the defendant committed murder in the first degree."

We lunched that first day at Tom's Tavern. I ate a bowl of chili. Morgan moved a spoon around in a bowl of beef stew. "He doesn't have Rita," Morgan said, as absently he played with his food. "Did you watch him squirm up there? By God, he doesn't have her, and he knows he isn't going to make it to that jury." For the first time in weeks, a small elation seemed to bubble up in him.

"Listen, Dan," I said, "I made a list of all the things Frank Menendez and I came up with. I thought maybe you'd like to go over them to prepare to cross-examine Rita. Just in case she does show up, I mean. I think if you just ask her if Joanna Barnes visited her in the jail on that date, she'll know we found her out, and she'll shit, right there in front of the jury and they'll know she's lying."

"She isn't going to show."

"But what if she does? Don't you want to get ready?"

"Maybe later," he said.

We walked back to court.

"You may call your first witness, Mr. Hauser," Eldon Phelps announced.

"The State calls Dr. Robert Wallace, Your Honor."

I heard Morgan exhale, and I watched him ease back in his chair. His dogmatic prophecy about her nonappearance notwithstanding, Morgan was as nervous as I was about those doors opening upon Rita. Well, the appearance of the county medical examiner posed no threat. He came only to tell us that Travis was dead. He'd get no argument there. Morgan and I both relaxed.

The ballistics expert testified next. Midway through his testimony, the door behind me opened, and I jerked around reflexively. An old street woman squeezed vigorously onto a bench next to a pretty young television reporter. The ballistics man droned on interminably, and he was still on the stand when we broke for the afternoon recess.

Juan Menchaka sat on a bench in the hall. "You'll take Juan again," Morgan ordered.

I walked across the hall.

"Juan," I said, "you remember how you couldn't tell whether it was Rita who fired the gun?"

"Yes."

"The same goes for Miranda. Right?"

"That's right," Juan promised.

I walked around the fifth floor and then back to Morgan, who sat hunched on a concrete bench, his elbows on his knees and a cigarette between his fingers.

"Seen Rita?"

"She isn't on this floor," I told him. "I've looked everywhere. I even went into the ladies' room."

"You have to be careful with that. Sometimes there are jurors in there."

Back in the courtroom, Hauser went on for another half hour with ballistics—angles of entry, positions of the body, distances. I began to wonder if he'd come up with another theory, something intended to prove forensically that it had actually been Miranda who fired the gun. I scribbled a note along that line to Morgan, and he shoved back a reply: "He's stalling. They're still trying to find Rita. That's why nobody's with him at counsel table. They're all trying to find her." Suddenly he pulled the yellow pad back and added a postscript: "He knows his tit's in a big wringer."

The courtroom door squeaked. Once again I spun around. Juan Menchaka appeared. Hauser called him to the stand, and after forty-five minutes of direct testimony I asked my only question. "From what you observed, Mr. Menchaka," I said, without so much as a flutter in my voice, "you could not tell whether it was Miranda Eddington or her mother who fired the gun, could you?"

"That's right," Juan answered simply and directly.

"Thank you, Mr. Menchaka."

I moved toward my chair. As I was about to sit down, I heard Juan say one more thing: "If anybody, it was Rita who killed him." I looked up, this time more stunned than when he'd given me a small, unsolicited boost in Rita's defense. I couldn't believe it. Nor, apparently, could Max Hauser, who remained frozen in his chair. "It was Rita who did it," Juan declared emphatically.

Hauser awakened and rocketed to his feet. "Objection!" he exploded.

"Sustained!"

But Juan pressed on. "This is crap! Miranda didn't kill anybody."

"Sir!" Eldon Phelps yelled. "The court has sustained an objection! You be silent!"

"But this is ridiculous. This is—"

"Mister." Eldon Phelps pointed his finger.

But Juan would not stop. He kept on about the absurdity of the proceeding while the jury and I stared, rapt. I felt Morgan come up behind me. He gently eased me into my chair. As he took his own chair, he signaled with his hand that I was to stay out of the fray. I nodded, and he winked. We both watched Juan, who fought like a big fish, and Eldon Phelps, who worked like an angler with a small leader. As Juan struggled with the judge, I realized that he was trying to make amends for stretching the truth in the first trial. A small stretch, but we had both recognized it, and he felt guilty.

I looked over at Morgan. His head dipped. A sudden and deep kinship with Juan? A shared sense of guilt for having played fast and loose with the truth and, as a result, Miranda's life? Then Morgan glanced at the jury to see that no one was looking at him. He smiled.

"This is wrong!" Juan yelled.

"I renew my objection!" Hauser screamed.

"Is there any reason that this witness should not be excused?" the judge demanded.

"No, Your Honor."

"Sir, you are excused."

When Juan saw the bailiff begin to move toward him, he got down from the stand.

"We will be in recess until nine o'clock tomorrow morning," Phelps intoned. "The jury is excused until then. You ladies and gentlemen will remember the admonitions of the court. You are not to talk about this case. You are not to read the newspapers. You are not to watch the news on television or listen to it on the radio. And counsel will remain while I have a word with them." The judge stared coldly at me as he rattled out that last order.

The jury filed out, and I braced myself.

"Mr. McKenzie."

"Yes, Your Honor."

"I'm not sure what just happened here. I'm not sure how this happened. But it is never to happen again."

"I'm sorry, Your Honor."

"In the future—" He stopped. He pointed a long finger at me out of his robe. And I could see the blood pulsing in the veins along his neck. "In the future you prepare your witnesses so they don't offer that kind of scurrilous performance in this court. If anything like this happens again, I will have you before the governors of the bar within a minute. You make no mistake about that, sir."

I flushed, acutely aware of all the newspaper and television reporters in the gallery. I could feel the blood in my face as red as the judge's. I was about to say again that I was sorry, that I really did not mean for it to happen, that it would not happen again. But before I could say all those things, I heard one word erupt from Dan Morgan.

"Whoa!"

Then he slowly rose, and I knew that every eye in the room had moved to him.

"If it please the court," he said. "If it please the court, I would remind Your Honor that Mr. Menchaka was not Mr. McKenzie's witness."

The judge got redder, and Morgan went on.

"Mr. McKenzie asked one unobjectionable question on cross-examination. Your Honor will recall that it was Mr. Hauser who spent upwards of an hour asking for an excruciatingly detailed rendition of events, most of which tell us nothing. I would respectfully suggest that if Mr. Hauser can prepare his witness to bore us so effectively for so long, it is Mr. Hauser who might be urged to instruct his witness that he should not tell us what he knows to be the truth, so long as such distortion is the pleasure of the court."

Morgan turned his back to the bench and looked at the gallery. A reporter for the *Arizona Republic* smiled at him, and Morgan winked back. I watched the color come up in Max Hauser's already very red face. Then I realized that the judge had left the bench.

Morgan had just finished packing his briefcase when Max Hauser approached him. "You son of a bitch," Hauser said.

Morgan bent to his sock and pulled out a package of cigarettes and put one in his mouth. He flipped open his lighter, but before he struck the flint, he pulled the cigarette away in order to say something to our adversary. I moved toward them, thinking I might have to step between, but as I neared, Morgan returned the cigarette to its proper place, fired the lighter, and left the larger man standing in a great cloud of smoke.

Outside on the sidewalk, I heard Morgan mumble something. The only word I could make out was "asshole."

"I think he's just nervous," I offered. "I don't think he'd have called you that if he was really confident in his case."

"Not Hauser," Morgan said. "I was thinking about that fucking judge."

64 IN ACCORDANCE WITH a gruff command, I met Morgan at the Arizona Club for dinner at seven-thirty. "Thank you," I told him as we pulled up to the table.

"For what?" he said.

"For sort of getting me out of that situation in court today."

"Oh." He chuckled. "I think old Juan may have gotten that jury's attention."

"I know he did," I said.

"And there was fat boy jumping around in front of them like a fart on a skillet, looking like he had something to hide. That kind of stuff can lose cases. I really believe that."

"Well, thanks," I said. "The judge embarrassed me."

"Ha!" Morgan laughed. "Don't give him a second thought. He's an asshole, and he's going to do everything he can to sink us, and we may as well just live with it. But we don't have to take any crap off him."

I gave Morgan a chance to get most of a beer down before I raised the old subject again. "What about your cross-examination of Rita?" I finally asked. "I thought maybe tonight I could try to help you get ready."

"She isn't going to show," he said. "That's why Hauser's stalling with all his witnesses. He hasn't got her." Morgan closed his eyes and twisted his head a few degrees.

"Something wrong?" I asked.

"Just a little headache. It'll go away. Hey, Mason, can I have an aspirin and a steak over here? And another beer."

I worked on a large trout and watched Morgan's steak get cold as he stared silently out across the lights of the city. From time to time, he grimaced, and I could tell that the aspirin had not touched whatever it was that had gotten hold of him. I chewed my fish and sipped my wine, and I thought of all the stories I'd heard about how Daniel Morgan prepared for trial. If the other side called five witnesses, Morgan would be ready to cross-examine ten. If a hostile witness was dangerous, he would know everything that witness had ever said, everything he'd ever done, every inconsistency, every piece of dirt, everything that could impeach, discredit, embarrass, humiliate. . . . But there he sat on that chilly Arizona night, the fifth of the New Year, staring up North Central Avenue, telling me that we didn't have to worry because he had somehow divined that she wouldn't appear.

"He doesn't have her, Doug. She wouldn't come back and do that to Miranda."

I ordered another glass of wine, and by the time I finished half of it, I was telling myself that there was nothing I could do but wait and see what happened. I dared not broach the subject again. It was no longer my problem, I told myself. I raised my glass and filled my mouth.

"I'll tell you what, Doug," Morgan said, "I'll make you a little wager. If she shows up, you can cross-examine her."

It was a joke. I knew that when he said it. Then I saw his cold, hard stare, and I realized he wasn't kidding. I had once promised myself that never again would I balk when Daniel Morgan gave me a chance to do something in a courtroom. But at that moment I could think of nothing but the vacuum in my chest and the burning in my neck where the blood was running toward my face and the spot of wine that had fallen from my glass to the linen tablecloth. The memory of my reply is absolutely vivid.

"No fucking way," I told him. He pushed his chair back. "No way," I said.

He stood up. "I promised you that you could take the testimony of a witness. I promised you when you walked away from the golf tournament."

"You kept your promise. You let me do Juan."

He reached for the check. "That was nothing."

"You let me do Joanna Barnes, too."

"That wasn't anything either."

"It was good enough for me." He signed the check. "I can't," I said. "I don't know how." He pulled his jacket from the back of his chair. "It's too important, Dan."

"You'll do fine. You and Frank have your theory. If she shows—she won't, but if she does—you can go ahead and make your theory work."

He left the check on the white linen and walked toward the elevator. Now it was I who stared out at the lights that ran up North Central Avenue. Not for long, though. When I got to the elevator, the doors were closing, and I shoved my hand in and forced them back.

"How the hell am I supposed to get ready for this?"

"Frank can get you ready. He's done a pretty good job of taking over your education so far." I stepped back, the door closed, and Dan Morgan was gone.

When I dialed Frank Menendez's number it wasn't on Morgan's advice. I was following the only instinct I had.

"It's impossible, Douglas," Sue Menendez said. "It's simply impossible." She was crying as she hung up on me.

I left the men's reading room, where I'd gone to use the telephone, and in a daze I wandered into the billiards parlor, which was empty and dark save for the far corner where a single Tiffany lamp illuminated a two-man snooker game. I pulled myself into the tall chair at the dark end of the room, and I stared unconsciously at the light over the snooker table, and I heard the click of the balls. I tried to think. Rita would come. She would be beautiful, wearing one of the dresses that Morgan had selected for her courtroom appearances, probably the pale blue knit that Ann Hastings had worn when she let down her hair. She would tell the lie that Morgan so carefully provided the means for her to craft. And unless Douglas McKenzie, a year out of law school and never a threat for Boy Orator of Arizona, could ask her precisely the right questions, those that would elicit the right answers, she would cast her child into the hands of Eldon Phelps. I longed to be back in juvenile court.

I stared at the distant triangle of light the lamp shed on the two men moving around the green table. I lowered my head into my hands. Then suddenly I was in the elevator. Then I was out the front door of the First National Bank Building, running through the dark toward the Luhrs Building. I ran past the construction equipment for the new park and across the spot where Harry Wilson's bar had been torn down. I jumped over two winos and into the Luhrs lobby, where I fumbled for the key that would stop the elevator at our floor. When I finally made it, I ran for Morgan's office, and I leaped at the door. It was locked. I banged my shoulder into it, but it didn't budge. I picked up a chair, and as I was about to swing it, I heard a voice.

"What's going on?"

"I want that door opened!" I yelled. The maintenance man stood with his eyes very wide. "I work here. I'm Douglas McKenzie. Open that door."

"I've seen you before," the man said.

"Come on. Please. It's important." At last he reached for the keys that hung from his belt. Finally he found the one that turned. I went to the credenza behind Morgan's desk. It was locked also. I turned to the maintenance man frantically. "I've got to have that damned thing opened."

"Well, I sure don't have a key to that."

"Break it open."

"I can't do that."

"I've got to get in there."

"There's a crowbar in the utility closet, but I'm not going to use it."

"I'll get it," I said. I got the crowbar, and I used it, the credenza lock springing readily, and I reached inside. Then I walked slowly to my office, clutching Morgan's manual on cross-examination to my chest like a baby.

I read, and I sweated, and I began to realize that if Mor-

gan's attempt at scholarship was teaching me anything, it
was that the art of cross-examination was not something
one learned overnight by use of some worn, coffee-stained
manuscript and that I had no business trying it. I could see
between every line how afraid Dan Morgan was of smart
witnesses, and those spaces between the lines taught me
just how embarrassed I would be the following day when
perhaps the smartest witness I would ever see, the one
who'd been hand-polished by Morgan himself, would
come to devour me. As I read, I knew that this had to be
some cruel joke, but still I worked into the night. At least
I wouldn't have trouble getting to sleep. I knew from the
beginning that I would not even try.

I got out yellow pads, and I tried to organize everything
Frank Menendez ever told me he thought had happened.
Then I tried to figure out just how far I could go, in good
faith, in suggesting what we thought was the case, just
how much of it I could, to use words once spoken by Dan
Morgan, shove up Rita Eddington's ass. I sweated, and I
burned, and finally morning came.

65 TOM GALLAGHER'S FACE was the color of lead when he stepped off the elevator into the hallway outside Eldon Phelps's courtroom. "Where's Danny?" he asked.

"He hasn't gotten here yet," I told him.

It was very early, and Gallagher and I stood alone in the hallway, the only people on the fifth floor. I didn't ask why he wanted Morgan; from his expression I knew. He took his keys from his pocket, then put them back. He closed his eyes and massaged the bridge of his nose. He exhaled a long, audible breath. He stood silently in the same place until the elevator doors opened again and Morgan stepped out. Morgan stopped. Then Gallagher confirmed what Morgan and I already had read on his face.

"Frank's dead, Danny." Morgan started to speak, but then he just looked down to the floor. "He died about an hour ago," Gallagher said. "The last thing he told Sue was to have me come and tell you. He didn't want you hearing it from some newspaperman."

Morgan bit his lip. For an instant I thought it might begin to bleed. He made a fist and softly hit his forehead three times. He looked back to Gallagher, and his eyes began to moisten. "Tom," he said apologetically, "I've got to take this little girl's testimony today."

"I know."

Morgan threw his shoulders back and walked past

Gallagher into the courtroom, making me remember the marine who'd gotten up and walked out of the Baseline Tavern. Gallagher pushed the button and stepped into the elevator, leaving me alone in the hall.

Badly needing a private place where I could think about what I would likely have to do that day, I slipped into the men's room. A lucky thing I did. Within about ten seconds, I threw up. I hardly knew it was coming. If anyone should ever want to know where that ritual event happened for Douglas McKenzie, it happened in the room marked "Gentlemen" on the fifth floor of the Maricopa County Superior Courthouse, the courthouse at the corner of First Avenue and Jefferson Street. The men's room is at the northeast corner of the fifth-floor hallway. It happened in the stall nearest the door. I flushed, I rinsed out my mouth, and I walked back into the hallway and fixed my gaze on the elevator door. I waited for her.

Rita did not appear, and I went into the courtroom and slid into my chair. Morgan seemed unaware that I had arrived. Not one word of testimony registered on me that morning. I was too busy going over in my mind what I was going to ask Rita when I cross-examined her. I felt something burning inside me, very hot, and I felt sweat dripping down under my arms, and I felt something grinding somewhere around where my heart was supposed to be. But I was no longer scared. At least I didn't think I was.

Rita had not appeared by noon, and I followed Morgan to Tom's Tavern for beef stew and coffee. "I'm sorry about Frank," I choked out.

His face contorted for an instant, and then he raised his hands an inch or two off the table. "It had to be."

Max Hauser was in the hallway when we returned to the courtroom. He refused to acknowledge us when we stepped off the elevator. He paced back and forth nervously, much the way I had that morning. Morgan went into the courtroom, and I stayed behind in the hall, feeling great energy, feeling quite certain that I was no longer afraid. I stared at Max Hauser's enormous back as he watched the elevator doors. The elevator delivered a deputy sheriff to the hall-

way, and Max Hauser (he must not have realized that I was
still in the hall) spoke openly with the man. "Where the
hell is she?"

"She didn't show up."

"Find her. Find her, goddamn it."

"We can't find her, Mr. Hauser. God knows we've tried."

I folded onto the cool concrete bench, then gratefully
exhaled.

"Rita Eddington may as well never have existed, for all
we can find," said the deputy.

Hauser stormed into the courtroom. The deputy sheriff
took the elevator back down, and I sat there on the bench,
all alone in the hallway. I put my hands behind my head
and looked upward and felt myself breathe. At the far end
of the hall, the ladies'-room door opened. Joanna Barnes
stepped into the hallway. I jumped to my feet, trying to
think, trying to analyze whether Hauser could possibly
make a case against Miranda on her testimony alone.

"Douglas," Joanna said brightly. She wore her long
skirt, her knee-high boots, and a long-sleeved silk blouse.
No scarf. She began to move in my direction, as if to give
me a hug. The elevator doors parted once again, and Joanna Barnes stopped dead in her tracks. When I saw Rita
my eyes closed involuntarily, and I heard the echo of Frank
Menendez's voice: *"She'll come back. . . . Rita will come
and probably that other greedy bitch, too."* I opened my
eyes, and she stood framed in the elevator door, looking
just the way she'd looked in the elevator leaving the Arizona Club that time I'd last seen her. She wore the blue
dress. She wore the same shoes. She wore her hair exactly
the way Morgan had told her to. Then I saw something new.
Around her neck she wore Joanna Barnes's scarf. My eyes
widened. Frank Menendez had been right. It was all true.

Rita and Joanna looked at each other. They nodded
pleasantly, as do people who have seen each other but have
not been formally introduced. All cool and controlled.
Then Joanna noticed the scarf, and control evaporated. She
moved instinctively toward Rita. For an instant I thought
she would tear the expensive silk from Rita's neck. But then

she stopped and glanced at me, trying to gauge how much I knew. She blinked repeatedly. I pushed my cheek far out with my tongue. I nodded at her three times very slowly, and then I smiled and winked. Joanna Barnes shoved both hands between the closing elevator doors. She forced the doors open and ducked into the car. Gone. She didn't even say good-bye.

"Hello, Rita."

"Hello, Doug," she said calmly. She remained composed, cool and unruffled, as if Joanna Barnes, the complete stranger, had never been there. Suddenly I imagined the nights she'd lain awake planning this moment, polishing her wicked testimony, buttressing it for cross-examination by Dan Morgan himself. Was she afraid of Morgan? If she was, her eyes didn't show it. She was ice, and I knew she was ready for us. "How are you, Doug?"

"I'm okay," I lied.

"You're looking good," she said.

I suppose, right from the moment I decided to write it all down, after I'd begun to obsess about what happened all those years ago, I knew that there would come a time, if I were to tell the whole story, that I would have to tell what I've never told before—that which I never told Dan Morgan, that which I've never told Tom Gallagher, or Walter Smith, or Ann Hastings, or my mother, or my grandmother Belle. I never would have done it, but for Morgan's little practical joke. And it had from its beginning been a malicious little joke set up to punish me for my small infidelity with Frank Menendez. I was one year out of law school. I had spent one half-drunk night at the Arizona Club listening to him go on about his theories of cross-examination. *Come on, Morgan, it's a first-degree-murder case.*

I stood in the hallway looking at the muted blues of Joanna Barnes's scarf and the bright turquoise of Rita Eddington's eyes. "Are you going to testify?" I asked.

"They subpoenaed me, Doug."

I looked both ways to make sure we were alone. And then I did it. I believe it may go by many names, beyond simple loss of nerve, and I remember that the one at the front of my mind that afternoon was obstruction of justice.

"We know, Rita," I told her. "We know all about you. Right down to where you got that scarf. You got it from the woman who just ran like hell when she saw you wearing it. She bought it at Helga Howie's boutique on Maiden Lane in San Francisco. You testify and Ferris Eddington finds out all about you and Joanna Barnes and all the rest of it."

And then she wasn't ready for us anymore. In an instant I learned how fast the eyes of a human being can become those of a frightened animal. I had told Morgan that if he confronted Rita with Joanna Barnes—with what we knew—Rita would defecate. I hadn't meant it literally. And then maybe that isn't what she did after I told her what I told her. All I know is that she turned with her eyes flashing, looking for cover. I could swear she perceived that the ladies' room was too far away, and that was why she went into the men's. And if she wasn't sitting down in there, she was bent over, right at the spot where I'd been not six hours before.

A juror got off the elevator and headed into the men's room. "I think you'd better wait, sir," I told him. "I think I just saw a lady go in there."

Minutes later Max Hauser made the announcement he'd been longing to make. "Call Rita Eddington, if the court please." She looked a little pallid as she walked past us to the witness stand, and when the clerk asked her if she swore to tell the truth, she only shook her head.

"You'll have to speak out loud," the court reporter firmly instructed.

Still, all Rita could manage was a pained whisper. "Yes, I swear to tell the truth."

"State your full name," Hauser demanded unceremoniously. She didn't state her name. All she did was look at me, and I could see that she was thinking about the incredible predicament she was in. She hadn't had sufficient time to think it all through in the men's room. "Mrs. Eddington, I must ask you to state your full name for the record." Silence. "Mrs. Eddington?"

Morgan pushed his chair back and rolled behind Miranda toward me. "I thought you told Ann there were only two of those scarves in existence," he whispered, head down.

"Right. And that one belongs to Joanna Barnes. She just neglected to tell Rita that I'd seen it. Rita never would have worn it if she'd known."

"Holy Christ."

"Frank Menendez had it figured out," I said.

"Do you have notes for your cross-examination?"

"Yes."

"Give them to me. I'll take her."

"But can you—"

"Just give me your notes, goddamn it."

I handed him the yellow pad, and he moved back to the table and began to read. So, you see, it had all been a cruel joke. There was no way Daniel Morgan would have let young Douglas McKenzie conduct a cross-examination of the only real witness in a murder case, not when that witness was as hostile as a witness could possibly be.

"Mrs. Eddington, I must ask you again to state your name." More silence.

I watched Morgan read, and once again I saw him turn to steel. Twice he bent back around our client in order to confirm details of certain events, such as the date on which the good-looking woman visited Rita in the jail, and the address of Joanna Barnes's apartment on Vallejo Street in San Francisco. At length he stopped reading and looked at the ceiling and took a deep breath. He wrote me a note: *"You've done well. If this all comes as a surprise, we have her."* I put my head in my hands.

"Mrs. Eddington, again, I ask you to state your name."

Morgan ran his hand through his hair, and his eyes moved around the courtroom, flashing first at the judge, then at the jury, then back into the overflowing gallery. Finally he turned back and fixed upon Rita Eddington. Rita continued to stare at me. So, too, I realized, was the judge staring at me, as was Hauser and the jury. I gazed straight ahead. I knew one thing: Rita would have to start talking

before anybody had grounds to arrest me for my conduct
in the hallway. (Even though I was a lawyer, I had a right
to remain silent—*Spevack v. Klein*.) And I knew that Rita
was not going to start talking. I remembered the smell of
fear in the conference room the day Ferris Eddington tacitly threatened not to pay our bill unless we agreed to do
his bidding and defend his granddaughter. (At least then we
thought she was his granddaughter.) We had all been afraid
of him, we lawyers, but what we'd felt that day was not
what Rita was feeling as she sat in that witness chair staring at me. What she felt moved out through her pores and
danced around on the green carpet. And I knew that when
back in the hall she had told me, "You're looking good,"
that was the only lie she was going to tell this afternoon.

"Will you tell us your name, Mrs. Eddington?"

She didn't move her gaze from me, and she didn't blink.
And she did not answer, even though now it was the judge
who was asking. I sensed movement next to me, and I
turned and saw Miranda Eddington staring at her mother.
Miranda was trembling. I had been so wrapped up in my
own anxiety I'd all but forgotten that our client was in the
room with us. Now, as I looked at her, I could see she was
about to cry. I put my arm around her, and I pulled her
close to me, then felt her grab my hand and squeeze it until
it hurt. "It's all right," I whispered. "You don't have to be
afraid. She can't harm you now."

Rita kept staring at me, still trying, I could tell, to sort it
all out, trying to figure out what to do. Suddenly she stood,
fully erect. She began to cry. "I'm sorry, Mr. Hauser. I cannot do it." She stepped down from the witness stand. "She's
my daughter," Rita said to Hauser as she passed him on her
way out of the courtroom.

Hauser just stood there, seemingly in shock, for a full
minute. Morgan stared up at him with a nasty grin. The
room was starkly quiet for that first minute. Then a few of
the newspeople in the back began to whisper, and in time
the gallery became very noisy. It was the judge who finally
brought Max Hauser back to the proceeding. "Mr. Hauser,
do I understand that Mrs. Eddington is under subpoena?"

"What?" Hauser said.

"Is Mrs. Eddington not under subpoena?"

"Oh. Yes, Your Honor, she is."

"Might it be appropriate for me to issue a material-witness warrant?"

"Yes, Your Honor. I request that."

The judge turned to his left and said, "Members of the jury, we will be in recess for thirty minutes. Remember the admonitions of the court."

Thirty minutes later Maximilian Hauser was explaining to Eldon Phelps that Rita Eddington was not to be found. "She simply disappeared, Your Honor."

"Do you have other witnesses, Mr. Hauser?"

"Your Honor, I intended to call a woman named Joanna Barnes, but I am now advised that we are unable to locate her as well."

"My impression is that the case cannot go to the jury unless we have Mrs. Eddington's testimony," observed the judge.

And if that had ended the matter, if Eldon Phelps, when it became inescapable to conclude that he was not to have Rita Eddington's testimony, had simply closed up shop and sent the jury and Miranda Eddington home, I likely would never have given a second thought to what I did with Rita in the hallway that day. Justice would have been done, and Dan Morgan and I would have gone to the Arizona Club for his beer and my champagne and the grand homage that most surely we would have been paid. But that was not the way things went.

"Your Honor, I believe we have an alternative," I heard Max Hauser announce, and my insides went cold. The judge peered down, most interested. "We have the transcripts of Mrs. Eddington's and Ms. Joanna Barnes's testimony from the prior trial. Taken together, that testimony proves conclusively that Miranda Eddington is guilty as charged. Both women, even though they are under subpoena, are now unavailable to testify. I propose to have that testimony read to the jury."

"But, Mr. Hauser," said the judge, "that would be rank hearsay."

"You're damned right it would be!" Morgan shouted.

"We'll have none of that language in this court."

"I'm sorry, Your Honor, but you are absolutely right."

"Your Honor, I have taken the liberty of briefing the question," Hauser said as he handed a thick memorandum up toward the bench. The judge was already reading eagerly by the time Hauser handed a copy to Morgan. The judge stopped reading and announced a twenty-minute recess in which we were to prepare to argue the issue.

In the hallway Morgan flew through Hauser's memorandum, turning the pages so fast that I had no hope of keeping up. "This is horseshit," he said.

"I don't know," I said. "I know there's something in the new—"

"Oh, come on, Doug. This is bullshit. Rita isn't testifying, and we're out of here."

"I know there is something in those new *Federal Rules of Evidence* about the use of prior testimony, when it's under oath, when all interests in a matter were represented. I just didn't think of it until Hauser started talking, but I know that Professor Cleary—he's the reporter on the new rules—was having debates on it out at the law school. The proponents were relying on cases from both state and federal jurisdictions."

"Christ," said Morgan, "we have a constitutional right to confront her. To cross-examine her."

"Hauser already cross-examined her."

"It didn't count. He was ineffectual. He broke every rule. This is horseshit, Doug. If Phelps lets it in, the Supreme Court will reverse him for sure." His voice was not as firm as his words, and as we walked back into the courtroom, I felt a deep depression settle in.

In the courtroom Morgan yelled, "A defendant's right to confront witnesses is fundamental, Your Honor! The right to cross-examine is as important as any—"

"Yes, Mr. Morgan. I don't mean to interrupt, but I notice that Mrs. Eddington was already cross-examined—by Mr. Hauser."

"She was not cross-examined on behalf of Miranda Eddington."

"Now, wait, Mr. Morgan. It was done at a time that Mrs. Eddington and you, sir, had set about to prove that Miranda was the guilty party. At that time Mr. Hauser's interests were identical to what your client's are now."

"He wasn't her lawyer."

"I don't know what difference that makes."

"What he did was inadequate."

Hauser snapped around.

"He should have been ashamed, Your Honor," said Morgan, without turning from the prosecutor.

Hauser reddened.

"Well," said the judge, "I know you trial lawyers delight in second-guessing each other. You all have your own pride. Your own arrogance——"

"Arrogance, hell! He's inept! Why do you think we won the first time around? He ought to turn in his ticket. And you can't call what he did cross-examination!" Hauser started to move toward Morgan, and I quickly pulled Miranda back to a protected corner. The bailiff managed to step between the two lawyers before the first punch was thrown.

As things calmed, the judge took another tack. "Mr. Morgan, I will tell you what I think distinguishes this matter and makes it more appropriate for what Mr. Hauser suggests than even those cases he has cited in his brief. You were the lawyer who elicited from Mrs. Eddington the testimony Mr. Hauser proposes to read. You had certain ethical obligations not to offer perjured testimony. You should not now be heard to complain of the testimony you, in what strikes me as a very real sense, created."

"I didn't create it!"

I choked, thinking of how carefully Morgan had set the stage for Rita to practice her craft.

"You elicited it from her, Mr. Morgan. And you were ethically bound not to do that unless it was true. And if it *was* true, then it *is* true, and further cross-examination would serve no purpose other than to distort the truth."

"You misstate my ethical duty when you say it was not to offer perjured testimony!" Morgan yelled. "My duty was not to offer testimony that I *knew* to be perjured."

"That, sir, is a pretty pathetic distinction!" the judge shouted back.

"We know things now, Your Honor, that we didn't know then, things I could use to expose her lie but which I will not be able to use because I cannot cross-examine a cold transcript."

"Well, if you do have things to put the lie to what Mrs. Eddington said, I suppose you can prove those things by extrinsic evidence."

"We don't have witnesses, Your Honor."

"Then it strikes me that any impeachment will be negligible." Morgan stood in shock, and the judge turned to Hauser. "Are you prepared to read the transcript of the two women's testimony?"

"Yes, Your Honor."

"In that case bring the jury back." Eldon Phelps paused. "And now, Mr. Morgan, I see no way I can avoid telling them about what went before."

The judge told the jury all about the first trial, and the jury turned their collective gaze upon our table. Some of them looked at the child beside me, but most of them looked at the man on the other side of the child, the one whose jaw was moving in and out, the one who was staring at the man on the bench in the black robe, and the gaze those jurors cast upon Morgan was equal to the one Morgan cast upon the judge.

Max Hauser didn't simply read the transcript of Rita's testimony to them. He had a young woman lawyer from his office come in, take the stand, and read Rita's answers as he read Morgan's questions. The woman, though not nearly as lovely as Rita, made an excellent witness. Though unable to manage the perfectly timed tears, she seemed entirely as credible as Rita was when she had originally performed the part. And, I noticed, Hauser seemed better when he was reading Morgan's questions instead of his own.

As I listened to the young woman in the blue gabardine

suit read Rita Eddington's words, it slowly but fully dawned on me what had happened. We had been deprived altogether of the right to cross-examine Rita herself. We would have no opportunity to attack her with all we knew about her and Joanna Barnes, no chance to ask her where she got that scarf. We had no real evidence to link her to Joanna Barnes and her perjury. We had only a good-faith basis to surprise her with it and then let the jury watch her react. Had the jury been able to see her react the way she had earlier that day, they would have seen the truth.

But that would not happen. All because Dan Morgan could not bring himself to see the truth. *Oh, come on, Douglas! It was all because you were too much a coward to face her in the courtroom. You had to do it in the hallway, and because of that, she did the thing that told the truth in the men's room and not in front of the jury.* I looked at Miranda, and I looked at Morgan, and there in the very bottom of my chair I learned what it felt like to burn with shame.

"Make him read the cross-examination." Morgan had jumped to his feet.

"Your Honor, there was no substantive evidence offered in my cross-examination."

"The basis for allowing this to be read, Your Honor, was that it had been cross-examined."

"But I thought I heard you say, Mr. Morgan, that you did not think much of Mr. Hauser's cross."

"I want it read!"

The judge considered Morgan's demand, then apologetically ordered Hauser to read it. Hauser read, and he only colored a little bit as he did.

When he presented Joanna Barnes's testimony, Hauser brought in another woman to read it, a stout woman who looked to me more like a telephone operator than the real witness had. Almost before I knew it, they finished, and Joanna Barnes had managed to do in absentia that which she did not dare show her face to try.

"On behalf of the State of Arizona, Your Honor, the prosecution rests."

"You may call your first witness, Mr. Morgan."

And, for Morgan, she was his only witness. "Call the defendant, Your Honor."

Miranda Eddington walked shyly to the stand, and sitting there in a blue cotton dress, she told the story I had by then heard so many times. She told the jury what had happened, and the jury watched and seemed to listen, but often I would see their eyes linger on the man who was asking the questions, and their eyes, when they would do that, hardened. It didn't take long, and when Morgan announced that he rested, the judge told the jurors that they were excused until the following morning, when they would hear closing arguments.

It was over. There was nothing for me to do but wait until morning and watch Morgan argue. I remember that as Morgan and I walked across First Avenue, the thought crossed my mind that at least Miranda had the best lawyer she could get to make the argument. The thought was fleeting, however, for in my mind's eye I saw once again the hardened faces of the jury as they watched Morgan question his young client so smoothly and so skillfully. I thought I might be sick for a second time that day. As we walked on, I looked at Morgan, surprised by how white he'd become. I wondered if he knew that I'd done something to scare Rita into her silence, that it was I who had put him in the fix he was then in. He'd hardly spoken to me since lunch, and I was worried.

We moved on toward the Luhrs Building, and as we neared, he said, "Doug?" I jerked around. "Do you think there's any way the Supreme Court will affirm a conviction based on those transcripts?"

I breathed. "I don't know," I told him. "I can do some research."

"You may as well start," he said sadly. "We don't have a fucking chance with that jury."

At first I thought I would go home and go to bed, since I hadn't slept the night before. But then I knew I couldn't

sleep, so when I realized that Morgan had disappeared from
the office, I drove to Durant's by myself. I thought I would
have one drink, then dinner, then go home to bed. My first
bourbon was so good, though, that I had another and then
another. I remembered the last time I'd sat at that bar, when
Ann Hastings had come in, and I indulged a small fantasy
that she might do the same thing this evening. She didn't,
of course, and I sat and drank my whiskey alone, and I felt
it dull me from the inside out, and I thought about how all
my worst fears had materialized, about how Rita Eddington had come for us and in some great poetic irony she had
done us in. Then I thought about Miranda and how she
shook when she looked up at her mother sitting in the witness stand.

I thought back to my grand epiphany on the hallowed
fairways of the Olympic Country Club, when I concluded
that it was beneath the calling of any decent man to defend
a person he knows is guilty. *What sanctimonious crap.* I
didn't even have the question right, let alone the answer.
The question isn't how can a lawyer live with himself when
he's defending a person he knows is guilty. It's how can he
sleep when he's defending one he knows is innocent.

I ordered another drink and tried to tell myself that
it wasn't my fault, that if only Morgan had listened to
me—no, if only he had listened to Frank Menendez—it
never would have happened. He would have gotten ready,
and he would have burned Rita down. He would have evis-
cerated her. Whatever it was she'd done in the men's room
that afternoon she would have done in front of the jury. The
jury would have acquitted, the media would have broad-
cast the entire story of our brilliance, and we would have
had a party, and someone, at some point in the festivities,
would have yelled out that Frank Menendez would have
been proud. But that was not to be, and I could not think
any more about what had really happened, so I finished my
drink and ordered another.

66

"WHAT?" I GROANED, barely able to hold the telephone.

"It's Ann."

"What?"

"Doug? It's Ann Hastings."

"It's the middle of the night." I calculated that I'd been asleep for about an hour. I also determined that I was still drunk, and maybe sick, from all the bourbon I'd swilled at Durant's.

"Doug. There's trouble. Morgan's in jail."

"What?!"

"Morgan's in jail."

"How do you know?"

"Some guy from the jail—he said his name was Shorty—"

"Yeah, I know Shorty."

"Well, Shorty just called and said that Dan told him to call me and tell me that he, Dan, is in jail. I think perhaps I should come over. Would it be okay if I came over?"

"I think maybe you'd better."

I managed to brush away some of whatever it was that was in my mouth, and I threw some water in my face, and by the time I got a pair of pants on, I was pretty sure I was sober. I had a terrible headache, and I was very shaky, but I could think well enough to get scared. I put on a shirt. I couldn't find any clean socks, so I just slid on a pair of shoes. I finally found a belt, and after I'd managed to buckle it, I saw that I was still shaking.

Then I did something I'd never done before, never, not once in my life. I had a drink to steady myself. I remembered that my mother had passed on to me a bottle of whiskey that someone had given her (may God forgive her, Grandma), a bottle of rye, Old Overholt. The bottle had remained untouched in the cabinet above my sink since the day I'd moved into that dingy apartment. I broke the seal, I poured a healthy shot into a glass, and then I drank it down neat and felt the merciful burn. Ann arrived, and as we drove toward the jail, I was calm, no shakes. The Old Overholt had done its work.

"If we can only find Shorty, I'm sure he'll help us," I said.

"I doubt we'll get him out without a court order of some kind."

"What the hell did Dan do?"

"I have no idea," Ann said as we rolled down the ramp into the darkness of the jail parking basement.

"Morgan was drinking at the Baseline Tavern," Shorty told us. "He was up at the bar all by himself. He'd been drinking straight bourbon for almost three hours. Then some guy from Gilbert, who used to drink with Travis Eddington, finds out who Morgan is. He walks up to Danny, and he says, 'How the hell do assholes like you sleep at night when you're defending people you know are guilty?' " Shorty stopped there and took a deep breath.

"Well, come on, Shorty, what happened?"

"Danny went through the guy like shit through a goose," Shorty said with pride. "He just went apeshit."

"Oh, Lord." Ann Hastings sighed.

"It took about five cowboys to pull Danny off him. They were afraid Danny was going to kill him."

"Oh, my God!" cried Ann.

"Morgan walked out the door and took off in his car," Shorty continued. "Somebody called the cops, and they finally found him in front of the Luhrs Building. He'd parked there and passed out. They figure he had stopped somewhere along the way and really started drinking. He sure wouldn't have been able to whip up on anybody, not as drunk as he is now."

Shorty showed me the booking sheet.

"Only drunk driving?"

"It was Gunnar Thude who brought him in," Shorty said. "You know him?"

"No."

"Well, Danny does. And Gunnar knows the guy from Gilbert. For now it's only DWI, but I can't release him without a court order. You get me an order from any judge of the superior court, and I'll fix it so he's out real quick. For all the good that's going to do you."

"Maybe I can go in in the morning and tell Judge Phelps what happened and move for a continuance until we can get him out on bail."

"Good luck," Ann said sardonically.

"What's that supposed to mean?"

"If he's got a jury there, the judge will probably just tell you to argue."

"Oh, come on."

"Well, what do you think he'll do? Have them wait around all day on the chance you can get Morgan released?"

"Oh God," I exhaled. "This isn't even funny."

"And what do you suppose Ferris Eddington will think about you doing the closing argument, when it was Dan Morgan he demanded and Dan Morgan he's paying for?"

"To hell with Ferris Eddington. What do you think I'll think about when they convict Miranda?"

"If we go over to the office, you can call and explain to the judge what's happened and see if he'll sign an order."

"What kind of order?"

"An order authorizing Morgan's release."

"It's three o'clock in the morning."

"Do you want to start preparing your closing argument?"

"Let's go!"

"You'll probably want to call Max Hauser first," Ann

advised. "He can speak for the State. Get him to let you tell the judge he has no objection to Dan's release. Then you're three-fourths of the way there."

Hauser's anger at being awakened at such an hour dissipated when he heard the reason for the call. Still, he would not agree. "How do you expect me to stipulate to his release? I know nothing of the circumstances of the crime."

"Come on!" I yelled. "Do you think there's any question he'll be released? You think Dan Morgan's going to skip out on a misdemeanor charge?"

"Why can't *you* argue it, McKenzie?" Hauser asked. "Morgan seems to be a little preoccupied anyway. You'll probably do a better job than he. You saw the look on those jurors' faces when they found out Morgan already got Rita acquitted. You saw them looking at him. They're going to convict, no matter what Morgan has to say. He may be good, but he isn't that good."

I stared at the receiver until I felt Ann take it from my hand. "Listen, Hauser," Ann yelled into the telephone, "when we call the judge, do you want us to try to patch you into a conference call so you can argue, or shall we just tell him you oppose release?" Ann handed the phone back to me. "Just tell Phelps that Hauser won't agree."

If the judge was angry about the hour, he didn't let it show. And somehow his voice betrayed the same delight that Hauser's had registered upon hearing the news. "I'm sorry, Mr. McKenzie, but without the consent of the State, in the absence of an evidentiary hearing, I don't feel I have authority to order release."

"But, Judge, the only question is whether he'll make court appearances in the future."

"Still, I know nothing of the facts."

"But, Judge—"

"Did you know that I'm acquainted with your family, Mr. McKenzie?"

"Yes, sir."

"I saw your grandmother only last Sunday at sacrament meeting."

"But, Judge—"

"She told me about how you decided to transfer up to BYU."

"Yes, sir, but I really need to—"

"I thought it was a wonderful story. I know your mother also, and other people who speak very highly of you. I expect that you will make a very able closing argument."

The judge hung up, leaving me with my head in my hands, mumbling something about the whole thing being a bad joke. Ann Hastings looked at me with horror and pity.

"I spent the whole of last night preparing to cross-examine Rita, because Morgan wouldn't get ready."

"Well," said Ann, "you'd better spend the rest of tonight getting ready for your argument."

I looked at my watch and saw that it was three-fifteen. I also saw that I was beginning to shake again. I wondered if Morgan kept anything stronger than beer in his office. "No," I said to Ann. "No way."

"Then what are you going to do?"

I reached for the directory and dialed the number listed next to "Adair, Pauline."

"Hello," came the husky voice.

"Ms. Adair?"

"Yes."

"This is Doug McKenzie, and I don't have time to take any crap for calling you at this hour." I spewed the whole story into the telephone, and then I waited.

"Can you type, McKenzie?"

"Not without a lot of mistakes."

"Did you say Ann Hastings is there?"

"Yes, she is."

"Push that button to put me on a speaker." I pushed the button. "Ann, can you type with any competence?" blared out into the office.

"Yes."

"Then put a piece of paper in a typewriter and put a superior court caption on it with a title 'Petition for Writ of Habeas Corpus.' Tell me when you've done that, and then I'll dictate something for you." She dictated a very technical pleading that contained precise citation to cases the veteran litigator knew off the top of her head. Five minutes later Ann reported that she had finalized both a petition and an order for signature by a superior court judge.

"Good. Now, I'll meet you at Henry Penrod's house in twenty minutes, if I don't see any cops. I'll call him and tell him we'll be there. Do you know where he lives?"

There was a moon, and the palm trees that lined Central Avenue were absolutely still in the moonlight, and all was calm as Ann and I drove toward the judge's house. We rolled up Monte Vista Street until we saw him sitting in a wicker chair under the light on the front porch of a house across from the museum. He wore a robe over pajamas, and he smoked a large cigar.

"Good morning!" he shouted as Ann and I got out of my Mustang.

As we walked up to the house, I heard tires squeal, and I snapped around to see a Jaguar XKE screaming up the street. The low, sleek roadster screeched to a stop, and Pauline Adair, wearing a tattered sweatshirt and faded Levi's and canvas sneakers, jumped out. "Let me see those," she said, grabbing the pleadings from my hand. She read as we all walked toward the judge, and when we got to the porch, she handed up the package.

"If Ms. Hastings had anything to do with them, I'm sure they are as they should be," Judge Penrod said. He put the petition and the order under the porch light. Looking down through his half glasses and across the glow of his cigar, he read very carefully.

That was when I got my first taste of the eloquence of the woman Ann Hastings had once characterized as one of the very finest advocates in Arizona. "Christ, Henry. Would you sign the goddamned thing?"

"I'm just wondering whether there is some way I can avoid stepping on Eldon Phelps's toes," drawled the judge.

"Do you really give a damn what that cold-blooded bastard thinks?"

Henry Penrod reached for the fountain pen I held extended and with a bold stroke ordered that Daniel Morgan be released on his own recognizance. I said thank you and, clutching the writ of habeas corpus, turned to walk off the porch, but the judge spoke again. "Things are bad, huh?" he said to me.

"Yes, sir."

"That Eddington woman show up to testify, did she?"

"Yes, sir."

"I kind of thought she might." The judge chewed on his cigar. "She say the same thing she did when she was before me?"

"No, sir. She showed up, but she didn't testify." He raised his bushy eyebrows. "She just sat on the stand, Judge, completely mute. She never said a word, no matter how much they tried to encourage her. Then she took off."

"So how in the world is that case going to a jury?" When I told him about how Eldon Phelps had let them read the testimony from the prior trial, Henry Penrod looked incredulous. I told him that we were pretty certain it was reversible error. "Well, I surely wouldn't have let it in," he said. I was comforted, but then the judge puffed and pondered. "You know," he said, "this business of admitting prior testimony given under oath is gaining currency. I've read they put something about it in those new federal rules. Hell, the Supreme Court may affirm him." The knot to which my chest was becoming accustomed reasserted itself. "Anyway," the judge said, "I figured that woman would be eager to testify."

"Why do you say that, sir?"

"Well, to get all that money, that fortune."

"Did you think Rita killed him?" I asked the judge.

"Oh, yes. She was lying through her teeth."

"How did you know?"

"Christ," Pauline Adair interjected, "was there ever any question?"

"I just knew," the judge said soberly. "Dan did an awfully good job with her, but I had no doubt that she was lying."

"What about Joanna Barnes?" I asked. The judge gave me a curious look. "The telephone operator."

"Oh, yes, the girl from San Francisco. I couldn't quite

figure that out. There's something dirty there, though. I couldn't help thinking she gave you a little more help than the circumstances warranted." He raised his cigar to his mouth again, and I watched the smoke drift up toward the insects that buzzed around his porch light. "I assume you believed her story when you took her testimony."

"Yes, sir, I did."

"He and Danny both started believing their own bullshit," Pauline Adair interjected. I stared at her. "Haven't you learned about that little occupational hazard yet?" she asked.

"Well, the irony," the judge said, "is that if Dan Morgan had been prosecuting that woman and Mr. Hauser defending, that jury wouldn't have taken long to convict. Dan would have found the dirt long before your San Francisco woman came to town." I didn't know how to respond, and I was getting edgy to show Shorty the order I held in my hand, but as I tried to make some sort of graceful exit, the judge kept talking. "Had I any idea that Mr. Hauser would prosecute that unfortunate little girl," he said, "I might have tried somehow to influence the jury. You know. The way federal judges sometimes do. But I just sort of felt that it should be a fair fight, that Mr. Hauser should have been able to take care of himself." He turned and looked down the street, and I knew that Morgan and I and Juan Menchaka were not the only ones who were suffering poisonous second thoughts about what we had let happen. "I suppose," said the judge, "Danny had a pretty strong need to get drunk. Anyway, you take that order and get him. If anybody's got a chance of talking that jury out of a double miscarriage of justice, he's the one. You go get him. You sober him up."

Ann and I did get him. With Shorty's help we humored him, cajoled him, rolled him, pulled him, and finally threw him into the backseat of my open car. "I just want to sleep, goddamn it," he whined repeatedly through that first leg of our ordeal. As we drove to the Kendall House, he changed his tune to, "Who in the Christ took the top down on this car?" And when we got there, when Ann took over the whole operation, he moved into, "Pretty woman." He even tried to put those words to music. He certainly didn't sound like Roy Orbison, but at least he was alive.

He had squeezed himself down toward the floorboard. "Come on, Dan," Ann said. "You have to get out of there."

"Oh, what a lovely woman," he purred. He moved, and I felt a bit more calm, a little further from that jury.

"Now, come on. We have to get you up to Doug's apartment."

"Oh what a beautiful woman." His left hand struggled up to the top of the front seat.

"Can I help you up?" I begged.

"An exquisite woman." He pulled himself up, managed to stand, then stepped down out of the car to where I was waiting and offering a small prayer of thanks. "A woman," he warbled, and he stumbled toward her, and he threw both arms around her. I expected at least some ambivalence on Ann's part, but I saw none as she kissed him on the cheek, then wriggled away and took his hand. And she only laughed when he squeezed her fanny as they ascended the stairs toward the second-floor landing. I was behind them then, climbing the stairs, and that event took place inches from my face. As he staggered down the landing toward my door, I saw him put his arm around her shoulder and move it down, and I knew what he was squeezing then, and she showed no resistance.

"You put some coffee on," Ann instructed once we were in my apartment. While I was lighting the stove and pouring the water, I heard her say, "Well, this suit has had it." When I went back to them, she was pulling off his pants.

His speech was still slurred, but at least he was talking. "I feel like somebody beat the shit out of me," he said. I looked at my watch: four-thirty.

"We heard it was the other way around," Ann said. She slid off his shorts, leaving him naked, the way I'd seen him at her apartment. I inspected the tattoo. Somehow it seemed to have faded since the last time I'd seen it. Faded or not, the words on the banner below the globe with the anchor through it could still be read: SEMPER FIDELIS.

"You've got four and a half hours to get ready," I said.

He leaned back in the chair and, bleary-eyed, studied Ann's face. "What do you mean, 'the other way around'?"

"They say you beat up on the other guy," she informed him.

He dropped his head between his knees. "Oh, my God! What happened?" He reared back and gazed at the high ceiling above the loft, searching for some recollection. After a while he put his head back down between his knees. "I gotta think," he said, groaning. "I gotta think." He kept going back and forth between the ceiling and his knees, all panicky, until at last he looked at Ann, tacitly asking for help. Ann said nothing.

"I think I hit that guy real hard," Morgan said. Then he looked down at his right hand, and for the first time I noticed that it was swollen and that spots had begun to scab over where the skin had been torn off. Morgan turned to me. "Get ready for what?"

"The argument. You've got to get ready to argue."

Ann went for the coffeepot. "Drink this, Dan." She gave him a large, steaming cup, and he drank dutifully. He kept closing his eyes, as if trying to pull up out of somewhere what had happened to him. At times, when it looked as though he remembered something, he would give out small moans. When he finished the first cup, Ann poured another, and there he sat, naked, shriveled, both hands around the coffee cup.

"Now you've got four hours and fifteen minutes," I said.

"Drink the coffee, Dan."

"Oh, yeah. Eddington. Got to get ready. Got to stop Hauser. That son of a bitch."

"Right," I said. "That's right."

"Oh," he said, "what do I say?" Ann and I watched him drink that cup of coffee, then another. He seemed to be thinking about what he would say to the jury. He seemed to be coming back to life. "Anybody got a cigarette?" he asked. I went through his coat, saw where it had been torn, and I found a pack of Camels. When he lit one, he began to look like himself, and I knew then that there was hope. He even laughed a little as he exhaled a long draft of smoke through his nose and gazed lovingly at Ann. "I really did smack that bastard," he told her boastfully.

"Why don't you start the shower running," Ann said to me. "We need to get him in there."

"Where'd you learn so much about sobering up drunks?"

"It's the only thing I got out of being in a sorority in college," she said.

"Watch who you're calling drunk," Morgan chimed in lamely.

I ran the shower, and I helped her get him into it, then stood and watched, as unabashed, in the steam of my filthy bathroom, she soaped him down. The steam loosened her thick blond hair, and it began to fall about her shoulders. The spray soaked her, and I could see that she'd gotten dressed so fast that night that she hadn't put on a bra. The next thing I knew, Morgan was trying to take off her blouse, and she let him get two buttons undone before she slapped his hand away. At that point I walked out and sat down on my sofa and stared at a half-empty coffeepot. How did I feel about what was going on between the two of them? I don't remember. Maybe I repressed it. All I remember thinking about is how desperately I needed him out of that shower, shaved, dressed, and propped up in Eldon Phelps's courtroom by nine o'clock.

"You've got four hours," I told him when Ann brought him back from the bathroom, dripping all over my carpet.

"For what?"

"To get prepared." He gave me a blank stare, and I knew he was still drunk. I had equated his ability to walk with sobriety, with an ability to think clearly. But that wasn't the case. He was still drunk. "The closing argument. The Eddington case. The jury!"

"Oh, yeah," he remembered. "I gotta get ready. I gotta get to the office."

"I'll drive you."

"I need some clothes. Don't I?"

"Right."

"They're up in my apartment. Clean. I've got some clean suits up there. Fresh shirts."

"I'll go up and find something," Ann said, searching his pants for his keys.

"Ann," Morgan called. She stopped. "I want a blue suit. Navy blue. And a light blue shirt and a maroon-colored tie."

"All right."

"You make sure."

Ann left, and Morgan turned to me. "I really nailed that shit-kickin' motherfucker." He wasn't laughing now, but still the flash of pride was there. He wanted me to know that he had struck a blow for the entire legal profession.

The telephone rang. It was Ann. "Ask him where he keeps his ties and his socks," she ordered.

"Don't you know?" That set her back, I could tell, and it made me sorry I'd said it.

"The only time I was ever here, his wife ran me off."

"I'll come up and help you look," I volunteered.

I left him alone, still naked, still sitting in the chair by my door. I climbed the stairs to his penthouse, and I went through the door Ann had left open, and I could hear her in his bedroom.

"I found his socks," Ann said. "But I can't find any ties. I've looked everywhere."

I began to search through his closet, where everything was ordered to perfection. Blue suits hung together. Gray suits formed their own bloc. Shoes all had trees and sat next to each other as if in formation. It gave the impression of a locker ready for Saturday-morning inspection. There were belts in proper place and shirts hung precisely. There were sweaters neatly stacked. But there were no ties.

"I can't figure it out," Ann puzzled.

I found a set of drawers, and I began opening them from the top, where there were undershirts. In the next drawer there were undershorts and in the next knit shirts. Then I saw a large mahogany box. It had a brass plate on the top: DANIEL MORGAN, USMC. I opened the box, and there were the ties, each rolled so that it fit into its own little space the way ties are sometimes displayed in fancy men's stores.

"My God, do you suppose he rolls his tie up every night?" Ann wondered.

"I don't know," I said, grabbing a maroon one, "but let's just take this stuff and get it on him."

Well, we never did get it on him. This is what happened, as best I could reconstruct it. While Ann and I were gone, he went to my kitchen looking for yet another cup of coffee. I say that because I found his empty cup there. But while he was in there, he spotted the bottle of Old Overholt that I had opened a few hours before. It must have looked better than the dregs in the coffeepot, for he'd taken the bottle and a glass back to the chair that he, by then, had made his own. And that was where he and the bottle and the glass were when Ann and I returned with his fresh clothes. The bottle was half gone.

Neither Ann nor I said a word. Morgan said two things. First he said, "Fuck it." Then he said, "I gotta get to the bathroom." He didn't make it. Halfway there he vomited all over the carpet, then stood stock-still for an instant, then, in slow motion, crumpled to the floor. Ann rushed to him and gently tried to shake him back to life.

I had my clothes off before I hit the bathroom door. When I came out of the shower, I wrapped myself in a towel, more, at least, than Morgan had had the decency to do. Somehow Ann had managed to drag him to the sofa, where she was cleaning him up.

I ran up the stairs to the loft where I slept and where my clothes were hung, and I picked a navy blue suit, a light blue shirt, and a maroon tie. I found a pair of dirty socks. As I hurried past the chair by the door, Morgan's chair, I reached for the Old Overholt one more time.

67 "MR. MCKENZIE," SAID Eldon Phelps, "you may address the jury."

And there I stood, up in front of all of them, under all those bright lights. To my left and above was the terrible man in the black robe, the one who had forced me to stand there. To my right, the newspeople were crawling over each other, making sure against sure they would not miss a word I would utter. Behind sat the child who had only me. And in front was the wall of faces that belonged to the twelve men and women whose names I could not remember, the faces that had gazed so approvingly as, minutes before, Maximilian Hauser had given his summation. (And Hauser had been compelling as he show-cased Rita Eddington's testimony from the first trial, then set its veracity in concrete with the unimpeachable corroboration provided by Joanna Barnes. "Proof of the defendant's guilt has not been beyond a reasonable doubt, members of the jury. Her guilt has been proved beyond a shadow of a doubt.") I had a cup of water, because my mouth was so dry I knew I would be unable to speak without it, and even with it, I knew that my voice would shake.

"I have a most unenviable task," I told the wall of faces. "I stand here to ask you to write yet another chapter in the legend of a fiercely shrewd and clever lawyer." I took a long, deep breath. "We know this much. A man was in a room, and two people walked into that room, and one of those people murdered the man. Now, what if a lawyer could defend both those people? What if he could persuade first one jury, then another, that each of those people, in turn, should be found not guilty? What if that lawyer could get them both off when we all know, beyond any question, that one of them committed cold-blooded murder? What do you suppose would happen to that lawyer's stock around town? I mean, what would happen after the newspapermen had run for the telephones and after the lights had shone and the cameras had rolled?"

Some of the jurors looked to their left where the media were crowded into the gallery.

"Do I really need to talk about the clients that would come? The cases? The money? Or may I just leave it here? Years and years from now, that would be the lawyer remembered when the old lawyers sat and talked. 'You remember Dan Morgan?' they would say. 'Now, there was a trial man. There was a man who could wrap a jury around his finger. There was a man who could mesmerize. There was the man to go to, the lawyer who could set a guilty client free.' " I stopped for a moment, and a few of the jurors moved their heads in a knowing way, and I saw that I had found a nerve. "Should a decent system support that kind of a result?" I asked them. "Should a system that decent people can be proud of support that kind of a lawyer?" A few more heads moved, and a number of eyes narrowed. "You might well wonder why I come so bluntly to this nasty point."

"I wonder," Hauser said behind me, "what the point is, Your Honor, and what it has to do with the facts of this case."

"Perhaps you wonder," I continued, as if I had not heard him, "why I shake as I stand before you. Well, it isn't only my lack of experience and my lack of confidence that makes me shake. You see, I am afraid that maybe—and I say 'maybe' because I am a lawyer and I am not sure—but maybe that question should be answered no. And should you say no to my question, I could not fault you for your conclusion. But it is not my fear that you may conclude no decent system should allow for such a result that makes me shake. I shake because I know that if you take it upon yourselves collectively, as this jury you constitute, to announce that the fierce and shrewd and clever Mr. Morgan is to be repudiated, if you take it upon yourselves to say no, you will not let Dan Morgan get away with it, the only way you have to do that is to find guilty the one person in this whole tragic fiasco who is completely innocent."

At that point I turned to the bench, and, continuing with my argument, I let my gaze remain on the Honorable Eldon Phelps. "To judge Dan Morgan is to prejudge Miranda Eddington." When I saw the way Phelps looked back at me, after I had made my impertinent little attempt to communicate with him, I was suddenly afraid that my head was coming off right in front of the jury.

Max Hauser also smelled the blood, and he rose. "Your Honor, perhaps Mr. McKenzie could be admonished on proper argument," he pleaded.

The judge measured me, and I braced myself, and, curiously, as I waited for the eruption, I noticed that I had almost stopped shaking. I recalled Morgan's admonition that we didn't have to take any crap off him. But the judge didn't explode. There was a great silence in the courtroom, and a strange questioning look came across his face. "Do you have an objection, Mr. Hauser?" the judge asked at last.

"Yes, Your Honor," Hauser eagerly affirmed.

"Overruled. You go on with your argument, Mr. McKenzie."

When I turned back to the jury, I saw in their eyes a spark of something, and I had a feeling for the first time that they wanted to hear what I had to say.

"You see, what Dan Morgan did—the evil alchemy that he performed—he did in the other trial. And what he did was to get a guilty woman off. The simple fact of this case is that Miranda Eddington did not kill her father. How do we know that? We know that because she *said* she did not kill her father. She took the stand, raised her hand, swore to tell the truth, and then she told what happened. And it was her mother, that strange woman who sat before you but refused to talk to you, who murdered Travis Eddington. Why are we here? Not because this child committed murder but because Dan Morgan made it look like she did. And I helped him do it, ladies and gentlemen. I helped him do it. Dan Morgan, with just a little help from me, did what lawyers do. He brought out the facts that helped his client, and he suppressed, at least where he could, the facts that hurt her. He twisted, he distorted, he tortured, and in the end he won. He created a great illusion, which made it appear that it was Miranda who was guilty.

"He had to do that. You see, if Miranda wasn't guilty, her mother certainly was, and if Daniel Morgan didn't persuade that other jury that Miranda was guilty, he could not have won. And to lawyers who play for the stakes Daniel Morgan plays for, winning is everything."

"Your Honor," Hauser beseeched. "This has nothing to do with this case."

"Yes it does!" I yelled. "It has everything to do with it!" I turned to the bench to await the ruling, and when the judge remained quiet, thinking, I said again, "It has everything to do with it, Your Honor."

Judge Phelps appraised me silently, and I had a strange feeling that he was coming to believe, just a little, the things he'd said about me, the graduate of Brigham Young University, on the telephone the night before. I had the feeling that he imagined he saw something of my grandmother in me. And in that moment I became absolutely certain that he had not earlier been close enough to smell the bourbon and the rye. "Ladies and gentlemen," he finally said. "As I have told you before, arguments of counsel are not evidence. You are to be governed by the evidence that came to you from the witness stand. Having told you that again, I am going to allow Mr. McKenzie some latitude in what he says to you. I assume that you will not let him, to borrow his word, mesmerize you."

"Would that I could mesmerize you. Had I that skill, I would most assuredly use it. I would do anything the judge would let me do to persuade you to find this little girl not guilty. Like I said, lawyers who play for these stakes will do anything to win. Anything. I don't know for sure why that is. I don't know if it's the joy of winning, which I tell you borders on ecstasy, or if it's the fear of losing, the emotion that now engulfs me and makes me shake."

Again I heard Hauser's booming voice. "Your Honor, I know it's a common tactic to try to gain sympathy for a defendant. But is Mr. McKenzie trying to gain sympathy for himself?"

"No," I said to the jury, without looking back. "But it is important to me that you understand how it was in the spirit of the combat they call a trial that Dan Morgan made it look to that first jury as if this girl was guilty. You know, ladies and gentlemen, when it finally dawned on me early this morning that I would be the one here arguing to you, I considered giving you a lecture right out of law school. I was going to tell you we never really did prove that Miranda was guilty the first time around; we only showed that there was a reasonable doubt that her mother was guilty. Then I was going to argue to you that there is equally a doubt that Miranda is guilty. Just one party's word against another. No way to know which one did it. That's not true, though. First, we did prove that Miranda was guilty; we broke our backs to do it. Second, it was a lie. And indeed it is the evidence in this case that what we did, what Dan Morgan did, what Rita Eddington did, was a lie. And it is not only the testimony of Miranda that proves that so. It was the testimony you did not hear from her mother.

"I'm going to talk about what you did not hear from Rita Eddington in a moment, but I want to touch on something else first. You know, a few minutes ago Mr. Hauser told you something he really doesn't believe. Still, it was something that is absolutely true. He told you that Daniel Morgan is a better lawyer than he is. You remember that Mr. Hauser began so modestly a while ago by reminding you that this case should not be decided on the relative skills of the lawyers, because if it were so decided, Daniel Morgan would surely win, since Mr. Morgan is the more skilled and clever advocate? Why did Mr. Hauser come on with all that palaver, all that gush? Because he believed it? No. Weren't his little left-handed compliments, if you really think about them, intended to poison you just one small bit more against the shrewd and clever lawyer who was forced to try to work his magic before you? Now, there is nothing wrong with Mr. Hauser's praising his adversary, ladies and gentlemen. It's just a standard lawyer's tactic, a trick they teach you in law school. What is really tragic in this case, though, is that what Mr. Hauser said is so true."

"Objection," protested Max Hauser. Eldon Phelps looked down at him. "This is all irrelevant, if it please the court."

"But you raised the point, Mr. Hauser. You opened the door," said the judge. "You proceed, Mr. McKenzie."

"It has taken some time for me to figure this out, but Mr. Hauser really *isn't* very good." I noticed a small crack of a smile on one of the women's faces. "I wish I could take you all back to the evening after we got Rita Eddington acquitted. We had a party at a place over here called the Arizona Club, our whole law firm. And for a long time, Daniel Morgan regaled us that night with stories of how stupid Max Hauser was."

"Objection!"

"Stories of how we had blindsided him at every turn."

"I object!!"

"How Mr. Hauser had let our witnesses run over him like Sherman tanks."

By watching the jurors' eyes follow him, I could pretty well tell where Hauser was as he jumped around behind me (if I may take a phrase from the lexicon of Daniel Morgan) like a fart on a skillet. "I object, if it please the court. I object!!!"

"Do you see now, ladies and gentlemen?" I asked as they watched him make his shrill objections. "He tells it to you, but Mr. Hauser does not really believe that Mr. Morgan is the better lawyer. Is it possible that Mr. Hauser has an ego as big as most trial lawyers'?" I swear that a juror in the second row shook his head in the affirmative. "And it does, Your Honor, have everything to do with this case,"

I said, turning to answer Hauser's objections, fearful that I might have gone too far and that the blast I had assumed inevitable would now be coming from the bench.

"I don't think you intend to dwell on the point, do you, Mr. McKenzie?" said Eldon Phelps mercifully.

"No I don't, Your Honor, but I do contend that it is this foul competition gone awry between these two lawyers that has put us here today."

"Well, you go ahead and argue to the jury."

"Ladies and gentlemen, this business of lawyers getting carried away when they play for high stakes can be a two-way street. As I said, Dan Morgan pulled out a few stops when he defended Rita Eddington. I can tell you this, also: He is now paying for what he did as he lies in a guilt-ridden drunken heap, unable to face you, unable to—"

"Objection!"

Once again the judge was circumspect, taking time to consider his ruling. "Sustained," he finally declared. "Yes, Mr. McKenzie, I think you had better stick more closely to the evidence."

"In this case, members of the jury, it is not the treacherous Mr. Morgan who has done anything wrong. Indeed, you saw everything Daniel Morgan did in this case, and you saw that he did nothing, other than let Miranda tell you what happened. No, in this case we walk the other side of that two-way street. In this case it was Mr. Hauser who got carried away with the competitive urge. You know, lawyers are officers of the court, and as such they have an obligation not to suggest things that they do not believe to be true. Indeed, when a lawyer cross-examines a witness, that lawyer is not to suggest something to the witness that he does not have a basis in good faith to allege as true."

"Objection!"

Dan Morgan once told me he really believed that too many objections can lose cases for a lawyer. Many years have passed since that night at the Arizona Club, yet I'm still not sure whether I have come wholly to his theory. But I did learn one thing that winter day as I stood before the jury. I learned that irrespective of whether incessant objections have much effect on verdicts, jurors do not like to hear them. I say that because while Max Hauser stood behind me having bellowed yet again, I heard one of the jurors speak to another. It was Juror Number One, who sat in the front row all the way to my left. During the quiet while Eldon Phelps considered Hauser's objection, the woman whispered to the man who sat next to her, "I wish Hauser would sit down and shut up." When the woman saw that I had heard, she put her hand to her mouth and flushed. Then she smiled at me, and I smiled at her, and I quit shaking completely.

"Your Honor," argued Hauser in support of his objection, "it is for the court, not counsel, to instruct the jury on the law. There has been no discussion of an instruction in this case on a good-faith requirement in cross-examination."

"Well, Mr. Hauser," the judge replied, "you certainly don't quarrel with that proposition, do you?" That slowed the big man down. "You would agree, sir," said the judge, "that a lawyer must have a good-faith basis before asserting a fact at any time in court, either on cross-examination or otherwise, would you not?"

"Yes, Your Honor," Hauser conceded, and he sat down.

"You go ahead, Mr. McKenzie."

"Let me remind you, members of the jury, of a series of questions Mr. Hauser asked Rita Eddington when he cross-examined her in the first trial, a number of points he demanded she admit. No, I won't only remind you of the things he contended Rita Eddington should concede. I'll read them to you, just to make sure that I don't get it wrong. Your Honor, I think maybe I'm supposed to note for the record that I am reading from page sixty-two, line seventeen of volume four of the transcript of the trial of Rita Eddington. It is part of what Mr. Hauser read into evidence in this trial."

"So noted," said the judge.

I opened the transcript, and I read from Max Hauser's cross-examination of Rita Eddington, the cross-examination Dan Morgan had insisted Hauser read, the thing Hauser had been reluctant to do.

" 'You carried the gun into the house?' Mr. Hauser put to Mrs. Eddington.

" 'Yes,' was her answer.

"After that, members of the jury, you will recall that Mr. Hauser demanded Mrs. Eddington admit a number of things which he knew had happened. Mrs. Eddington, the woman whose very life hung in the balance, denied Mr. Hauser's allegations. It is not her denials, however, but the allegations made by the prosecutor that tell the true story."

"Objection, if Your Honor please. The questions I asked are irrelevant. What was relevant was the testimony given in response to my questions."

I let my gaze drift to Juror Number One, and I saw her shake her head, then look up at me and give a near-imperceptible smile.

"But, Mr. Hauser," came the answer from the bench, "those transcripts are in evidence, and it was you who put them in evidence. And Counsel may argue the evidence as he sees fit. The objection is overruled." I was turning back to the transcript when a miracle occurred in the person of the Honorable Eldon Phelps. "Even though statements made by counsel are generally not evidence," the thin-haired man told the jury, "what Mr. McKenzie said is right. No lawyer may suggest something in a courtroom that he does not in good faith believe to be based in fact. And I so charge you, ladies and gentlemen of the jury. That is the law." Then, as if that weren't enough of a nose rubbing for the man who had made the objection, the judge turned to Hauser and blessed him with one more afterthought. "Certainly, Mr. Hauser, you would not have sought a concession on cross-examination of a fact you did not reasonably believe to be the truth?" Then the judge waited for an answer. Oh, if Dan Morgan could have seen him now. Eldon Phelps was not an asshole after all. He was doing the best he could, and I could have crawled up on that bench and kissed him.

"No," Max Hauser finally answered grudgingly. "I would not do that."

"And this, ladies and gentlemen," I told them, making sure they saw that I was reading his exact words from the transcript, "is what Mr. Hauser stated to Rita Eddington: 'And you pulled the gun from your purse . . . And you pointed it at your husband, didn't you, Mrs. Eddington? . . . You held it on him. . . . And you pulled the trigger. . . . You shot your husband six times. . . . And you watched him die.'

"The point is, members of the jury, that Mr. Hauser had it right. He had it precisely the way Miranda said it happened. He just hadn't figured out what Travis Eddington had figured out. Mr. Hauser didn't know that Rita Eddington was homosexual. But now we all know that she was. How? Through Miranda Eddington's testimony. You remember that right before he died, Travis Eddington asked his wife if she was a lesbian. Did she deny it? No. She simply killed him. Exactly the way Mr. Hauser said she did. If Mr. Hauser did not have a basis to conclude it happened that way, it's like Judge Phelps just instructed you, he had no business saying those things. And the horrible question becomes, if he had a good-faith basis to state the case against Rita Eddington so precisely and so accurately, how on earth can he now proceed in good faith against this child?"

"Perhaps, if it please the court," came a rumbling sneer from behind me as Hauser went to his feet once again, "perhaps I learned a few things from Mr. Morgan, and that is why we are here."

"He trusted Daniel Morgan?" I said to the people in the box before Hauser had sat back down. "He tells us he accepted what Daniel Morgan showed him about his case? When Daniel Morgan was being paid what he was being paid to get that woman off? Come on!

"What happened is this: Mr. Hauser simply got beaten by Daniel Morgan. Badly beaten. But he could not bring himself to accept it gracefully and walk away. He had to have a scapegoat, and the only scapegoat in sight was this innocent girl."

Max Hauser was still standing when I said that, and I knew he was trying to articulate another objection. He didn't get one out, though, and I watched a number of the jurors shift their eyes to him and fix him with a look not unlike the one they had cast upon Dan Morgan when first they heard about what had happened in Rita's trial.

"The sorrow," I continued, "is that Mr. Hauser had it right when he prosecuted this girl's mother. He had it right, but he did not have the wherewithal to stop Daniel Morgan from blinding that other jury. And the greater sorrow, the real pity, is that I may not have the wherewithal to stop Daniel Morgan from convincing you of the great lie. For you must see now that my battle here is not with Maximilian Hauser. It was not Mr. Hauser who groomed and then presented the testimony of Rita Eddington. That was Mr. Morgan's dirty work. And it is upon that dirty work and that alone that this case stands or falls. Without the testimony that Rita Eddington gave when she and Daniel Morgan needed so badly to save her skin, there is no evidence that Miranda did anything in this case besides shoot a blackbird off a wire. Do you not see the great irony, ladies and gentlemen? My real adversary is the man who is not in the courtroom, the man for whom I work. And the greater irony is that it should be he, Daniel Morgan, not I, who stands before you arguing to get out from under the case he put together so shrewdly before. But, you see, although he encountered no real problems in trying a case against Maximilian Hauser, when it came to standing up against himself, Daniel Morgan could not bring himself to the occasion. So here I stand, the second chair, doing my best not to shake.

"And the greatest irony of all? If Daniel Morgan beats me, he will never live another guilt-free day. On the other hand, should I beat Daniel Morgan, he becomes a legend in his time.

"I told you I would turn to what was lacking in Rita Eddington's testimony. Ladies and gentlemen, everything was lacking. She would not talk to you. She sat in that chair, and she would not speak. Why would she not testify to you? Why would she only sit and look at me in that strange way? Mr. Hauser tells us he feels he learned something about his case after the first trial. Do you not think maybe I learned something about Rita Eddington after we put her case on?"

"I object! Counsel is testifying."

"I'm not testifying, Your Honor. I'm not going to tell the jury a thing about what I know that did not get into evidence. I understand how improper that would be. But I contend that I may ask the jury to draw their own inferences from the way Mrs. Eddington regarded me during that time she sat here, under oath, seemingly petrified."

Eldon Phelps's eyes widened, and he bent forward and measured me with a mixture of suspicion and curiosity, and I knew that another light had gone on. I said a small prayer that there would be no further inquiry about how Rita might have learned what I knew.

"Yes," the judge said very slowly, with continued suspicion. "There may be an inference to be drawn."

"And what," I asked the jury, "about the telephone operator who was an architect? The woman named Joanna Barnes. Why wasn't she here to testify this time around? Why, despite all his efforts, using all the resources of the State, could Mr. Hauser not find her? It was easy enough for me to find her and bring her down from San Francisco. Why couldn't he find her? What strange relationship was there between these two women? Is Joanna Barnes homosexual, too?

"I object! Your Honor, there is no evidence of any relationship between those women."

"The evidence, Your Honor," I stated loudly and emphatically, without turning from the jury, "is that Rita Eddington is a lesbian. Miranda told us that her father asked her mother, 'Are you a lesbian, Rita?' And with that, Mrs. Eddington killed him. Now, there has to be a reason for Joanna Barnes to come to court and lie and then run beyond where she can be found. I contend that the jury may reasonably infer that Joanna Barnes and Rita Eddington were lovers."

I turned from the jury to the bench to learn how Eldon Phelps would rule, and when I did, I knew full well that I was not indisputably beyond that inevitable blast. I wasn't sure how far across the line I had traveled in wafting nasty speculation toward those twelve people who by then had been so well tutored in the principle that before I could suggest it, I had to have reason to know it. I had told them that I would do anything I could get away with to persuade them to acquit Miranda. I knew I'd been pushing it, and I remember that as I turned to the bench, I was preparing to duck.

But when I looked up, I saw that Eldon Phelps was not looking at me, and I knew he was not thinking about what I said or how he would judge its propriety. I saw that the judge, with a strange expression that mixed horror and compassion, was looking down to the table where my client sat. I followed his eyes, and I saw Miranda sitting there, all alone in her blue starched-cotton dress, her chest convulsing gently and tears much larger than any shed by her mother running down her cheeks. Oh, no! I never had, until then, told her what a lesbian was.

And there we stood, the hulking Hauser on one side of the pretty girl who was still a child, I on the other, and the judge with the pasted hair looking down from above. There was no sound in the courtroom save for the faint sobs coming from Miranda.

I spun around and looked at the jurors, all of whom were staring at Miranda with expressions much the same as that of Judge Phelps. And I knew that the time had come for me to sit down. I knew that if they didn't have the message by then, they weren't going to get it, and I lowered myself into my chair and gave Miranda's hand a squeeze, and then I watched Max Hauser as he waded through the heavy silence to address the jury one more time.

I didn't even listen to Hauser's closing. I just sat collapsed in my chair, exhausted, and tried to give what little comfort I could to the girl who sat beside me. I did hear Hauser sputter a good deal, but I had the feeling that the jury was sick of listening to lawyers and that they were not paying him much heed. And in time I saw that the belligerent man was sitting down, too.

I listened to Eldon Phelps after Hauser had finished, as he instructed the jury on the law. I figured he might say something to which I should take exception, so I pulled myself up and got out a pen and a piece of paper. That, however, was not necessary, because the judge, having come 180 degrees gave Morgan's and my proposed instructions wholesale, including the one on reasonable doubt that Morgan had made me draft so many times before Rita's trial. He even added one that I hadn't thought to request: He repeated to the jury one more time that lawyers were not to say things in court that they did not have a good-faith basis to believe.

Suddenly it was all over, and the bailiff was escorting the jury toward the jury room for their deliberation. The judge left the bench; the media moved out to the hallway, where smoke was coming up from freshly lit tobacco; Max Hauser went out through the side door; and finally Miranda Eddington and I were alone at our table. I was trying to think of something to say to her when the nurse appeared and asked if she could take her downstairs for a soft drink.

"I'm sure it will be okay," I said. "Just stay close by, in case there's an early verdict."

"We will," the nurse promised.

"You okay, Miranda?" I asked.

"Yes, I am," she assured me.

And then I was all alone in the icky little veneer-covered courtroom, slumped back down in my chair, lifeless, feeling all that adrenaline, which was mixed up with all that rye and bourbon, begin to drain away and move out through my pores. I hadn't slept in two nights, and I was sure that I was near death. I was in that posture, just trying to feel my insides, when I became aware that someone had slid into the chair next to me. I labored to turn my head, and when I got it around, I was staring into the face of Dan Morgan.

"How you doing?" he asked in an airy tone suggesting that nothing out of the ordinary had happened the night before. I didn't say anything to him, only nodded to show I was aware of his presence. Then, very casually, he began to let his gaze roam around the empty courtroom. He looked at the bench and then the witness stand and then the clerk's table, and finally he looked over to the empty chair where the bailiff had sat.

As he did so, I watched him closely. He was shaved, his hair was combed, and his eyes were bright and no longer bloodshot. He wore a bone-colored gabardine suit, which his wife no doubt had ordered, for it was tailored to perfection. The morning-fresh shirt was pale blue, his tie an olive-and-blue paisley. On his feet I saw soft brown Italian loafers. There sat the man whom, just a few hours before, I'd pulled out of the Maricopa County drunk tank, the man I'd watched do what he had done in my apartment, and he was not at all the guilt-ridden drunken pile I'd told the jury about. He was bright-eyed and bushy-tailed.

"These sure are crappy-looking courtrooms, aren't they?" he said. Again I refused to speak to him, and he moved his gaze from the bailiff's chair to my face, where he left it for a few seconds before moving on to the empty jury box. "I hear I puked on your carpet," he said as he stared at the chairs that were still warm from the jurors.

"Right," I corroborated.

"Sorry about that," he told me, with about as much remorse as if he'd bumped me on a dance floor.

I said nothing. I just stared in silent disbelief, knowing as I slumped there that I looked like death warmed over and finding inescapable the fact that Morgan looked like he'd just stepped from the pages of *Gentlemen's Quarterly*.

Again he rested his eyes on mine. "You did a good job," he said, deadly serious.

"What?"

"Your argument. It was very good."

"How would you know?" I said with a nasty edge.

"I watched you."

"What?"

"Yes. I watched you."

"How?"

"Through a crack in the door."

"You're kidding."

"No."

"You were out there the whole time?"

"That's right."

I turned toward the jury box. I thought for just a minute. Then I turned back. "You dirty son of a bitch."

"Oh, come on, Doug," he drawled. "The rug was already rotten. Besides that, I've got a couple of guys up at your place right now, recarpeting the whole thing. Just to show you how sorry I am."

"I'm not talking about the carpet, and you know it."

"Oh?" he questioned.

"This was the all-time ultimate mushroom treatment," I said.

"What's the mushroom treatment?" he asked.

"You know damned well what it is," I said. "You keep me in the dark and you feed me shit. But this time it was spectacular. Unbelievable." He only stared, and I kept talking. "You knew you couldn't come in here and say the things I said to them."

"You did make me sound a little more evil than I like to think I am."

"So you just threw me in here; you fixed it so I didn't have a choice. Didn't you? I just can't figure out when you finally decided to do it. Was it before or after I got you out of jail?"

I was moving around in my chair with ever-growing anger.

"You know something, Doug?"

"What?"

"I think you may have saved her." He said it to me with cold sobriety, and there was something almost sad in the way he said it, something that gave me the feeling that he might choke up if he kept talking. He nodded his head and raised his eyebrows, all in a way that made it understood he did not intend to discuss the matter further. The subject, I knew, was closed. "I came in here because I need to talk to you about something else."

"Yeah?" I replied petulantly.

"A man in Tucson unloaded a forty-five into his wife late last night. A fellow named Pettibone. He's rolling in money. He's already wired me a hundred-thousand-dollar retainer. I was wondering if you'd like to take the second chair on this one?"

"I don't think I ever want to work with you again."

"Well, I'm asking you to think about it. I kind of need to know by this evening. I'll be driving down to Tucson in the morning, and I'd like to have whoever's going to help me come along."

I didn't say anything after that, and neither did Morgan. We just sat there, the two of us, alone together in the cold, empty, quiet courtroom. I could not remember ever having been so tired. Then suddenly the side door flew open, and the clerk burst through with wide eyes and a startled expression. "They have a verdict!" she announced.

I came straight up in my chair. "Oh, God," I whispered.

"Congratulations," said Morgan. "There's no way they're going to convict her that fast."

"Oh, Lord," I breathed. "I don't know."

"I'm outta here," Morgan said.

"You're not leaving?"

"I don't think it would look too kosher for me to be here. You know—under the circumstances."

I went to the snack bar, and I found my client. "We have to go back to the courtroom, Miranda."

"Okay," she said, and she grabbed my hand and held on as we walked. "They have good Cokes in there," she told me.

"What?"

"I like the way they mix their Coca-Cola."

"Oh," I said. "Yes."

When we got back up to the courtroom, the gallery was full again, but this time I saw that Tom Gallagher and Walter Smith and Ann Hastings and Chet Johnson and even Lester Pierce were sitting in the front row. They all just stared at me as I walked Miranda up the center aisle and through the gate. Miranda still held on to my hand, and she would not let go, even after we sat down.

The jury filed in, and Miranda squeezed my hand harder. And before they reached their seats, they looked at her, each of them, every last one looked at her. It remained only for the clerk to read, "Not guilty," which she did with tears running down her cheeks. And then there was noise all over the courtroom.

I do not remember what it felt like. I try sometimes to remember, but it will not come. I must, I think, have been numb. All I can recall is the noise, and that Eldon Phelps was thanking the jury for their service to the community, and that afterward one of the jurors, a woman who was crying, came over and put her arms around Miranda and squeezed her and said, "Oh, I've been wanting to do this all week long." And I remember we were suddenly surrounded by people, and some were slapping me on the back and telling me nice going.

I bent close to Miranda. "Are you okay?" I asked.

"Yes. I think I'm going to be okay." Only then did she let go of my hand.

Then I saw that another hand was reaching toward Miranda's, a hand with aristocratically long, square fingers and a large diamond ring, one with which I was so very familiar. I looked up and into the face of Ferris Eddington. Miranda took his hand and stood up and squeezed against him. "Thank you, Douglas," the old man said. Then he turned, and the crowd parted, and I watched as the two of them, both ramrod straight, walked out of the courtroom.

Max Hauser went out the side door and slammed it.

After that I was telling a group of television people that I did not want to be interviewed on camera and that I really did not want to comment on what the jury had done. Sometime in all of this, I saw that Ann Hastings had come up beside me and was touching my arm and that Tom Gallagher and Walter Smith and the rest of them were there, all standing back as though they didn't want to intrude. "We thought," said Ann, "you might like to go and get a drink."

"Thanks," I said, "but I think I just want to go home and go to bed." They all nodded understandingly—there was no "Oh, come on, Doug, just one drink"—and they moved out through the double doors.

And soon I was alone again in the empty courtroom.

I stayed there for a time, hoping the crowd outside would clear and I could get away without the television people chasing me. I looked around the room, and I remember that it didn't look so bad to me as it had. It still wasn't sweet, not like the big old courtroom in the other building with the hand-painted beams and the sunlight pouring through the venetian blinds. But it wasn't so bad. For a moment I thought about the crying juror who had hugged Miranda and said she'd been wanting to do that all along, and I wondered if maybe we had never been in as much trouble as we thought. And then I walked away. I went down in the elevator and out through the big glass doors into the bright, warm sunlight of the afternoon. There, on the low-rising front steps, a television crew had cornered one of the jurors, a big, rawboned man in Levi's and a golf shirt. There was a man with blown-dry hair and a very large voice who was asking the juror what he thought of his recent experience.

"They ought to kill all the lawyers, that's what we decided," said the juryman.

I skirted the small crowd that had gathered, and quickly I was across First Avenue without their seeing me. I made it to the Kendall House, where at first I stood in dismay, looking at the brand-new carpet that covered my entire apartment. Achingly tired as I was, I suddenly knew there was no way I would sleep. I changed my clothes, and I pulled my golf clubs from under the bed, and I carried them out to my car, and I took down the top. I took a deep breath, and once again I drove across the roads that marked my childhood—Guadalupe and McClintock and Alma School and Southern and Baseline and Williams Field. Of course the alfalfa was not yet coming up, and the cotton had not been planted. But there were still Herefords there that day, and Anguses, and quarter horses. And there were the sheep.

I drove on to the San Marcos Country Club, and all alone that warm and quiet winter afternoon, I began to walk the almost-empty golf course, down the Bermuda fairways yellow in their dormancy, past the dusty old tamarack trees, along the cotton field that ran down beside the fourth hole, and across the bentgrass greens. And in my state of near somnambulance, I tried to think about all that had happened. I walked as far as the seventh green, giving no real thought to how I was swinging the golf club, and then I found myself veering off the course toward the parking lot. I have no witness to that which I now report, but I swear it's true, as true as it was that Miranda Eddington did not kill her half brother: When I walked off the San Marcos golf course that warm winter afternoon, after seven holes, I was two under par.

By the time I reached the Luhrs Building, the sun was gone, and when the elevator reached our floor, the empty office was dark. I walked down the hall, and when I turned the corner toward Dan Morgan's office, I could see a shaft of light. I pushed the door and stepped inside, and he looked up from what he was reading. "You're going to Tucson with me," he said.

"Yes," I said. "I'll go."

He held a book entitled *The Insanity Defense*. His hair stood straight up, and there was electricity in his eyes and a can of Coors on his desk. And he was smoking a cigarette.

EPILOGUE

I DID GO TO TUCSON with Morgan that next morning, and after that I tried cases with him for four years. Some we won, some we lost. For some we were paid handsomely, for most we received no fee at all. Fortunately, write-offs presented little problem during those years, since both Morgan and I were regarded as the saviors of the Eddington account and all it promised for the years to come. Even Paul Butler eventually boasted about the amount of pro bono work the firm did.

But that all changed after a winter morning when Ferris Eddington fell dead at his desk, much the way my father had nine years before. The official diagnosis: cardiac arrest. I was probably the only person on this earth who knew enough to suspect that he'd died of a broken heart. (Rita never returned after she sneaked out of court that afternoon.)

Sadly, Ferris Eddington did not live to watch his only daughter grow up. I remember the day Dr. Hardy told me that if Miranda could only stay out of mental hospitals, she might just grow up to have a decent life. He was right. She married a man from Kentucky, where she has raised children and Thoroughbreds. Not too many years ago, I visited Lexington, and Miranda and I rode her horses across green hills that had white fences, none of which she ever tried to jump.

Almost immediately after Ferris Eddington's death, his executors sold the ranch, including all the land on the border and that up near Prescott, to a huge development company in California. The new owner relied on Los Angeles counsel as it turned a good chunk of the Salt River Valley into subdivisions and golf courses and strip malls. Losing the dreamed-of business changed the mood at Butler and Menendez, and within the year Dan Morgan, with almost nothing in the way of paying clientele, found himself once again in Paul Butler's crosshairs.

One evening after a partner's meeting, Tom Gallagher came into my office. He looked ashen. "You want the good news or the bad news?" he asked.

"I always like the good news first," I said.

"We all just voted to offer you a partnership." He slid a piece of paper across the desk.

"What's that?" I asked.

"The amount of your proposed monthly draw and an immediate bonus."

"Wow."

"Yeah," said Gallagher. "Congratulations."

"So what's the bad news?"

Tom took a deep breath. "Maybe," he said, "I'll let Dan give you that."

Minutes later Morgan came in and dropped into one of my chairs. "I just stood up in that meeting," he said, "and told them all to fuck themselves. I'm outta here, Doug. I'm getting space over in the new Valley National Bank Building. I hope you'll go with me. We'll be partners. I'm inviting Chet Johnson and Lester Pierce, too. How about it?"

I looked at the piece of paper Gallagher had left on my desk, and I studied the figures carefully. "Can I think about it for a while?"

"Take your time."

I thought about it for a week. Telling him no was about the hardest thing I've ever done. And for the next months, I worried obsessively about whether the day would come when I would deeply regret my decision.

That day never came. In September of that year, Morgan called me. "Doug?"

"Hey, what's going on?"

"I just had a doctor tell me that if I don't stop working so hard and take up some physical activity, I'm going to die. I think I want to play golf. How do you learn it?"

"You find a good teacher. Then you treat practice balls like beads on a rosary. And you go to church every single day."

"I want to try it. Can you fix me up with a good teacher?"

Five days later I picked up the *Arizona Republic* to see, on the front page, that the nationally prominent trial lawyer Daniel Morgan had died of a heart attack while taking his first golf lesson at the Moon Valley Country Club.

A. L. Moore's funeral home filled to overflowing, and more than three hundred people from both sides of the law stood outside listening to loudspeakers in the rain. Supreme Court justices spoke. Ex-convicts spoke. Walter Smith told us that Daniel Morgan had a gift for knowing what would win a case and, through some invisible alchemy, the uncanny ability to make that thing happen within the rules— always within the rules—almost every time he went out. That, Walter declared, amounted to a form of genius. Elias Butler said Danny Morgan had so much musk on him that when he walked into a courtroom, he made the rest of us feel like fairies, and it was a goddamned chickenshit shame that a wannabe blue-chip firm in Phoenix, Arizona, could not accommodate such a lawyer. (When he said that, Elias was looking right at his son.) Tom Gallagher tried, but he could not speak at all. I walked across from Tom and ahead of Walter Smith and Jake Asher and Morgan's two sons as we carried the casket to the hearse.

At the grave I stood next to Ann Hastings under an umbrella in the drizzling rain. She wore a simple black dress. At the neck I could see a sliver of blue, the edge of the scarf I'd bought for her in San Francisco. I stared at the lovely silk as I heard the first muddy clods hit the casket. Ann caught me looking. "What are you thinking?" she asked.

"You want the truth?"

"Yes."

"I was wondering if someday you might consider marrying me." The words were out before I could bite them off, and I could feel the blood rushing to my face. I searched frantically for something to say, something to stanch this final embarrassment. I tried to laugh. Ann looked down into the darkness of the hole beside us. "It's just that I saw you wearing that scarf, and I somehow—"

"Yes, Doug. If that was a proposal, I will marry you."

Ann Hastings and I live on the third fairway of the Phoenix Country Club. Our children are away now. Sometimes Ann plays golf with me.

ACKNOWLEDGMENTS

MY DEEPEST APPRECIATION goes to the following people:

Betsy Burton, who owns the King's English bookstore in Salt Lake City, has, over the years, made clear to me the value of the independent bookseller. Recently she has given me more help with this novel than I could ever have imagined. She read it. She critiqued it. She introduced me to her own freelance editor (Betsy recently published a fascinating account of her life selling good books), Ruth Greenstein of Greenline Publishing, who arranged to have Charlotte Carter, a fine mystery writer, give me editorial help. And it was Betsy who threw the manuscript over HarperCollins's transom at a woman named Carolyn Marino.

The "acknowledgments" of almost every novel I've read lately have lavished praise upon Carolyn Marino. I am here to testify that all of it is wholly deserved. What a pleasure it is to have your paper graded by a real pro. And it doesn't escape me that a big component of the gratitude I'm trying to express to her is naked, shameless bragging. It really sets me up to be able to tell people my editor is Carolyn Marino.

And (since I'm on a boastful tack) my agent is Richard Pine. I hear people say he's the best in the business. For all I can tell, so far, that's very likely true. It's just that it always takes at least a month for me finally to realize how sound his advice is.

I have to thank a couple of other people at HarperCollins. John Zeck helped Betsy Burton target Carolyn Marino. Wendy Lee not only sneaks me books but listens patiently to my naïve questions, then provides invaluable tutoring in the ways of big-time publishing.

I want to thank Kit Burton, Esquire, who practiced law in the courts of Utah for many years and read an early draft of my book, providing insightful advice as well as encouragement. As for encouragement, the most important I got came from Jedediah Purdy, an extraordinary author and a law professor at Duke University. On about the tenth time I'd given up, Jed told me not to. When I was in law school, I took courses in procedure and trial practice from a professor named Michael Berch, who not only nudged me toward a career at the bar but taught me that the art of the trial was something that could be studied. It's about time I thanked him. I owe a debt to my longtime friend and fishing companion, Don Bruemmer, for reading the final draft and correcting errors neither I nor my editors had yet caught.

Deepest thanks go to my wife, Tena Campbell, who used to be a very able trial lawyer and now is the hardest-working judge I've ever known. Without Tena's love and support I could not have completed this project.

Last, and most important, I have to thank my daughter, Mary Campbell, a real smart lawyer and an exceptionally gifted wordsmith. When her friend Jedediah told me to keep going, it was Mary who put her money (if a lawyer's time is money) where her mouth is. She pulled my manuscript out of the closet and spent the better part of a summer teaching her father how to tell a story with language that he might someday persuade someone to read. I will be forever grateful.

A final note: When I was in law school and for a time afterward, I had the good fortune of working for a trial lawyer in Phoenix, Arizona, named John J. Flynn. John had taken Ernesto Miranda to the Supreme Court of the United States. Remarkably, establishing our right to remain silent was considered one of John's lesser accomplishments. Many people considered him the best criminal defense attorney of his time. My character, Dan Morgan, is not John Flynn. Lamentably I did not know him well enough to write his incredible story. Still I do know that any inspiration I had for this project came from my time with this wild man who affected me profoundly so many years ago. Later I joined the Phoenix law firm of Lewis & Roca and was lucky enough to work for the likes of John P. Frank, Walter Cheifetz, Bill Grainger, and Monroe McKay. Had it not been for the influence of those men and the other very talented lawyers of that distinguished firm, I would not have been able to write this book.